TEA FOR TWO AT THE LITTLE CORNISH KITCHEN

JANE LINFOOT

One More Chapter
a division of HarperCollins*Publishers* Ltd
1 London Bridge Street
London SE1 9GF
www.harpercollins.co.uk
HarperCollins*Publishers*
1st Floor, Watermarque Building, Ringsend Road
Dublin 4, Ireland

This paperback edition 2022

1

First published in Great Britain in ebook format
by HarperCollins*Publishers* 2022
Copyright © Jane Linfoot 2022
Jane Linfoot asserts the moral right to
be identified as the author of this work

A catalogue record of this book is available from the British Library

ISBN: 978-0-00-840812-1

Printed and bound in the UK using 100% Renewable Electricity
by CPI Group (UK) Ltd

Jane L[...]ntic fiction with feisty heroines and a bit of an edge. Writing romance is c[...] because [...] pretty shoes instead of wellies. She lives in a mountain kingdom in Derbyshire, where her family and pets are kind enough to ignore the domestic chaos. Happily, they are in walking distance of a supermarket. Jane loves hearts, flowers, happy endings, all things vintage, and most things French. When she's not on Facebook, and can't find an excuse for shopping, she'll be walking or gardening. On days when she wants to be really scared, she rides a tandem.

www.janelinfoot.co.uk

twitter.com/janelinfoot
instagram.com/janelinfoot

ALSO BY JANE LINFOOT

The Little Cornish Kitchen Series

The Little Cornish Kitchen

The Little Wedding Shop by the Sea Series

The Little Wedding Shop by the Sea

Christmas at the Little Wedding Shop

Summer at the Little Wedding Shop

Christmas Promises at the Little Wedding Shop

Love at the Little Wedding Shop by the Sea

Standalones

How to Win a Guy in 10 Dates

The Right Side of Mr Wrong

High Heels & Bicycle Wheels

The Vintage Cinema Club

A Cornish Cottage by the Sea

A Cosy Christmas in Cornwall

For Anette, with love.
You sent Herbie and Bear when we needed them most.
Ruffleups Old English Sheepdogs –
filling every day with boundless love, mud and happiness since
2004 xx

It's no use going back to yesterday because I was a different person then.

ALICE IN WONDERLAND

When you can't look on the bright side I will sit with you in the dark.

ALICE IN WONDERLAND

The Surf Shack Café, St Aidan, Cornwall
Slippery slopes and caramel crispies
Friday

'Hi, I'm Cressy, I'm *so* sorry we're late.'
Above my head the bunting is flapping against a cornflower blue sky, and across the Surf Shack Café's hewn plank table I'm looking at three smiling yet expectant faces.

I take it the women round the table all know Diesel, the dog, already as he pretty much wrenched my arm off to get to them. Let's face it, with his huge grey head and his long lollopy legs that are mostly out of control, he's quite a local icon in St Aidan. When we finally got here he leaped up the steps so fast my sparkly flipflops barely touched the ground, then he careered across the beachside deck like a guided missile. Now he's finally come to a standstill in front of the group, he's shoving his big black nose into each of their faces in turn and giving them the licking of their lives.

As his tail finally slows to a normal wag I can see a major slick on the one in the check shirt, who I think is called Nell. Then his bottom thumps down on my foot and he stares up at me. If a guy were playing me like this I'd push him into the harbour. But with those heart-melting brown eyes I forgive Diesel every time.

Nell swipes a hand across her cheek to clear the slobber and gives his hairy shoulder a last pat. 'Lovely to see you too, Diesel, I hope you're being good.' She turns to me. 'You're out of breath, is everything okay?'

Even if these are friends of a friend rather than work, I was *so* hoping to make a good impression here. I flap my once white T-shirt and pray that the sweat halo around my scalp isn't turning my carefully prepped hair to frizz as they watch. 'Don't worry, I always hyperventilate when I'm excited to meet people.' Hopefully that explains why I sound like I just finished an iron man.

As for Diesel, I've known him since he was a puppy, but when I agreed to look after him and Pancake, the cat, while my brother Charlie and his lovely partner Clemmie go off on an extended trip to Scandinavia, I had no idea he'd be this much of a handful. Charlie and Clemmie's flat is just along the beach, but the second Diesel's paws hit the sand he legged it, and we had a wild half hour of chasing before I finally grabbed him again. From Nell's hard stare it's almost like she's guessed.

In the end, wading into the shallows was the only way I was going to catch him. Looking at the tide line on my otherwise pristine belted boyfriend jeans and my long dripping cardigan, you'd never know I spent the best part of this morning getting ready. It might sound over the top to some people, and neat wasn't my natural state. But since I had success with my internet baking clips, I'm expected to be picture-perfect every time I leave the house.

I've no doubt that if the handover had been left to Charlie he would have tossed me the flat keys as he left for the airport saying, *You know where everything is, see you in three months' time.* But Clemmie has made me a manual to cover every eventuality. If she missed the bit about how to catch Diesel, it's because he never normally runs off. I'm guessing Clemmie took charge of the instructions because her part of the top floor where I'll be staying is vintage with lots of quirks. But she also added an hour-by-hour pet-care log, as well as personality profiles of most people in St Aidan, and then insisted on handing me into the care of her besties, who are welcoming me now with afternoon tea.

It's lovely of them to treat me, but it's more looking-after than I need. I'm the youngest of six, and what the family forget is that I'm thirty-two, independent and completely capable of taking care of myself as well as Charlie's pets.

If ever you want proof that life can flip from good to the worst kind of bad then back again, you only have to look at Charlie. Thirteen years ago, on the eve of their wedding, his wonderful fiancée, Faye, got ill and died. He had ten long, desolate years. Then Clemmie moved into the flat next to his, and made his life happy again.

If I'm a little bit wary of being engulfed by Clemmie's childhood friend group, it's because I've always hung out with one bestie rather than a crowd. This lot still call themselves 'the mermaids' and they haven't even met me, but they've already offered to make me an honorary member.

It would be lovely if that were my kind of thing. Don't get me wrong – I love the sound of waves crashing on the shore and the higgledy village of St Aidan with its colourful cottages stacked up the hillside and the novelty of a café that's made out of a thousand bits of driftwood nailed together. But I have no intention of reaching for my own personal mer-persona any time soon.

Spending a few weeks by the sea in early summer is the kind of treat I wouldn't have had if I hadn't been pet sitting, and I've really been looking forward to the change; I've bought my Salt-Water sandals and I've vowed to eat my body weight in clotted cream while I'm here. But that's the limit of me turning native because I actually love my life in London. I know it's gone a bit tits-up lately, which is why I'm extra pleased to have the chance to lie low in Cornwall for a while. Fingers crossed, by the time Charlie and Clemmie come home my troubles will have blown over. Then I'll head back to civilisation and pick up where I was before everything went wrong.

'We've been so looking forward to meeting you, Cressy. We don't often get stars in St Aidan.' The woman speaking now is blonde and her eyes are shining. But her aqua blue top and matching chinos are straight out of Clemmie's file notes.

Sophie, mum of four, owns a hundred identical T-shirts the colour of mint ice cream, started her multi-million-pound skincare brand making cosmetics on her kitchen table, now owns a castle and rules the world. Hot tip: super-organisational, be prepared to resist her on her forceful days.

However starstruck Sophie sounds today, she shouldn't be. Most women who breathe and read *Good Housekeeping* use her Sophie May products, whereas I got one accidental lucky online break that I ran with and milked for all it was worth.

Nell rubs her nose and nods. 'Kate Humble once popped in for a sticky toffee pudding at The Yellow Canary, so we know you're the real deal, Cressy. With celebrity presenters it's all in the polish.'

I'm not about to share this, but when my career is based on something as flimsy as my on-camera sparkle and a few iced buns, I have to put the hours in. I'm hoping my all-day miracle foundation has withstood the assault of chasing after Diesel.

The woman in the paint-splattered boiler suit chimes in. 'It's your superhuman glow that's the giveaway. When Patrick Grant came to open the Fish Quay Festival he glowed too – but way less than you.' That has to be Plum, from the gallery on the steep cobbled hill above the bakery. She shakes her dark ponytail and grins straight at me. 'You're exactly the same as when you cook on YouTube – except without the pinny and the flour smudges.'

Nell flaps her fingers in front of her face. 'You'll have to excuse us having our fan girl moments. At least ten million of your billion views came from us watching your videos when Clemmie was learning to bake.'

Plum's screwing up her face. 'Please – before you sit

down, could you possibly say what you do at the start of your baking clips?'

People ask me this all the time and I always respond because it acts like an icebreaker; once it's out of the way we can get back to being normal.

I widen my eyes, lock onto an imaginary selfie stick and fire. 'Hi, Cressida Cupcake here, bringing love to the world one blondie at a time.' Given the depth of Plum's contented sigh, I have to put it into context. 'It's a very niche audience, internet fame is very fleeting.'

If anyone knows how fickle social media success is, it's me. Until recently I'd always have said my ambition in life was to fill the world with *cake*; but that was before I publicly humiliated myself in front of gazillions of TV viewers.

Plum gives me a sideways smile. 'We all saw you on the fabulous Channel 5 baking show too, don't forget.'

It would have been too much to hope they weren't going to mention it. I force a smile. 'My time on there was sweet but very short.'

Going on a bake-off show for internet bakers sounded so much fun, and better still, it landed me my dream commission for two recipe books. But getting sent home the second week because my oven wouldn't heat up wasn't how it was supposed to end. And even worse, the editing made my gateau look way more raw than it was in real life and blew my baking disaster out of all proportion. But by that time it was out of my hands. And given the fallout I'm dealing with now, I'd say it was cracking bad judgement too.

Sophie gives me a wink. 'Don't undersell yourself, Cressy Cupcake, it was amazing to get on *Social's Biggest*

Bakers! at all.' She nods at the giant tower of fancies and muffins at the centre of the table, pushes back a chair for me and starts handing round plates. 'Anyway I'm Sophie, this is Nell, and that's Plum. It's wonderful to meet you, let's get on with the tea.'

As my phone pings in the depths of my bag I know it'll be more hate comments about uncooked middles. Despite the lack of phone signal at this far end of England where the last bit of land pokes out into the sea, there's still a deluge of the damned things. It won't last for ever. This is just a temporary downturn I've got to ride out.

So long as I keep my eye on the bigger picture I can side-step a total meltdown. I've got twelve blissful weeks ahead of me with nothing to do but bake and look after the pets. The sun is sparking off the bright azure sea and Diesel's curled up next to my chair. Sophie waves the cake tongs and I nod to a popping candy cupcake, a white chocolate muffin, a sticky slab of chocolate brownie and a flapjack slab the size of a bath sponge. Then as Nell passes round cups of tea my watering mouth tells me for the moment there's no need to fake it. As far as true happiness goes, for me the next hour is sorted.

The blueberry muffin Plum is biting into is almost as big as her head. 'You're going to love being in Clemmie's side of the attic flat, Cressy, it's *so* cosy and you can see right around the bay.'

It's great to move the focus off me, and she's right; it's the most amazing place to stay. Before Clemmie and Charlie got together, they were neighbours on the top floor of Seaspray Cottage, which is a pebble's throw from here, just round the corner from the harbour's end. Clemmie's place belonged to her grandmother, who crammed it with jewel colours and random clutter that's all still there, whereas Charlie's side of the top floor has a more minimalist, luxury vibe.

I laugh. 'And while I enjoy the views of the sea from Clemmie's ancient pink sofa, the decorators are taking over next door at Charlie's.' The downside of huge white spaces is how often they need repainting, especially with Diesel living there.

Sophie's eyes are bright. 'Clemmie mentioned you'll be busy working on your first book?'

'That's the plan.' The contracts are due any day, and the stonking advance is what I'm counting on to see me through until the bake-off bollocks dies down and the book writing is done. Living in London doesn't come cheap, but thanks to this windfall my finances are looking rosy for the first time ever. The money hasn't hit my account yet, but the moment it does, my agent will let me know, which is why, despite the patchy signal, my nose is glued to my phone screen. 'I'll be using the next few weeks to check all the recipes and make the final selections.'

Sophie's laughing. 'Clemmie was convinced you'd be bored out here in the sticks, so we've promised to keep you entertained.'

Her offer is making my chest tighten because I'd counted on today being the end of the mermaid intervention. 'Truly, I'm looking forward to relaxing at home.' Not wanting to be rude, but my life has been all kinds of crazy since my Cressida Cupcake blog took off. More importantly,

I have to get the book fully completed and submitted while I'm here.

From the way her jaw drops, she's not used to getting knocked back, but she recovers fast. 'Lucky for you, I'm over every meditation class in the area. Give me a yell and we'll pencil in some chill time.'

Nell's lips are twitching. 'And if you'd rather have fun rather than fall asleep, there are our singles events. We're very inclusive, couples and committeds are welcome too.'

I should have known this was coming because Nell's singles club was all over Clemmie's notes, but the kick in my gut now she mentions it catches me off-guard.

'I fly solo, and that's how I'll be staying.' We're already being quite shouty, but that comes out so loud, the people at the nearby tables turn to look. Except for a guy with fabulous shoulders rippling through his shirt, who doesn't flinch but runs his fingers through his dark hair and stares resolutely along the beach. I kick myself for my shriek, lower my voice and try again. 'Thanks all the same, but I'll probably give those a miss.'

Couple-y activities, in St Aidan of all places, hold too many echoes for me. The one and only time I lost my head to anything resembling love was over a decade ago and that was when I was here on holiday.

Soon after Faye died Charlie had moved down to Cornwall and a load of us came to keep him company over Christmas and ended up renting a big house on the coast road. There I was, bursting with the certainty that goes with turning twenty, holed up at the end of the world with Charlie's best friend from uni, Ross Bradbury, whom I'd fancied the pants off since I first gasped at his pecs and stubble shadows as a sassy fourteen-year-old. I like to pretend it was mutual attraction but I suspect I flung myself at him so hard there was nothing he could do but catch me.

The images of those few days used to be sharp as laser cuts in my mind, but over-viewing has blurred them to softer focus. All I know is, nothing since ever came even halfway close. But that was maybe because, like all the best holiday flings, there was a water-tight guarantee that it was for now, not for ever. We kept it under wraps because the last thing Charlie needed back then was his best friend and his sister making out under the mistletoe.

Even as the waves thrashed over the promenade and I leaned in to grab that first searing kiss, the end was already written in the sand. However tightly Ross wrapped me inside his coat and told me he'd never let go, we both knew the second we'd waved in the New Year that he was flying off for an exchange at a veterinary faculty in the States and I was going back to my media studies at uni in Brighton. As things panned out, it ran on to a more painful conclusion we hadn't foreseen. But what that time taught me made me who I am today; since then the only person I'll ever ask anything of is myself.

What's more, I'm shocked at how stirred up I am now. All those years ago I promised myself to put what happened behind me. To take note, and move on. And until my wobble a moment ago I'd have sworn that's what I'd done.

Nell gives a shrug. 'No pressure at all to join in. Unless

you're into gardening clubs or OAP discos, the social scene isn't exactly buzzing here otherwise.'

'I'll most likely be working flat-out. The recipes are my priority.' I'm racking my brain to remember what else Clemmie wrote about Nell so I can smooth this over.

Loves a pork sandwich, parents live at Forget-me-not Farm…

I seize my chance. 'Talking of baking, aren't you my go-to woman for eggs? Three dozen would be brilliant to start off with, please.' So long as I act like everything's fine, no one will ever guess any different. That was one of Charlie's hot tips for getting through the bad times, although compared to him losing his life partner, my problems have been the teensiest of blips. The one positive thing about a tragedy in the family is that difficulties that come after feel like nothing at all.

Nell brightens. 'The eggs are all free range, I can even tell you the names of the hens that laid them. I'll pop them round later.'

It might work best if I take control of the invitations here. 'I'll be doing my try-outs every day so there will be cake, tea and colourful cushions any time you fancy dropping in.' Seriously, with the amount of stairs they have to stagger up to reach the flat, they definitely won't.

Plum waves her ginger slice at me. 'Cressida Cupcake's personal handiwork *and* the views from Seaspray Cottage? I'm in!'

'You're welcome any time.' I hide my surprise by reaching down and scratching the top of Diesel's head. It's his flat more than mine, so I feel like I should be including him in this. 'Isn't that right, boy?'

I bite into the pile of popping candy on my cupcake and let the first delicious mouthful melt on my tongue. Smile as Diesel opens one lazy eye under the table. Sit back and listen to the sound of the waves rushing up the sand, then pulling back down again.

Then from nowhere there's a clatter and a whoosh of grey and Diesel jumps to his feet. Before I can protest, his paws are on my knee and he's snatched the cupcake out of my hand. A second later it's gone, paper and all. There's a flash of pink as he licks his lips, then he's down resting his head on the deck again.

My shriek finally breaks free. 'Oh my days! What happened there?' He was full of mischief as a pup, but that was almost a third of my life ago. Apart from the time he made a midnight raid on my mum's specially iced Christmas cake, he's always been so good.

Diesel's stare is inscrutable. If it wasn't for the sandy footprints decorating my jeans and top, I could almost be persuaded he had nothing to do with this.

Nell's wagging her finger. 'Bad boy, Diesel.'

Plum's brow wrinkles. 'The entire cake went without him swallowing.'

I'm scrubbing the marks off my shirt, leaping in to cover for Diesel. 'I'm sure it won't happen again.' I'm aiming to laugh this off, so I frown down at my thighs, which have to be double the size of Sophie's and are way larger than they were before all the bake-off tasting. 'It's probably Diesel's way of reminding me not to grow too big for my apron.' The great advantage of Insta and YouTube is you can keep the bulges out of shot. And as Diesel's got one over on me twice already this afternoon, we might be better quitting while we're ahead and making a run for home. At walking pace this time.

I smile around the table. 'It's been lovely meeting you all, but Diesel will be wanting his next walk.'

Nell squints at me. '*Another?* We've barely started on the cakes.'

'They were awesome but I've had more than my share.' It was touch-and-go getting my jeans to zip up earlier.

Sophie's running her fingers through her perfectly cut blonde hair, watching me as I stand up. 'If you really can't stay, don't forget – anything you need, we're all here on standby.'

It's fab of them to offer, even if I won't be taking them up on it. I'm closing my fingers round Diesel's lead as he scrambles to his feet. I've had a delicious half hour, but I as I told them earlier, I really will be fine on my own. 'Thanks then, see you soon…'

As I wave them goodbye I'm giving silent hurrahs for getting away without making any definite arrangements, and before Diesel did anything worse. I'm on my third whoop when I feel the lead slide across my palm. I make a grab but it's already gone – and Diesel's way ahead of it.

2

The Surf Shack Café, St Aidan, Cornwall
Toast toppings and where to stick them
Friday

I close my eyes and curse under my breath as I feel the gap in my hand where Diesel's lead should be. When I open them I'm ready to see Diesel lolloping off, tail held high as he disappears around the curve of the bay. But he's much closer. And it's *so* much worse. He's made a beeline for the guy sitting on his own at a café table by the steps and his paws are already on his shoulders.

I groan. It's one thing Diesel clambering all over Clemmie's friends, a stranger not so much. And not that I've got a choice, but I wish Diesel had chosen someone ordinary rather than the most ripped guy in the place.

Two leaps and I'm across the deck and ready to grovel. 'I'm *so* sorry, my dog's not attacking you, he's just super friendly.' If I personalise this he may react better. 'His name is Diesel... Obviously I'll replace any food of yours he's breathed on.' I'm under the table trying to find the end of the lead before Diesel takes off again.

'Diesel and I already know each other well.'

'You do?' As Diesel seems to be besties with most of Cornwall, that's no surprise. But there's something catchingly familiar about that laid-back gravelly tone that makes me jolt so hard, I bang my head on the table. As for recognising the pull of taut denim, or the giveaway curve of a thighbone in the shadows, that's ridiculous. But as I finally close my fingers around the leather and scramble back to my feet, my insides have turned to jelly.

'Egg-and-Cress Hobson, who'd have thought? It is you, Cressy, isn't it?'

It's that same dark chocolate voice that used to inexplicably turn me from a shy teenager into a mouthy princess desperate to be noticed. Now there's a huge hole where my stomach should be and, worse still, hearing my childhood nickname has made me clamp my eyes tight shut.

'That's right.' Except my head's spinning so fast I'm not sure I know who I am at all as I try to work it out and fail. *Ross? Surely it can't be?*

Except one flick of my eyes, and I can see it's him. What's more, he's still got the whole rugged jaw and devastating dark eyes thing going on. Not that I'd be shallow enough to fall for that whole knockout, sex-on-legs vibe now. These days, if I were looking – which obviously I'm not – I'd look a lot more at the whole person.

'Still just as extraordinary too, from what I just overheard.' He's peering at me past Diesel's back. 'No surprise there! You were always going to do something astonishing.'

'You were listening in?' I'm praying he didn't hear me acting like a celebrity. As for him catching me on my frizziest hair day since time began, well, isn't that just typical?

He pulls a face. 'It wasn't deliberate. You *were* talking quite loudly.'

That fires me up enough to make me focus again. 'What the hell are *you* doing *here* anyway?' More to the point, what the hell went wrong with that unspoken agreement we had? He took Scotland, which he never left due to being a workaholic, and I got the rest of the world. For all those years I've been totally confident that he was never going to accidentally waft into a city bar and start ordering pints of craft ale. Secure that the scar on his left cheek where he got kicked by a cow wasn't about to jump out from behind a postcard rack and make my knees do what they're doing now. Legs as sturdy as mine shouldn't ever give way, but I grasp the table edge just in case.

He clears his throat. 'I'm doing a bit of locum work at the local vets'.'

'*Excuse me?*' With Charlie so established in Cornwall now, it's easy to forget that Ross is the one who grew up here. However surprising it is that he's returned to his roots after so long away, we both know guys with as many letters after their names as Ross has don't work as temporary stand-ins.

He sniffs. 'Charlie mentioned you were arriving, but I thought that was tomorrow. And my placement ran on

17

unexpectedly, which is why I'm here having a last blowout.' He's drumming his fingers on the table, then his voice rises sharply. 'Hey, don't let Diesel eat my toast!'

The crusts I'm wrestling out of Diesel's mouth are green and slimy, but it's a matter of pride to get the whole slice back onto the plate again.

To be fair to Diesel, he might have done Ross a favour here. Considering all the yummy cake on offer, grilled sludge looks a terrible choice. 'Why not give Diesel the dodgy toast and I'll shout you an extra-large slice of death-by-chocolate instead?' I'm appalled that I can even recall his soft spot for cocoa, but if I'm plagued with unwelcome insider knowledge, I might as well use it.

That's brought on a frown like a storm cloud. 'You are joking? Of course Diesel can't have the toast. Avocado's bad for dogs. *You must know that?*'

I do now. What's more, as a trusted pet sitter, it's more than my life's worth to admit the gaping hole in my doggy knowledge. 'So *that's* what the slime is! Lucky super-vet's here to put me straight.'

These guys and their health kicks. Plus, he's looking at me like I'm about two inches high. I know he's got a gazillion more qualifications than me, but other attributes count too. In my world I look guys in the eye as equals until proven otherwise. And didn't he used to laugh out loud rather than have a tiny ironic twist to his smile? It's like I'm staring at someone who hit thirty-five and had a total sense of humour bypass.

Looking at that stony expression, it hits me how dismal

my life could have become if things between us had worked out differently.

I did not have that thought. More than that, I have spent the last twelve years making sure I never let my mind go anywhere close to there. What am I thinking?

He's staring out to sea like there's no hope for any of us. 'If you're responsible for Diesel, I'd better drop you a chart off.'

'A chart?' I'm talking in the voice of a strangled hedgehog. 'You're surely not *coming round*?' It's bad enough seeing him here. If I had to face him in Clemmie's tiny flat, I might actually expire.

'Don't worry, I'm not about to invade your space. *Foods dogs need to avoid – a visual reminder.* It'll fit through the letterbox.' He rubs Diesel's ears. 'Charlie worships this boy, we can't be too careful while he's away.'

If there had been any other way, Charlie and Clemmie would never have left him. But I'm damned if I'll let Ross see the responsibility petrifies me. Instead I give a tug on the lead. 'So can I get you that cake before we go? Or more toast?'

He pulls a face. 'I'll give that a miss, thanks. I'm suddenly less hungry than I was.'

'Great!' It's not, but as we've totalled his visit to the Surf Shack and he's pretty much wrecked my afternoon, no other ironic answer springs to mind. I toss in a final throwaway line before I run. 'We'll see you around then.'

He leans back in his seat. Narrows his eyes like he's giving this his full consideration, but there's also an extra flicker to the scar on his cheekbone that gives away how uncomfortable he is. 'It might be best if I leave the beach to you from now on.'

The last time I saw that same pained frown and the twitch on his cheek, I'd just lost our baby and he was backing out of the room, heading back to the States. And I hadn't ever planned on seeing him again. To the extent that you have no idea of the effort I've put in to make sure I didn't. As far as I know it's been forever since he was down in Cornwall, and I had no reason to think that would change. If I'd had the slightest suspicion he'd be here, I'd have headed for the other end of the country.

If I've ever let that unlikely accidental meet-up scenario play out in my head, it certainly didn't end with us glaring at each other as we divvied up who could go where in the village. Of all the shocks, I was not ready for this one. When I think how much I've looked forward to chilling by the sea and reconnecting with my happy place. And now I feel like a tidal wave has picked up my entire ordered, nicely level life and tumbled it to chaos.

The full implication of what he's said is dawning on me. 'You mean you'll *still be here?*'

He closes his eyes. 'Only for a couple of days.'

I make sure my smile is the brightest ever. 'In which case we *won't* see you. Around or anywhere else. Which is fine by *us*.' Including Diesel makes us sound stronger, but better still it makes this less about him and me. I'm about to tell him to have a nice life, but I manage to bite it back. Even a very breezy 'laters' feels too loaded with threat that I'll be stalking him, so I end up being my mum doing her impersonation of her old hockey teacher. 'We'll say cheerio, then – toodlepip!'

And for once when I turn to march off, Diesel wags beside me. And somehow we manage to make it across the deck and down the steps without me falling off my flipflops. And then we're sinking into the soft sand, hurrying to the ocean's edge where the lacy-edged breakers are frothing over the watery shine below.

3

Clemmie's flat at Seaspray Cottage, St Aidan
Sweet fillings and sticky ends
The next morning, Saturday

'Chocolate chips, walnut, white chocolate chunks and Oreo, dark chocolate and mint...'

As I come through into the living room next morning Nell's eggs are stacked and waiting on the apple-green dresser in the kitchen, and I'm running my favourite brownie mixes past Diesel. I've already re-smoothed half my rather salty hair and messaged Clemmie and Charlie with some early-morning views from St Aidan – Diesel lying by the open bedroom door, enjoying the breeze from the balcony. And Pancake giving me a disgusted-of-St-Aidan dead eye. That was for being two hours behind Clemmie's morning schedule serving up today's prawn and bamboo-shoot kitty-soup breakfast. Which was pretty mean of Pancake. After all, she was the one who kept me awake most of the night lying on my pillow mountain purring in my ear.

I can't *really* blame my lack of sleep on Pancake. And it wasn't down to the noise of the waves breaking on the beach below the window either. And the bedroom itself is dreamy, with the comfiest bed with the prettiest floral-print eiderdowns and picture-covered walls painted in a patchwork of dusky rose colours. If I was still thrashing around under the soft floaty duvet as the dawn light crept across the sky, it was because the afternoon at the Surf Shack was running through my head like an everlasting film loop. And if I ever managed to stop it, the gap simply filled with half-forgotten montages from years ago instead.

And sure, in those long dark hours before daybreak I was cursing myself for not having given Charlie a subtle yet thorough grilling about Ross's movements before I arrived. I should have realised I need to be just as vigilant now as I was all those years ago when I was constantly scanning the horizon, triple-checking the coast was clear.

Yet it's hard to stay down in St Aidan. Especially when you wake up to the sun glinting off a pale turquoise sea, the seagulls wheeling against a sky filled with cotton-white clouds, and surf lines stretching right across the width of the bay. Sure, Ross may have hurt me because he didn't turn out to be the guy I thought he was. And with me falling accidentally pregnant, and then getting over the loss of not being, the fallout was out of all proportion to our very short time together. But it was a long time ago.

All those times, over the years before, when Charlie brought Ross home, he'd never been anything less than his smiling, very clever, hugely fanciable and charming self. But that's not to say he was perfect to the point of being boring. In fact he was pretty all-round flawless in the most interesting and off-beat quirky ways.

He teased us five sisters in exactly the right amounts to make us tease him back. He brought my mum her favourite dark blue anemones when the rest of us hadn't even noticed she liked flowers. And not only did he know all the characters in *The Archers*, he was up for discussing the plot twists with her too. He chatted to my dad about the *Today* programme and Frank Zappa. I mean, who else did that without falling asleep?

Basically, as far as our entire family were concerned, the sun shone out through the strategically placed rips in his tight, Levi-clad tush. What's more, it wasn't just at home where he excelled. He was always telling us about the times at vet college when he'd taken on entire herds of cows and got the better of them. Once he'd even anaesthetised an elephant with a bloody tranquillising dart. This was the kind of superman we were dealing with.

Which was why it was such a shock when he and I got into metaphorical deep water and I discovered when it came to the big stuff, he couldn't actually swim. There's that Eleanor Roosevelt quote about women being like tea bags – you only know how strong they are when you get them into hot water. In Ross's case the tea he made had no colour at all. You could say the whole damned bag pretty much collapsed. Which wasn't what I was expecting, because it simply wasn't what he'd led us to believe.

But, hey! That was then and this is now. I found out I

could do it on my own anyway, which was the best lesson in empowerment I could have had. More importantly, I'm not the kind of woman to let a reappearing ex ruin my working holiday. Especially an ex as insignificant as Ross. So I'm determined to make things better in the best way I know – by baking. Which is why I'll be throwing myself straight into my brownie trials.

'I mustn't overlook caramel and custard cream. But then I also love Nutella ones…'

I plug in my hair tongs, curl up on the deep-pink velvet sofa, and smooth down my favourite ditsy-print shift dress. Then Diesel flops down beside me, and as my phone pings I reach to check it.

I'd trust the meringue tips more if that cake hadn't been #totallyraw

What a pretender! #CrappyCupcake

These are the comments I've been rising above ever since the baking show went on air, with two more wonderful new hashtags today. You have to hand it to the haters for their creativity; who'd have thought there'd be so many different ways to say 'not quite cooked'.

It must be at least an hour since I checked my emails too, and as I flip through my inbox and see the name Martha Channing I almost choke. Isn't it always the way? You refresh every two minutes for three months and the moment you turn your back, the mail you've been aching for drops into the inbox.

Martha is my agent, and this will be her letting me know the book contract has come through from the publisher, which also means the mahoosive advance will be dropping into my bank account as soon as I sort my digital signature.

I squint at the email.

Cressy, Are you around for a call later this morning? Martha x

Even in the media and magazine world, having an agent is the kind of big thing that only happens on the back of a TV show. And this is how lovely Martha is; she's actually taking the time to tell me in person that the cash is on its way.

I write *Hell, yes!* Then delete that and try to sound more like the pro I'm going to be.

Martha, Lovely, eleven thirty would be fab. HUGE thanks, Cressy xxxxx

Then as I press send it hits me; she usually does a face-to-face call, so both sides of my hair have to be the same *and* I need makeup. And Diesel needs a walk before then. And I can't take a high-calibre call like this without some serious calories on board to get my sugar levels up. So that means pulling in a trip to the bakery too. Which luckily is just around the corner, because seeing it's already ten, my feet aren't going to touch the ground.

It's that same sod's law with my hair. When it doesn't matter it's a dream to do, but when I'm trying for perfect it's a pig. The only way I can calm myself down enough to smooth anything out is by thinking of champagne. Not that I'm going to go crazy, but something this big is worth popping a cork over. And I'll treat myself to fish and chips with all the trimmings to go with it. Then wave a finger at all the #soggybottom miseries as I enjoy it.

This is a whole new jumping-off point for Cressida Cupcake, and as we set off through the village it feels like Diesel's upping his game too. By the time we're tearing up the hill to Crusty Cobs he's trotting beside me like an obedience champion. For me, splashing out on a box of four strawberry tarts is both a treat *and* an investment, and just to celebrate how much in the money I'm going to be, I buy a couple of almond croissants to eat on my way home too. All we've got to do now is make it up the stairs to the flat without expiring, and then I'll take the call on the pink sofa where the signal's strong. With a few well-placed patchwork cushions and the turquoise and green stripy wall behind me, it'll be job done. No one could accuse me of not going the extra mile on my prep.

It's all going so brilliantly as we cross the harbour on our way back to the flat, there's even enough time to loop beyond the stacks of lobster pots and wind along the quay edge where the bright coloured fishing boats are bobbing beside the piles of nets, which Diesel likes to sniff. When I hear my ringtone, I stuff the last of the first croissant into my mouth and the second into my cardigan pocket. Then I fish the phone out of my bag, hang onto Diesel and answer automatically, thinking it's probably Charlie or Clemmie. It's only as my finger hits accept on the call that I clock that it's Martha ten minutes before she's due.

As I pull Diesel closer there's a cascade of pastry flakes falling from my mouth as I try to speak. 'Maaaarrrfff... How lufffly...'

'Cressy, great to see you. I'm a little earlier than we said, but you're obviously ready and looking fantastic.'

I was right about the face-to-face call, and she's on speaker phone, but I'm not going to risk changing that now. 'Mwaaaaaaaa...eeeee...' This isn't a reply, it's my protest as Diesel's nose homes in on the spare croissant and edges it out of my pocket. For once he doesn't gulp it, but the way he holds it down on the cobbles with his paw and takes little tugs with his teeth, it's as if he's trying to torture me.

Martha's screen is entirely filled with my exploding face but she's pushing on. Her voice is booming around the harbour, which is fine because I feel like whooping too.

'There's been a tiny hitch, Cressy, but it's not unexpected after all the hashtag-soggy-bottoms we're contending with.' The lovely thing about Martha is she's so cheery and supportive, she always makes me feel like a winner. It's too bad she's telling the whole of St Aidan about the hashtag. Worse still that she's seen them at all.

'Mmmmhmmm...' I'm letting out silent wails for my disappearing pastry but as the word 'hitch' sinks in, my attention snaps back to Martha. More fool me for seeing this as my own *private* nightmare.

Martha carries on. 'We can't blame the marketing department for getting chilly feet!'

Damn, damn, damn. When the backlash is so public, of course the publishers will know about it too. But she sounds so bright it can't be that bad.

'So for now they've withdrawn their contract offer!'

It takes a couple of seconds for her words to echo back off the row of fishermen's cottages and sink into my brain. As my heart judders to a halt I stagger to a nearby bench. Then my gulp is huge enough for me to swallow the rest of what is left in my mouth. 'So they won't be paying *anything* upfront?' It's meant to be a hyena shriek but it comes out as a whimper.

'Not at this stage. And they won't be taking the books from you either. But if you're still keen to do one, go ahead. We can try to place it once it's complete.'

I can't believe she sounds so matter of fact. For me it's like I won the lottery and now I've lost the ticket. But I need to get this clear. 'So that's all the work, but none of the cash? And no guarantees either?'

More to the point, how am I going to survive for the next six months without the money? It felt so rock-solid, I've based all my financial forecasts on it and my life plans too. Which sounds a lot more fancy than it is. But if you think there's a wodge coming your way, you're a lot less careful with the cash you have left. I mean, five minutes ago I was splurging at the bakery. What I blew there would have kept me in soup for a month. Now I'm counting every almond flake, thank Christmas I didn't buy the fizz.

Martha's smile is pained. 'Get your book under your belt while the ice age is here, and pray like mad for a thaw. It's speculative, but it's my best suggestion, given the—'

I can't help my yell. 'The hashtag raw-as-effing-rainbows?' What use is cash that may never materialise when you need the damn stuff in your hand today?

30

She's got her calm-the-client voice on now. 'It's all very unfortunate. Let's talk again soon, we'll firm up when you've had time to think it over.'

Then Diesel gives a yank on his lead, and as I lurch to my feet and follow him to a sandwich crust across the cobbles, the signal's breaking up. A moment later Martha's call has ended.

Then another yank on the lead takes me by surprise and before I know it Diesel's haring across the car park with so much momentum that all I can do is follow. It's lucky for us the traffic here is crawling. We dodge in front of a tractor pulling a trailer piled with boxes of fish, narrowly miss two cars, and then we've got a clear run to the end of the harbour parking area.

'So, I've got a runaway dog, no income, and just like my dreams of a book, my tarts will be bashed into a million pieces. This has to be the worst it gets.'

I'm muttering to myself as we reach the corner where the tarmac gives way to the dune path, then I twist for a moment as I clutch the stitch in my side. And in that split-second view over my shoulder I catch a figure standing by a mud-spattered estate car, head tilted against the morning sun as he watches me.

If that was Ross and he saw Diesel out of control *again*, my day just went downhill a whole lot further.

4

Clemmie's flat at Seaspray Cottage
Gate crashers and garden parties
Later that day, Saturday

Take it from me. When your whole world is imploding, the fastest way to feel better is to make cake.

Martha's call and my impromptu run with Diesel left me in such a whirl that I was hyperventilating even before I reached the entrance to Seaspray Cottage. But then as I wound my way up around the stairs with their creaky waxed floorboards and took in the scent of thyme and lavender on the landings, instead of gasping I started to breathe again.

And when I reach the top floor, Nell's eggs are on the side next to the butter I took out of the fridge to soften when I got up this morning. And as Clemmie's store cupboards are bursting with ingredients and come with an open invitation to help myself, all I have to do is set myself to autopilot and press go.

One of the best things to bake in a crisis is brownies. From the mental lists I was making as I woke up today, it's almost as if I knew what was coming. They're straightforward to make, so as I weigh the ingredients and set Clemmie's baby-pink mixer to beat the batter, my mind is free to wander. But best of all is that thick, sweet, chocolatey mixture that swirls around the spoon as I fold in the walnuts. The way the chunks of dark mint chocolate in the second batch shine with promise as I spread the mixture out into the tins. Imagining the dense fudgy middle and those dark delicious flavours as the tops of the Nutella batch firm in the heat. By the time the oven door opens and blasts the kitchen with a steam-shot of pure cocoa, my brain is flooded with endorphins. I still have no idea how I'm going to live when my bank account runs dry, but now I mind about it less.

Exactly three hours after ground zero – with ground zero being the point when the signal expired on my call to Martha – I'm wiping my hands on my apron, and looking at a row of Clemmie's colourful tin trays, each piled high with a delicious stack of sticky chocolatey squares. And even though I've avoided posting baking on my pages lately because every time I do, I get a backlash of nasty comments, they look so delish I can't resist taking some photos. Just for me.

Getting the kitchen spick and span immediately after baking isn't my biggest strength, but I get as far as piling the sink with dishes and baking sheets, and then I take a breather.

I give Diesel a rueful grin as I fill the kettle. 'The shit is still the same, but the day is definitely brighter.' Then I cross the living room and he follows me onto the long sunny balcony that runs the across the front of both Clemmie's and Charlie's flats.

The breeze is playing havoc with my hair, but the air is so fresh I carry on anyway, ignoring that the slits under my bare feet give me glimpses all the way down to the sand below. I edge past the vintage table and chairs and get as far as the hand rail. Then a shout from below startles me so much I practically fall over the edge.

'Cressy, how are you doing up there?'

I lean out and see Nell's sandy head, Sophie's blonder one and a clutch of children, their faces all tilting upwards. 'Diesel and I are having a ball.'

Nell chortles. 'We heard he gave you a run for your money down the harbourside this morning.'

And damn that we were spotted when I'd hoped to get away with it.

Sophie digs her in the ribs and shouts up. 'Her other half has his office there. Don't worry, you're only the most interesting thing in town because you're new.'

Nell chokes into her fist. 'That's not strictly true. Everyone here always knows what everyone else is doing, sometimes before they've even done it.'

Sophie shakes her head. 'It's not as bad as it sounds. We're just off to the Surf Shack for a late lunch, if you'd like to come too?'

I hesitate for a second. Even if I didn't need to save every penny I can, yesterday's girl chat was quite enough to last me. On the other hand, I may feel elated now I've made a cake stack the height of the cliffs, but I didn't think it through as far as who was going to eat them. I can't possibly have them all to myself. Growing out of my jeans would push me off the financial cliff.

'Or I have a batch of warm brownies and the kettle just boiled. We could have tea in the garden?' If Sophie and Nell are here with a small, hungry army it's a no-brainer to put my reservations to one side and reach out instead. They'll be able to give me feedback I need on how they taste, and enjoy the cake mountain too. I mean, I haven't completely embraced Martha's suggestion of carrying on with my book regardless, but as I've got this block of time allocated to recipe testing, it might be a waste not to use it.

Sophie's voice goes dreamy. 'Brownies, you say?'

Nell nods. 'With a pot of strong tea? Now you're talking! Sophie can sort out the seats down here, I'll come up and help you carry.'

I'm hesitating. 'So long as you promise not to judge me on how messy the kitchen is.'

Nell seems to find that funny. 'As if! Sophie might, but I was practically brought up in a farmyard, so I never would.'

Which reminds me that these 'instant' best friends really belong to someone else. It's funny how little I know about their backstory and what makes them tick. But whatever, ten minutes later I'm handing out Clemmie's pretty, mismatched plates. Even worse, there was no time to check how woozy my hair was. After being out on that balcony, I probably look like a haystack that got stuck in a wind tunnel.

Sophie's already dipping into the mini taster-squares as she shunts the pale green metal table into position on the patio made of faded criss-crossed bricks. 'This end of the garden is less private, but it's more sheltered here today and we can still see the sea.'

Nell's looking over the low wall to the beach path beyond. 'Better still, we can introduce you to anyone we know who walks past. And Diesel should behave himself today because he's at home.'

Sophie watches as the older kids take a lump of cake in each hand then run off through the picket gate and throw themselves down on the grass underneath the apple trees. 'They love this garden. Clemmie does afternoon teas here for our Mums and Bumps group in summer.'

Nell's nodding. 'And it's great for outdoor singles evenings when the nights are warmer. Everyone loves a pudding night – they could be right up your street too.'

What they're talking about is Clemmie's amazing Little Cornish Kitchen business, which she started upstairs a couple of years ago and then moved down to the ground floor when it took off. I came and did my hygiene courses with Clemmie a couple of months ago, because I think she'd hoped I might keep the business going while she was away. But we both decided I wasn't up to the challenge.

As for the way Nell's directing this at me, I'm not sure where she's going with that.

She's giving me a hard stare. 'Just saying. They bring

good money in. I'm sure Clemmie wouldn't mind you putting a couple on yourself – if you're short.'

I know I'm panicking about money, but I didn't know I was *that* transparent. 'Short of *what*?'

Sophie lets out a sigh and pulls the smallest child up onto her knee. 'We'll come clean. Nell's other half accidentally overheard your call down at the harbour this morning. We're here to help.'

Nell chimes in. 'If you're having cash-flow problems, events at Seaspray Cottage are definitely your answer.'

This makes yesterday's afternoon-tea intervention look like nothing. Quite apart from anything else, I'd never use Charlie and Clemmie's place to earn money when we hadn't planned it in advance.

However well-meaning they are, I need to put them right on this. As for getting it right on the night enough to put on events, forget it! Bake-off-gate has taught me my lesson – from now on I'm going to stick to what I know. The thought of veering this far off course is making my palms sweat all over again.

Like a lot of people, my career hasn't turned out as I expected and I definitely haven't been turning out perfect flans since the age of two. I went to uni with dreams of working on a make-up magazine and I didn't even begin to bake until I was twenty. But me using my baking professionally was completely accidental. I was working for a stable of upmarket lifestyle magazines and in a mad moment I filmed myself on my phone showing a friend how to pipe buttercream. She uploaded the clip to YouTube the same week the entire world went crazy for cupcakes and the rest is history. But it's completely different from the fabulous parties Clemmie's told me about that made her a local legend; even in my biggest, most inflated dreams, I'm not in that league.

Sophie's wiggling her eyebrows. 'Clemmie was a total beginner when she started. We made it work for her, we can do it for you too.' Her eyes are fixing me to the spot.

Unlike Clemmie, who worked bars right around the world, I have zero face-to-face customer skills and no hospitality experience. I'm desperate to make them understand how wildly off-target they are here. 'I film myself doing simple baking, but I'm like an actor. Everything I do is a pretence, it doesn't relate to *real* life at all.'

Nell sniffs. 'These brownies taste pretty damn real to me.'

Then another, more concrete excuse flashes into my head. 'It's out of the question anyway. The builders are knocking down walls in Clemmie's work kitchen while she's away, and all the tables and chairs have gone to be repainted.'

Sophie slaps her knee. 'Damn, I'd forgotten. *That's* why the garden looks so empty.'

I force out a smile. 'Maybe you can help me another way. I actually hoped selling brownies over the wall would plug the hole in my finances.' That shows what pressure can do for on-the-hoof brainwaves. I dip sideways and do a little jazz-hands wiggle behind one of the trays. 'So what do you think?'

Sophie sits back in her chair and peels her child's hands off her T-shirt. 'Lovely and sticky, I've got great coverage here.' She stares down at her cocoa-covered boobs. 'This is why I have two hundred identical tops – did Clemmie mention it?'

Nell pulls a face. 'One brownie at a time? Speaking honestly as an accountant, it's going to be an uphill struggle.'

My stomach deflates. 'I meant *the flavours*.'

There's a moment of silence as it hits us how badly we've all blundered. We're opening and closing our mouths around the table, but then something much worse happens.

'I came to drop that poster off, but if those are brownies, I'm a world authority.'

Damn, damn, damn. I don't even have to look to know whose deep gravelly voice that is. And then, just when I think it can't get any worse than bloody Ross Bradbury crashing the tea party, Diesel leaps up, sails over to the wrong side of the wall like a Grand National steeplechaser and tries to eat his face off.

'*Food that's unsuitable for dogs.*' I beam round at Sophie and Nell. 'That's the poster. And meet Ross, he's the guy who first introduced Charlie to Cornwall. He's been in St Aidan very briefly and he's leaving any day.' That pretty much covers it. And hopefully sends him off-stage as fast as he came on.

Sophie wrinkles her nose. 'We know who Ross is, we grew up together.' She turns to Ross. 'And luckily for us, he's been here for a proper stay this time. Blossom and Bluebell love going to see Ross.'

The alarm bells are pinging in my brain. He's obviously been back a lot longer than he implied. And how unsettling that they all know each other, even if it was from back in the day. And so like Sophie to choose those fab names. I'm looking along the garden. 'So which ones are Bluebell and Blossom?'

Sophie grins. 'They're actually our guinea pigs.'

Nell spits her tea across the table as her laugh explodes. 'The trick to remembering Sophie's *kids*, all their names begin with M. From small to large, Maisie, Marco, Matilda and Millie-Vanilla. How did we not introduce them earlier?'

I'm puzzling as I take in the stubble shadows on Ross's jaw. I thought he worked with hippos and tranquilliser darts, not small things that squeak. 'Don't you specialise in large game?' I'm remembering America. 'Or presidents' puppies.'

He's shaking his head. 'Keep up, Cressy, that was one working holiday. As there's not much call for rhino sedation in St Aidan, hamsters are also welcome.'

Sophie's smiling at him in such an easy way. 'There aren't any jobs up your end of town, Ross, are there? Cressy could do with a few extra hours to add in alongside her baking.'

I'm so busy doing my impression of a guppy with lock-jaw, my shriek of protest at this interference doesn't ever make it into the air.

Whatever Ross does with his face, he's definitely not smiling. But he still gets those killer creases down the middle of his cheeks. 'The smallholding next to the surgery is looking for someone to feed their calves.'

'Excuse me!' I'm pointing upwards to my hair, and holding out my fingers. My very pretty red nails are all my own and took a full thirty minutes to bake in my mini acrylic-hardening oven last night and my entire life to grow, so he might as well get the full effect. And I know it was a rush job today, but I don't usually leave the house without at least two and a half hours of hard prep. 'I may look like a seagull roosted on my head, but we all have limits. Farm buckets and wellies are a long way past my safe word.'

'It's your call, I was only trying to help a friend.' His voice goes extra deep. 'The farmer, not you. He's out of action, so we've all rallied round, and as I'm closest that mostly means me. And FYI, seagulls mostly sleep on the beach or at sea.'

What an unbelievable know-it-all. When did Ross become such an arse?

Nell turns to Ross. 'Is that our Walter from Snowdrop Farm you're talking about? How's he doing?'

Ross sighs. 'Not great, I'm afraid. But he *is* ninety-two.'

Nell's straight back at Ross with another question. But now the heat's off me I don't waste time. I dart for the serviettes, and before Nell's finished her rundown of St Aidan's OAPs I've wrapped two brownie parcels and delivered them to the wall.

'Here you go, Ross. One for you and one for your friend Walter. I hope he feels better soon.'

Ross gives a shrug. 'His condition's terminal so on balance he probably won't. But thanks anyway.' As he reaches out to take the package a flash of angry skin on his fingers makes me wince.

'What have you done to your hand?' It's none of my business, but it's out before I can stop it.

'Nothing. Nothing at all.' A millisecond later he's shifted the parcels and buried his fist under his other arm. Then his eyes narrow and he's scrutinising my face. 'Your eyebrows look different – have they grown?'

Of all the things to pick up on. 'It's over ten years, a lot of things are larger than they were, Ross.' My hips. The size of cupcakes. The rips in his jeans. How much I dislike him. How I can't imagine what I ever saw in him.

He's holding up the parcel. 'We'll get back to you with our verdicts later in the week.'

'You'll still be around?' My stomach sinks. 'That's really not necessary.' He's still standing there. 'Tell Nell. If you must.'

'And you'll keep Diesel away from car parks and avocados from now on?'

So he did see us at the harbour earlier. 'And chocolate, cherries, limes and macadamia nuts. Not to mention chives, mushrooms, grapefruit and broccoli.' Like I'd get Diesel to eat any of those if I tried. But all the same, I'm mentally punching the air that thanks to Google I've got the danger list word-perfect. As I march through the gate and coax Diesel back into the garden I'm racking my brains for a way to express how much I don't want to see Ross ever again that's suitable to say in front of the kids.

'A pictorial reminder is so much more effective than lists reeled off.' He's still talking about the bloody poster. 'Hang it above the work surface. And just to make sure, my mobile number's on there in case of emergencies.'

Like I'd allow that to happen to Clemmie's kitchen on

my watch. As for the number, what the eff? 'Now please …
just piddle off and don't come back.'

There's an echo around the garden. 'Piddle off! That's a
good one! Did you hear that, Mum?' But Sophie doesn't
react because she's stripped off and diving into a clean but
identical top she's pulled out of her changing bag.

All of which seems to leave more questions hanging
than answered as Ross strides off around the front of the
house.

5

In the garden at Seaspray Cottage
Pink hair and sudden changes of plan
Tuesday

Three days later, Diesel and I are back in the garden at
Seaspray Cottage. He's lying, nose in the air, sniffing
the sea breeze as it ruffles the grass around him. Despite
racking my brains for a better option, in the end a stall by
the garden gate seemed the best way to bring in instant
cash. So I'm sitting on a wall by the criss-cross brick terrace,
one eye on my laptop, the other on the gingham-covered
table I carried out to the beach path earlier today. But five
hours on from putting out my tray bakes and a £1.50 *each*
sign, they're still all there under the two glass domes.

As a familiar check shirt appears at the table, I sigh and
confess. 'You were right, Nell, I won't get rich anytime soon
selling cakes over the wall.'

'I'll have a dozen.' She pulls a note out of her pocket and

starts to fill some of the bags I've left under a smooth stone from the beach.

I sigh. 'You're my financial adviser, take them as a gift. At least that idea's been tested to destruction now.'

She smiles. 'It's nothing to do with your baking. Between the harbourside donut stall and the Surf Shack isn't the best location; lots of passing trade but all on their way to eat or full already.' She tucks the bag of buns in the crook of her arm. 'Anyway, I'm here to pick you up for this afternoon. Clemmie did tell you?'

'Of course. It said on the schedule, *Dog therapy at two with Nell*.' I've already been thinking about it. 'Maybe we could sit out here and talk to Diesel about his running off? Or would he prefer a massage?'

The corners of Nell's mouth are curling. 'Diesel's the one *giving* the therapy, not getting it.' She's battling my bemused stare. 'On Tuesdays I take him up to the community retirement home to say hi to the residents. So if you're ready…'

I'm reading her expectant expression. 'You want me *and* Diesel?'

'I did promise I'd take you along. They love meeting new people, especially famous ones.'

In which case they're going to be disappointed, but I close my laptop and check the time on my phone. 'How long have I got?'

'I have Diesel's harness and jacket here. Is five minutes enough for you?'

Considering the state of my hair, five hours would be better. Plus however long it's going to take to clear up the kitchen, which looks like an explosion in an icing sugar factory after my baking earlier. That's the other good thing about film clips, you never have to show the mess out of shot. I might be a neat and tidy cook on screen, but off camera I'm a total disaster area. 'A smudge of lippy and a cardi and I'll be back.' I'm thinking of the countertop full of boxes upstairs I was hoping to have sold that will now be going to waste. 'Would they like some free millionaire's shortbread? They're best eaten while they're fresh.'

Nell's face lights up. 'Turn up at Kittiwake Court with Diesel *and* baking, you'll be a popular woman.'

Quick changes and fast getaways are not my best thing. But half an hour later we're outside a big Georgian villa out along the road to Comet Cove and I'm as ready as I can hope for. At least one of us looks awesome; as Nell presses the bell Diesel's resplendent in his personalised yellow therapy-dog coat. And Nell's looking pretty dapper in her matching handler's waistcoat.

I shiver and wrap the cardi tightly around my polka-dot dress as a woman comes towards the door. 'I wasn't expecting nurses.'

Nell sniffs. 'It's a care home, carers go with the territory.'

'Wouldn't you just hate to be in a place like this?' Her uniform makes it feel very medical and not in a good way. I've known hospitals were places to avoid since I broke my arm when I fell out of a top bunk at a sleepover party when I was seven. Not many people hate injections as much as me, so getting pregnant really wasn't on my to-do list. Those eighteen weeks seemed to last for ever. With all the problems I had enough scans and blood tests to last me a lifetime. Even as we wait here now, that unmistakable mix of antiseptic smell and the taste of cold, bitter coffee out of wobbly plastic cups is as fresh in my mind as if it were yesterday. And it's making my stomach disintegrate.

Nell laughs. 'Actually, I'd love to live here. It's owned and run by the village. I've got my name down already. It's like a luxury hotel in there.'

As the door opens the scent that hits us is a mix of fresh linen and vanilla. There's a washing machine where my tummy should be, but as I take in the biggest smile I've seen since I arrived in St Aidan, the fast spin cycle slows.

'Hi, come in.' As the woman pauses to drop a kiss on Diesel's head, I catch a flash of fuchsia in the crown of her spiky bleached blonde hair and for once he doesn't try to eat her. 'I'm Nell's Aunty Jen. How are you travelling, Cressida? Loving the lustre of your lip colour, do you mind if I ask what it is?'

'Victoria Beckham's Posh.' It's not the first thing I was expecting to talk about, but I was lucky enough to get some promo samples before I dropped into obscurity. And at least she's overlooking my cheeks that must be a pale shade of green after the shock of her uniform.

As she leans in, the waft of Diorella that comes off her is a world away from sterilising fluid. 'It's a favourite pastime here. We women love looking in each other's make-up bags.'

Nell winks and hisses behind her hand. 'People aren't here to end their days, they're here to whoop it up.'

'We're doing a *Grease* singalong later, if you'd like to stay on.' Jen is striding along the wide entrance hall where the cream wool carpet is so deep it almost buries my pink suede Converse trainers, while the walls are painted a turquoise blue that's bright enough to make me feel normal again.

Nell nudges me, and points to one of the pictures. 'Plum painted all these, they're here on loan.'

'They're amazing.' The canvases I'm looking at are six feet high and make me feel like I'm standing right in the middle of a breaking wave. They also explain why there was so much paint on Plum's dungarees the other day.

Jen looks over her shoulder. 'We call this corridor Ocean Boulevard.' Then she pushes through a wide door and we're in a glass room looking straight out over the bay. 'And this is Sea View Lounge, which is exactly what it says on the tin.'

I turn to Nell as I gaze through a wall of floor-to-ceiling windows to the ocean beyond. 'It's duck-egg blue today. Clemmie told me to look out for the way the colour changes with the sky.'

Jen turns to the residents, who look up from stylish checked armchairs. 'Diesel and Nell are here, and they've brought Cressida Cupcake with them.'

Suddenly every face in the room turns to me. When they all start to clap I fight the impulse to dive behind the nearest recliner and instead manage a wave and a mumble. 'My real name's Cressy.' I hand Jen the boxes I'm carrying. 'There's some baking too.'

Jen's face breaks into a beam again. 'Thank you. We'll have that with tea.'

There's a cough from the open double doors. 'Any pasties in there?'

Jen wags her finger at a man pushing his way in from the patio outside, wearing what looks like Plum's boiler suit minus the paint, and a tweed cap. 'Any more cheek from you, Walter, you won't be getting any.' Jen turns to the others. 'Okay, who'd like to see Diesel first?'

There are more enthusiastic cries from round the room and before I have the chance to check if this Walter is any relation to the one from the other day, Nell's already chatting to their first customer while Diesel stands patiently having his head patted.

I perch on a footstool, and watch as Nell takes him from one chair to the next. As Jen comes to stand nearby I can't contain my smile. 'Isn't it amazing the way everyone lights up when they talk to Diesel? He's never this good with me.'

Jen smiles. 'Is it too much to hope you'll pop in with him on your own sometimes while you're here?'

I give a cough. 'Unless you want mayhem, I'll save you the trouble.'

Jen laughs. 'We can handle mischief. You may have noticed, Walter's our biggest tease here.'

I'm opening my mouth with the same question I was going to ask Nell but Jen gets in first. 'There was another favour I was going to ask – could you possibly do a little activity with us one day?'

I wasn't ready for this, but the sea air seems to be great for thinking on my feet. 'I could do manicures. I've got some very pretty nail-art sequins.'

Jen's clicking her tongue in disapproval. 'We can't waste Cressida Cupcake on nails! How about something more kitchen-based? Maybe later this week?'

There's no time to say I'll think about it. 'I could bring in some buns to ice?' It sounds a lot easier than keeping Diesel under control.

Jen gives a cough. 'I think they were hoping to see you in action, perhaps with your mixer?'

It was bad enough having the whole room looking at me just before. 'If I tried to cook with people watching, I'd be so nervous I'd drop things.'

Jen's lips are twitching. 'They all have their iPads for facetiming their friends and families. When Nell heard you were coming she loaded you up and they've watched your baking clips non-stop ever since.'

'It never occurred to me that I'd appeal to this demographic.' I hope that sums it up without giving offence. My views have to come from somewhere, but I'd always imagined they were from people like me, not my grandparents.

Jen shrugs. 'Better still, it reminds them of being at home again, even though most of them have made the decision to give them up.'

There's a loud shout from the doorway. 'Speak for yourself, Jennifer Crawley, I'm not staying here a moment longer than I have to.'

Jen cups her hand to her mouth and calls back. 'There's obviously no problems with your hearing, Walter. Or your hollering.'

He gives a chuckle. 'I've had plenty of practice over the years calling them cows in.'

I think that may have answered my question.

Jen's eyes flash towards the ceiling. 'Why not come over here, Walter, so you don't have to shout?' But as he sits down in a chair where he is, she turns to me again. 'So what do you think, are you going to come and bake for us?'

If I play for time, something – most likely Diesel – will save me. It's the first time I've been willing him to be naughty, but until he is I'll steer the conversation away from food. I nod at the nurse across the room in a very pretty overall. 'Is that Sanderson dandelion-clock print she's wearing?' When I moved into my latest rental share I made two cushions in the same print with bobble fringe to make the room more mine.

From the way Jen's face brightens, I've hit another of her sweet spots. 'We have our scrubs specially made up here in the village.' She smooths down her own tunic. 'Mine's Fairyland.'

'So it is.' More fool me for thinking she was in operating-theatre pink earlier. Now I'm close up I can see it's covered in delicate woodland flowers and tiny winged creatures.

'Tanya's got it in blue. She's coming now with the drinks.'

From the way Nell and Diesel are both looking up three chairs along, they've heard the clink of china way before the trolley trundles into the room.

'Tea's up!' Tanya grins around as she dips and pulls on the brake. 'And there's a visitor for you, Walter.'

Talk about being caught off-guard. It's the total wrong place for Ross to turn up, and the total wrong time. But as I look up and see his figure by the tea trolley, that's not the worst of it. Because the way he's standing behind the nurse in a pale blue uniform is like an exact recreation of the scene twelve years ago, the day he flew in from

America and took me by surprise at the hospital. As my insides collapse to nothing, the breath goes out of my lungs, and as my head spins the words are echoing in my ears.

> *'But I told you I could do this by myself.'*
>
> *'I'm here because I want to support you.'*
>
> *'You're way too late.' As if he could just switch on the caring, months down the line. And there I was, still stunned by how ferocious the labour had been. 'There isn't going to be a baby after all.'*

As for now, I don't know what to do first: throw up, or slide down on the floor. But then as the voices in my head quieten I catch sight of Ross's wide-eyed blinking. The way he's blowing out his cheeks, I reckon I might have the edge in the surprise stakes this time round. And that thought acts like a blast of rescue remedy.

As my sagging spine stiffens, I swallow hard, and try to sound super-bright. 'Ross, you're visiting Walter! You must be here to say goodbye?'

Ross's jaw is still hanging open, but Walter's straight in there.

'I'm not dying that quick, Mrs Cakeface.'

I'm cursing silently at how wrong that went. 'I'm talking about Ross leaving, not you, Walter.'

Ross's eyes disappear into his head, but at least he's got his jaw into gear. 'And the bad news is, I'll be around for a while longer.' He pulls in a breath as he turns away. 'Walter, you're in the lounge, how about taking your hat off?'

Walter lets out a loud laugh. 'You know my motto, lad. Cap on at all times – unless I'm getting my leg over!'

Nell's spluttering into her hand. 'Walter, what are you like?'

Walter grins at her. 'Being in here gets my hopes up on an hourly basis.'

Nell's heading him off. 'Cressy's the one who made the brownies Ross brought you, Walter. She was wondering if you liked them. Seeing she's here, why don't you tell her yourself?'

With Walter as he is, I'm bracing myself for his reply.

'Baking that tasty? I'd say you need to put a ring on it, pronto, Ross.'

Now I've heard it all. But it was worth it, if only to see the look of horror on Ross's face. As for me, seeing there are no available holes to crawl into, the only option is to play this for laughs.

I grin at Nell. 'And to think I thought a bad hair day was the worst it could get.'

Nell laughs. 'He'll have to catch her first, Walter. Cressy's got very high standards, she won't say "yes" to just anyone.' She winks at Ross. 'Not even the hottest vet in St Aidan.'

It's as if her wink makes Diesel notice Ross for the first time. His nose quivers and his ears prick up, then he's leaping to his feet, claws scratching on the polished pine floorboards. Two huge bounds later, he crashes past the tea trolley and comes to a halt with a front paw on each of Ross's shoulders.

Nell sighs as she walks across to Jen and me. 'Something

tells me that's the end of our calm therapy-dog for today. Poor Diesel, he's still getting used to Charlie being away.'

I'm feeling so guilty for hoping he'd do this. I'm also truly grateful he's saved me from a long afternoon sitting in the same room as Ross. It's out before I know what I'm saying. 'We'll come back and do bun icing later in the week.'

Jen's straight back. 'Thursday would be lovely.'

I just hope that's enough to keep them happy, because that's definitely the most I can offer. And I'll have to have a word with Nell to make sure Ross is at the other end of Cornwall that day.

6

In Clemmie's flat at Seaspray Cottage
Excruciating suggestions and decisive action
The next evening, Wednesday

I n spite of me sending Clemmie and Charlie photos of
their fur babies at least once an hour, at some time every
day they do a FaceTime call for a proper catch-up. It's top
secret, but they're not *only* in Sweden for a holiday. Charlie's lifelong friend is a consultant at one of the top fertility
clinics out there, so when they found they were unlikely to
have a baby without IVF, he was the one they turned to for
help. Luckily they can afford both the private treatment and
the travel, and they've got some embryos now. But after
their first short trip for treatment came to nothing, this time
they've opted for a longer stay so they can relax and boost
their chances of success.

This evening we started the FaceTime call showing them
Pancake blissing out on my cardi. My screen fills with

Clemmie's tumble of auburn curls as she comes in for a closer look. 'Typical Pancake, and I see Diesel's comfy on the pink velvet sofa. I hope the girls are looking after *you*?'

'They've given me a great welcome.' I point the phone to give her the full benefit of Diesel asleep on his back, legs in the air, and move the conversation on before she has time for more mermaid suggestions. 'We walked right round to Comet Cove earlier.' It was Diesel's idea, not mine, and my legs feel like they might be dropping off.

Charlie's low voice cuts in. 'Who'd have thought we'd ever see Egbert walk so far?'

If Charlie's calling me by my childhood nickname Egbert he must be especially grateful. Egbert began with Egg-and-cress-y, and I was glad of anything less stuffy than Cressida. When I first came up with Cressida Cupcake for my YouTube clips, it was a joke. But then nothing else had the same ring, so in the end it stuck.

Clemmie's laughing. 'Just warning you, if Pancake's wheedled her way onto your cashmere, she'll be there until we get home. Any other news?'

I shiver as I think about yesterday. 'There was dog therapy which went *really* well, and I'm just doing *lots and lots* of recipe testing. Truly, I'm in baking heaven.'

I've been washing-up non-stop since I got here, but it's still way more chaotic than it was when Clemmie left it, so I keep the mess out of shot. And I definitely mustn't let them know about the lost book contract, or Charlie will insist on filling up my bank account. The point is, he's rich because he worked his ass off and I've never taken handouts. Me supporting myself is a matter of honour; I'd metaphorically die before I asked for help. They have three months of enforced relaxation to cover on top of their clinic bills, and the beautiful Scandi beach houses they've chosen must be costing shedloads. Rich as they are, they really do need every penny for themselves right now, so I cram the next few minutes with pet details so they won't guess anything's wrong.

And just when I think I've got away with it, Clemmie fills the screen again. 'There's a Polaroid camera and film in the green dresser. You're welcome to use it, then you can show me what you've baked. It'll be wonderful to see your recipe book coming together, day by day!'

Damn. I hadn't thought that one through. 'Thanks, Clemmie, Polaroids would be useful for making the final selections. And I could run my chapter ideas past you too – that's if you don't mind?'

Clemmie's eyes are bright. 'I'd love to be involved. I'm really missing the Little Cornish Kitchen, it'll make me feel useful.'

'Great, that's sorted then!' I hope no one from the village accidentally tells them the truth. But if I was looking for an incentive to do the book on spec, this might be it.

As Clemmie waves goodbye Charlie's face fills my screen again. 'One last thing before I go – I was talking to Ross last night.'

My stomach drops. 'Really?' I hate that his name sends bits of my body into freefall. 'He was visiting up at Kitti-wake Court when we were there.' Charlie has no idea about my complications in the past with Ross; as the timing was so bad, we kept it from him.

Charlie pauses. 'He offered to come and stay at the flat to give you a hand with the crew.'

'*He did what?*' Shit, he can't possibly be thinking of it seriously?

'You two always got on so well and Ross is literally sleeping in a cupboard up at the surgery.' Charlie sounds hell bent on pushing this. 'Another pair of hands might be good for *you* if you're finding it hard.'

I'm definitely not going to echo *that* negative language. 'Who says I'm not breezing through this?'

He coughs. 'No one – *absolutely no one* – has mentioned you're struggling, okay?'

It's getting worse. This can only be one person, and even for him it's low. Ross plants the metaphorical seeds of doubt then rides in on his bloody white charger to take over the spare room. Of all the unexpected disasters I've had lately, this would be the hugest yet! I need to put this fire out before it takes hold.

'Ross and I both have *huge* personalities and masses of professional accessories. There just isn't enough room here for both of us *and* a dog the size of Diesel.' I don't give Charlie time to remember that I'm the youngest of six kids, so making do with small is what I'm good at. Instead I whizz on. 'Let's talk again tomorrow and revisit this in a couple of weeks. Okay, byeeeeeee.'

And then I do something I never do: I end the call.

7

At Kittiwake Court
Carnage, chaos and random chatter
The next afternoon, Thursday

'Has everyone got a cupcake?'

As I look at the faces around the table the next afternoon, I can already see they have. I'm also aware that my voice is wobbling with nerves in a way it never does on the film clips, which is why I've minimised the risk by keeping this simple. I've brought along three dozen small sponge buns I baked this morning, and now the icing sugar is rising in a cloud as I pour water into the bowl in front of me and start to stir to make the glacé icing.

This is as hard as it gets, so there's no reason for me to have quite so many flutters in my tummy. But as it's a live performance with no possibility of retakes, and thanks to me reliving the horrors of those few days baking at the TV

61

studio, I woke up worrying at four and didn't go back to sleep again. At least the head-start meant I had time for my full hair-washing and make-up routine; it's just a shame I've had to tie my hair back on the one day it's really shiny and smooth.

I know flipping my hair about is one of my accidental signature moves on YouTube, but *those* cakes aren't going to get eaten by the public. Given the minefield of health and safety these days, we're probably lucky we aren't wrapped up in hairnets here today. As it is, all Jen suggested apart from my ponytail was plastic aprons for the residents.

Pam shifts in her wheelchair, and runs her finger over the crinkly edge of her blue spotty bun case. 'They didn't always make cases this fancy! Back in the sixties we only had two choices: white or white with flowers.'

Kathleen picks hers up and sighs. 'When I think of how many of these I've made in my time… My Den used to have them every day in his snap box.'

Joanie looks at hers. 'When our kids were small it wasn't a birthday party if you didn't have fairy cakes. With orange squash to go with them, and paper straws that always went soggy.'

I smile because it's funny how one small cake can bring so many memories flooding back, and I may as well share mine too. 'My mum hung ours off strings on her Sheila Maid drying rack and we used to eat them with our hands tied behind our backs at Halloween.'

Joanie nudges Pam. 'I bet that was a sticky business.'

'But so worth it.' I grin at her. 'You can't beat the icing and sponge combination.'

Simple iced buns are extra special for me because these were the first thing Charlie and I ever made together, the summer he taught me to bake. Family legend has it that our mum refused to let Charlie leave home until he was fully house-trained, although we tease her that she thought a guy who could cook, bake and clean like a dream would get better girlfriends. By the time she got to her sixth child, she was understandably flagging, so I made it all the way to the age of twenty before Charlie decided to put that right himself.

Jen's listening in further down the room, where Nell is taking Diesel round to the people who aren't joining in with me. She calls to us. 'Buns on strings – I'll put that in my diary for October.'

After Faye died Charlie and Diesel took refuge at home with our mum and dad, and I was there too, on my summer break from uni, working as a mother's help. Every evening after work we'd pull on our pinnies and roll up our sleeves. It wasn't just about the therapy of doing something practical to take his mind off the agony he was going through. All the delicious cakes we cooked had to have helped too.

You can't ever mend fully after a loss as huge as Charlie's. By the end of the summer he was in good enough shape to venture down to Cornwall, just him and Diesel. And when I went back to my last year at uni I was able to cook, even though at the time I had no idea how much I'd be using it a few years later.

As I always say in my videos, never underestimate the power of sugar! Just stirring now, watching the shiny icing run slowly off the spoon and back into the bowl, I feel more relaxed and in control of my life, even if I'm not.

Pam nudges Roger, who's sitting next to her. 'Looking forward to having a try?'

Roger looks as doubtful as I feel. 'I'm afraid cooking was Cynthia's department, not mine.'

Jen raises an eyebrow. 'You've built power stations, Roger, you can do this.'

I smile at Roger. 'I'll come and show you. All we do is spread the icing on the top of the cake.' On the upside, at least we're not dealing with Walter and his wisecracks today. I don't know where he is, but I'm thanking my lucky stars he's not at our table.

Joanie holds up a finger. 'But that icing's white!'

I smile. 'White icing with bright coloured hundreds and thousands, that's what we always had at home.'

Joanie's shaking her head. 'Oh, no! Mine always had pink icing.'

Kathleen frowns. 'And my Den only liked yellow. Mine won't feel right if they're not yellow.'

I drag in a breath and count to ten. I may as well ask. 'How about anyone else?'

Pam gives a little shrug. 'Duck-egg blue is my favourite. I made them every Sports Day, they went with the girls' PE shirts.'

Ian coughs next to Roger. 'I support Exeter City, they play in red and white stripes.'

Oh my days. Jen's wading straight in to help. 'We've all enjoyed a trip down Memory Lane, but this is your activity, Cressy. It's fine to stick with white for today.'

I'm nodding in relief and agreement when I see Kathleen's expression. It reminds me of Diesel's when he wants an extra biscuit and I say no. And what's worse, I crack *every time*. And not that I'm comparing Kathleen to Diesel, but a second later I'm looking at Jen. 'If you've got some extra bowls and food colouring, I've brought enough icing sugar.' It's my one and only time here, I might as well go for broke. 'Let's have pink, yellow, white and blue too.'

Twenty minutes later, as I beat the icing in the fourth bowl to a lovely pale turquoise and push it into the centre of the table, I'm hoping three varieties of hundreds and thousands will be enough to hit the spot. But there's no time to worry about that as everyone's spoons hit the bowls together. Pam, Joanie and Madge are making a meticulous job, but some of the others need more help. There's icing flying everywhere but I'm too stressed running from person to person to think about the mess.

It's only as I stand up to brush off a splat of icing that landed on my cheek that I take in that we've actually got a second audience. This one's resting his shoulder on the wall, right next to where Walter is sitting by the door to Ocean Boulevard, and the shadows playing on his stubble make him look drawn and distant. For all I know, he's probably day-dreaming about how he's going to take over Clemmie's living room. And damn that I whip my eyes away too late, because he catches my gaze and comes to life.

'This is nothing like YouTube, Cressy – that table looks more like one of Plum's seascapes.'

'You know Plum too?' Of course he does. And he's been watching my clips as well, which makes my heart hit the floor before it bounces back into my chest again. 'I thought Nell said you worked Thursdays?' That's one advantage of everyone knowing everyone. It took one call to Sophie's receptionist sister-in-law. Not that I wanted to give anything away, but it was well worth sharing with Nell and Sophie that Ross wasn't my favourite old friend of Charlie's, if it meant I didn't have to bump into him.

Ross shrugs. 'Walter had an appointment today.'

Not only has Ross wrecked my forward planning, he also told Charlie about my disasters with Diesel. I might as well get this over. 'And to save disappointment, Ross – I'm not looking for a roomie at Seaspray Cottage.'

Joanie looks up. 'What's a roomie again?'

Oops. I make my voice airy. 'Sorry, everyone, we'll move on to sprinkles in a second.' Then I hiss through my teeth at Ross, 'And telling tales isn't cool.'

He narrows his eyes. 'About what?'

Nice try there. I look down the room to where Diesel's in his high-vis coat next to Nell in hers, giving his paw to a resident as if butter wouldn't melt. 'Diesel not always being as perfectly behaved as he is today. Now if you'll excuse me, I need to get back to my cakes.'

Ross's voice rises. 'Call me many things, but I'm not a dobber.'

But I'm back at the table, taking the tops off the decoration boxes. 'Let's move on with the hundreds and thousands.' I'm looking at Roger, who's got as much icing on his ear as on his bun. 'Take a pinch and sprinkle them on top of the icing.'

Pam nods. 'That's why they're called sprinkles, Roger.'

Joanie smiles. 'The icing is wet, and as it sets the sprinkles stick to the top.'

Roger is nodding as if something major is falling into place in his mind. 'Well, well, isn't that cunning?'

Pam's carrying on. 'Did you know, each molecule of sugar contains twelve carbon atoms, twenty-two hydrogen atoms and eleven oxygen atoms?'

'I must remember that.' Jen's shaking her head at me. 'You learn something every day with this lot around.'

I push the boxes towards them before they start asking *me* about science. 'What are you waiting for? Go, go, go!' Approximately five minutes from now my ordeal will be over. I know my first job on a slimming magazine was sometimes an eye-opener, but my mental picture of older people spending all day snoozing has been seriously challenged this afternoon.

Walter is peering from under his cap, and lifting his walking stick. 'My Sarah always won first prize with her little cakes at that women's place she went to on Monday nights.'

Joanie's eyes light up. 'Yes! Your Sarah was queen of the butterfly buns at the WI.'

Jen's smiling at me. 'They sound like a great idea to try next time.' She lowers her voice. 'They might make Walter feel more at home here.' Then she raises it again. 'Does the same time next week suit you, Cressy?'

My stomach deflates. 'You want more next Thursday?'

'Unless you can fit us in before.'

The splatters across the table look more like an explosion in a paintball park than cooking in a care home lounge. I'm staring down to where Ian and Roger are dipping their icing-covered hands into the sprinkle boxes. They hold up fingers encrusted with sugar strands. 'So what do we do next, Cressy?'

Pam's shaking her head at them. 'How many Captain of Industry Awards do you two have between you? Grab a paper towel each before you go any further.'

Then a cough behind me makes me turn. 'Actually the snitch wasn't Ross, it was me.'

'Nell?'

Her hands are deep in the pockets of her Day-Glo waistcoat and Diesel's wagging beside her. 'I may have *inadvertently* mentioned Diesel's escapades to Clemmie.'

'So what about Ross?' My gut tells me he's in this too.

But we never get to answer that question, because Diesel's nose is at table level, and a second later he strikes. But I'm learning fast.

What do they say about never working with dogs or children? As I dive in and swipe Joanie's bun to safety right out from under Diesel's nose, I turn to see a tribe of kids filing in, with Sophie waving at me from behind them.

'Are you up for a few more customers? We couldn't resist joining in with fairy cakes!'

The eldest girl takes in my wide-eyed blinking. 'Don't worry, I'll help the littlies. We won't be here long, we're on our way to dancing.'

Jen's right behind her. 'And you will bring your mixer

with you next time, Cressy? We can't wait to watch you make buttercream in person.'

Maybe this is the way in St Aidan. You can't fight it, you simply have to go with it. Which might be fine for kids icing cupcakes. But it certainly doesn't extend to Ross Bradbury making moves on my flat.

8

At Clemmie's flat
Waaaaahhh – that's all
Saturday

My afternoon icing buns with the residents at Kittiwake Court leaves me feeling more like I've been trampled by a large herd of heavy animals than rubbing shoulders with octogenarians. My news is that after another chat with Martha I've decided to press on with the book while I have time and an agent. And if she can't place it when it's done – I'll self-publish. So I'm pushing straight on with recipe selecting, and I have a week – maybe two – to come up with ideas for making cash before my finances hit rock bottom.

If I want to make progress I can't be out in the garden or in view on the balcony where I might get ambushed. So for the last couple of days I've thrown the living-room doors open and worked sitting on the floor. With the late spring sunshine spilling in from outside I'm in the perfect position to catch the diamond glints off the sky-blue sea through the balcony balustrade.

So far I've been baking items as they popped into my head, but in an effort to be methodical rather than random I've decided to go through my blog and the YouTube clips. But it turns out to be a bigger job than I imagined; by the evening of the second day I'm nowhere near finished.

As I watch the sun sinking towards the horizon I give Diesel a nudge where he's lying against my knee. 'I feel a lot like Alice when she fell down the rabbit hole.' I've seriously underestimated how many pieces I've produced over the years, which is wonderful in one way, but makes it harder to sort.

The way Diesel opens one eye then closes it again, he's telling me that unless there's food or an outing coming his way he's not about to engage. It's funny because a few days ago I had no idea at all what Diesel was thinking because I hadn't quite tuned in. But if I'm getting to the cupcakes before he does, we've definitely crossed a bridge in our relationship. If we carry on like this, I'll soon be the one deciding the routes we take on our walks too.

When I first arrived I was completely up for being pulled around the bay. But with Ross Bradbury breathing down my neck it would be useful to look like I'm in control, even if I'm not. I get that Diesel's being more of handful than normal if he's missing Charlie and Clemmie. But what the hell does Ross think he can add that I'm not doing already?

And if I sound antsy, that's because I am! It's not only

that the man is irritating beyond belief; I'm also cross with myself. I can excuse my teenage incarnation for panting with excitement whenever he turned up because that's just what happens when you're a hormone-charged fourteen-year-old. Obviously I cringe that I was ever sad enough to stick my chest out while wearing teensy crop-tops to try to make him notice my boobs, or use actual black felt tip trying to get eyes as sooty as Avril Lavigne's.

But what I can't excuse is getting that same rush now. When I *know* the inside in no way matches up to the sizzling-hot exterior, it makes no sense at all for my tummy to still be turning somersaults whenever I catch sight of him. And the more I think about the way Ross is manipulating Charlie into letting him stay at the flat, the more appalled I am. I know from experience that Ross is an emotional coward; but somehow it's shocking all over again to find he's a self-seeking opportunist too.

Rant over, and back to my life looking after the animals. As for Pancake, she's adoring me giving her a daily brush, and up until today she's been devouring her gourmet fish dishes faster than I could put them out. Apart for this morning, that is. When I deliver her Taste of the Sea with crab a few minutes from now, I know she's going to get all purry and try to devour it before I get the pack open, because she loves that flavour so much she even knows the name.

I get up to call her through. 'Panpan, it's dinner time, you're having cr-a-a-a-a-b…'

Instead of the patter of kitty paws and those bright blue eyes instantly peeping round the door to the hall, Diesel sidles towards me but there's no other movement. As I go through to the bedroom to see where Pancake has got to, I notice the litter tray hasn't been used since this morning either.

'Hey, Mrs Lazy, you can't stay on your cashmere *all* day.' I lean across the pillow and give her ear a tickle. She barely stirs and it takes a few moments before she blinks at me. As she drops her head back onto the cardi there's an uneasy twang in my chest.

'Come to Aunty Cressy.' I ease her off the bed, and as her weight sinks onto my waist it's like a hot water bottle bursting. I let out a shriek as tepid liquid runs down my legs. 'Panpan, you're peeing!!!' I worked as a mother's help so it's not the wee itself that's alarming. But she shouldn't be as floppy as she is unless she's ill. And she never wets out of the litter tray.

I snatch a towel, then take her through to the kitchen and start leafing through Clemmie's manual.

I sink onto a bright blue chair and let out a groan. 'You can't be ill, Pancake, because I don't know what to do.' Then my moan deepens. 'Oh my, *what if she dies?*'

The St Aidan vets' phone number is there in large font, and somehow I think it's best to find out what we're dealing with here before worrying Charlie and Clemmie. There's a different number for emergencies but it's for an out-of-hours vet in Penzance half an hour away.

As I take my phone out of my pocket I can see it's already after eight. And then I catch sight of the damned poster Ross gave me, still folded under a pile of post. I peel back the corner and sure enough there's a line of neat numbers in black marker next to his name. And he's also printed:

Any worries, any time, I'll be happy to help.

Except he wasn't exactly happy to help when I called all those years ago, was he? It's a fleeting thought and now's not the time. He's the last guy in the world I'd want to ring. But he's only five minutes away. And I'm ringing for Pancake and Charlie and Clemmie, not me.

I've pressed call before it hits me I have no idea what to say if he picks up. But one ring later he does.

'Ross Bradbury?'

I'm floundering. 'It's Cressy, there's something wrong with Pancake...'

'I'll come straight over.'

My gulp is so huge, I almost swallow the phone. 'Actually, we'll come to you.'

'Straight up the hill from the harbour, we're half a mile on the left along the Rosehill road. I'll wait for you out in the car park.'

He's as good as his word. Never in my wildest nightmares have I ever imagined I'd be pleased to see Ross. But as the car tyres scrunch across the gravel towards a long low converted barn with a sign that says *Veterinary Surgery*, and I catch sight of a familiar figure, jeans sliding down off his hips, I'm close to ecstatic.

As I pull to a halt he opens the back door of Charlie's runaround and takes Diesel, and by the time I'm out of the driver's side he's already got Pancake's basket out too. It's a good thing he's got his hands full, because it helps me to hold back from throwing my arms around him. Instead, as he strides off towards the door saying not to bother locking the car, I'm running to keep up.

'Come on in.' Somehow he hangs onto both animals *and* holds the door open for me.

I scoot past getting a blast of something that's disturbingly more man-scent than vet disinfectant. It's only as I inhale that it hits me – I ran out of the flat without a thought. My mouth is still operating with no input from me. 'Excuse me being covered in cat wee.' That probably over-rides that I barely brushed my hair today.

'It goes with the territory.' He gives a sardonic grimace and leads the way through a lofty white-painted waiting room and into a smaller side room and we come to a halt either side of a tall table. As the door clicks closed behind me Ross wipes down the table surface and checks the details he's brought up on a screen. 'We're short on state-of-the-art equipment here, but hopefully the care makes up for that.' He's already easing Pancake out of her basket. 'So what have you been up to, old girl?' He hooks his stetho-scope in his ears and starts moving the other end around Pancake.

I'm spouting random snippets that might help. 'She'd been off her food and sleeping a lot, then I picked her up and she exploded.'

He's squeezing her tummy, then he lifts her tail and pops a thermometer into her bottom. 'You should protest a lot more about this too, Pancake.' He turns to me after a couple of minutes. 'Her chest is clear, but she's running a temperature. I'd say we're looking at a bladder infection. A urine sample will confirm that, but in the meantime we'll give her an antibiotic injection and some painkillers.'

I'm stammering. 'So she's n-not going to b-burst and she's not going to die?'

'Hopefully not this week.' As he moves her over to some scales on the windowsill he's so laid back, I'm asking myself if I've made the wrong call here.

'And it could have waited until morning?'

He shrugs. 'It's always best to get them checked out sooner rather than later.'

'Especially when they aren't yours.' It's not lost on me. On the way here I was working out how the hell I'd break the news to Charlie if anything happened to Pancake. As Ross looks down to read the numbers off the scales, my eyes are glued to the stubble shadows on his jaw. His hair curling over the collar of his polo shirt. Obviously I wouldn't usually be careless enough to stare but I'm just so damned thankful Pancake's okay, for now I mind less.

His cough makes me look up again. 'She's a heavy lady. That was a lot of stairs for you to carry a five-kilo cat down with Diesel in tow too.'

'It was totally fine.' My arms did literally feel like they were going to fall off my shoulders. And every time I changed hands with the cat carrier Diesel's lead tied my knees together. But it was still better than having a house call.

As I watch Ross drawing up an injection, there's a tiny alarm bell ringing in my brain. If he's questioning my capability again, I can't let it go.

I clear my throat. 'I'm hugely grateful for you stepping

in like a hero and helping Pancake out tonight. But it's not fair to imply I can't cope, just to twist things to your advantage.'

He pulls up a piece of Pancake's fur, pushes in the needle, then rubs it as he pulls it out again. Then he draws up some liquid from another bottle, squirts that into her mouth, and slips her back into her basket again.

He carries on without a reply. 'Come through, I'll get you some syrup to take with you.'

'Thank you.' I follow him into what looks like an office-cum-kitchen where he unlocks a tall cabinet and picks a box off a shelf. 'So is there an upstairs?'

He blinks. 'The sloping ceilings are the giveaway. The operating suite is at the other end, and that's it.'

'So where do you sleep?' If I'm asking it's out of sheer puzzlement, not nosiness.

He pulls a face as he sets off the printer. 'There's a drop-down bed.'

'Charlie mentioned you slept in a cupboard, that's all.'

There's another shrug. 'Nothing so luxurious. The bed gets the cupboard, not me. Then there's a microwave, and I share the fridge with the vaccines.'

There's barely room for the desk chair, let alone a bed. 'I get why Clemmie's flat seems so attractive, even with all the drawbacks.' The stairs, the teensy size, me being there. It's good to get this properly in the open.

His eyes narrow then his voice goes up. 'You surely didn't think *that came from me*?'

'It's hardly come from anyone else, has it?'

He lets out a sigh. 'I'm used to roughing it, a few more

weeks makes no odds to me. Staying at Seaspray Cottage is the last thing I'd suggest.' He takes a label from the printer, presses it into place and holds out the box.

'Great to know we're on the same page with this.' Then I see the knots of red skin inside his fingers and my stomach clenches. 'And that's your hand again.'

He's shaking his head. 'There's a lot to clear up here, Cressy. It was Charlie who had the crazy idea I should move into the flat, not me. Charlie was worried about *you*, and I wanted to help *him*. Heaven knows why, but he thought it might be good if I were there in case of emergencies.'

'Like tonight.' I'm feeling about two inches tall, because Charlie's right. And obviously it's his call to make. And there's no way I'm going to rake up the past to explain to him why I'd hate Ross to stay. So I'm going to back down here. And then I'm going to go. And however tough it is to be sharing a small space with someone I dislike, because of how badly they let me down, I'll just have to get on with it and be the bigger person. 'The single room's spare at Clemmie's. Or better still, I'll move and leave you the big one.'

He rolls his eyes, then they turn flinty. 'That won't be necessary. As for my hands, I don't need anyone's pity. *Especially not yours!*'

And then he marches out to the waiting room, and swings Pancake in her basket out to the car, and I'm left staring at Diesel. 'That went well. *Not*. And we still don't know if he's coming.' Then Diesel gives my hand a lick, and we follow Ross out into the dusk.

By the time we reach the car Pancake's back on the front

seat and Ross is already closing the door. 'Bring her in first thing Monday. We'll check her over again and take some bloods.' He tosses me a small plastic pot. 'And bring a pee sample too.'

'Thanks for sorting this, Ross.' However ungracious I feel, and however much I wish I hadn't had to turn to him, I'm still truly grateful for what he's done here. And that's not all, but this comes out less easily. 'I'll find you a spare key for Clemmie's. Will Monday be soon enough?'

'There's no rush.' He steps back from the car, digs his hands in his pockets, and swallows. 'I always try to be there for the people I care about, Cressy. That's my way, it's all this is.'

Except we both know that's not true. Because when I needed him, he wasn't there at all.

9

At Kittiwake Court
Icing and anarchy
Tuesday afternoon

'Hello, everyone, I'm Cressida Cupcake and I'm here to fill the world with love and butterfly buns.'

It's the next Tuesday afternoon, we're back at Kittiwake Court again and, believe me, as I look over the heads in front of me my smile is a lot more dazzling than I feel inside. When I agreed to whizz up some buttercream it was supposed to be me and a few residents at a table. If I'd known I'd be standing up in front of an audience there's no way I'd have come.

There are times in life where you just have to stop hyperventilating and go with the flow. The only way forward is to tie up my apron, plug in the lovely pink mixer I've borrowed from Clemmie's and go.

Joanie is calling from the centre. 'You don't *really* mind, do you, Cressy? It's lovely to see you as you are on screen, that's all.'

I can't help smiling at her. 'It's fine just this once. But I can't *always* do all the work.' I can't believe I'm talking as if this is going to be a regular gig.

I turn to where Nell is adding a chair to the end of the row. 'What about Diesel and his therapy visits?'

She's already tucking him in at her feet. 'We'll do those afterwards. Plum and Sophie are here to help me keep an eye on him.'

Diesel's resigned sigh is halfway to a snore so it's hardly going to take three of them. I'm just hoping I've brought enough cupcakes.

It's as if Jen's read my mind. 'Don't worry about numbers, Cressy, we're expecting quite a few visitors today, so chef made up extra buns this morning.' She's not joking; there are as many young people here as there are older ones. She lifts an eyebrow. 'All the off-duty staff are here, and there are family members too. And then friends. And friends of friends.' As she nods across at the terrace doors another group slides around the edge of the room.

'Great!' My tummy is turning cartwheels with so many eyes on me, but as I flick back my ponytail I also catch sight of all the lovely people from last week at the front. And without realising, I'm smiling a proper smile at them as I raise my voice to reach the people at the back. 'If I don't get this right first time I'll just have to do another take. Are you all okay with that?'

There's a series of nods and Pam and Joanie chorus, 'Absolutely.'

The truth is, now it's happening it really doesn't bother me how many people are watching, so long as a certain vet isn't anywhere near.

Talking of animals, my furry patient at home picked up as soon as she'd had her antibiotic shot and by Sunday she was eating for England again. When we staggered all the way down the stairs and drove her up to the surgery yesterday I'd been dreading our Monday appointment pretty much since we'd left the first time. But more fool me, because Ross wasn't even there. Instead we saw Elise, who was young and pretty and sang Ross's praises so long and loud, she has to have a crush. By the time Pancake's blood was in the tube I was feeling quite pale.

Then I left Ross's keys to the flat at the reception desk, which means I've been on a knife edge ever since waiting for him to arrive – but he didn't. In fact it's a relief to be out so I don't have to listen for the sound of his key turning in the flat door.

As I look at my friends in the front I'm wondering how to play this. My YouTube clips make things look effortlessly perfect thanks to the editing, but I always try to be completely myself.

I give a little grimace. 'I'll let you all into a secret. I had to look up how to make butterfly buns, because I've never actually made them before.' I can only think Charlie and I missed them out in the rush to get from iced buns onto meringues. 'But luckily for me there's a picnic basket in the kitchen where I'm staying that's filled with Clemmie's gran,

Laura's, recipe cards.' The instructions for butterfly buns from there were brilliant, right down to the last sprinkling of icing sugar. Then something else strikes me. 'Even counting the baking programme, this is the first time I've worked with *this* many people in the kitchen.'

Joanie smiles back at me. 'Knowing Laura's baking, they'll be good. Don't worry, my lovely, there's a first time for everything.'

Pam nods. 'I remember my first day as deputy head-mistress up at the school, it was terrifying.'

Madge joins in. 'When I married my Bert I knew nothing about being a farmer's wife. That first year was terrible, even the hens used to scare me.'

I'm sorting out my scales and ingredients as they talk. 'As some of you probably know, I *have* made buttercream once or twice before. The butter is nice and soft so for this first batch I'm going to use eight ounces and a pound of icing sugar with half a teaspoon of vanilla essence, and see how we go.' I know they'll never have to use the amounts, but they'll want me to stay as close to my usual routine as I can.

Walter gives a laugh. 'My Sarah used to scare me. She'd chase me back out into the yard if I didn't take my boots off at the back step.'

Kathleen's shaking her head at him. 'You should have known better than to drop mud on your Sarah's clean floor, you dozy heffalump. She used to scrub those quarry tiles on her hands and knees until they shone.'

Roger joins in from the back. 'My Cynthia used to chase

me out onto the golf course when I first retired so I didn't get under her feet.'

I smile at Walter. 'It was talking about your Sarah that reminded us about butterfly buns. There must be lots of other recipes we can remember too.' It's only going to take a minute or two to make the icing, so chatting will make it last. And leafing through the basket at Clemmie's, there were so many variations from the past I hadn't seen before. If I'm wanting to hear more about vintage cooking, I'm talking to the right people.

Kathleen smiles. 'My eldest girl has my recipe book. We used to write them in by hand, and if anyone at the WI came across anything new, we'd copy them out and pass them around between us.'

Joanie laughs. 'Do you remember those things called mucky golf balls back in the seventies? We all made them.'

Madge's eyes light up. 'Ground almond, dipped in chocolate. Once you ate one you had to eat them all.'

Pam's got a faraway look in her eye. 'I've still got my recipe books in the storage unit. My *pièce de resistance* was my rum trifle, I made it every July for the end-of-year staff party.'

Ian nods. 'You can't beat a good rhubarb crumble with custard. But I'm talking about eating it, not making it!'

Jen's nodding too. 'And what about custard tart? Did anyone make that?'

It's at least another ten minutes before they've finished discussing blind baking and how much nutmeg is the perfect amount. At this rate it'll be teatime before I begin.

As they start to flag, I tip the icing sugar into the bowl and clear my throat. 'I've borrowed this mixer from Clemmie, but I have the same one in red, which is what my apron matches.'

Nell laughs. 'If this is going to be a regular thing we'll get you an apron with *pink* stripes, Cressy.'

We all know this is my one and only performance, so before she gets any more carried away I start up the mixer. Hopefully by the time I'm looking in at smooth creamy swirls and breathing in the scent of vanilla, Nell will have moved on to something else.

'Thanks to the magic of this fabulous Smeg mixer, we've got lovely buttercream already.' I do a little ta-da, then lift the bowl off and parade it round so everyone can have a look. And I know that promo will be lost on people who don't have their own kitchens, but as Smeg are among my website sponsors I do it anyway.

I get as far along the line as Nell and she opens her eyes wide. 'And another thing …' anything different will be good, '… it's Sophie's Kittiwake Court fundraiser garden party up at Siren House on Saturday.'

'Brilliant.' I'm not sure why they'd mention it to me, but I'm already back at my table ready to push this on. I look up at the room. 'Before I show you how to scoop the little pieces of sponge out of the buns, did everyone get Nell's shout-out for the fundraiser there?'

Sophie's bright blue eyes are fixed on mine. 'One o'clock prompt to set up, the gates open at two! We've put you in charge of the bring-and-buy cake stall, Cressy.'

'You want me to come too?' Of course I'm happy to help

if it's for Kittiwake Court; I'm only sighing because that's another free day I won't be working on my book.

Nell beams around the room. 'So anyone wanting to meet Cressida Cupcake again, make sure you come along on Saturday.'

Sophie's still looking directly at me. 'Don't worry, Cressy, cake stalls in St Aidan sell out faster than you can say Victoria sandwich, you'll be home in no time.' Her perfect eyebrows have lifted. 'But if you have any spare baking time before, rainbow cupcakes are very popular. I'll drop off some unicorn horns for you to put on too. A few dozen of those would really boost our effort. And vegan versions are mandatory too, don't forget – we're very hot on inclusion.'

And there goes my Saturday morning, obliterated by Sophie's rolling juggernaut. And probably my Friday evening too.

Kathleen's nudging Joanie. 'Talking of Victoria sandwiches, do you remember Mrs Hawksley's fatless sponge recipe? That made the best raspberry jam and cream cake ever.'

Walter's stick is in the air. 'Bugger Mrs Hawksley, what I want to know is who gets to lick the bowl out today?'

I have to smile at the way Walter gets straight to the point, and at least he's brought us back on task here. 'Seeing as you asked first, you can do the honours, Walter. Once the bowl is empty you can come up to the table.'

Walter's stick is going again. 'Make sure you leave plenty in there then, I'm not walking all that way for nothing!'

Which has given me another idea. With so many willing hands I should take a note out of Sophie's book and set them to work. 'Next I'm going to show you how to take the centres out of the buns to make the holes for the icing. Who'd like to come to the table and carry on with that afterwards?'

'We will!' Pam's already got Jen wheeling her chair to the front, and Joanie's up on her walking frame.

I'm breaking it down into tasks. 'And let's have Kathleen to spoon the buttercream into the holes. And then Madge and Ian can come and cut the sponge discs into halves, and stick them in the icing so they look like butterfly wings. And then I'll help Roger sprinkle them with icing sugar.'

There's a voice from the back. 'Aren't you piping the buttercream?'

After last week's icing explosion, I know better than to let this lot anywhere near a full piping bag, which is why I stuck to the spoon method. I know I'm trying to be honest, but sometimes you can't be. 'We're doing the fast cheat for this week because I was saving piping for next time.' And damn if I've just committed myself again there.

Jen's beaming. 'We knew you'd want to make this a weekly event once you got started.'

At which point someone arrives from the kitchen with more boxes of cakes, and before I know it I'm stalling Walter and making up more buttercream instead. By the time the tea trolley trundles in half an hour later, we've got plates of butterfly buns stretching right along the table, and everyone is starting to chat amongst themselves. I'm just neatening the final plate of buns, thinking how pretty their icing sugar dusting looks on the cocked sponge wings, when a voice by the window makes me look up.

'That went well! I'll just come in closer for a couple more shots of Walter with his icing bowl.'

I get the goosebumps on my spine before I fully recognise who it is. And then there's a flick of a curtain and as a figure in jeans and a purple St Aidan vet surgery polo steps out onto the lounge rug, my jaw drops. The only good thing about any of this is the speed of my recovery. 'Ross, what the hell are you here for this time? Is it a runaway tortoise or a gerbil having a heart attack?' Then as he arrives and I catch sight of his phone screen my heart drops in horror. A moment later my voice is soaring. 'Please tell me you aren't filming?'

From his tone he doesn't give a damn. 'Don't knock it, Egbert, it's come out really well.'

I'm so cross I'm spitting. 'Most decent people would have asked permission first.' I bring out my scariest scowl. 'And if you upload *any* of this *anywhere* on the internet, I'll sue your butt off!' It's bollocks but at least I sound like I'm not to be messed with.

But instead of backing down, or – perish the thought – apologising, he just laughs. 'That's just the same face you used to use when you were fourteen and Charlie teased you to distraction.' There's a twist to his lips. 'It's a good thing I was there to defend you.'

'Excuse me?' I don't appreciate him bringing this up now. In any case, if we're talking about teasing, he dished it as much as the rest of them.

He sniffs. 'And I know you're used to the spotlight being all yours, but this is for Walter's son in Australia, to show him how his dad's settling in here. And *of course* I'll run it past you before I ping it off around the world.'

I'm kicking myself for walking into another of Ross's traps. I really *don't* think it's all about me, but I feel about two inches tall. Again.

He clears his throat. 'You did a pretty good job there, making him feel at home.'

'So is there anything else?' I'm not going to back off if he looks like he's in the wrong, but I will tread more carefully in future.

He shrugs. 'Elise says Pancake seems to be making a good recovery.'

'Thanks for your help with that.' I wince as I think of how he and Elise will have to breathe in to pass each other in that tiny surgery office. Especially with the way the fabric of his jeans is stretching across his thighs.

'And it might be worth making an extra unicorn cake or two.'

And some people sound like they rule the world. Just saying. 'And why would I do that?'

'I'll be moving in on Friday. Rainbow buttercream sounds like as good a way as any for me to donate to the Kittiwake Court cause. If that's okay with you?'

Damn, damn, damn. 'Absolutely tickety boo.' It couldn't be further from okay and I'm talking like my mum again. But it's happening. I can't fight it, so I've got to deal with it.

His eyes darken. 'And just so you know, any icing bowls, I'm exactly like Walter.'

If I could cock one eyebrow this is where I'd do it. 'And your point is?'

'Put me down for licking them out.'

Which is terrible news, but it's not my main worry right now. Because I'm another four days closer to the end of my cash and still haven't come up with a way to earn.

10

In the garden at Siren House
Panic buying and wild claims
Saturday afternoon

'The bakers of St Aidan certainly know how to fill a cake stall. If we sell this lot it should be enough to pay for a good few blocks in the extension wall!'

This is me on Saturday afternoon, talking to Sophie's eldest, Millie, my designated helper, as the first early-bird visitors are trickling into the garden party.

Nell filled me in on the fundraising details on our way back home the other day. Kittiwake Court was left to the community as a bequest, to be a homely place to live for people from the village who couldn't manage on their own anymore. Over the years it's been upgraded using gifts from grateful – departed – residents, but lately it's been a victim of both its own success and a raft of new regulations.

Long story cut short, without new kitchen facilities and

bathroom refits to bring the place up to current standards, the council is threatening to close it down. But thanks to Kittiwake taking such good care of people, there's been a dramatic drop-off in legacies. And the eye-watering sum immediately needed to ensure the care home has a future is around a hundred thousand pounds.

There are certain grants available, and fundraising has already begun. But there's still an outstanding amount that's big enough to make Nell whistle. As time is running out fast, the younger residents of St Aidan are going all out to come to the rescue. Knowing all that, I was happy to stay up until gone one making cupcakes and be up again at six to get myself ready.

When Diesel and I arrived here earlier Sophie's husband Nathan and Nell's other half George were lugging the huge pine kitchen table across the garden, and we loaded it with the goods people had dropped off in advance. And now, with Diesel and his water bowl tucked safely underneath, we're looking at the kind of variety you only get at a bring-and-buy event: thistle-printed shortbread biscuits tied in cellophane and finished with tartan bows, a glossy glazed apricot tart that wouldn't look out of place in a French patisserie, a strawberry and cream gateau that looks large enough to feed a rugby team.

And then there are gingerbread men with Smarties buttons and cheeky icing grins, and chocolate cornflake clusters in pretty paper cases made by the playgroup kids, not to mention chocolate banana loaves, lemon drizzles, cherry scones and brownie stacks. And thanks to Sophie's talent for covering every aspect, behind us – believe it or not

– we have a second, empty table and a roll of labels, where people can leave what they aren't going to eat immediately to pick up later.

As for my week and my impending visitor – Ross finally called my mobile yesterday to say he'd be dropping by the flat. Then while Diesel and I were on the beach for our afternoon walk one tiny bag appeared in the small bedroom, along with a note pinned to the kitchen door saying *Back tomorrow*. And as tomorrow's here and we've made it all the way to two o'clock and still haven't seen him, we're taking that as a win. Although the constant waiting's not exactly relaxing; it might be better to get him there, and deal with it. And I'm no further forward with my job ideas either. My mum's sister Nessie does astrology, and I'm currently what she'd describe as stuck. I feel like a damn great planetary shove to move me forward would be good.

Millie looks up as she gets the piles of paper bags and cake boxes ready for the customers. 'It's actually going to take loads of money to save the care home. And the people who live there mustn't find out it could close, in case they worry.' She pulls her fingers across her lips. 'As Mum always says, it's good we know how to zip it in this village.'

The way my own classified information spreads like wildfire, discretion isn't a concept I personally associate with the residents of St Aidan, so I gaze around the lawns to find something to discuss where we'll have more common ground. It should be easy because the whole place is amazing; on one side the grass ends on a cliff edge, and beyond it the navy-blue sea stretches straight out to the horizon. And as I look past the bring-and-buy stalls and the curly metal tables where people are already sitting with cups of tea, I take in a huge stone house with wall tops that zigzag across the cobalt sky. 'It must be nice living in a castle.'

Millie rolls her eyes. 'Don't be taken in. Everyone knows Mum got carried away and bought a wreck. They'll be doing it up for ever and we haven't got two pennies to rub together. But at least my room's cool.' She lets out a sigh then she grins. 'I based my colours on Clemmie's flat.'

She sounds closer to a hundred than eleven. More importantly, for someone who claims to keep secrets, she's alarmingly frank. 'Let me guess. You've got orange, and bright pink and apple green?'

Millie's nodding. 'And Clemmie making rainbow cupcakes for *my* party was what started the craze.' Her face goes serious as she looks at the cupcake towers at the end of the table. 'Yours are even nicer. It's true what Mum says, with your cakes and your celebrity pulling-power, you'll make us a mint.'

For now I'm ignoring that Sophie rushed past a moment ago and added a large sign saying *Unicorn Cakes by Cressida Cupcake*, and doubled my price. Instead I'm watching as Nell hitches up George's pirate britches. He's got a patch over one eye and a fake parrot on his shoulder and as he climbs into some mediaeval stocks, she's swilling sponges in buckets of water.

Meanwhile Millie's waving at Plum as she comes out of the French windows in an ice-blue silk sheath dress with an over-skirt that looks a lot like a sequin-covered fish. Millie turns to me again. 'I've got a mermaid outfit too, but I decided jeans were more practical for helping with Diesel.'

She looks at me. 'What a shame we didn't think, you could have borrowed Mum's tail. Nell's putting hers on soon too.'

'Really, I'm fine as I am. In any case, people will recognise me more easily in my apron.' It's not a refuge I'd usually take, but I reckon I've had a very narrow escape there. I'm up for a lot of things, but a full mermaid costume isn't one of them.

Millie's grinning. 'It's okay anyway, they'll all know it's you because of your amazing shiny hair.' She gives her hair a little swish over her shoulder that's a lot like the one I do, then looks at me. 'I've been practising all week, did I get that right?'

I'm not sure whether to be horrified or appalled, so it's a shock when I spin around from Millie and my face hits a purple chest with a vets' surgery logo on it. I allow myself one second to let my stomach descend like a high-speed lift, then I force myself into action. 'Ross! Customers on the other side of the table, please!' I'm looking past him to a crowd clustered at the far end of the lawn. 'Whatever's going on over there seems popular, you might like a look at that.'

Millie peers past me. 'That's Nell's singles club, they've got a speed-dating table and a lucky-in-love bran tub.'

Ross nods at the bulging pocket of his jeans. 'Already been, and believe me, there's nothing lucky about that tub. I pulled out a "Get to Know Your Partner" quiz game, which is zero use to me when I don't have one.' He takes a step back, which in some ways makes things worse not better, because instead of looking at a small square of polo shirt piqué I now have a view of the whole smiling guy. And truly, absolutely *no* part of me is whooping to find out he's unattached. Then he runs his fingers through his curls and gives the kind of inscrutable grin that used to finish me off. 'I saw Diesel's lead was tangled round the table leg. If that means I'm also rubbing shoulders with Cressida's world-famous cupcake tower, it's entirely accidental.'

It might help if I close my eyes. 'Just sort Diesel, help yourself to a sugar hit and—' how to say bugger off in public? '—go and throw some sponges at a pirate.' I open them again expecting he'll be long gone, but he's still in exactly the same spot.

He lets out a breath. 'The stocks are next to the Roaring Waves beer tent. I just left Walter there with all his mates from the market. In any case, I wanted a word.'

The gates must have opened, because the garden is suddenly heaving and people are already lining up in front of us. I take the money for a Victoria sandwich, four bags of fudge and half a dozen unicorn cakes that Millie packs into a cake box, then push a cupcake at Ross to hide how much my heart just sank at the thought of talking to him. 'Eat this and come back when we're quieter.'

For the next two hours there'd be no space for Ross to get a look in even if he were here. All I'm doing is taking money while Millie wraps whatever is needed and shuffles the cakes around. Better still, I hit on a brilliant way to direct people's attention away from the whole Cressida Cupcake thing; I ask them what their favourite cakes are, and after that there's only time for me to say, 'Hope you enjoy' as I give them their change and move on to the next customer. It's so busy I don't give Ross another thought until there's finally a lull and I see him coming towards us from the house carrying a tray of mugs.

'You're still here.' It's a statement, not a question, seeing as he's next to us.

Millie grins. 'He's been working really hard the whole time, bringing cakes over from the kitchen.'

'He has?'

Millie's beam widens. 'So I could fill the gaps on the stall. He's what Mum calls a natural helper.'

Ross gives a shrug. 'Only doing what Sophie told me. Now it's quietened down I grabbed us all some tea.'

Millie beams at me. 'Also very helpful, you see? He just can't stop himself.' And she could be right.

'Great.' The mug's already in front of me so it looks like a done deal, but at least we're standing up, which makes it less of a commitment.

Ross coughs as he picks up his own. 'I take it you've seen my rucksack back at the flat? I put off coming for as long as I could, but I'm sure you'll agree that keeping Charlie's stress levels low is the priority here.'

'Sure.' It's a good point, I'm just loath to agree with anything Ross says, on principle.

'We have to put Clemmie and Charlie's wellbeing ahead of our personal reluctance.' He's still sounding super serious.

'Of course.' From where I stand personal reluctance is a bit of an understatement.

The questioning frown lines on his forehead deepen. 'You *do know* why they're away?'

Oh crap. Looks like I'm going to have to head him off

fast before he drops them in it completely. 'Absolutely! They're doing a tour of Wallander's favourite haunts, Nordic baking research, and pulling in visits to eco-friendly building projects.' I'm not about to discuss Clemmie and Charlie's confidential fertility problems in front of an entire lawnful of garden party revellers, so I'm sticking with the complete official version, which I'm pretty proud I can remember in full. 'Because Scandi housing leads the world in cutting-edge low-energy technology.'

Further along the table Millie's looking like she's going to burst. 'Excuse me, but that's a load of cobblers. Clemmie and Charlie aren't really cooking, they've actually gone to get one of those ITV babies that they make in a dish!'

If the castle turret had fallen on his head Ross couldn't look any more shocked. 'They told *you* about the *IVF*?'

Millie's beaming. 'Not just *me* – *everyone* knows. We even had a lesson about it at school. Sometimes when the sperm and egg don't get together normally you have to help things along.' She gives Ross a hard stare. 'I'd have thought you'd know all about this if you're a vet.'

He's shaking his head. 'Cats with UT infections are more my thing. But thanks for explaining.'

It's almost worth the secret being village-wide to see the appalled look on Ross's face. It's so funny I'm biting my lip to hold in my smile.

Millie's grinning at him. 'Not everyone needs IVF. I actually arrived a lot earlier than my mum planned. She got pregnant with me when she was at uni.'

That came out of nowhere, and hits me like a punch in the chest. And it serves me right for laughing at

Ross. In front of anyone else I'd just let it pass until I'd recovered enough to get my breath back. But with Ross here watching I have to beat away that winded feeling. From somewhere I find enough air to sound really bright and make a very important point. 'I *just know* your mum would have been really happy you came along, Millie.'

Millie nods. 'I was a surprise, but the nicest sort.' She wrinkles her nose. 'For a while it was just Mum and me, then we found Nate, who's my dad now, then Mum had the twins and Maisie, and now there are loads of us.'

I wink at her. 'So many you need a castle to live in.'

There's a twang in my chest as I see this real, amazing, lovely, three-dimensional person here in front of me. And I know children grow in all shapes and sizes, and their personalities and talents are all completely individual. But I can't help thinking that if *my* uni baby had been born and grown up she would have been approximately Millie's size now.

Ours, even.

There's a bigger pang still. Their ages might have been close enough for them to have been in the same class at school. Which is a ridiculous thing to think at all, because there's no way I'd have lived in St Aidan. Which is exactly why I've always tried not to think about what might have been. Because when you do, it is mind-blowing as well as upsetting.

I deliberately try not to look at Ross unless I can help it. But when I accidentally catch a glimpse of the shadows under his cheekbones he isn't even thinking about what

JANE LINFOOT

Millie's said at all because his eyes are locked on a fishing boat halfway across the bay.

Millie's cry makes him jump. 'You can't afford to hang around, Ross, even male fertility doesn't last for ever. You definitely need to have a go on the speed-dating table.'

Then he must sense my gaze on the back of his neck, because he jerks his head round to look at Millie. 'You talk a lot, don't you?' He breaks off to laugh, which makes it more of a joke than the accusation it first sounded like. 'You remind me a lot of Cressy when she was a couple of years older than you.'

He has to be told. 'It's never a good thing to rake up the past, Ross. Especially bits about me as a teenager.'

He's straight back at me. 'Let's talk about the future then.' If he's made my stomach turn a cartwheel, that's only more proof of how inconsiderate he is. 'If you're still looking for work there are some hours at the surgery. We have a filing cabinet full of client notes that all need to be transferred to the computer. It pays, it's a lot cleaner than feeding cows, and I can't personally think of any reason you wouldn't jump at it.'

He seems to think he's doing me a favour, which just goes to show how out of touch he is with bloody everything. If it were the last job in the world, I'd still rather jump in the sea than work with Ross. Even if it meant ruining my beloved pink suede Converse. Which means I've got approximately ten seconds to come up with some better work, and more importantly it has to sound real.

As Nell and Plum wander towards the table there's a

collective shimmer of turquoise and pink and my shout is heartfelt. 'Hey, saved by the Nell!'

As Plum does a twirl there's a clatter of shells as her hair braids collide. 'How do you like our mermaid tails?'

'They're totally fab, but there's an idea I'm bursting to tell you about.' It's one tiny thought, but I need to make it sound huge. 'There's been so much interest in the cakes this afternoon, I've decided to run some small-group baking tuition evenings.' It's mad, it's crazy, and it's as much of a surprise to me to hear the words that are tumbling out of my mouth as it must be for everyone else.

Considering how tightly her ankles are tied together by her mermaid tail, Nell's star jump is spectacular. 'Now that's what I call a brainwave, Cressy!'

Plum's laughing. 'There'll definitely be takers for that!'

I'm thinking as I speak, making this up as I go along. 'I wouldn't want to use Clemmie's flat, so I'd do them in people's homes instead. Like at Kittiwake Court, but scaled down.' I'm emphasising the small, because I don't want to talk myself into anything I can't handle. But I also want to make it sound like I've thought it through. 'I'll put up posters in the local shops tomorrow and a post on the village Facebook page, and take it from there.'

Plum's smiling. 'Great idea. I can put some flyers in the gallery for you too.'

Nell's eyes are wide. 'It's like Clemmie did with her pudding evenings, but back to front. People paid to come to *her* kitchen – this way they'd be paying you to go to theirs.'

The more I'm setting the scene, the more it's sounding

like something I could manage that might also bring in some cash. 'I'd arrive with drinks and all my own ingredients, and the guests could watch me whizz up a cake or two while knocking back their fizz and eating ones I'd made earlier.'

Ross's eyes are narrowing. 'It's very *Blue Peter* and spur of the moment. And much less reliable than office work.'

Plum's holding back her smile. 'Spontaneous ideas are often the most successful, Ross.'

Sophie's hurrying over, keen to join in. 'And small equals exclusive, so you can pitch the price higher too.'

My own grin is so wide my cheeks are tight. 'I'll run it past Clemmie, but I'm thinking I could call it The Little Cornish Kitchen On Tour.' If she was eager for me to take over the reins while she wasn't here, I'm sure she won't mind this.

Plum grins. 'Brilliant, it'll keep the name out there while she's away.'

There's already a chorus round the garden. 'The Little Cornish Kitchen's going on tour? The Little Cornish Kitchen's going on tour!'

I'm keeping my smile going. 'It's not as if it's going to be for long – it's only to tide me over while I'm stuck here in St Aidan.' Three months down the line I'm hoping the haters will have grown tired of making their hateful comments on every word I post, and I can go back to London and gently pick up the YouTube clips and the recipe blog again.

Sophie's beaming. 'We'll clear it with Clemmie, I know she won't mind.' Her fingers close on my arm. 'And don't worry! We'll all be here to give you a hand.'

As I look around at Clemmie's friends, I'm grateful for

their enthusiasm but I hope they're not expecting to be *too* involved. When it comes to work, I'm used to doing things on my own. I'd actually find it easier to put on a mermaid's tail than accept their help with this, and we all know how much I'd hate to do that!

And while the idea of cooking in front of strangers in someone else's house is enough to scare the bejesus out of me, being without money would be worse. And the nightmare of working with Ross would be even more unbearable than that. So I'm just going to have to grit my teeth and get on and make this off-the-wall idea a success.

To think I thought that Ross moving in was as bad as it was going to get! But alongside the scary shivers, there's a tiny part of me that feels inexplicably excited too. If this is me moving forward with my earning, it's to a completely new place. And that's got to be good as well as terrifying.

11

In Clemmie's flat at Seaspray Cottage
Last orders and dirty dishes
Sunday morning

Walter and his mates were so intent on sampling every craft ale going at the beer tent yesterday, by the time they wobbled across the grass to the cake stall we were clearing the last crumbs off the table. But their bulk order for ten boxes of what Walter called 'them sticky chocolate bricks' was too big to miss, especially as they paid up-front and added a tip so mahoosive, it had to be down to the amount of Rip Curl brew they'd put away, as much as their generosity.

As for Ross, he went off with Walter and his merry men shortly after. As I didn't hear the thunder of Clemmie's high-flush loo other than when I pulled the chain myself, I can only assume that, yet again, he found somewhere better to stay. Which is fine by me.

So this morning, despite the rain that was hammering on the balcony outside my window, I woke up powered by the double adrenalin-shot of a cake order *and* my new idea for generating cash. By six I was crossing the garden with Diesel in his waxed jacket and me in Charlie's, ready for a dash along the beach before I got down to my big bake. But Diesel had other ideas; given the horizontal rain was whipping up enough grit from the beach to sting our faces, I couldn't blame him for having one leg-cock then diving straight back into the hall and bolting upstairs.

So while we waited for better weather I weighed out sugar and butter, sloshed around vanilla essence, jotted my umpteenth version of house rules for Ross and made notes for my posters, all with the whirr of the mixer beating brownie batter in the background. And Diesel curled up on the rug by the kitchen doorway in the perfect spot to keep one eye on me working in the kitchen and the other on Pancake, who was sitting by the French windows trying to catch the raindrops as they rolled sideways on the balcony side of the glass, driven by the wind blowing straight off the sea.

By the time I'd got four cooling racks stacked with glossy brownies my poster and rules were still works in progress. The kitchen smelled divine but it looked like an explosion in a cocoa factory and the sink was piled to the ceiling with baking tins and mixing bowls. But with a break in the rain and a sudden burst of blue in the sky Diesel was gently nosing my leg telling me he might be up for a walk after all. As all busy women will tell you, the secret to successful multi-tasking is knowing how to prioritise. So I decided the only way forward was to close the door on the mess and make a run for the beach before the clouds came in again.

When Diesel and I burst back into the flat an hour later shaking our heads and wiping the salt spray out of our eyes, we both look like we've been caught in a hurricane. It's only when I hear the clatter from the kitchen and Diesel lets out a little bark that it hits me we're not alone. As his legs start to fly the rug whips out behind him, then he powers across the living room. I follow and arrive at the kitchen door in time to see a pile of baking trays cascading to the floor as Diesel launches himself at shoulder height, and Ross in yellow Marigolds whirling away from the sink, soap bubbles clinging to all the way up to his elbows.

I wait for the face licking to subside, but when it comes to my turn to say hello I'm less enthusiastic. 'Ross, thanks all the same, but I *really don't* need you to do my washing up!' Talk about taking over! He couldn't have made a more territorial statement if he'd marched in and flown his family flag off the balcony.

Not that I need reminding, but now he's here he's taking up even more of the space than I'd imagined he would. The scent of dark chocolate is already completely overlaid with his man-scent too; fabric conditioner mixed with the kind of body spray that's so delicious it makes your knees go wobbly.

He gives a shrug. 'Don't get your cardi in a twist, Egbert, it's no big deal. In small spaces I find it's better to tidy as I go, that's all.'

It'd be folly to let him call the shots this early in the

game. 'Except this isn't your area, it's mine. If we're split-ting up the flat you can take the living room, and I'll stick to the kitchen and the balcony.' Thank goodness I've thought this through enough to write it down in advance.

He picks up a tray from the floor and lifts one eyebrow. 'You're talking about the list of house rules you left out on the table?'

'They're not completely finished.'

He lets out a laugh. 'They're not entirely workable *or* applicable either. *No walking round in boxers?* Like I'd do that when I go commando.'

That makes my eyes snap open. 'Please tell me you don't…' I hate that I can even remember how achingly irre-sistible he was in his tight-legged Calvin Kleins, but this is a whole awful new twist I hadn't bargained for.

'You've no idea how much washing it saves.' His expres-sion is inscrutable then he takes in my shudder and his lips start to twist. 'Ahh, Bertie, you still fall for them every time, don't you?'

I'm rising above this. 'I think you're about to find I totally don't.'

'We'll see about that.' He pulls a face then it straightens again. 'Don't worry, I'm really not about to horrify you with views of my underpants. And forget the bathroom rota, I'll shower at the surgery.'

'I'm sure there's no need for that.' Now he's making me feel guilty.

'I do Walter's animals after work, it makes sense to clean up before I get in the car.' He's sounding very matter of fact. 'I promise I'll be fully dressed in public areas. And if you insist on me covering up every inch of exposed skin at all times, I'm happy to go along with that – so long as you do the same.'

'So that means no shorts?' Or skirts above the ankle. Or low necks on hot days.

He shrugs. 'You're the one hung up on over-exposure and personal space, not me.'

I'm having a hasty rethink here. 'Maybe we could simplify…'

He nods. 'How about we both use the whole flat with consideration. And if anything offends we let each other know.'

'Great!' I make myself sound as bright as if this had been my idea all along. I'd have saved myself hours of agonising if he'd said this in the first place, but whatever. 'I can't think why you're making such a big thing about it.'

He lets out a long sigh. 'You really have no idea how tough this is for me, have you?'

I'm so appalled I let out my trapped hedgehog shriek. 'Hard *for you*? Why the hell would it be hard for you?' I was the one who lost my baby, let's not forget. I refuse to say *our* baby when *he* was the one who made a beeline for the proverbial door the moment he found out there was one.

He clears his throat. 'When I see you every day it's a constant reminder of how badly I stuffed up and I'm sorry, but it makes me feel like shit. I hate mistakes, and that one has to be the worst of my life.'

Oh my stars. I don't believe what I'm hearing. All this time later, and all he's still kicking himself for is getting drawn into our fling. And only a guy would make this all about him and his ego. I thought I'd put this behind me, but hearing him say this is like a knife twisting in my chest, opening up the wound all over again. But the sudden searing shot of pain sparks my anger too, and I'm hissing through my teeth. 'I'm very sorry to have caused you so much anguish and regret, both in the past and now.'

He's opening his mouth to reply and I'm scouring my brain for another withering comment I can get in first, when there's a knocking out in the hall and the sound of voices.

'Hey, don't worry, we'll let ourselves in...'

As I pop my head around the door edge Nell, Sophie and her band of littlies are trooping across the living room and into the kitchen. 'Wow, you're *all* here! Again! Come in! Great timing! How lovely to see you!'

As interruptions go, they couldn't have come at a worse moment. Though maybe it's for the best; if we hadn't been forced to hit the pause button the argument could only have escalated. I'm not one for full-blown shouting matches, but this is so raw I'd have found it hard to hold back. It's just a shock to find out that Ross is reacting. There I was, thinking it hadn't touched him, when all along he's been silently raging inside for letting it happen at all.

Sophie laughs as they squeeze past me and slide onto the chairs around the table. 'Not quite all of us. Plum was busy at the gallery.'

Nell nods towards the other end of the kitchen as she pulls up the pink chair. 'And Ross too! Good to see you've already set him to work, Cressy.'

Millie's grinning at me. 'I knew he'd love washing up, you could just tell.' Her eyes light up as she sees the brownie stacks. 'Are these for Walter's friends? We've brought you some cake boxes, shall I fill them?'

'Please.' As I nod to her I'm sending silent thank-yous to my imaginary fairy godmother that they've missed the ice flow between Ross and me.

Sophie pulls Maisie onto her knee then snatches up my poster sketches, so I take that as my cue. 'I ran things past Clemmie last night and she loves that The Little Cornish Kitchen is getting out into the world while she's away.'

'You won't be needing these after you've heard our news.' Sophie pats the sketches, and gives Nell a shove. 'Go on, then, tell her.'

Nell leans back in her chair and adjusts her padded waistcoat. 'Not that we want to tread on your toes, but after you left the garden party yesterday there was *so* much interest from the members of the singles club. We couldn't let it go to waste.' She pulls a sheaf of papers out of her pocket. 'So here's the first four On Tour evenings fully sorted with attendees, dates and venues, another ten pencilled in, and a huge list of more people all fighting for their turn.'

In terms of standing on toes this is the equivalent of having an entire football team in hobnail boots not just treading on my feet – they're actually jumping. 'Do I get to do anything?'

Sophie's missing the irony and purring. 'You'll be full on with your planning and handouts.'

Nell's eyes narrow. 'And we'll need your input with the fizz and all the future dates. Otherwise, the favourite requests were for meringues, chocolate cake, blondies and millionaire's shortbread.'

Sophie carries straight on. 'The hosts are all close by in the village, we've hand-picked the nicest people with the best kitchens to ease you in, we've pitched the price so high you can't lose. And we'll all be there to smooth you through.'

I'm smiling round the table at them. 'Put like that, it's a win-win-win! What's not to like?'

Millie's nodding. 'And Ross can come too!'

What's that saying about picking your battles? If I need to insist on one thing, Ross not coming will be it. 'I'm sure with all of us there, we don't need to inconvenience Ross.'

Millie lets out a wail. 'But we can't miss Ross out! He's proved that he's great at washing up, and he's also on the lookout for a wife. And as Mum says, he currently has the social life of a water snail.'

Ross gives a groan from the sink. 'Thanks so much for bigging me up there.'

With a build-up like that for him, I'm feeling generous enough to give way on this. 'Fine, he can come the first time. But he has to take responsibility for his own social life after that.' I know they're all only trying to help, but if I'm being overruled on Ross there has to be a little bit more of me in there too, because I have to feel like I'm in charge of my own destiny. 'If it's okay with all of you, I'd actually like to kick off the first evening with a selection of cupcakes.'

Millie lets out a whoop as she closes a brownie box. 'You're Cressida Cupcake, you have to start with those!'

I do love this child. But there's one thing to get straight

before we start. 'I'm not sure I'll be able to afford to pay *all* of you for your time though.'

Nell gives a cough. 'We're coming to help as friends – we're free until you're up and running.'

That's a relief. 'Thank you. And if the first couple of evenings work out, we'll take it from there.' Hopefully by then I'll feel like I own this enough to manage on my own. Which only leaves one other crucial question. 'When are we doing this?'

Nell grins at me. 'You're at Kittiwake Court for butter-cream piping on Tuesday afternoon, which is perfect practice. So how does Wednesday evening sound?'

Crap crap crap! How can it be so soon? But I need to get this off the ground, and what's more, my mouth is moving with no help from me. 'Brilliant! Couldn't be better!'

I can't believe I just said that! It's not what I'd planned, I've never been less in control. But times are desperate. All I can tell myself is, like my ongoing soggy-bottom tweets, it's temporary, it won't be for ever. Before I know it my stay here will be over and my life will ease back to what it was before. Even if I embarrass myself hugely here in St Aidan, I'll never have to face these people again after I've left.

I beam along the faces at the table. 'Fabulous! So if anyone fancies some brownies to celebrate, how about I put the kettle on and make us a pot of tea?'

There's a cough by the sink. 'That's already done!' Somehow Ross is putting cups onto a tray next to a steaming teapot. 'Give it a couple of minutes to brew and you're good to go.'

I'm a sixth child, I'm completely used to fighting for everything. But this has left me open-mouthed and staring.

Nell sends me a wink. 'Great choice of housemate, Cressy. You may never have to make a hot drink ever again.'

Millie's catching my eye too. 'What did I tell you? Mum's right, this one could turn out to be a keeper.'

Sometimes the only way forward is to turn to cake. I smile at everyone as I head for Clemmie's tower of mismatched plates. 'Let me pass you all some brownies – before Ross beats me to it.' And something else crosses my mind. Sure, I need the cash, but I'm not the only one in need. 'This all grew from Kittiwake Court, and if all of you are helping, it's only right we give some of the proceeds to them.'

At least that way, when I'm having to rub hips with the awful Ross next to some stranger's microwave, it'll be easier to justify to myself that it's for a good cause. Truly, if it were only for my benefit, I might have to call it off.

12

*Cressy and The Little Cornish Kitchen, on tour at Saxifrage
Cottage*
False starts and green cupboard doors
Wednesday evening

'How about we call a truce? Just for tonight.'

This is Ross talking. We're one step away from the pink front door of the house we're heading into. It's my first cupcake evening, and as our frowns lock over the tops of the boxes of kitchen utensils we're both carrying, I have to say, the man has a talent for choosing his moments. As the huge car he's borrowed from Charlie is currently wedged in the steepest cobbled lane in St Aidan, I'm not about to argue. On the plus side, this should be our second-to-last load.

'Sure.' It's one word. After everything Ross has held against me for all these years, that's all he's getting. It's also massively more than we've exchanged in the last four days.

Since Nell and Sophie and the littlies left the flat on Sunday – for Ross's benefit, not mine – I've made every effort to avoid him. I've got out of bed extra early and dragged poor Diesel miles along the beach to be certain we didn't get back until Ross had left for the surgery.

Baking prep for this evening's event has been crammed into the day, then I've huddled Diesel and Pancake into my bedroom before Ross came home and stayed there reworking the running order for this evening until he shut himself away in his. I only tiptoed out to do more in the kitchen when I was certain he'd flushed the thunder-box in the bathroom and settled down to sleep.

The one exception was at the buttercream fest at Kitti-wake Court yesterday, where he showed up and pointed his mobile at me. If he wanted to film Walter enjoying resi-dents' activities, I wasn't going to stop him. And even when he came in close to catch how I was using different pipes to make the petal shapes on the flowery cupcake tops, I still managed to turn away so he didn't actually have to face me.

With a history like ours we were never going to be best friends; there will always be a chasm between us that can never be crossed. And being forced together in the flat is like bringing the same poles together on magnets – the proximity only increases the force that drives us apart.

And I'm really not one to hold a grudge. In my normal life I prefer to make the best of even the most difficult situa-tions and move on in a positive way. But with Ross it's as if he's hanging onto the darkest parts of his past, feeding on the negativity. Knowing he's still harbouring so much venom and animosity towards me has not just made me defensive; it's changed how I feel towards him too. Before this I'd lost all respect for him and was happy to pretend he didn't exist. But now I'd secretly like to flatten him. Which is why it's especially hard having him around this evening.

As I stare past his muscled forearms to the car I appreciate he's working like an actual removal man here entirely for my benefit, but Sophie pushed him into it, not me. Despite already making a massive number of journeys to the kitchen that's my temporary base for tonight, the boot still seems as rammed as a student's on their way to uni. It's a few cupcakes, so why the hell is most of Clemmie's flat here with me? I meant to stick to one word only, but I'm suddenly doubting myself.

'I've brought too much, haven't I?'

'I didn't say that.' He drops his eyes for a second, then his face breaks into a grin. 'You'll soon learn what you can leave behind. Next time you can bring a half-size removal lorry, not a full-sized one. Come on, let's get this lot in.'

I let out a groan. 'Saxifrage Cottage may be about to burst.'

'Or it could just fall into the sea due to being overloaded with every kind of spatula known to man.' He pushes open the door and glances back over his shoulder. 'I'll re-park the car, then once you've sorted out what you need I'll hide the rest away.' At least that way the paying customers might not notice.

Luckily for me the mermaids have kept their word and delivered a kitchen with a huge wow factor. Beyond the frontage the cottage is like a Tardis, and the living room opens out onto a wide extension at the back with a smooth limestone floor, windows onto the sky and views across the bay.

The last couple of days, as I baked a hundred one's-I-made-earlier cupcakes, practised my delivery non-stop and made an extra effort to look good, I've mostly been preoccupied with dodging Ross. But now I'm here and the fear is freezing my brain, it's hitting me that I should have worried more.

I smile at Chloé, the host and cottage owner, who's hugging the wall and looking as terrified as me. 'What a fabulous kitchen. I love your hanging plant holders.' From the on-trend pea-coloured units, it has to be new.

Chloé gives a shy shrug. 'The macramé is done by a local woman. She sells on the St Aidan For Sale and Wanted Group on Facebook.'

Plum gives me a nudge as she passes. 'You should take a look on there, it's a treasure trove.'

Chloé pulls a face. 'I'm afraid the kitchen hasn't had much use. I don't want to sound like a cliché, but it's usually meals-for-one in the microwave.'

Nell gives a chortle. 'Cressy will christen it in style.' Then she shoves me into the utility and hisses in my ear. 'Chloé's one of our more difficult-to-place singles, we're counting on a complete change of mood and pace to work wonders for her tonight.'

I let out a cry. 'You're using this evening for *matchmaking*?'

Nell puts a finger to her lips, reminding me to keep my voice down. 'Not everyone's as happy on their own as you are. For anyone lonely who would rather be a couple, every social interaction is an opportunity.' Clemmie wasn't exaggerating when she wrote about Nell being a singles-club evangelist, then. Nell beckons me closer. 'We think Chloé may like Gavin. So anything you can do to help that along...'

More fool me for thinking people were coming because they wanted to learn to make cupcakes. And I know I was desperate to stay independent, but I'm hugely grateful that Diesel is safe, watching TV with George round at Nell's place.

With so much still to do it's also a relief that Sophie's the one trying to prise words out of a very reticent Chloé while Nell puts the fizz in the dedicated wine fridge and sorts the glasses. As I set up my mixer and get out my bowls and ingredients Plum's filling the tiered cake stand and arranging Clemmie's pretty, mismatched plates opposite the six stools already around the island unit.

Then Ross comes in and whisks everything I don't need off to the utility room. He stops by the bank of ovens as he comes back in. 'You'll be wanting both of the big ones on. What temperature would you like?'

'A hundred and sixty, please.' I already noticed the fan symbol on them.

Millie's not here tonight, but I can still see her standing right behind Ross giving me an 'Isn't he a treasure?' thumbs up. What's more, with everyone rushing around it's completely possible that without his prompt I'd have forgotten to pre-heat. I shudder at how that would have wrecked my schedules, but there's no time to think because the ship's bell outside the front door is already ringing with the first guest.

Nell glances at her watch and raises her eyebrows at me. 'Ten minutes early shows how much they're looking forward to it!'

Plum waltzes over to me. 'I think you're all set.' She flaps some fabric out from behind her back. 'Here you go, your very own pink and white stripy apron for our St Aidan version of Cressy.'

Shit, how did I forget my apron? I slip the new one over my head and push my pile of cue cards in the pocket, thinking that's something else I need to add to my early-warning checklist for next time, as well as turning the oven on. Then as I look down at my front I notice a plain patch of fabric with embroidered writing.

Plum grins at me. '*Cressy Cupcake at The Little Cornish Kitchen*. We hope that's okay for you?'

I'm swallowing hard as I squeeze Plum's hand. 'Thank you, it's perfect.'

Sophie's behind me, straightening the collar of my red flowery dress as she ties my apron strings and frees my hair. 'And you're perfect too, Cressy! Be your very wonderful self and you'll knock them off their stools.'

And then it's happening! The guests – Gavin, Tash, Harry, Fi and Josh – are clambering up into their places around the island unit with Chloé, and I'm standing at the end telling them how lovely it is to see them. Then I say, 'I'm Cressida Cupcake, I'm here with The Little Cornish Kitchen bringing the baking love to St Aidan.' As I stop to gasp for air I catch sight of my white knuckles. 'Tonight I'm going to show you how to make cupcakes, so would anyone like a drink while you're watching?' As I carry on my echoing voice sounds slightly more like my own and I dare to let go of the hammered metal work surface.

And that's it. Nell hands round the fizz, Plum follows her giving out mini cupcake tasters and I'm straight into weighing and mixing and giving my running commentary. And I already know from Kittiwake Court that the minute they start to join in with some banter I'll be fine from there. Except they don't join in. Where there should be a clamour of questions and comments it's more silent than a Latin class. I send them a beam.

'How about an ice-breaker whilst I beat the butter and sugar together! Favourite cupcakes, anyone?'

Chloé mumbles 'Lavender.' And that's the most I get.

So I start listing as many as I can think of. 'Lemon ... vanilla ... chocolate fudge... I'm breaking in the eggs here, it's always good to keep your eggs at room temperature before you use them.'

As I look round the faces I'm so missing Pam and Madge and Joanie and their lovely friends telling me about their farmyards or their domestic science lessons or their sex lives back in the seventies. I'm also kicking myself. Sure, keeping it small cuts down the threat of hostile hecklers, but how did I think six would be anything other than excruciating if they were quiet rather than loud?

'I'm folding in the flour now. I'm doing it gently, and always with a metal spoon. Anyone tried Malteser cupcakes? Or key lime ones...' If they don't join in soon this will be over in no time and they'll all want their money back. 'Excuse me one moment...' As I catch Nell's eye across the kitchen she pulls a face and follows me out to the utility.

I let out a groan. 'I'm dying out there, Nell. If they were my mates I'd suggest a line of shots to liven them up.' Alcohol isn't always the answer, but as I stare around the shelves I'm desperate. 'How about we borrow that bottle of gin, raid the mint plant and cordial, and hit them with a prosecco cocktail.'

'Good thinking.' Nell's already got the Gordon's in her hand. 'Leave it with me.'

I take in the background music and Ross who's magically appeared to hover in the doorway. 'And please, please, please could you get those Bach Preludes off the speakers and put my *Cook Like Crazy* playlist on instead?' As I shove my phone at him I'm truly grateful to Millie for insisting that he came. 'Start it off with "Jump (For My Love)".'

If they all still stay like boards after this, at least I've done my best. I'm picking up my cue cards again when I have another thought. 'Maybe Chloe and Gavin could come over and help me put the plain mixture in the paper cases. And while I make the chocolate and lemon versions of the sponge mix I'll tell you all about when I worked at a slimming magazine and put on four stone.'

As I set the mixer going again, at least I'm having fun even if no one else is. By the time Chloé and Gavin's trays are ready I hope Nell's seen their heads have almost touched twice.

I whip up a full baking tray, show it round to everyone and wave my thermometer. 'It's always a good idea to double-check your oven temperature.' I'm still too raw to share the full story of my soggy-bottom day, so for now that's the most I can manage.

As I head across the room, I have to say I'm so relaxed, I've got time to think how exhausting it must be to have a kitchen where you have to hike from one side to the other. It's only as I pull open the oven door that it hits me that things aren't as they should be. I should be met by a faceful of hot air and the whirr of the fan, but instead there's just darkness. I jump across and wrench open the other oven too, but that's the same.

I give a little cough that turns into a squeal. 'I might not be needing my oven thermometer after all.' I turn to Ross. 'You did turn these on earlier?'

'Shit.' He's there in a nanosecond. 'Definitely. Is there a problem?'

It's *way* larger than that – failing to switch on the oven while cooking in front of an audience is more on the scale of a seismic world disaster. 'They don't seem to have – er – heated up.'

Chloé purses her lips. 'I can't help, I've never used them before.'

Gavin sends her a wink. 'Someone else who lives on microwave meals? We need to get together and compare our favourites.'

As Ross prods a button the oven light comes on and the fan springs to life. 'Damn, so sorry, beginner's mistake, they were both in timer mode so they didn't switch on. They're all good now.'

'Well, that's fabulous news. Thanks to our technical

expert, Ross, for saving the day!' I'm the only one to blame here; a pro would have checked. But I could have done without an extra fifteen minutes of heating-up time to fill.

Nell's waving a jug around. 'Anyone like more cocktails? Or a quick round of musical chairs while we wait?'

Chloé's panicked expression tells us it's a 'no' to that.

Ross looks directly at me. 'What about the game you used to play as a kid?'

'I don't think so.' Him dragging up my childhood now isn't helpful.

Across the kitchen Nell's doing star jumps. 'Eating iced buns dangling from the Sheila Maid! When you told us all about it at Kittiwake Court it sounded like *so much fun!*'

'Of course!' This might just save my bacon! I make a dive for the pile of cake boxes I made as going home gifts, thanking my lucky stars I brought too many. 'I have iced cupcakes here, so all we need now are some lengths of string, and a tablecloth to protect the floor.'

Ross is already staring up at the ceiling looking for places to hang them as he heads for the utility room. 'Your maximalist packing strategy is paying off! You have both of those in a bag through here.'

Gavin's down off his stool too. 'The saucepan rack will be a great place to suspend them.'

Two minutes later I'm spearing scissors through cupcakes, and tying knots in the strings. As everyone lines up, jostling to have a go, Nell sidles past me. 'Looks like we hit on the perfect warm-up activity.' She clears her throat and turns to the group. 'The only rule is, don't use your hands! Maybe get in pairs for this one, and come in for the cake from both sides.'

Now it's my turn to look horrified as I watch the waiting buns swinging in the air. 'Isn't that too much?'

Nell lets out a chortle. 'It's fully consensual. Any chance of breaking down the barriers this fast, we have to take it.'

Sophie watches Chloé go straight in. Seconds later she's pushing salt caramel buttercream and toffee drizzle across Gavin's cheek with her nose. 'All these years of your singles club, Nell, this could be the sweetest game yet!'

Nell gives me a bump with her elbow. 'Are you and Ross going to have a go then?'

I jump a yard across the kitchen. 'Absolutely not! I've got three lots of icing to make – immediately!' I nod at the sink stacked high with mixing bowls. 'And if Ross has offered to wash up there's plenty to keep him busy too.' And this really isn't me trying to keep him out of the action with Fi and Tash, who are both really pretty even when their faces are covered in chocolate buttercream. Ross can rub noses with who the hell he likes; if I'm feeling slightly queasy here, it's down to the shock of my evening coming so close to careering off the rails, not the threat of Ross ending up with his tongue in someone's ear.

I'm staring at the crumbs and icing lumps landing on the gingham tablecloth, mentally moving on to the next problem. 'How does polished limestone stand up to grease?'

Plum takes hold of my shoulders and turns me round. 'Leave the floor to me! You sort your icing and fill your piping bags; you're going to have six very hyped hands-on bakers to help you soon.' Her face splits into a smile as there's another whoop from under the saucepan rack. 'It's turning into a brilliant evening.'

That's the funny thing; once everyone starts having a great time the rest matters less. No one minded that I over-cooked some of the chocolate cupcakes because we'd all gone out onto the terrace to watch the sun go down. And Josh insisting on icing warm cakes instead of waiting for them to cool showed everyone why it was a bad idea when his buttercream melted to a puddle. But the time whizzed by, and before we'd reached the end of my playlist, we were giving Chloé her special hostess mixing bowl, and waving the rest of them out onto the street.

'Six very happy customers there.' Nell's patting me on the back as Plum and Sophie put the last of the boxes into the car.

As I try to get this into perspective for myself, I suspect she's exaggerating. 'On the up side, they all wanted aprons and piping bags too.'

Sophie gives my arm a squeeze. 'The merchandising opportunities are fabulous, aren't they?'

Ross comes out with the last of the rubbish bags. 'And we're doing it all over again in two days' time?'

'We are?' I'm buzzing, but if they're as shattered as me, they might not be up for it. And in any case, Ross was here for one night only.

Sophie, Nell and Plum all chorus together: 'For sure we are! For you and for Kittiwake. We'll go with the same arrangements until you take off properly.'

Ross gives a shrug. 'Another night, another kitchen. We might need to ask if Charlie has a larger vehicle.'

If we were still talking I might tell him he won't be needed. But I'm guessing that's our truce over, so I'll have to leave that to Sophie. While she and Plum get a lift back to the harbour with Ross, I go back to Nell's to pick up Diesel and walk him home.

As Diesel and I pass Charlie's car on the way back to Seaspray Cottage I stop to pick up the first of the bags to carry back to the flat. As the cottage is quite a way from the harbour I'm counting on taking the whole of tomorrow morning to unload. But instead I find the boot's completely empty, and when I get up the stairs to the flat everything's neatly stacked in the kitchen.

I know I love doing things my way. But just this once it's been so good to have some help. As for how long this will last – after a couple of nights as chaotic as tonight, the word will get around and the evenings may well die a natural death. But at least I've got enough in the coffers to keep me in cocoa for the next few days.

13

On St Aidan beach
Principles, climb-downs and online dating
Monday afternoon

By the end of the weekend I have two more Cressy Cupcake evenings behind me, but none of them have been what I'd count as a proper success. A new venue and a different group every time make it impossible to anticipate the pitfalls, and they've each had their own set of quirks and disasters.

Friday's was in a tiny cottage with a group of women who were as lively as Chloé's group were quiet. But where Chloé's place was spacious, this one was so small there was barely room to lift a cocktail glass let alone a piping bag. Mostly I remember hysterical laugher, gallons of Tequila Sunrise, and people falling off chairs. No one took their handouts away. In terms of learning outcomes they might as well have stayed at home and eaten Häagen-Dazs.

131

By contrast Saturday's group was mixed but horribly grown up. They waved away the fizz and drank iced water with lemon twists instead. Then they wrote down every word I said in personalised notebooks, fired questions at me faster than *Mastermind* and insisted on an impromptu competition for the neatest in-class piping! They were so fun-averse that the cakes on strings game got pushed right to the end, but when they came to that they were so competitive it was like a scene from *Fight Club*.

I was hoping to build demand from recommendations, but if any of this lot spread the word people will run a mile rather than sign up. The exciting thing about trying new things is the surprises; the evenings may be about to fizzle to nothing, but seeing the public face to face for the first time has highlighted how much they love baking accessories.

So on Monday afternoon I nip to the fabric shop in town with Diesel to check out the cost of having some customised aprons made up. Shop owner Helen is one of those people who goes the extra mile and works really fast. Once she'd given Diesel some fuss and a treat she whipped out some bales of lovely stripy fabric and took thirty seconds to help me decide which two would work best. She's coming back to me later with a special friends-and-family-rate price.

Obviously I need to get more cash up-front to cover this, which brings me to my next venture. Over the weekend I joined the St Aidan For Sale and Wanted Facebook group; it has posts for everything from friendly electricians to second-hand bridesmaid dresses, and from the speed the vintage dressing table disappeared it gets lots of traffic.

As I spent yesterday doing more recipe testing for what I'm now calling my speculative book project, I've got a kitchen overflowing with tray bakes. So I ran my prices past Sophie and just before I came out I posted a photo in the group with a little post offering variety bake boxes, for collection from Seaspray Cottage.

As Diesel and I make our way back from town and down to the beach for our afternoon walk I tap the pocket where my phone is. 'This has to be better than a stall in the garden, Diesel. All we have to do now is wait for the Facebook messages.'

As we walk along the bay I'm throwing pebbles into the shallows for Diesel to chase, and he's splashing about as he tries to find them. But mostly I'm anticipating the tell-tale vibration on my ribs saying I've got mail.

When we've walked all the way to Comet Cove and back without a peep, I can't help but share my disappointment. 'People in St Aidan obviously don't like cake as much as we thought, Diesel.'

My hope is fading as we wind our way back up to the flat, then I glimpse Ross from the landing window and my heart sinks as far as my Converse. 'Damn, now we'll have to grab some dinner supplies and make a dash for the bedroom.'

We just make it. Diesel's curling up in the bedside armchair as we hear Ross come in and the kettle going on. Then I finally pull my phone out of my pocket and the blank screen pretty much sums up the afternoon. 'And now the battery's died. At least I've got a charger handy.'

I'm popping open a can of Pepsi Max and tugging at the

pack of Pomme Bears I've brought through when the phone buzzes on the bedside table. And then it buzzes again. And again. By the time I open Messenger there are already eleven messages. They're all asking about the bake boxes and as I tap out the replies more are coming in. I'm working my way through them when a person called Dave Rave simply shoots the money for two boxes into my PayPal account, and says he'll be round to pick up in five.

As I dash to the kitchen I see Ross in one of the armchairs by the French windows, a squeeze ball in one hand, bent over his laptop. I take two cake boxes, drop in a selection of blondies, then bundle them under my jacket. As I hurtle across the living room and out onto the landing I shout to Ross. 'Sorry to disturb, just popping to the garden.'

I open the downstairs front door as Dave Rave is reaching for the bell, hand him the boxes, say 'Enjoy!' and I'm back up the stairs before you can say 'Cressy Cupcake's on a roll.'

I make up a couple more boxes, type in a couple more replies, and someone else is already on their way.

So I take another deep breath and stroll in front of Ross. 'Me again, back soon.'

This time he barely looks up from his screen. At some stage Diesel sneaks through to lie on the rug by the kitchen door, and by nine thirty I've made seven round trips and sold fifteen bake boxes and most of my tray bakes. Whatever Ross is watching must be riveting because apart from the odd grunt or hand stretch he hasn't reacted at all. I'm hitching up my shorts, standing by the green dresser sinking my teeth into the last piece of Jammie Dodger blondie, thinking this is so delicious it has to go in the book, when Ross's voice drifts through to me.

'Cressy, do you have a minute?'

As I push the last crumbs into my mouth I hope he's not rumbled me, because I have nothing at all against selling cupcakes, but I'd rather he *didn't* know I'm doing it at the door. I just feel very vulnerable when a few bake boxes mean the difference between having cash and not. Especially when not long ago I was being sent three-hundred-pound dresses and getting paid even more to wear them in the baking photos for my Insta posts. It's not that I'm proud, but I'd rather Ross thought of me as the success I used to be than as the temporary disaster-zone I am now.

I push my head around the door and try to sound business-like. 'How can I help?'

Ross tilts his laptop my way. 'Charlie's on Facetime, he wants the two of us.'

I tickle Diesel's ears as I pass. 'Time for a chat with your dad.' But as I cross the room Ross's frown and the half shake of his head make me leave Diesel where he is. I perch on a chair edge and immediately regret that I'm so close to Ross that we're practically breathing the same air.

The way Charlie rakes his hand through his hair as he waits for me to come into view isn't a great sign either. Behind his head I can see the pale timber-clad corner of the Swedish beachside house they gave me a FaceTime tour of yesterday, and the water beyond is rippled by the wind. He sinks properly into view and rests his chin on his fist. 'Just to bring you both up to speed – Clemmie's IVF hasn't worked, we won't be having a baby this time around.'

I feel my whole body deflating for how crushed he sounds. 'I'm *so* sorry, Charlie.' All I want to do is to hug him. I've been counting the days, knowing a pregnancy test would be coming up. Yet now he's saying the words, I know I was taking it for granted that if they got to one of the most respected clinics in the world with a director they knew personally, and had the best care, and stayed nearby, then this would definitely happen for them. If I'm unprepared for the let-down after all their effort to make this work, how awful must they feel?

Ross drags in a breath too then blows out his cheeks. 'I'm gutted for you both. But you do get the chance to try again?'

Charlie sighs. 'We do. But that will mean another six weeks before we get those results. I'm just checking you're both okay with the timescale.'

'Absolutely. We're in this for the long haul.' Ross's elbow hits my ribs. 'Aren't we, Cressy?'

'Totally.' Nothing I can say will make Charlie feel better right now, but I have to try. 'Send my love to Clemmie, and be kind to yourself too. Anything I can do, you know where I am.'

'Thanks. I'd better go and ring the oldies.'

His sigh is so long I have to offer. 'I could do that?'

He shakes his head. 'Nice thought, but it has to come from me. Give Diesel a hug for us, we'll talk again soon.' Then he gives a half wave and the screen goes blank.

I'm staring beyond the balcony to the darkening shadows on the beach, fixing my eyes on the invisible line where the sea meets the sky. 'To think I was worrying over tray bakes and all the time their hopes and dreams were in tatters.' I'm talking to myself more than Ross.

He shifts in his chair. 'It's not the end, they still have more embryos.'

The frustration is making me clench my fists so hard my nails are digging in my palms. 'It just doesn't seem fair, after everything else Charlie's been through.'

Ross clears his throat. 'It's ironic that it happened for us so easily, and yet it's so hard for them.' The words are so loaded they seem to hit the floor and bounce back at me.

I flop back into my chair and try to get to grips with saying anything about this at all when I've sworn to myself I never would again. Especially with him. 'We weren't *that* great at it. In case you've forgotten, we didn't get the whole way.' I let out a sigh because I'm so sad for Charlie and Clemmie, but I'm also appalled that Ross has twisted the focus onto us here. 'You're right though, they don't even know what it feels like to get a positive test.' Hopefully that will move this straight back to Clemmie and Charlie and their struggle.

Ross lets out a sigh. 'Do you know what's the strangest thing for me, all these years on?'

'And?' I have no wish to know how he feels about any of what happened to us, because I closed that door straight after. But I sense he's going to tell me anyway.

He narrows his eyes. 'I simply don't understand how what happened to us back then doesn't appear to have affected you at all.'

My jaw falls open and locks with my chin on my chest. I could ask how the hell he thinks he can see inside my head and read my mind, but when he's talking like an arse I'm not going to. 'Would you like to explain that further?'

He's stretching and clenching his fingers, staring at them. Then he stops and looks directly at me. 'You didn't tell your family. There wasn't even a pause. You carried straight on with your degree and your career trajectory as if nothing had happened.'

I'm damned if I'm going to justify myself. And if my insides just disintegrated in the face of those dark brown irises, it's a total one-off. I swear I'll be ready for his full-on gaze next time it comes. 'Everyone deals with things differently. I accepted I'd made a mistake, and moved on.'

He's rubbing his thumb across the stubble on his jaw. 'Whatever gets you through, I suppose. And good on you for being tough enough to do that. But not a day has gone by when I haven't thought about this; it's shaped every single thing I've done since.'

Which is a bit much to claim when he's failed to react to anything relating to it so far. At least that explains why he's so bitter.

But for me, to prolong anything that hurt *that* much would have been impossible. All I could do once the numb shock began to turn to pain was shut it out. Lock it tightly away in a place in my brain where I'd never visit it again. And hurl myself at the future. And for the most part that worked for me. Or it has until now.

Ross would be the last person I'd ever admit that to, but he's expecting *something* here. 'I did learn from it. Mostly it taught me to aim high.' *Seize every opportunity and rely on no one but myself.* I'm gritting my teeth, clamping my jaw. 'I refuse to apologise for making a success of my life since.'

He's shaking his head. 'And well done to you for everything you've achieved, Cressy. But that's another thing it's hard for me to get my head around. Your media persona and your polish are worlds away from the person you used to be.'

'*What?*' I'm opening and closing my mouth but nothing else is coming out.

He blows out a breath. 'I always had you down as full of heart. But you're so wrapped up with yourself these days, it's like no one else matters anymore.'

I bite back my shriek of protest. Make my voice low and level. 'That's a little bit damning.' There's no point defending myself against an onslaught like this. He has every right to think what he wants. I don't have to take it on board, less still let it drag me down.

Ross gives a snort. 'Take tonight, for example: you're running up and downstairs on Tinder instead of supporting your family.'

'Why would you say *Tinder*?' Maybe it's better he thinks that than knows the truth. 'And how does my family come into this?'

'Constant messaging and guys coming and going might be the giveaway.' He pulls a face and his attitude is so darned smug and know-it-all. 'No one really gives a damn about the detail, Cressy. What matters is that Charlie messaged you to talk earlier and you were too busy to respond.'

My eyes snap open. 'Surely he can't have? *Why didn't*

you say?' As I reach for my phone and scroll through the names my stomach feels like a steel hand is gripping it. And then way down the list, miles off the bottom of the screen, just below Dave Rave, there's Charlie's name highlighted showing an unopened message. I click on it and there it is.

Crap day here, Egbert, could use a chat if you've got time x

'Oh my stars. How the hell did I not see?' I swallow hard. Charlie needed to tell me about the baby, and I totally missed it. Ross might have his head up his bum and be wrong about everything else, but he's right about this. 'I should have been there for Charlie earlier. I let him down so badly.'

Ross closes his laptop. 'You've talked now. That's what matters.' He stands up, picks up his coffee mug from the side table. 'I'll take Diesel for a stroll before the tide comes in. If that's okay with you?'

'Great, he'll enjoy that.' I'm pleased he's running this by me. It's also a relief he doesn't rub my nose in it any further, because I couldn't feel any worse than I already do. But my mind is racing. After everything else Ross has said tonight, I really shouldn't be accepting his help. 'And thanks for all your effort with The Little Cornish Kitchen evenings, but I'll manage those without you from now on.'

His forehead creases into a frown. 'Nell said we were all Team Cupcake, and my jokes about bulldogs were what melted the ice with those hideous serious bakers. You do know how many bags I carry?'

I pull in a breath. 'I appreciate everything you've done,

but we can't change the past. At least this way you won't have to keep confronting it.' It's morally wrong to accept help when he despises me as much as he does. Sure, his dog jokes crack people up, but I need to be firm.

His eyes narrow. 'I don't know what Sophie's going to say about this.'

I'm staring past him to the clouds outside as they turn smoky purple. 'I'll make sure she understands.'

I'm being much truer to my principles this way. If tonight has underlined anything for me it's why it's imperative to rely on myself and no one else. If I'd stuck to that in the first place and kept my distance from Ross better I'd have avoided this trouble tonight.

He stops and rests his shoulder on the kitchen door frame. 'I'm not sure Charlie would approve of the dating app either. Meeting strangers without backup isn't good.'

I'm not using the app but this feels like him overstepping yet again. 'So is this Charlie disapproving, or you?'

Ross blinks. 'You're better than the guys who go on there, that's all.'

'This is the twenty-first century, Ross, catch up!' As I curl my fingers around the notes in my pocket from the bake boxes I'm reluctant to give this up. Ross has got the wrong idea, but as it's the perfect cover I'm going to play along for now. 'Rest assured, I won't do anything Charlie wouldn't be comfortable with, okay?'

'I suppose it'll have to be.' Ross is peering into the kitchen. 'Did I see cake in here earlier?'

'Cake? What kind?'

He's frowning again. 'That Jammie Dodger slice. There was quite a lot of it.'

Easy answer. 'Sorry, those were for orders. And I ate the rest.'

After everything he's said too. Some people's sweet tooth is way stronger than their ideals. Which is always worth remembering when you're holed up with an enemy as embittered as Ross Bradbury.

14

At Clemmie's flat
Dry mouths and bad judgement
A week later, the early hours of Monday morning

With another three baking evenings in the next few days without Ross's help there are times when my shoulders ache so much from heaving boxes around St Aidan I feel more like a delivery woman than a baker. I'm still a long way from a gym bunny, but let's just say, I'm firming up in places I never knew I had muscles. Nell tried her best to fill the gap left by Ross, and brought along a volunteer care assistant from the home to pitch in with carrying, banter and washing up, but as a first-timer he was bound to need more direction than Ross.

Having let the team's main powerhouse go, it made sense to cut down the effort at my end too. With that in mind I spoke to the builders working in Clemmie's venue downstairs at Seaspray Cottage, so I now have a small room for storage there which at least saves me dragging every single item up and down the stairs every time there's an event.

If I sound like I'm regretting losing the help, I admit giving it up was an emotional reaction that I didn't fully think through on a practical level. What not having Ross around has made clear is that if I'd tried to do this entirely on my own I'd have been in big trouble. I must have been crazy to ever think that would have worked! What it's mainly highlighted for me is how lucky I am to have Sophie, Plum and Nell, all so willing to be involved.

They all have busy lives of their own, but we've talked about it again; as this is only for a few weeks at most, they're willing to pitch in and cover the help I need between them. In return, I'll make a donation to the Kittiwake fund to cover the work they do each evening. And by making a donation for every bake box I sell too, that should keep the interest going and bring more cash in for me and Kittiwake.

As for Ross, since the night of Charlie's bad news I've hardly seen him at all. Tonight, by the time I've finished unloading after this weekend's second event, and Diesel and I are passing the harbour car park on the way back from his late-night leg-stretch, I'm checking the cars and thinking how warm it is considering it's almost midnight.

'There's still no sign of Ross's beaten-up estate, Diesel.' As I pull my cardigan round me and watch the moonlight splashing on the waves as they ripple up the beach I'm remembering the open bottle of prosecco I stowed in the fridge on my last trip up the stairs. 'Maybe I'll risk a glass of fizz out on the balcony under the stars, as a Sunday evening treat.' That way if Ross makes his way back, I can spot him and do my usual disappearing trick.

It's not only a treat. It's also a commiseration for something less good I've been too busy to acknowledge until now.

One of my biggest advertising sponsors has been wavering, but late on Friday I finally heard for certain that due to the 'negative publicity' surrounding me they'll be withdrawing from my platforms for the 'time being', which probably means for ever. Sure, we have a contract, but their get-out clauses are water-tight. Given the serious grovelling I had to do to get them on board in the first place, their loss should be gut-wrenching. But somehow it hasn't hit me yet. Due to being here, not in London, and up to my neck with The Little Cornish Kitchen, it still feels very distant. As if it's happening to someone else, not me.

The wonderful thing about dogs is, they mostly agree with you. From the way Diesel's wagging his tail he thinks drinkies on the balcony are a great idea. The drawback of sparkling white is how easily it slips down, especially when you're knackered. Four large glasses later I learn that fizz fired down really fast won't revive me or my future. Instead it knocks me out. As my head hits the pile of downy pillows and I turn out the light the room is spinning like it did when I was a tipsy teenager.

Four hours later as I wake up to the dawn light seeping through the muslin curtains, my head is pounding and my throat is like sandpaper, and there's one thought in my brain – ice-cold fizzy water.

My eyes are still closed as I pull on the doorknob and

stumble into the half-light of the corridor. I'm bumbling towards the kitchen when my head smacks straight into something warm and hard.

'Cressy! What the hell…?'

Damn. As Ross's strong fingers close on my shoulders, I'm breathing in a mix of hot skin and some familiar body spray that's even more heady up-close than from across the room. My cheek is rammed against his bare chest, and my knee is somehow all tangled up with hard-muscled legs under soft denim jeans.

'It's half-past four in the morning, Ross.' I try to sound less like Alexa telling the time. 'What the hell…? back at you.'

He's still hanging onto me. 'I just came in from an out-of-hours call. Elise was struggling with an abdominal torsion in a Doberman. I went to help out.'

I haven't got the first clue what he's talking about, but I'm still getting a picture flashing through my brain. Him and Elise, their heads bowed together under surgical lights, his tousled curls brushing against her sleek dark bob cut. Which is bloody ridiculous, because surely if they'd been operating they'd have had head coverings on. And there's no reason it should feel as much like the end of the effing world as it does.

'Where's your shirt?'

He nods down at the knot around his waist. 'No one told me I was going to run into the dress-code police. I took it off in the living room. How about you, out in your PJs, what's your story?'

'I had too much left-over fizz and now I'm getting a

glass of water.' There's no need for me to be hanging onto him. Even less for my knees to be sagging so much he's actually propping me up.

'It's really important to stay hydrated after drinking.' There's a short pause. 'Would you like me to get your water for you?'

And have him deliver it to my bedroom? 'Hell no!' That woke me up fast enough to sound decided.

He's staring down at me, surveying me in the shadows. 'So long as you're safe. We don't want any alcohol-related accidents.'

Sure, I'm leaning on him hard enough to feel the indent of his belt in my hip, but I'm not about to fall over. 'I'm thirsty, Ross, not off my face.'

'That's good to know. One last thing while we're here.'

There always has to be. 'And?'

'Walter's son asked me to upload the films of him to YouTube. Do you have a problem with that?'

Walter? It's the middle of the night and he's talking about Walter? 'Why are you asking *now*?'

'I haven't seen you. I never know how much time Walter's got.' He stops and takes a breath. 'They're clips from the care home, but you're in them and I don't want to overstep.'

'Thanks for checking.' They'll only be a few minutes each. And there's not much of my career left for them to ruin now anyway.

'It's my fault for filming a celebrity.' He gives a shrug. 'But we'd very much appreciate you giving your permission. So I'll leave you to get your drink if you're sure I can't help?'

'I totally am. And "yes" to the films.' At this time of night it's 'yes' to everything. Well, almost everything. Obviously not tray service to my room.

'Great. If you're sure, I'll get straight onto it in the morning.' He's releasing my shoulders. Easing me to my balance point. Backing off. Flattening himself against the wall so I can pass.

Even then it's still the kind of squeeze that has my head spinning all over again when I get to the kitchen, and it's nothing to do with the fizz.

All I can think as I splash Perrier into the glass and I get the satisfying sting as it hits the back of my throat – it could have been worse. If I'd crashed into him going the other way I'd definitely have poured water over both of us.

Ross's voice echoes from the corridor. 'And I'll tag you in as Cressy Cupcake, shall I?'

'Why not? Knock yourself out.' Right now I give no shits; all I want to do is get back to sleep. Then my sensible self wakes up and intervenes. 'Or you could send them over to me to put up. You might get more views that way.' And at least that lets me stay in control with the content.

As for the thought of being rammed against Ross's wet chest, in a soaking, skimpy pyjama top with no bra if I had collided with him – that's so wrong it keeps me awake pretty much until it's time to get up.

15

At Kittiwake Court
Teenage kicks and casual help
Tuesday afternoon

'Okay, let's check what colour icing everyone wants, and then I'll put the colouring in.'

It's Tuesday again. This morning Clemmie and I had a very useful brainstorming session and firmed up chapter headings for my spec-bakes. And now I've got a group gathered around the table in Sea View Lounge having a hands-on residents-only cooking session. Everyone had a go at rolling out the dough and cutting biscuit shapes of their choice and we've been chatting while they've been in the oven. And – surprise, surprise! – now I'm standing in front of a catering-size mixing bowl making icing.

As I lift my wooden spoon the smooth white liquid falls back to make ripples in the shiny surface below and I check around the table. 'So I'm doing green for your rabbits,

149

Walter; Ian and Roger are going for multi-coloured zig-zags; Joanie's flowers are having white petals and yellow centres; Madge's will be pink and orange; Jen's having her hearts pink; Pam's pigs will be cornflower blue; and everyone else is happy to mix and match.'

Joanie brushes a smudge of flour off her chest. 'We'll have to be careful, these aprons you've brought us are much too nice to spill on, Cressy.'

I can't help laughing. 'That's what they're for, Joanie. Don't worry, they're washable.'

Walter gives a chortle. 'I can't see why I need a pinny at all when I'm already wearing my overalls.' Jen's still not persuaded him out of his farmer's dungarees and into his real clothes because he insists those are only for special occasions. Even with the promise of licking the icing bowls he was still reluctant to put his apron on, so he's sitting next to me to be sure I keep my side of the bargain.

Joanie is up at this end of the table too because the biscuits were her special request for today. She pats his arm. 'I bet it's the first time you've ever worn pinstripe for work, our Walter.'

Madge, who's sitting round the corner, gives Pam a wink. 'I'm not sure the pinstripe goes with that flat cap of yours, Walter. We need to ask Cressy to get you a chef's hat for next time. Or maybe a bowler.' She eases back in her chair. 'You're not the first farm man to wear a pinny though – when the blacksmiths used to come to shoe our carthorses years ago they always wore leather ones.'

I picked up the aprons this morning, paid for them with my bake box money, and gave them to everyone here as my treat. If they hadn't all been so insistent, I'd never have baked in front of an audience, so this is my way of thanking them for giving me that push.

Helen's advice on fabric was spot on, with the pink and white stripes which most of the women have opted for looking really fresh, while the charcoal and white stripes are a smart alternative. As for the logo, she insisted on adding *Cressy Cupcake @ The Little Cornish Kitchen* at no extra cost, which is great for Clemmie *and* me. And as some sticky labels saying the same thing arrived in the post yesterday to put on the bake boxes, I'm feeling temporary, yet official.

Jen smiles as she brings the cooling trays back from the kitchen and arranges them along the centre of the table. 'So Shrewsbury biscuits have egg in and shortbreads don't. If I'm wearing a pinny I need to remember that!'

Which reminds me, I may as well talk everyone through the plans now. 'We've agreed to make Roger's shortbreads next time.' They were his wife Cynthia's favourite, and his daughter brought in her recipe specially. 'And we'll make Madge's cookies next week too, and Kathleen's keen we try her ginger cake, and Ian's asked for flapjacks.'

Jen's eyebrows lift. 'A couple more recipes arrived for you in the office. I'll give you them before you go.' When I suggested baking their recipes, not mine, I had no idea we'd have such an enthusiastic response.

Millie catches my eye from the stool where she's perched next to her friend. 'I'm just going to swap to the other side so everyone gets a chance to be in the shots.' They're here this afternoon as part of their school outreach project, and standing in for Ross with the video. More fool me for even thinking they might be too young to film; the clips they showed me when the biscuits went to the kitchen are easily as good as mine.

Joanie taps Walter's shoulder. 'Make sure you tilt your cap the right way, we can't have our leading man hiding his face.' Before Walter has time to reply she's leaned across and done it for him.

Madge turns to me. 'So where's your young man today, Cressy? He's usually in charge of filming.'

I'm opening my mouth to deny that he's *anything* to do with me, but Millie gets in first.

'Ross is at the surgery, but he's not Cressy's. She's very happy to be single. For now, anyway.' Except for the last bit, an answer like that makes me want to hug her.

I hold back a grin. 'I was hoping young Walter would ask me out, but he hasn't.'

Jen sends me a wink. 'You'll have to get in the queue, he's very popular here in the lounge. We're hoping all the attention will make you want to stay with us, aren't we, Walter?'

I smile at him. 'There you go, Walter, that's what being a YouTube star does for you.'

Walter laughs. 'Pam says we've had another thousand "looks" since this morning.'

'Brilliant.' So far Ross has only sent me the film from the fairy cake afternoon, but when I whizzed through it before I uploaded it yesterday afternoon I had no idea it would take off this fast. Obviously it was lovely seeing everyone joining in. But with the wonky camera angles I hadn't tipped it for Oscar nominations.

Jen circles the table delivering biscuits back to their makers. 'St Aidan is riveted, and everyone's shared us on Facebook and Twitter. If people all over the world are watching, we'll likely be famous.'

'In which case, we'd better get on, and we'll upload this one too.' As I smile up at Millie and add inky drops of colour to each bowl of icing, I'm thinking back to the time my first-ever buttercream video took off. That whoosh of excitement when I saw how fast the number of views was rising; when it reached a hundred thousand I actually felt like my chest was going to burst.

I was such a different woman before those videos took off. Life was so simple when all I had to do was turn up to the magazine offices from Monday to Friday with a few ideas for lifestyle features to slip in alongside the slimming articles. But once my social media career took off there was pressure every minute of every day. I'd wake up knowing I had to find more ideas that were ahead of everyone else's, that my posts had to be better than the day before, that I'd always have to stay two jumps ahead of the copycats. My entire being depended on likes and views and followers, on keeping my sponsors interested and happy and on board. And all the time I'd have my antennae out searching for new ones.

It's not that I'm not delighted the way things have turned out for me; how could I be anything else? But having clawed my way up this particular ladder, I'm fully aware of the downsides. The drawbacks outsiders don't see.

Looking along the lines of faces here I feel very protective. There was that group of pensioners who filmed themselves singing heavy metal songs in their sheltered housing complex; the clips went viral and the media took over their lives.

It's a hard call. If you've only got a few months to live, would you rather spend it being whisked off to London in stretch limos to have cocktails with pop stars and photo-shoots with the *Daily Mail*? Or would it be better to stay quietly at home on a Cornish clifftop surrounded by friends who love you, watching the seagulls wheeling and the sun sparking off the sea?

Obviously as a young person I'd choose London every time, but I live there *because* I love the buzz. More impor-tantly, I'll have plenty of time to watch the surf lines when I'm not young any more. But for my friends here, I want the best for them. And something deep inside tells me they're lovely as they are. I'd really hate to spoil that.

It's a fleeting thought, and as I push the bowls of coloured icing out along the table it's broken by Millie's shout.

'Is that a wave in your hair, Cressy?'

I smack my hand to my head. 'Please tell me it isn't.'

Millie's grinning. 'I was wondering how you'd done it, it looks cool.'

I run my fingers over the back of my scalp and sure enough, there are kinks all the way down. I give a grimace. 'That'll teach me to rush my straightening.' There simply isn't as much time to fit it in as there used to be. And possibly there's less motivation; I'm still on show here, but no one is as judgemental.

Millie's looking at her friend. 'Waves are in, aren't they, Luce?'

Luce nods and tosses back a mass of curls. 'We were just saying, you should give them a try.'

'I'm so busy, I may have to.' Obviously I'm joking. The last time I let my hair express itself I was twelve. In any case everyone knows perfect waves take even longer to achieve than sleek. I'm just hoping they don't turn their eleven-year-old judgement on my dress, because I took a short-cut with that too, and wore it straight from the hanger without giving it a second press. The last six weeks my standards have slipped so far I can't even think about it. It's all very well having a holiday, but there's the panic that if I let things go too far I may lose them for ever. That it'll be hell on earth to get back to the Cressy I was before.

I pull a bobble out of my pocket and hurry my hair into a ponytail to hide the damage, but I'm not quick enough for Nell.

'Beachy waves would suit our Cornish Cressy.' She's been at the other end of the lounge, socialising with Diesel, but as she's here alone I'm guessing he's crashed out after all the attention. 'I've come to give you the good news on camera.' She turns to Millie. 'Make sure you get this.'

I get up to hand out the spoons, but Jen has already done that so I lean across to help Walter push the icing all the way to his rabbit's tail. 'Give me a clue?'

Nell's beaming. 'I'm very happy to tell you, the feedback data on your evenings so far has been phenomenal.'

I'm puzzled. 'But they've all been disasters. I haven't got

onto trouble-shooting once. Where did this data come from anyway?'

She gives a shrug. 'The singles club members fill in scores online for *all* the events in the village.'

I'm so appalled I'm shrieking. 'Scores? *For what?*'

Nell's got a mischievous glint in her eye. 'For lots of things, but mostly it's a measure of enjoyment. Yours are among the best ratings we've ever had.'

It's a horrible thought even now it's over. 'If I'd known I was being marked I'd never have dared do them. I can't believe people liked them either. I assumed word of mouth would kill them off.'

Nell's stealing one of Jen's hearts, pushing the crumbs into her mouth. 'Completely the opposite. Demand was through the roof before, but since the video went live it's exponential.'

Jen runs her finger over her icing spoon and gives it a lick. 'That's *very* sweet news for our fundraising – so long as no one minds carrying on?'

I smile at the expectantly raised eyebrow she turns on me. 'If the demand is there, why not? I'm up for maxing it out.'

Nell's finishing her third iced heart. 'You wanted to take over the bookings, Cressy. If we're going to do this and go for broke, I'm happy to carry on with those while you concentrate on the baking?'

It's not in my nature to delegate or give up control, but this time it sounds like a lifesaver. 'So long as you give me time to prep between shows, that's a great idea, thanks,

Nell. But your lives are already crammed. Are you sure you can carry on?'

Nell smiles. 'If you want help always ask a busy person.'

I'm thinking of Sophie in particular. 'But there can't be much time left in the day with a multinational company and four children.'

Nell looks serious as she considers. 'Nate's an angel, he's very hands on, and Sophie's good at delegating.' Then her face breaks into a grin. 'She wouldn't miss a minute after she gave Clemmie her word. Which brings me to Saturday...'

'Yes?' I'm standing behind Joanie and Madge, watching as they ice each individual segment of their flower-shaped biscuits. Then a shadowy figure steals into my sightline and when I look up and see who it is I jump so much I nudge Jen's elbow. 'Ross! Creeping up on people! Now I've made Jen drop her biscuit.'

Madge is beaming at me. 'We knew he'd be here. He always comes when you do.'

Nell gives a cough and carries straight on. 'We have an *extra-special* request for Saturday – a customer with a fabulously large kitchen and lovely outdoor terrace would like a meringue evening for twelve!'

'Twelve?' The shock makes me repeat the word *and* state the obvious. 'That's twice as many as six.'

'Or, another way of looking at it, no awkward silences and double the profit.' Nell's looking jubilant. 'Sophie and I will both be there, and Blake's free to help out again too. He's getting the idea now he's done it a few times.'

Not that I'm looking at Ross. But I still catch his face falling as he hears that.

'Fabulous!' I'd have put up more resistance, but I really hadn't meant to let Ross know he'd been replaced in such a public way, so I'm trying to rush this on. 'In that case I'll text you my egg order later.'

Ever get the feeling you can't win? He hated helping, but he's not keen on someone else stepping in. But at the same time when I see that hurt expression in his eyes, it twists my heart in a really peculiar way.

Nell laughs. 'At this rate we're going to need more hens.'

I'm thinking aloud. 'And I'll get Helen to run up more aprons too.'

Jen pushes back her chair. 'And while you're thinking big, I'll go and get that recipe envelope.' When she comes back a few minutes later she's hugging a folder to her chest. 'Here you go.'

I have to put her right. 'That's not an envelope, it's a large expanding box file.'

She stares at the ceiling. 'Folder, file, whatever. Once people got wind we were collecting favourite recipes, I couldn't stop them. They came from all over the village.'

Even though there's more than we could ever use I'm touched at how many people have taken the trouble to look them out. 'That's brilliant. I'll look through and make a list so people can look forward to their choice coming up.'

I don't like to mention it, but I'll be gone before the people at the table have had their turn, without throwing staff and friends into the mix too. I'm sure Jen will find someone I can hand my head-baker's apron on to when the time comes. But there's another twang in my chest when I think in a few weeks' time I won't see any of the gang again.

Jen laughs as she hands the file over. 'How about we let you off the washing up for today?'

Nell gives a chortle. 'With the number of events we've got coming up, I'd say that's the least you can do.'

Which leaves me thinking: how the hell did I let myself get talked into something I had no intention of doing? It's not the first time. And something tells me, it won't be the last.

Then just as Jen turns she whispers in my ear, 'You've no idea how much we need this, Cressy.'

No pressure there then.

16

At Clemmie's flat
Short cuts and hungry horses
Saturday morning

I t's Saturday morning, Ross is long gone, and Diesel and I are back from our race along the beach. To help psych myself up to face twelve people tonight we called in at Crusty Cobs on the way home and invested in some croissants for a lunchtime treat. The kitchen is piled high with boxes of meringues and cupcakes ready for later, but as I'm well ahead with the preparations I had another quick chat with Clemmie and I now have a rock-solid chapter list based on themes. And to celebrate that milestone I've come out onto the balcony to dip into the file Jen gave me on Tuesday.

There are even more recipes than I first thought and they're a wonderfully mixed collection. Some are jotted on scraps of paper, others carefully copied out in beautiful handwriting, some typed and printed with perfect margins and clip-art illustrations. As I pore over the method for Dorset Apple Cake and come to profiteroles that Jen's mum sent in with the side note 'simply delicious', my mouth is watering. There are personalised ones, like Mrs Baxter's Honey and Pecan Pie and Marsha's Rum Bumble, and it would be a shame for Gossipy Pudding and Moon Mountains not to reach a wider audience.

I've spent so much time lately trying out my own recipes, I'm hooked on the idea of books. Which is why as I'm leafing through these recipes all I can think is that collecting these into a little pamphlet would be a lovely way for me to say thank you for all our afternoons at Kittiwake Court.

I'm filling the kettle to make a coffee when I hear the click of a key in the lock, and a second later Ross appears in the kitchen doorway with Diesel wagging and jumping around his legs as if he hadn't seen him for days.

'Sorry, I wasn't expecting you.' If I'd known he was going to ambush me I'd definitely be wearing much bigger shorts. Not that I'm going to draw attention to them by explaining.

'I'm back to pick up some different boots.' He stares at my legs for a nano-second then his gaze lifts to my face. 'You look happy.'

I'm not expecting a personal comment like that either. 'Who wouldn't be? I'm about to sit down with coffee and a box of fresh croissants.' I'm also pleased with my idea for the recipes and where we've got to with my own book, but I'm not going to bore Ross with baking talk.

He looks up to scan the worktop. 'I skipped breakfast, is there any spare cake?'

'There are mini meringues for tonight.' Pink, white, and chocolate chip, which I'll be sticking together with butter-cream later to have with the fizz as an appetiser. Then the plan is to make meringues from scratch and go on to build mini Pavlovas with meringues I've made already while they're in the oven. I pull off a lid and push the container towards him. 'Take a couple, see how they are.'

One crunch and he's done. 'Delicious. But over very quickly.'

'That's meringues for you.' I pull off the next lid. 'These cakes haven't been iced yet, but they're more weighty.' They're for the sticky-buns-on-string game, which Nell insists is a must-have. As for Ross, if he's *that* hungry he'd be better off dropping by the chippy.

He takes a cake in each hand. 'Elise had some kind of cake box full of blondies at the surgery earlier but they'd gone before I got back from the out-of-hours meeting. They said they were very moreish.'

I hitch in a breath. 'Too bad about that.' When I ordered my bake box labels I didn't think as far as Ross meeting them out in the world.

His eyes are roving over the other containers. 'Cakes in boxes sound like a good idea. You could make those in your sleep.'

Oh my stars. 'Except I'm probably too busy. What with Tinder and everything.' It's more me reinforcing the wrong conclusion he jumped to earlier than an outright lie. I've never had the kind of cash I could splash without thinking, but I just feel very embarrassed to have got into a situation where I'm scrambling around not knowing where my next pound is coming from. And I'm extra anxious that Ross doesn't find out when he's so high flying and sorted himself.

'*I'd* buy them from you…' Lucky for me he's cut off in mid-protest by my phone ringing.

It's Nell checking in, so I give her an update. 'Hey, I'm all on track for this evening, not too much panicking. How about you?'

There's a beat of silence at Nell's end that makes my heart sink.

She gives a sniff. 'All great, except Blake's mum's had a fall so he's had to go to Truro.'

'So we're a man down for tonight?' St Aidan's buzzing, and Nell, Plum and Sophie know the whole village; there must be loads of other potential helpers we can call on.

Nell groans. 'Everyone else I've asked so far is tied up with the Lip Sync Finals at The Hungry Shark.' Which means I could be on my own to sort out this one.

'Give me a few minutes and I'll ring you back.' I really didn't want to ask for Ross's help, but if everyone else has said no already, I may have to.

He's peeling the last piece of sponge off his bun case. 'Staffing problems?' He gives a shrug. 'Not the best night either, the women at the surgery were telling me, there's some entertainment night on. It's huge apparently.'

I'm too used to him having the social life of a spider. Even worse, it's exactly the kind of thing Elise would ask him to. I'm willing my fairy g-mother to fly over, because if ever I need her powers it's now. 'You're not going to it?'

He pulls a face. 'On balance, probably not.'

I give a silent phew to that. But I'm still steeling myself here, remembering it's for Jen and everyone at Kittiwake Court too, and not just for me. 'In that case could you possibly keep an eye on Diesel later? George was going to look after him, but we're going to need him at the meringue night.'

Ross gives a sigh. 'I'm not dissing George, he's a great solicitor – but he's not exactly a domestic goddess.'

'So?'

Ross blows out his cheeks. 'Just saying. He's more likely to smash your plates than wash them up.' He pauses to let that sink in. 'It's probably better all round to leave Diesel with him as planned and let me give you a hand?'

It's the last thing I'd want or choose, but I'm also out of other options. And there has to be a way of making this feel less awkward. 'I can only accept your help if there's some- thing I can do in return.' Not that I'm in a position to make conditions, but I do have my limits. 'But please not filing at the surgery.'

I thought it would wear off, but as the weeks went by I actually felt worse about rubbing up against him in that little office, not better. Possibly since the close encounter the other night in the hall here, or maybe it's the salty air. But my weakness for muscles in threadbare denim seems to have kicked into overdrive lately.

'Fair enough.' His lips curve into a smile. 'I'm about to

JANE LINFOOT

move the sheep at Walter's place. I could do with an extra pair of hands right away if you've got an hour to spare.'

'Now?' I'm staring at my nails, wondering if they'll survive. I mean, how many sheep is he talking here? But I do have a soft spot for the babies; I saw lambs on my best-ever school visit. Obviously not counting the music department trip to see Avril Lavigne.

It's as if Ross has read my mind. 'Don't worry, you don't have to grapple the rams, it's more to open and close the gates.' He's frowning and blinking. 'Unless you've got other plans—' he coughs, '—or Tinder commitments.'

'Not Tinder. Not today.' My voice is tiny, because it seems so insignificant and shallow beside what he's doing. 'Twelve 'til three thirty was actually set aside for me to get ready.' I catch hold of my ponytail and flick it back over my shoulder.

His voice rises in shock. 'It takes three and a half hours?' Then he lets it drop. 'Sorry, of course it does, I know that already. So, some other time then.'

If I run out on this he'll come tonight regardless, because that's what he's like. And I'll just feel shit about it. We've both got our weaknesses. I'm the woman who spends hours every day making sure my appearance is beyond reproach. He's the world's most reliable man who can't stop himself from leaping in to help people, whatever the cost to himself.

There's only one thing for it. 'I washed my hair yesterday evening, I'm going to have to step right out of my comfort zone and make do with a much more minor spritz and style for now.' It's one day. I'll survive. It never needs to happen again. I reach across for the Crusty Cobs box. 'If we eat lunch on the way, I'll make up the time later.'

His smile widens to a beam. 'Croissants!'

I'm suddenly thinking of his car upholstery. 'Unless they're too messy?'

'My car's full of mud, I don't care about pastry flakes.' His smile fades to a frown. 'You aren't expecting pristine seats, are you? You don't mind sitting on straw?'

'I can live with it.' Which sounded way too long-term for a five-minute drive.

'Great, I'll get us some coffees-to-go from the kiosk on the quay.'

I look down my bare thighs all the way to the rhine-stones on my flipflops. 'I'll grab some trainers. And longer trousers.'

Ross's eyes snap open. 'No need to spend too long getting ready.' He gives a cough. 'Shorts will be fine.'

And just like that, the Saturday I've meticulously timetabled down to the last minute has been turned entirely upside down.

Ten minutes later we're bumping along the Rose Hill road, Diesel's fur flattened to his face by the wind as he sticks it out of the back window, heading for Walter's farm.

17

On the way to Snowdrop Farm, High Hopes Hill
Bare legs and wild skies
Saturday lunchtime

'Not too much hay in the footwell then?'

This is Ross finally making conversation as we wind our way up and out of the village and turn off onto a bumpy lane behind the surgery. Thanks to the croissants we've been munching, we've driven the whole way without having to talk at all. But that isn't to say we've been sitting in silence. Far from it – the speakers in the car doors have been belting out Pink Floyd all the way up from the harbour car park.

I'm shouting to be heard over the number 13 volume. 'Definitely no complaints about the dirt.' He practically works in a field, it would be more of a surprise if it were spotless. Plus, you can't beat pastries eaten in the wild. And I'm not a moaner, but I can't let his choice of backing track go without comment. 'But listening to *Dark Side of the Moon* is like falling into a time warp. And not in a good way.'

He gives me a wounded stare. 'It's *so* iconic, how can you not like it?'

I pull a face. 'For me it's less about icons, and more like I'm a teenager again, walking in on Dad having a full-blown midlife crisis, trying to relive his lost youth on a Saturday afternoon in our living room.' Complete with flared trousers four inches too small, a skin-tight purple velvet T-shirt and platform-soled boots.

There's a smile playing around Ross's lips. 'Your dad was the one who first played it for me. And time proved him right, it *did* influence so much that came since. Better still, it's having a resurgence; hipsters love it.'

I can't let him get away with this. 'Shit, Ross, next thing you'll be telling me you listen to Fleetwood Mac.'

The guilty sideways stare he shoots me is the giveaway. Of course he bloody does. I let out a groan. 'Why, when we've got so much great music of our own, would you immerse yourself in dad music?'

He gives a shrug. 'I loved those times I spent at your house. You have no idea how lucky you are to have a family like yours.' He's tapping his fingers on the steering wheel. 'My parents never listened to music, they were always too busy being worried to have time for my friends. But the worst thing was they had no inkling that anything could be different, no ambition to make things better. That was *so* hard to live with.'

'Right.' That's confirmed my status as the spoiled, entitled child here.

He lets out a sigh. 'It's not only the nostalgia; sometimes music resonates because of how you are in a certain moment. This does that for me now.'

The clue is in the name. 'That *Dark Side* album came from a very *dark* place.' I'm thinking out loud rather than being profound. Not that my dad took it that way when he played air guitar and jived around wailing about people losing their minds and the sun being eclipsed. We kids used to rip the shit out of him because he used his Mick Jagger moves, regardless of what he was singing along to. And then the bigger implication hits me. 'Shit, Ross, you *are* okay?'

He tilts his head as he thinks. 'I'm as fine as I've ever been.' His knuckles whiten on the steering wheel as the car hits a pothole, and he wrestles it out of the nettles and back onto the track again. 'Just don't assume everyone's life is as full of rainbow buttercream as yours is, Cressy.'

I'm not convinced that he's as fine as he's pretending to be. But I give a silent hurrah that he's *so* oblivious to how far I'm falling and how fast. 'Point taken. I'll make sure I bear that in mind in future.'

Then we round a bend and a cluster of stone buildings with shiny slate roofs comes into view, surrounded by a sea of green meadows, and Ross clears his throat. 'So this is Walter's place.'

There's a loud thrum and my whole body shakes as we hit a cattle grid, and then as we lurch into another pothole I catch sight of the signboard in the verge. '*Snowdrop Farm, High Hopes Hill*. What a wonderful name!'

Ross gives an eye roll. 'Ever the optimist. I'm afraid it's a lot less picturesque than it sounds right now.'

I might be broke and I'm fully resigned to being #CCsoggybottom for ever. But no one can stop me looking for the good stuff. 'There's always a bright side, Ross.' As he pulls to a halt in a cobbled yard, a group of hens scatter, Diesel gives a bark and I rub my hands together like I really mean business. 'So what are we waiting for. Let's go and rustle up some sheep!'

Which might sound enthusiastic for Ross's benefit but is actually total bullshit. And this really mustn't take all day, because I've got meringues to fill. And after that I really do need to get ready!

18

At Snowdrop Farm, High Hopes Hill
Amateurs, meadowsweet and a nasty slip-up
Saturday lunchtime

'**Y**our mum must have been a tiny bit romantic to call you after *Poldark*.'

My throat is burning and I'm running to keep up with the guy in question, which I don't mind if it means we get this sheep chase over asap. Somehow I can't believe his home life was as bleak as he's making out.

Ross stops for half a step to look back. 'You're forgetting how old I am. Aidan Turner only ripped his shirt off five years ago.'

'There was a 1975 version.' I know, because my mum is *on* this. Even after five series of the new one she still prefers Demelza from the seventies. 'That would tie in.'

Ross is still pausing. 'Sorry to wreck your illusions but

my parents were driven by tradition. I'm named after my great-grandfather.'

I'm not giving in on this. 'It's *possible* they called you after *both*.'

I've got my hands in the pockets of my long cardigan trying to stop it catching on the thistles and cow parsley. I'm mighty pleased I brought it, because even though I put bigger shorts on, the minute I bent my legs to get in the car the bare bits expanded horribly and the cashmere hid a multitude.

'Have your parents moved on?' He'd hardly be sleeping on the surgery put-you-up if they were still in St Aidan. It's funny; when you're younger you accept people as they are, and it's only now I'm wondering where he came from and why he turned out as he did, but he's not giving much away.

'My sister's near Plymouth. She found them a little place overlooking the Tamar.'

I'm drawing level with him now. 'A big move if they'd been here all their lives. Do they like it?'

He shrugs. 'Who knows? They go to Dunelm to choose cushions, so I guess the new start has changed something for the better.' He takes a run at the fence we're approaching and hops over. 'Two more fields, and we'll be there.'

I catch sight of his outstretched hand ready to help me down from the stile and wince again at the liver-coloured scars on the inside of his fingers. I'm looking down on him as I hesitate on the wooden step, and there's a twang in my chest as I think of metal bucket handles cutting into those wounds. 'So how do you manage farm work with your injuries?'

He shoves his spare hand into the pocket of his jeans. 'It's not ideal, and I'm sometimes pushed for time. That's why I was searching for someone to help feed the animals.'

'You said cows. Aren't they huge?' I might as well explore this while I'm here.

His throat constricts as he swallows. 'Nell's parents have got most of the herd at their place for now; the ones that are here are youngsters. Any time you're up for job swaps, you know where to find me.'

However much I may need his help, I'm wary of committing at this stage. 'Let's see how today goes first.' I drop onto the grass on my own but as I land his gaze snags on my chest. 'What?' It takes me a nanosecond to get that he's scrutinising my T-shirt, not what's under it. I pulled it on without thinking before we left and as I squint down at the words on the front my heart sinks.

Ross frowns. '*I love you will u marry me?* What kind of message does that send out? No wonder your phone's always buzzing.'

I shake my head in despair that I've made so many single-lady declarations, yet he's missed them all. 'The T-shirt's ironic, Ross. If you can't see the funny side that'll be because your sense of humour's gone AWOL.'

He stops, and gives me a reproachful stare. 'I *laugh*. I laugh loads.'

I've pushed this too far. 'Yes, of course you do. All the time.' I just haven't been around to hear him.

His voice rises in protest. 'Not *everyone's* life is a riot,

Cressy. Some of us work in areas with serious responsibility. I wouldn't want it any other way, but it's not always fun-packed. Things don't always go to plan.'

I have a point to make here before he starts banging on about me basking in the glow of iridescent fairy wings. 'Which is why some of us have irony on our T-shirts – to lighten things up.' And now I need to change the subject, so it might be time to show how at one with the countryside I am before we meet the live animals. 'The yellow flowers are nice.'

'Do you mean the dandelions, the buttercups, the yellow rattle or the lady's bed straw?'

I'm kicking myself for forgetting the name for butter-cups when I'm trying so hard. 'All of them really.'

He turns and does a fake punch on my elbow. 'Only winding you up – see, I can still see the funny side some-times.' A pace later he picks up speed again. 'Walter's hay meadows are wonderful, all thanks to good old-fashioned cow muck and no chemicals.'

I'm panting as we approach the next gate, but at least that's another field crossed. 'You sound like you've known him for ever?'

Ross sounds thoughtful. 'I got to know him properly when I helped at the surgery when I was still at school. He must have been close to seventy even then; he'd already lost Sarah.'

'He's managed on his own for a long time.' I caught a glimpse of the front of the farmhouse behind a tangle of climbing roses, opening onto a courtyard with higgledy barns and mismatched doors and rusty corrugated-iron roofs. 'It's a lovely setting, but it's all very tumbledown.'

Ross stares back at the cluster of buildings in the distance. 'It's seen better days, but it's home to Walter. I'm not sure he'll ever come back to live here, but I'd like to keep it going for him as long as I can.'

There's a lump in my throat at the thought of what Walter is losing. 'At least he's not too far away.'

Ross smiles to himself. 'He's better looked after now than he has been for a long time, and whatever he says, he enjoys the company.' His mouth straightens. 'It would be such a loss to the village if Kittiwake Court wasn't there.'

My eyes pop open. 'But surely that won't really happen?'

'They're a lot closer to the edge than people know. But please don't mention it, we mustn't alarm the residents at this stage.'

My next thought makes my blood run cold. 'Where will he go if Kittiwake Court closes?' But it's not just Walter, is it? 'Where would they all go?'

Ross winces. 'They'd have to move on. There are various places, but they're all further away.'

I let out a cry as I think of Madge and Pam and Kathleen not sitting together any more. 'But they're like a family, they couldn't be split up.'

He gives me a hard stare over his shoulder as he reaches out for the gate. 'That's why it's so important we find the money to keep them where they are.' He bangs the steel rod sticking up from the gate post, strides forwards as the gate swings, then stands to hold it open for me.

However many baking evenings it takes to get that cash, I make a silent vow to do them. Then as I step forward I catch the glint in Ross's eye. If he's mocking me again, I need to show him where to get off.

'Thanks, but I can take it from here. I might be a townie, but I should be able to shut a gate.' I grasp the top rail, push the gate back to meet the post, and lean over to double-check that the clang has closed the catch. Job done. I stick my nose in the air and I'm walking away when a sudden tug drags me backwards, and I lurch to find my shoulder pinned to the gatepost. 'What the eff?'

Ross is coughing into his hand. 'Cardigan caught on the gate closer?'

Damn. Crap. 'Right. Thanks for that.' I unhook my cardi neck, readjust my sleeves, and when I try again I walk away fine. 'Are you okay?'

Ross is doubled up and looks like he could be choking. He pulls his hand over his face, and when he finally looks at me again he's pretty much back to normal. 'Don't worry, it could happen to anyone, gates attack people all the time.'

'Really.' He's taking the piss again but I'm not going to rise.

'And I admit, I might have been laughing there. Just a little.' He's pointing at the ground. 'Sorry, I meant to say, the cows have been in this field, so watch out for... Oops, too late.'

There's no other sensation like it – the sole of your shoe sliding, and you know you've stepped in something awful. Except when I look down and see the greeny-brown sludge squelching out of the crust and over my foot it's a hundred times more dreadful than the picture in my head. Worse still, I'd like to play this down but the shriek is already long gone. 'Waaaaaaaaaaahhhh…'

From somewhere Ross has found an even deeper tone than usual. 'It's only a cowpat, Cress, try to think of it as digested grass.'

Number one, if he thinks deeper equals soothing, it doesn't work for me. All it does is bring me out in goose-bumps. As for implying that I'm over-reacting… 'It's okay for you, you aren't the one with cow crap all over your third-best trainers.' It's my own fault. It's a farm field, I should have looked where I was walking. I can't believe I made such a silly mistake when I was trying to look like a cool country person. 'I know it'll wash off and they'll be good as new, but it's just a bit bleugh until they are.'

His face contorts. 'I'm fairly certain it won't come off. Not off that light suede. I'm sorry, we'll get you some boots for next time.' He's scanning my eyes to see how much he needs to throw in. 'And some more trainers. Pink ones. Definitely. For sure.'

I can't believe he thinks I'd be up for this again. 'Remind me to stick to parks in future.' I'm scraping my foot along the grass to get the worst of the dung off.

His face crumples. 'Don't say that. I always assumed you'd like the countryside.'

That gets the eye roll it deserves. 'I admit I'm looking forward to seeing the lambs. We saw some at a farm park when I was seven, and it was my life's ambition to take one home and keep it in the garden. They *are* the white ones that skip around with those cute wiggly tails?' I'm pretty sure that's right, but this is such a minefield, I'd better check. Now I think about it, an entire field of lambs will more than make up for one ruined trainer.

Ross gives me a strange sideways stare. 'You *are* messing with me, aren't you, Bertie?'

'When have *I* ever teased *you*?' He's the one who rips the shit out of me.

He takes a deep breath. 'The lambs are a few months old, they're not little anymore.' The frown lines on his forehead deepen. 'That's not the only reason you came?'

I'm not going to let him see I'm disappointed. 'No, Ross. I'm here so I don't have to feel guilty when you help me tonight, remember?'

Which reminds me; it's easy to lose track of time when the wind's blowing off the sea making the buttercups shiver in the sunlight, but I haven't got all day. And from what I know now, it's more important than ever that I make tonight amazing.

'Shall we get on?' And then I look over the next fence and see a row of sheep with black faces and droopy ears staring straight at us, stamping their feet. And not that I'm panicking, but the crowd surging behind them looks a lot like Euston on a Friday afternoon but more woolly. 'How many are there?'

Ross lets out a sigh. 'About thirty.'

I'm an optimist, but my heart's faltering here. 'The big ones are very…'

'Big?' Ross is nodding. 'They're Suffolks, but don't worry, these ones are quiet and friendly.'

I'm not sure that's reassuring. 'And what are we doing?'

'Moving them into the next field, and bringing the water tractor through with them.' He's biting his lip. 'You don't have to carry them, they walk on their own.'

And to think I was worried about broken nails. I *so* should have stayed at home making icing.

As for him making fun of me, in an ideal world that's not how I'd have chosen for him to reconnect with his lost sense of humour. But an idea is forming that makes a smile spread right across my face – I've got the perfect way to get my own back on him tonight.

The meringue night at Comet Cove
Frizz and spinning sugar
Saturday evening

I t's a good thing this evening's venue is only five
minutes' drive around the bay, because by the time
we've loaded up and Ross finally pulls out of the harbour
car park we should already be there.

I admit, the lateness is all down to me. With so many
sheep hurtling past me earlier this afternoon, it felt more
like I was on the set of *Far from the Madding Crowd* than in a
meadow in St Aidan. Whatever the excuse, I forgot to do
the one thing I was supposed to, which was shut the gate.
As Ross drove through into the field pulling the water tank
he swung the tractor around and I got distracted for a
moment watching him in the cab silhouetted against the sky
and the sea. Next thing I knew the whole damn flock was

stampeding back to where they'd come from. Which meant we had to start all over again, except this time they'd got wise and flighty too, and put up way more resistance to our polite suggestion that they should move a few yards the other side of the fence a second time.

Let's just say, I'm really pleased I opted for media studies, because I have no aptitude whatsoever as a sheep rearer.

I'll give you one guess what suffered. Obviously getting the mini meringues stuck together and stowed in their pretty multicoloured bun-cases and making sure everything got loaded into the car took priority over how I looked. So just for tonight the hair I'll be flicking back has no resemblance at all to mine, and has a lot more to do with getting shoved through a proverbial hedge backwards. Except in this case the hedge was actually real. It's a shame because I'd wanted to look my shiniest for this double-sized evening. But by the end the minutes were disappearing so fast that after a two-minute shower and the same for make-up I yanked on my clean jeans and a vest, pulled my blue spotty shirt off the bed on a hanger to put on when we get there, knotted a twisted scarf around my head for a hair-band, and ran for the stairs.

All I can do once we pull up outside the low, long-roofed detached cottage is accept things as they are, smile at Bonnie and Marc, the hosts, as they wave us in through the navy-blue painted front door, and be truly grateful to Nell for getting everyone to help carry in the gear and make it feel like fun. Chloe and Gavin are following behind me, their arms piled with cake boxes, and as I pass others in the hall I'm recognising a lot of them from the previous evenings we've done.

As I arrive in a kitchen which is large, but very lived in, Plum swoops across and puts a glass into my hand. 'Here, have this and get your breath back. The guests are a long way ahead, they've been here knocking back the fizz for most of the afternoon.'

'Thanks.' I swig it back before I remember I don't usually drink until afterwards, but the effect is instant. As soon as the liquid hits the back of my throat the tension in my neck eases.

Millie's putting a stack of egg boxes down on the table, and Sophie follows with the mixer. She leans across to my ear. 'You don't mind if Millie films again? The clip from Tuesday has had so much reaction, she's desperate to have another go.'

I laugh. 'It's a shame we won't have Walter and his wise-cracks tonight.'

Sophie grins. 'You were up at his place today, I hear – *with Ross?*'

I'm not too happy with the emphasis she's put on that. 'Only to secure extra hands for this evening.' I need to make myself clear about this. 'It's the first and last time I'll ever chase sheep around a field.'

Nell chortles as she fills the cake stands. 'You can't let one cowpat put you off, Cressy. We'll make a country girl of you yet.'

That detail didn't come from me. If I wanted to keep that

blunder secret I should have known better than to let Ross take my trainers somewhere as public as the surgery car park to jet-wash them. But there's no time to worry about that, because the bag of aprons arrives and they're all sold and being worn by people coming in and out of the French windows to the garden patio before I can say Little Cornish Kitchen.

Then just as I'm ready to begin Nell presses another glass of fizz into my hand at the same moment Ross delivers the mixing bowl I'd asked him to get, and I'm so relaxed the second glass goes down as fast as the first. Then some guests pull up stools and chairs around the table, others perch on the work surfaces, and before I know it I'm saying the bit about filling the world with love and meringues and I'm off. Talking about the different ways of separating eggs, showing them my preferred way, cradling the yolk in the half shell, and within minutes I'm standing back watching the mixer beating up the egg whites, talking as I wait.

'Meringues are fabulously simple to shop for, all you need are egg whites and sugar.' After being so far out of my comfort zone earlier, it's great to be back where I know what I'm doing. And having a teensy trick up my sleeve to get my own back on Ross for all this afternoon's teasing makes it all the sweeter.

Except this isn't going as it should. Pavlova was my party piece once I'd learned to cook, I've made meringue mixture so many times I can literally do it with my eyes closed. And I've timed myself making enough batches this week to know the mixture should be a lot stiffer than it is by this stage. I always intend to get to troubleshooting questions at the end and never have, but tonight I'll be talking about what can go wrong at the start – because it has!

I clear my throat. 'These egg whites aren't thickening as they should, so I'm going to call in my regular side-kick and funny guy, Ross, to find out why that might be.' This is nothing to do with the joke I'd planned at his expense. This is totally unscheduled. As I turn to catch Ross's eye I'm winging it.

From the way he jumps forward, he's definitely a thwarted performer. 'Have you heard the one about the spider and the cheese mountain?'

I give a cough. 'Skipping the jokes for now, did you do anything to the mixing bowl before you gave it to me?' I'd cleaned them all with vinegar and dried them meticulously before we set out to avoid this exact situation.

He grins and winks at the audience. 'I gave it a quick rinse on the way in just to be doubly sure it was spotless.' His face falls as he hears me curse under my breath.

'How well did you dry it?' I watch his eyes widen. 'Because if there's even a tiny bit of water or dirt in the bowl, the egg white won't whisk.'

'Damn. Sorry. That's your answer – I barely dried it at all.'

Gavin's calling from the far end of the table. 'It's the naughty corner for you, Ross.'

'Make sure you stay there a full ten minutes, Ross.' I'm smiling from sheer relief that it's nothing more complicated as I reach for the eggs. 'If you could bring me another mixing bowl while I clean the beaters, we'll start again. And I'll keep this one here so you can all see the comparison when the next batch does go right.'

Ross is back in a second with the next bowl and a piece of kitchen towel. 'There you go!' He cracks two wooden spatulas together and winks at Millie. 'If everyone's ready we'll move to Take Two!'

This time the egg whites fly into the bowl, and moments later I'm back on track. 'They're already turning white and fluffy. Be careful not to over-mix, stop when the mixture rises to peaks. Then Ross is going to help me show you the best way to tell they're ready.'

I take a step back from the table and smile at Ross, knowing he'll have no idea what's going on here. 'Okay, Ross, pick up the bowl, please.'

'All done.' He picks it up and does a little flourish for the audience to see how it looks.

I smile at him. 'Now tip it upside down over my head.'

His eyebrows shoot up. 'You *are* joking?'

I'm so enjoying this. 'I'm absolutely not. You'll have to trust me on this one. Perfectly mixed meringue mixture will cling to the bowl when it's turned upside down and will never fall out.' It's one of my signature moves on my videos and I always love doing it.

His voice rises in disbelief. 'Surely not? I mean...'

I'm laughing now. 'No more arguments, just move the bowl right above my head and turn it upside down.'

Around the table everyone's holding their breath. As he

steps towards me I breathe in his scent and my head spins. Then he drops back and puts the bowl back on the table again.

He's looking at me with one eyebrow raised. 'Just in case this is a trap to make me look an idiot, I'm going to cover the floor.' He disappears to the hallway then comes back and starts to spread out the tablecloth we put down for the buns-on-string activity.

If this is his attempt to ramp up the tension, it's working. He makes a big deal of standing me in the centre of the cloth, then squares up my shoulders. Which is great except if he carries on like this we'll never get the damn things in the oven.

I'm pushing him on. 'Right, let's do this, just grab the bowl and tip it – *now!*'

Ross is playing this to the maximum. If he's used to laying on the one-to-one charm with his patients' owners, times that by twelve. He's keeping so much eye contact with the audience he's barely looking at the bowl he's picking up.

There's a murmur around the table as he swings it high above my head, and as I glance down I see there's a bowl of sticky white egg mixture on the table in front of me. Maybe it's those two glasses of wine, perhaps it's having Ross so damned close that's distracting me. But whichever it is, I'm a second too late as I spot that he's picked up the wrong bowl, which means the one he's about to tip upside down is the one full of sloppy *unbeaten* egg white.

'St-o-o-o-o-p!' I put up my hand to catch his arm before

he tips, but it's too late! The mix of slime and bubbles is already cascading, hitting my head, sliding through my hair and frothing down my forehead and onto my cheeks.

There's a roar from the guests, then they all start to clap their hands and cheer.

Ross is hissing at me. 'What the eff?'

As I wipe the drips off my nose with my fist I'm dying inside but I manage to force out a grin. 'So just to say to the doubters, this is why big eyebrows are really, really useful.' Then I pick up the second bowl from the table, and hold it upside down over my head. 'And for comparison, this is what would have happened if I'd told Ross to pick up the right bowl – the mixture would have defied gravity in a way the unbeaten mixture hasn't.'

Ross is joining in. 'And the funniest thing of all is, Cressy's nickname as a kid used to be *Egg* and Cressy, isn't that right, Egbert?' He's murmuring in my ear: 'So sorry, but if we play this for laughs, we might get away with it.' He turns to the room again. 'I'm more than happy to step in and tell you a few of my dog jokes while Cressy gets cleaned up?'

Nell's already at my side, taking towels from Bonnie. 'Fabulous, Ross, super-helpful as usual. I'll come with you, Cressy.'

Every experience is there to learn from, and what I'll take from this isn't that I should choose my helpers more carefully – it's that however bad I think my hair is, it *could* always be worse.

And if we're talking rock bottoms, I'm truly hoping I've hit it. This *has* to be the worst things get – doesn't it?

As for this evening, thanks to no one else but me, it's totally ruined. And the saddest thing is that all due to me trying to get my own back on Ross for his teasing, I'll have wrecked what promised to be a great way of raising funds for Kittiwake Court.

20

The meringue night at Comet Cove
Punch lines and second chances
Saturday evening

'No one in St Aidan is ever going to take anything I say seriously after this. I've lost all credibility.' You can come back from a lot of things, but I'm pretty sure telling someone to throw sloppy egg over your own head isn't one of them. When you're a guest in someone else's house too, it's unforgivable.

I'm sitting on the bed in Bonnie's spare bedroom, talking to Sophie, Millie and Nell through the towel as I rub my newly-scrubbed hair. In the end my hair and shirt soaked up most of the egg, so they've been washed, but my jeans and vest are still wearable. And Ross decided to dedicate himself to wiping the worst off my Converse rather than entertaining the crowd.

As for me, I'm pretty much resigned; after what just

happened here my attempt to be a roving baking tutor in St Aidan will be over as quickly as it began.

As I put the towel down and shake my hair out, Nell's searching my face for clues. 'But you *are* going back out there?'

One glimpse of myself in the dressing-table mirror tells me it's way worse than it felt when my head was buried in Bonnie's navy-blue velour. With my hair hanging in rat tails, and my face stripped bare except for some inky mascara blotches under my eyes, I'm about as glamorous as a broad bean that's been trodden on.

I blow out a breath. 'Even forgetting the rest, I can hardly carry on when I'm such a mess.' I pull my cardi over my vest so I'm ready to make a run for it and let out a smaller sigh. 'If I were at home, getting properly ready from this stage would take me until way past midnight.'

Nell's eyes pop open in horror. 'Blinking Nora, that's hours of your life!'

Sophie's nodding. 'That's why you're such a pro, Cressy – you make it look effortless.'

Millie's frowning. 'That's the trap though. We've talked about this at school. The more make-up you use, the more you have to put on to make yourself feel normal. You might need to go back to zero and try a more natural look.'

I let out a groan, because she's so young, yet probably also so right. 'But that beauty regime of mine has propped me up for years. It's who I am!' I give a sniff as I get down to the real truth. 'Sometimes I think it's *all* I am. Which is why I can't possibly go out there in front of everyone like this.'

Nell gives a cough. 'With all due respect, there are twelve people downstairs who won't give a crap about your panda eyes. However, they *are* desperate to get their hands on your Pavlovas!'

So she *has* seen the ink stains, but it's such a straightforward take on the situation it makes me smile.

Millie's straight back at me. 'I've done the "be true to yourself and fabulous too" workshops. I promise I can make you beautiful in ten minutes.'

There's something so compelling about her as she stands there with her eyes shining, for a moment I almost believe her. And that's not all that hits me. Watching her here, self-possessed and confident, striking and persuasive, with so much power to help people, it's resonating with me for another reason. Reminding me how right I was to be happy and excited when I thought I was going to have a baby of my own.

Millie is living, breathing proof that having an unexpected baby at uni didn't have to be a life disaster. Sure, in my case it would have been hard work, and tough, and sent me on a different path. But if I'd had the chance I'd have *worked my socks off* to make that work. But Ross never got past that negative perception. And however many pairs of shoes he cleans for me – for which I'm obviously hugely grateful – this deep and fundamental difference back then will always stand between us.

Sophie's eyes focus on me. 'Don't forget, this is St Aidan, Cressy. Unfiltered is our big thing.'

She's so right about that – and it's not just with photos. No one holds back, they come straight out and say exactly what they're thinking. In some ways it's bruising, but it cuts straight through the pretence. There's a lot less room here for fakery; if you're into artifice there's no place to hide. But on the plus side you know exactly where you are.

Millie's already standing over me with the hair brush in hand. 'If you don't like the result, *then* you can leave. But please, please, *please* let me try before you go.'

I smile up at her, and pull myself back to the present. 'Put like that, it's very persuasive. So what are you going to do?'

She's standing back, staring at my face. 'Some plaits to hold back your hair at the side, a ponytail with a twist, dark pink lippy...'

Sophie joins in, propping my chin on her fingers. 'Eyebrows, a flash of eyeliner, a little contouring.'

Nell's wagging her finger at me. 'And a nice clean apron! Then you'll be good as new. Better even!'

Millie grasps my fingers and squeezes them. 'You're so much more amazing than you realise, Cressy. We'll work on that once tonight is over.'

Sophie pulls me into a hug. 'What she says, Mrs. She might be small, but she's very wise. And scarily on-the-nail most of the time.'

I'm biting my lip, swallowing back the saliva. To think when I first met them I thought I wouldn't need their help. And now I couldn't do without it. They're all so different, yet so much themselves, and so sure of who they are. And maybe they're right, I might need to think about me. And what went wrong. Because compared to them I seem to be floating along, not knowing who I am at all. Which is ridiculous, when they're the mermaids, and I'm the woman with her feet based firmly on the shore, who's been shooting for the stars for the last twelve years. I'm just not so sure how well that's working out for me anymore.

And there's another thought. Since I came upstairs it's that thing – nothing has changed, yet everything's different – and it's all down to them. If I'd known this was what having women friends was like, I might have wanted some sooner.

I take a deep breath. 'Okay, ladies, what are you waiting for? There are people downstairs wanting their puddings!'

And then I close my eyes, and brace myself for what's coming next.

21

Back on the Harbourside
Skill swaps and natural talent
Very late Saturday evening

'I was wrong when I said my life was never riotous. It was tonight!'

It's Ross, and we're in the harbourside car park with Diesel collecting the last load of the night from Charlie's car. And he's right about this evening being lively.

Kicking off by having meringue mix that didn't stiffen, followed swiftly by me asking to have runny egg poured over my head, wasn't the best start. Millie and Sophie worked their magic but when I came down after my mini-make-over I was still so bedraggled that there really was nothing left to lose. Somewhere between handing out the individual Pavlovas I'd made earlier and beating up gallons of whipped cream to put on them I stopped worrying and started to have fun, and the audience picked up on that. By the time we got to the buns on strings you'd have thought it was a party of fifty rather than twelve.

It's great they had a good time, but I can't claim the credit for *every* whoop. 'They'd all had a lot to drink, that's why there was so much hilarity and helpless laughter.'

Ross pulls the last box of dishes from the car boot and closes the lid quietly, so as not to disturb the people in the cottages around the quayside. 'Count me in for next time. If a social life is this much fun, I need one.'

'Lovely Millie's right again.'

He frowns. 'Lovely Millie's very full of herself at times.'

After the way she helped me, I won't hear a word against her. 'Or maybe the truths she comes out with are too close for comfort for some people.' I give him a hard stare. As for his rush to volunteer, I know *he* hasn't been drinking, but he might be getting carried away with the atmosphere. 'Nell's got a lot more larger evenings lined up. You might like to think about it again in the morning before you commit.'

He wrinkles his face. 'No, I'll do them.'

I can only think he must have decided to put his personal distaste to one side because the Kittiwake cause is so important.

He rests the box on the back of a harbourside bench, and clicks the key to lock the car. 'It's not only for the fun – it's also for the help up at Walter's. If you're up for that, I'll be there to pour egg over you as often as you need me to.'

I'm hoping Walter's won't always be as time-consuming

as it was today, or I'll never fit any baking in. As for the egg moment, as it flashes through my mind again my insides are withering with embarrassment, but if he knows that he'll only push it more.

I make my voice airy. 'Whenever you want to show me what to do at Walter's, let me know.' I'm sending frantic fairy-g messages into the ether, asking please can it not involve too many animals. 'And for the evenings, I've decided the key to success is to keep things simple.' I'm learning from experience. The fewer complications I have to worry about, the more smoothly they go.

He shrugs. 'People love it whatever you do, you're so bubbly and entertaining to watch. And your baking is delicious.'

I let out a groan. 'I was definitely *not* bubbly when my head was over the bath and I watched my face disappearing down the plughole.'

He gives a choke that's very close to a laugh. 'You have to admit, the natural disaster made for such a memorable evening, we could always do a replay?'

I'm suddenly getting where he's going with this. 'We are *so not* doing that every time!'

He doesn't seem to be hearing me. 'Or *you* could pour the egg on *me*? I don't mind taking one for the team!'

As I stare out at the lights twinkling around the bay, and the muted lines of surf frothing up the beach in the darkness, it hits me – he isn't even meant to be on the team. But there's something else too. I know he's a lot more morose now, and nothing like he used to be when he was young and boisterous and came around to our place with Charlie. But there's still this undeniable feeling that a room comes alive when he walks into it. And this isn't just me, I can tell it's something everyone picks up on; things are much better when he's there than when he isn't. Obviously on a personal level, it's completely the opposite of that; when he turns up, more often than not my day goes downhill very fast. But for the next few weeks, I'm resigned to working with that. If having him around means more cash for Kitti- wake Court, that has to take priority and I need to put my own preferences to one side.

I'm overcome by a sudden rush of gratitude for the way he's throwing himself into this. 'Thank you, Bradbury, I really appreciate what you're doing here.'

His brow wrinkles in a puzzled frown. 'What are you thanking me for?'

'For being a fabulous assistant. And all the rest, obviously.'

'You're welcome.' He pauses. 'It's actually been forever since anyone called me Bradbury.'

Damn. I'm kicking myself for the slip. 'It probably won't happen again.' Not if I have anything to do with it.

He sighs. 'And I owe you an apology – I was wrong to question your direction that day you missed Charlie's message, I see that now.'

'Another thank you for saying that too, Bradbury.' That really will be the last time. But it must have taken guts for him to make that climb-down.

He stares out at a boat heading for the horizon, then his gaze flashes back to me. 'Not many people light up a room the way you can. You're so good at what you do, but it's your warmth that people respond to. You being your very special self is what's made you a star.' He gives me a nudge. 'If I was Walter, I'd take my hat off to you.'

Walter only takes his cap off to get his leg over, but I'm not going to remind him of that. As for the rest, I have to come clean. 'I was doing well, but the ladder I was climbing was very fragile and now it's all come crashing down. That's the trouble with castles made of sugar.'

He's still heaping on the praise. 'You've got right to the top of your game, and you deserve total respect for that success.'

I pull in a breath, because I need to stop talking in metaphors and say it how it is. 'I was successful once, but it really is all over now. People took against me after the TV show, and it's all gone tits up as fast as it came. The publishers withdrew their offer, my sponsors are pulling out too. For now I'm getting by with these evenings and selling boxes of cakes at the doorstep.' It's a relief now it's out. I feel lighter for telling him the truth. Less of a pretender. Speaking the words makes it more real, but it's more than that. As if saying it out loud here I'm facing it properly myself for the first time too.

'Shit, Cressy, I could have helped. Why didn't you say?'

It's a good question, and the answer is that I'm too proud. 'I didn't want anyone who mattered to know until I'd turned things around.' Especially people like him and Charlie. 'And you *are* helping, but I *will* manage. And it'll be easier once I'm back in London.'

'London?' He's more bemused than I thought. 'But surely that's not for ages?'

'I live there, remember? I will be going back.' I'm saying this for myself as much as for him. It may feel far away now but I'll be back there in no time. And whatever I have to do to pull myself back up from the bottom, I'll do it. I'm confident, so long as I work my socks off, the future will be rosy and I want to convey that. 'Who knows? I may find I have an aptitude for farming!'

Ross has stopped a few yards short of the house. 'So you're not on Tinder after all?'

'Of course I'm not on bloody Tinder.' As if that mattered. 'I run up and down stairs selling bits of cake.'

'Thank Saturday for that.' He blows out a breath. 'And I knew cake boxes would work! Have you got any up at the flat? I can buy them off you straightaway. How about I take six?'

I roll my eyes because we're back to his stomach again. 'If I didn't have cake at lunchtime, how will I have any now? In case you forgot, I spent the afternoon chasing sheep.' Just saying. Then I remember – there could be a lot more of that to come, so I need to sound more upbeat about it. 'I could do my induction up at Walter's tomorrow?'

He's straight back at me. 'I'll be up there first thing, or late afternoon.' He pushes his way through the picket gate at the side of the house. 'Do you fancy chips?'

'Chips?' I don't usually repeat what people say. But I just caught sight of the contours of his throat in the moonlight as he swallowed and it blew all sensible thoughts out of my head. It takes me a nanosecond to whip myself into line again. 'Isn't it too late?' It's after midnight and we're at the end of the world, not in the city.

'My treat. There must be somewhere in town still open.'

'And afternoon will be good for Walter's.' It's one thing dropping my standards for a couple of hours. I've got a lot of catching up to do tomorrow.

His mouth is slanting in the half-light reflected off the sea. 'We'll make a farmer of you yet.' He wiggles his eyebrows. 'No need to look so horrified, I'm only joking.'

'Yay, you made a joke! That's two in one day!' I'm looking at my nails. And wondering how the hell they're going to mix with metal buckets and farm gates.

But as I stand there by the garden wall, staring out across the water, watching the cloud shadows shifting in the sky, there's another feeling too. When I arrived here I assumed my problems were a temporary blip that would last a couple of weeks. That I'd drop out of sight, brush myself off, then pop back up and carry on exactly as I was before. Only right now I feel a very long way away from that super-confident person who arrived in St Aidan with an advance on its way and her life still on track. And saying it out loud earlier was like waking up. Six weeks on, it all feels so distant. I may only be acknowledging the separation now, but my old life has been drifting further away with every day that has passed. And it might just be so distant that I may never get it back. Which is a truly horrible thought. So I pull my mind back to something better.

'If you're serious about chips, I need to run upstairs for ketchup.' It's one of those stupid things I should have grown out of but I haven't. Chips just aren't worth the bother if the sauce isn't right. 'I only do Heinz, remember?'

I sense Ross is rolling his eyes. Either that or he's doing an in-depth examination of the moon. 'As if I'd ever forget that, Bertie.'

It's a question I should never have asked. And that's definitely the wrong answer.

22

At Snowdrop Farm, High Hopes Hill
Country living and putting it down on paper
Sunday

'So next must be … the calves?'

We're up at Snowdrop Farm, and Ross has already talked me through filling up the hen water, how many nuts to give the pigs, and techniques for shaking out sheep food without getting trampled – tip the bag out really fast then run like hell. By a process of elimination, there can't be much else left.

As Ross says, while I'm here, he may as well show me around properly. What he doesn't realise is, it's hard to remember things when they're so alien. As it is, the Cath Kidston Meadow Flowers notebook I brought along in case of emergency is pretty much full already. Worse still, Ross keeps spotting it.

'You don't have to write this bit down, Bertie, it's four

scoops of milk powder, and then fill the mixing bucket to the top with water and stir like mad with the broom handle. Then share it out between the calf buckets.' There's a row of slobbery noses pushing past the railings; so long as they stay on that side of the fence I'm completely able to appreciate their doe-y blue eyes, and the furry topknots on their heads.

He said the same about my book when we went to see the pigs. They turned out to be the size of small cars, and they really do snuffle round in the mud and grunt. The best news is there are only two of them. The worry is that Walter goes in for rare breeds which means it'll be impossible to find replacements if I do happen to kill any of them. But so long as I hang on to my notebook, fingers crossed it won't come to that.

'Would you like to try mixing this?' Ross works so fast he's already got a line of smaller buckets laid out and now he's holding out the broom handle to me. 'You may need to put your pencil down first.'

'Sure.' I ram my book into my bag and tug down the hem of my flowery shorts-dress, then I grasp the stick and spin the liquid and powder round in the tub. 'If this was home, I'd be using my electric hand blender for this.'

Ross gives a grimace. 'Walter likes to keep things traditional. When he bought the calves in a few weeks ago he had no idea he wouldn't be here to look after them. There are more round the back by the caravans, up towards the cider orchard.'

'So people stay here?' That's the most identifiable snippet I've heard all afternoon.

Ross shakes his head. 'Not any more. But it's more a smallholding than a big farm, so back in the day the holiday trade and Walter's home-brewed cider made up for the lack of acres.' He sighs again. 'The hens have mostly taken over the vans. You'll likely find more eggs there than in the nesting boxes I showed you earlier.'

The one saving grace of all this is the extra egg supply, but it sounds like they'll be hard-earned if I have to play hide and seek to find them.

Ross takes hold of the tub and splashes the creamy liquid into the buckets. 'You'll need to watch them while they drink to make sure the stronger ones don't push the others out of the way and steal their food.' He gives a grunt. 'You'll get to know which ones to look out for.'

I prop up the mixing stick and reach for my notebook before I forget it. 'There's a lot more to this than I thought. If I have to get in and wrestle with them it's good I've got Sophie's spare wellies.'

There's a smile playing round Ross's lips. 'I won't leave you on your own until you find your feet.' His face cracks into something very close to a smile. 'Bright blue boots with purple spots might just scare them into behaving themselves.'

It's not *exactly* a dig, but it's close enough to nudge me into explaining what I touched on last night. 'There you go, you're taking the pee again.'

He gives a shrug. 'It's what I do, it's only for fun.'

I let out a snort. 'It might be that for you. I've had five brothers and sisters teasing me incessantly from when I was born until they left home, and every time I've seen them

209

since.' Big noisy families aren't always the jolly places they seem from the outside. Ours is loving and supportive, and obviously I wouldn't swap it for the world. But the older ones always ripped the shit out of me, and there were so many of them ahead of me, even if four of them laid off, there would always be one left to make fun of me. At school I didn't have many friends because I was mostly enjoying the quiet, and the same at uni.

I blow out a breath. 'My sisters are all so sorted and grown up and professional and weighty with kids and relationships. And they all have their stellar careers, and their intellectual pursuits.' It's not just Charlie. Bella's a therapist for bereaved children, Zoe is an art historian for the National bloody Trust, Laura is a top epidemiologist, Jo does behavioural psychology. And their children are all amazing too. 'They try to be nice but they all look down on me for being trivial and insubstantial, because compared to them, I am! That's why it was so important for me to succeed, even though what I achieved was worthless compared to them.'

Ross's look is a mix of anxious and searching. 'But you were excelling yourself, at the top of your field. Surely that's what counts?' He frowns. 'In any case, you're the Hobsons, you're legendary, I just assumed you'd all share everything.'

I let out a groan. 'This was why I was *so* desperate for no one to find out when it all began to unravel. And why I *had* to cover up how much I was floundering here. *I always hide my fails from them!*'

He props his foot up on the bottom rail of the fence, and looks at me sideways. 'But what about with the baby? I know we agreed not to tell Charlie, but surely the others supported you with that?'

I'm appalled we've got onto this again. 'I couldn't possibly tell them what a mess I'd made there!' I'm not talking about the pregnancy here; two minutes after I saw the lines on the test I'd already fallen in love with the idea. And I knew all the family would be the same. The biggest blunder was letting it happen with someone who wasn't interested in sharing it. And then that I lost it.

There's a sudden pain in his eyes. 'Of course, I should have known. But when things are really tough, sharing can be helpful.'

Looking back, if I had already told them they'd all have been as devastated as I was when I lost the baby. When they were already in pieces about Charlie losing Faye, I'm so pleased I saved them that.

In any case, something else strikes me. 'You can't tell me off for keeping things to myself. You're not exactly famous for *your* over-sharing.' As for bringing this back to the present, he doesn't have a clue about losing what's important. 'Do you have any idea how helpless you feel when you lose everything you've ever worked for?'

His shoulders are bumping mine as he grasps the tube of the scaffold pole fence. 'I get what you've been through, I fully appreciate how awful it feels.'

This is *my* stuff-up; him pretending he understands only diminishes it. 'It's lovely of you to empathise, but you can't have the first clue unless you've lived it.' But now I've made my point, I need to show him I'll turn things around, however that may be. 'Things will pick up; in a couple of months, I'll be fine. But I'd rather people didn't know until I'm there.'

Beside me Ross's sigh is so big his shoulders visibly drop. 'I wish I could be as optimistic for my own future – but I can't.'

As the meaning of his words sink in, I feel my heart stop in my chest. 'Hang on! Ross, *what is it?*'

His voice has sunk to a husky drawl. 'I'm not being kind. I'm living the same nightmare you are. And whatever I hoped, there's no way back for me.' He's pushed back off the fence, and he's holding out his fists, stretching and clenching his fingers. 'I came down here to take time to recuperate, but nothing is improving.'

'Your hands!'

He's closed his eyes, and he's shaking his head. 'It wasn't even heroic – I slipped on a mud run, ripped my fingers on some buried barbed wire. There's nerve damage on both and I can barely feel a thing.'

My stomach has turned to stone. 'But touch is vital for a surgeon – how can you operate without it?'

He pulls a face. 'It's quite simple – *I can't.*' He's kicking at the rough tufts of grass sprouting between the cobbles of the yard. 'At the surgery the younger staff cover for me. You saw me with Pancake, I couldn't have taken a blood sample from her to save my life. I'm overseeing things here to give myself a chance to get better. In Scotland there's an internationally renowned orthopaedic practice I've spent my whole career creating, a team of colleagues all waiting for me to get my act together. And every day I'm here, not there, I'm failing all of them too.'

'But time by the sea can only be good.' Even as I say it, I know it's meaningless.

He gives a cough. 'Expecting to get better was asking for a miracle. But every day that passes without the feeling in my fingers coming back is a day closer to me being finished. My life as I know it could well be over.'

My mouth is dry as the enormity of his disaster seeps in. But he told me before, he doesn't want pity. 'So what are you going to do?'

'I'm playing for time. Helping Walter for as long as he needs me. And when that's done, I could be heading for a desk job and winding down to an early retirement.'

I let out a cry. 'We're on High Hopes Hill. You can't give up that easily.' However much he hurt me, I'd never wish this on him. 'I'm sorry, Ross.' I reach out and squeeze the back of his hand. 'However bad it is, I'm here for you.'

'I've got more tests coming up, but I'm bracing myself for the worst. And right now the future looming ahead of me is like a huge black hole.' And this is Ross all over. He's brilliantly clever and obsessed with facts, but he doesn't have the capacity to dream. He can't see beyond this to imagine any kind of silver lining. He turns and gives me a grimace. 'You can't deny it, we're both in the shit here.'

Except that's not true. Compared to him, my challenges are non-existent. I'll pull myself together and move on to the next thing. If I'm really lucky, I'll maybe even sneak back to doing what I used to do. Whereas his suffering is real, because there may be no way back.

'How about showing me how to make calves behave? And then I need to find where the chickens hide the eggs.'

It's the last thing I feel like doing, but if he's marching round bossing me about, it may take his mind off the rest.

He gives a shrug. 'You could take a few selfies with the animals. I can see a country version of Cressy Cupcake going down well with your followers.'

I'm not sure we need to go that far, but I'll go with it if it keeps him occupied. 'And I could make some of that high-octane brownie once we go home?'

He's gazing at me through half-closed eyes. 'That's the sticky one you describe in your blog as the closest you'll get to a chocolate orgasm?'

'Something like that.' *Crap crap crap.* When I write this stuff it's not meant to come back and bite me on the bum. Obviously I had no idea Ross bloody Bradbury would ever set eyes on it, less still that he'd quote it back at me.

He pulls a face. 'You know me so well. Maybe that was what Eeyore needed to cheer him up – orgasmic chocolate cake or mouthfuls of thistles, I know which I'd choose, don't you?'

However we got onto this, I need to move us off, and fast. 'Jo says Eeyore had major depressive disorder, he needed behavioural therapy, not cocoa.' This is one of the rare times I'm grateful for having a sister who's a psychologist. And moving this on: 'Where are Walter's donkeys anyway? I'd happily tickle donkey ears all day.'

Ross is blinking, struggling to keep up. 'He hasn't got any at the moment, but I'm sure he'd ask around if you'd like one – or several.'

Now we're on better ground I let a grin go. 'There's enough here to be going on with. So shall we get on?'

As for me, it's going to take a lot more than a quick chocolate fix to cure my problems too. But Ross, as I used to perceive him, was untouchable and off limits. Whereas the vulnerable new version of Ross is twisting my heart so hard there's an ache in my chest. And that definitely isn't good for anyone.

23

At Clemmie's flat
90 per cent cocoa and dropping standards
Sunday

By the time I've come home from Walter's and taken Diesel out it's early Sunday evening before I get back to work in Clemmie's kitchen again. Ross's brownie squares are on the cooling rack, and I'm just putting another batch of meringues in the oven as the flat door opens.

'I'm back.' It's horribly domestic, but Ross calling out is only because of the expectation of cake; he never does it usually.

I clear my throat and make my reply loud enough for him to know where I am. 'And your brownies are *here*.' They're definitely ready rather than waiting, because waiting implies so much more. 'Would you like them in one container or two? To eat in or take out?'

'That depends.' He grins, heads straight to the green

dresser, takes one and sinks his teeth into it. His voice is thick with chocolate as he speaks again. 'Will you make me these whenever I ask or have these ones got to last me a lifetime?'

I'm trying not to smile. 'I *may* be persuaded to bake to order. It depends how many eggs you throw over me.'

'Right answer.' He's already waving his next brownie at me on the way to his mouth. 'Thanks for these, they're delicious, I'll have half for here for later and half to take with me in the morning, please.'

As he reaches out for a third I can't help laughing. 'The rate you're eating that'll be two *empty* boxes, then.'

Whatever they say about chocolate boosting endorphins, it certainly works for Ross. He's definitely at his happiest biting into cocoa and while that might be great for him, it's less good for me. His dark irises blurring with pleasure, as he eventually slows down enough to half close his eyes and savour a mouthful, make my chest constrict so much that the next thing I know, the beater I'm taking out of the mixer is spinning across the floor and has come to a halt against Ross's battered Timberland boot.

In one fluid movement he stoops, picks it up and presses it back into my hand. 'What are you like, Bertie? I washed the floor this morning too.' Before there's time to ask when the hell he fitted that in he's down again, wiping up the splodges of egg white with kitchen roll. He looks up at me. 'Before I forget, I met Sophie and the gang by the harbour. They've sent me something to run past you.'

I drag my eyes away from the taut denim on the inside of his bent knees, and force myself to concentrate. 'What's that?' After the view I've just had, he needs to start from the beginning again.

He stands up, pops the last of the brownie into his mouth and then kills me all over again as he wriggles to pull his phone out of the front pocket of his jeans and over his belt. 'Millie's made a little clip of the egg-on-the-head thing. Come and see, it's hilarious.'

As he heads towards me I dive for cover behind a fuchsia-pink chair, then once the table's between us I lean across the top, craning to see the screen. After watching it three times, my neck is cramping but at least I've kept a safe distance.

'Great.' It's everything it says on the tin. As a sixth child I'm well trained to laugh at myself, so I smile, and cross my fingers that'll be the end of it.

'And?' Ross's gaze is fixed on me. 'Millie's put a lot of work into this, so keep going.'

My heart drops so far so fast I feel it hit the floor. 'Please tell me she's not expecting me to upload it?'

Ross gives a grimace. 'I think she's hoping you will. Why wouldn't you? It's hysterical.'

I take a deep breath and work out how to explain. I don't want to sound up myself, but, truly, this is roll-on-the-floor laughing while falling off the sofa too. My usual slick yet bright signature moves couldn't be any further away from it. 'This simply doesn't fit the target audience I usually aim for.'

He lets out a snort. 'So, maybe you should be broadening your appeal?'

I try again. 'When I've spent *every second* of the last few years making sure *every single thing* I upload makes me and everything I do look perfect, why would I wreck that? That's not just approximately perfect, by the way. It's completely, utterly, dazzlingly, couldn't be any better, flawless.'

'Oka-a-y.' His sniff says it isn't at all. 'But you put Walter's stuff up?'

I pull myself up to my full height and tug my pinny straight. If we're going to argue about this, I need to look serious enough to fight my corner. 'Due to circumstances and the overriding considerations of compassion, I've been prepared to compromise the polish slightly with the Cressy at Kittiwake Court clips – but *this* is something else.'

He's staring at me as if he can see straight into my soul. 'And how is that idealised, impossible-to-achieve, better-than-everyone-else image working out for you?'

I shoot him the most withering look I can manage while still sneaking a finger full of meringue mixture off the beater. 'It *was* going amazingly, thank you. And as I told you, there's a good chance it *will* again so long as I'm patient and don't try to go back too soon.'

Ross swallows, and when he starts talking again his voice is really low. 'I've actually been thinking about it a lot; maybe it's time to stop pretending. Maybe you'd be better *as yourself*?'

For a few seconds all I can do is open and close my mouth. Then I find my voice. 'Frigging heck, Ross, don't hold back, will you?'

The wrinkles in his brow show how hard he's thinking about this. 'On this clip you're more like you used to be—'

I have to break in here, and it's more of a wail than I mean it to be too. 'I'd been out chasing sheep with no time to get ready, I didn't make my nose shine more than my hair on purpose!' And then something else strikes me. 'It's pointless comparing me to how I was in the past, I was a different person then.' Even at twenty-one when I almost became a mother, deep down I was still more a child than an adult.

Ross's frown deepens. 'I'm not saying you aren't fabulous as Cressida Cupcake. It's just for me, personally, you're more relatable when you're bubbly and beautiful *but real*. Other people may think that too.'

That'll teach me. I should never have fessed up to him about my failures. I can see him looking at his phone. 'Me watching it again won't change my mind; that's my final decision.'

His eyebrows have shot up. 'No, this is something else. I'm going to have to go, there's an emergency finance meeting at Kittiwake Court.'

'How's that anything to do with you?' It's out before I can stop it. He's not even a full-time resident here, yet he seems to push himself into everything.

He blinks. 'Don't ask! Sorry, I have to rush. I'll send you the clip, it's obviously up to you what you do with it. But have a think, Bertie – it's something about your expressions and the timing, it gets a perfect from me, every time. Sophie, Nate and Millie all agree, you're the only doubter.'

Five minutes ago I was fixating on his thighs, and now listen to him. It just shows, you should always go with your judgement and your gut. Lean, muscled legs and dreamy come-to-bed eyes count for nothing. What's worse, they can blow you right off course.

I bundle some brownies into a box and push them across the table. 'Take these for the journey, have a fabulous evening, I'll see you later.'

He hesitates in the doorway. 'I'm not sure when – I mean, best not wait up.'

As if I'd do that, I'm *totally* oblivious to when he comes and goes. I give a mental eye roll that a few brownies can make him feel so obligated. 'Good luck with balancing those books.'

And if I'm feeling a slight sense of anticlimax that he's leaving so fast, that's crazy. As I'll be telling Diesel the minute Ross is gone, I have a hundred and one jobs to be getting on with; there's no space in my life for anything other than the next thousand meringues. Especially not anything Ross-shaped.

He's still there in the doorway. 'I'll let you know how it goes.'

'Let go of the architrave, and bugger off, Bradbury.' It was fleeting, but I'd almost swear I saw a grin as he finally strides off across the living room.

'Laters, Bertie.' The words echo across the room, then the flat door closes with a bang.

When *I* casually said, 'See you around' on my first day here he practically had a meltdown. I know a lot can change in seven short weeks, but such relaxed banter from him is confusing for lots of reasons. And I'm not sure any of them are good. It would have been so much easier if we'd kept to what we agreed the first day, and our paths had never crossed again.

As for the clip, three batches of meringues later, I'm out on the balcony, treating myself to a Sunday evening mini-bottle of prosecco because I've also decided on my final inclusions for my meringue chapter. As I watch the moonlight washing the sea with silver, the wine bubbles are tickling my nose. And I'm also having a rethink. I know I hate taking Ross's suggestions, on principle. But however much I protested earlier, I waved goodbye to my 'perfect' reputation the day the soggy bottom TV show went out. However much I'd love to get back to being goody-two-shoes Cressida, I'm afraid she's long gone. I really have very little to lose by putting this clip up. And if Millie and Sophie get a thrill from Millie's film collecting a few likes, it would be mean of me to stand in their way.

And if I'm the one unleashing this on the world, I might as well have fun with the hashtags and give it an honest launch. It is what it is. #TheLittleCornishKitchenOnTour #CressidaCupcakeCalamities #WeLoveKittiwakeCourt #How*Not*ToMakeMeringues!

I'm just about to press upload when a message pings into my phone. It's from Ross.

Things aren't great for Kittiwake Court – promised you'll have loads of ideas for BIG fundraisers. They're counting on you, Bertie Buncase.

My heart is breaking as I think of Walter, Pam and the

others. As I tap out a quick reply my mind is already racing through the possibilities.

Okay, Cakeface, I'll have a think.

Obviously I don't mention it, but given how balmy the evening breeze is, I *might* still be here when he gets home. A brainstorming session on the balcony could be just what we need. Then my phone pings again.

Elise has a difficult out-of-hours calving, just off to help her through. This may take a long time.

And damn damn damn for that. And even more damns that I even mind. And still more to the bitter twangs in my chest when I think of those tight jeans, squatting beside Elise. And how many more excuses she'll have to big him up after this.

I nudge Diesel, who's asleep with his head resting on my foot. 'Sometimes there really is nothing to lose, Diesel.'

I press upload on the clip, swig back the last of the fizz, and then we go inside to bed.

24

On the deck at Plum's gallery
Deep cuts and good ideas
Tuesday

It's Tuesday lunchtime and after yesterday's sessions at Walter's it was blissful to get back to Clemmie's kitchen. As I finally got down to making the dough for some cookie box orders, while also adding ideas to my long list for my cookie chapter, I never wanted to set foot on a farm ever again. But that's not what farming is like. There are living breathing animals who need almost as many meals as we do, so here I was again this morning, whisking up milk for the calves' breakfast.

The bake boxes have taken off so well, a lot of the time they're spoken for without even advertising. So when I got home today I pulled in a cupcake and rocky road bake, which means there's something to put up on Facebook for this evening to keep the interest going. And then Clemmie and I looked through my cupcake snaps. We were still a long way from deciding whether to lean towards out-there and unusual or tried-and-tested favourites, but then we had the sudden brainwave that there might be a place for two chapters – so trad and edgy it's going to be.

And now Diesel and I have come up the hill from the harbour to Plum's gallery for a quick lunchtime meet-up with half the mermaids for an urgent fundraising chat. Then afterwards Diesel and I are heading straight off to meet Nell for this afternoon's baking session at Kittiwake Court.

I know I was hoping to use my time in St Aidan to chill, but as the weeks go by I'm busier and busier. Using the recipe tests for the book to fill the bake boxes has been a win-win and thanks to Clemmie's china and the flat, my blog photo-library grows every day. I've tweaked my methods and written introductions as I've gone along too, so I'm making good progress there. And with each Face-Time bake chat with Clemmie, the book is becoming firmer. I know I was busy before, filming and prepping my blog posts and keeping across what was going on all over the net, but from where I am now, it's feeling as if I'll be getting my rest when I go back home again.

Plum converted her gallery a few years ago from an old chandler's store, and Diesel and I waft through lofty white spaces filled with seascapes, past the postcard stands and shelves of jewellery and gifts, and out onto the deck where Plum, Sophie and little Maisie are already sitting at a table with the sea shimmering pale blue in the distance.

Sophie hands Maisie a slice of watermelon then looks up at me. 'So how's it going for our land girl?'

I grin. 'It turns out your Joules wellies are fab for keeping calves in line. And I still have six and a half finger-nails left.' Another one went this morning. It's such a horrible feeling when they crack, I'm coming round to the idea of wearing them shorter. I'm pinning my hopes on getting faster with the farm jobs; if I carry on as I am now, I'll be in the fields more than I'm in the kitchen.

Plum glances at her own paint-streaked fingers. 'It'll be helpful for Ross to have an extra pair of hands up there.'

I wince as that reminds me. 'I had no idea his accident was so bad.'

Sophie's brows furrow. 'It's a lot more serious than he lets on.' Which confirms that like everything else here, they're all aware of it. Then her anxiety melts to a smile. 'You two seem to have put your differences behind you?'

Knowing how fast the gossip line works here, I'm not going to fan any flames. 'It's easier now I'm getting to know him more. Millie was right, he's great at washing up.' Hope-fully that's made him sound suitably distant and insignifi-cant, and what I pull from the top of my bag should distract them. 'I've brought you some old-school sponge, which is deep cake topped with glacé icing and sprinkles, cut into squares.'

Plum licks her lips as she lifts the lid. 'Just like we had for school dinner seconds back in the day, with pink custard!' She puts some slices onto a big plate. 'How is the cake so yellow?'

I've got a confession. 'It's made from Walter's eggs, laid by hens with feathers on their feet, collected from the toilet cubicle in one of Walter's broken-down vintage caravans.'

Sophie's holding her piece in the air. 'That's quite a back story. Baked by a Londoner, who's been here so long you've almost got St Aidan residency.' She gives a cough. 'And whose other claim to fame is getting twenty thousand likes in two days for her film clip *How not to make meringues*.'

I can feel my eyebrows shoot upwards with the shock. 'You're joking me?' I checked that it had all loaded up okay on Sunday night, and, I'm ashamed to say, since then I've been more concerned with hungry calves. I know how unpredictable social media can be, but this reaction is so much more than I'd imagined.

Plum's beaming. 'Millie's made up, she was texting me all day yesterday as the numbers rose.'

Sophie's eyes are shining. 'She was simply there with her phone at the right time. The reaction is all down to your followers, Cressy. And your comedy timing, of course!'

I pull a face. 'Even I have to admit, it is funny.'

Plum gives my hand a squeeze. 'Well done for putting it out there. It takes a big person to be comfortable as the fall guy.'

Sophie smacks her palm against mine. 'Thank you for having the guts, we all appreciate it.' She's peering at my bag. 'What else have you got in there?'

I laugh. 'Nothing edible, just ideas for fundraisers.' However many people have seen me getting egg poured on my head, I haven't completely ditched the pretty things in life, so I've rewritten my ideas neatly into my lily flower notebook because they're symbols of prosperity. At a time like this we need all the help we can get.

Plum's eyes are popping as she pours us coffees from a

large pot. 'What do you say to a *Mamma Mia!* singalong film screening on the beach?'

Sophie claps her hands. 'With fancy dress!'

I can already see it. 'And moussaka!'

Plum's noting it down on a large pad in thick black felt tip. 'That's a dead cert. What else?'

Sophie's holding up a finger. 'I promised Nell that we'd think about hen races. And George suggested a St Aidan Wrong Trousers Day, where you get sponsored to go to work wearing something different from usual on your legs.'

Plum's writing. 'Poor George, he's always in his suit at the solicitors' office. They're both good ideas.'

Sophie's nodding. 'Nate thinks a mud run would be good for all ages. And I'd like to offer a wellbeing day at Siren House.'

Plum's mouth twists into a smile as she turns to me. 'She's been desperate to run wellbeing weekends ever since she moved in.'

Sophie looks smug. 'It's the perfect opportunity to try one out *and* showcase our Sophie May products. I'll put you down for art tuition, Plum, and we definitely need feel-good bake sessions, Cressy. I'll let you know more when I've put the programme together, but we could do two weeks from Saturday?'

I don't know why I'm blinking, I should know by now that everything happens immediately round here.

'How about you, Cressy, any more ideas?' Plum's tilting her head towards me, pushing cake crumbs and icing into her mouth.

I take a deep breath, dip to the bottom of my bag and

cross my fingers they're going to like this. I open Jen's file and push it towards them. 'Jen's been collecting favourite recipes from everyone up at the care home for me to bake on Tuesday afternoons. I was hoping to make them up into a booklet before I left.'

Plum's leafing through. 'Australian caramel cake, melting moments, dumpsie dearie jam – these are wonderful!' Her eyes are shining with excitement. 'Look at the comments too: "tasty and quick to make for unexpected visitors", "very moreish", "easy to make and never any left over".'

I'm so relieved they like them as much as I do. 'If we organised them into a collection, and had them printed nicely, I wondered if we could sell them?'

Plum slams her hand down on the table. 'What a brilliant idea! We could broaden it out to the whole village, and get more recipes and even more sales.'

Sophie's breathy with excitement. 'If everyone pays five pounds to get their recipe in the book, that would go towards the cost of a print run. And if we sell a thousand at a fiver each, that's an immediate chunk of pure profit.' She claps her hands. 'Great. So what about the title?'

They're looking at me again. 'How about *A Slice of St Aidan – Recipes from a Cornish Village*?'

Plum's nodding. 'With a foreword by Cressy Cupcake! I'll spread the word on Facebook and pop some notices in the shop windows.' She's turning to me again. 'So can you make the selections and sort out the order, Cressy?'

With my magazine skills I can do more than that. 'I'll sort a first layout too.'

Sophie's beaming. 'Our art department at the office will take it from there and they can whizz up a cover design too. It might be nice to have one of your photos on there, Cressy?'

Talk about fast work, but I already know the right one. I flick through my phone all the way back to one from the day we made butterfly cakes. 'How about this? Cake, buttercream and a dusting of icing sugar, in close up.'

Sophie's holding up a half-eaten slice of old-school sponge. 'My mouth's already full, and that's still making it water.'

Plum's looking too. 'It's a dynamite combo – these books are going to fly! Do we have a timescale?'

Sophie turns to me. 'Once we have the file sorted, I'll get our printers straight onto it. We're talking a matter of days.'

Plum bites her lip as she thinks. 'I'll collect the recipes and the cash, then it's over to Cressy.'

Sophie's obviously used to powering forward with her company, and she's looking straight at me. 'So could we be looking at a book launch for a month's time?'

I'm doing my guppy impression again because that means a couple of weeks for me to get it all together. Realistically, if it takes much longer than that, I might not be around to see it. 'I don't see why not.'

Sophie's rubbing her hands. 'Wonderful work!' Her face drops. 'Nell's going to be beside herself for missing this!'

'Does she work every morning?' We're at Kittiwake Court very soon, so I can only think she's on her way back from an out-of-town audit as we speak.

Plum crosses her paint-splashed legs and pulls a face. 'She's actually been for a check-up.'

Sophie must have read my mind. 'Nell's never ill, but a couple of months ago she had a cyst and lost an ovary.'

'Shit. We women need all the ovaries we can get.' It's out before I think, but with Clemmie and Charlie where they are, I'm very aware of the issues.

Plum's nodding. 'Luckily she's still got one left. But they won't be putting off their family plans for a moment longer after this.'

I'm speaking without really thinking. 'At least she's already settled with George.' I know the first day I met the mermaids I was adamant about being on my own, but I get a new kind of panic lately as I hear of real people I'm close to having fertility problems. 'I don't ever meet anyone I fancy.' The one very uncomfortable exception counted himself out of the running years ago.

And this is my private, most hideous fear that keeps me awake at night: not finding anyone I care enough about to have kids with until it's too late. Because as I know to my cost, it's not just about a guy being able to turn my insides to molten toffee, and loving me as much I deserve to be loved. They also have to be reliable, and strong enough to carry both of us, in the toughest of times, not just for the easy stuff.

As for the fancying, that's another awful part. You-know-who was the only one I've ever met whom I literally couldn't keep my hands off. And it's not that I'm looking for his clone, but no one I've kissed has ever given me that same out-of-control blood rush. Once you've had that it's hard to settle for anything less.

Plum laughs. 'That's exactly what Clemmie used to say until your brother came along.' Her grin widens. 'That's how it happens: one day you think you'll be happy rocking the single life for ever, and the next thing, you're a goner.'

Sophie's spooning yogurt into Maisie's open mouth. 'Everyone's journey is different too. Luckily not many of us have to go through what Charlie and Clemmie are doing.'

I'm musing to myself as much as to them. 'Our sisters all have kids already.'

Plum smiles. 'We've met a lot of them.'

And this is the other funny thing about coming away. My ordinary life in London is full of kitchens and baking, but it's also full of bars and films and drinks evenings and late nights on the tube. Apart from when I go home to family get-togethers, I rarely see any children close up, let alone think about having babies. Yet since I've been here, there are kids of all sizes popping up round every corner. And once you see them every day you realise how amazing they are. And funny. And once you see people parenting close up, it lets you see you all the things that children add to your life. And then after a few weeks it hits: how very much I'd like one of my own.

And at first you dismiss the feelings as ridiculous. Then you let them in a little. Turn them around in your mind. Play with them even. Act out little scenarios in your head. Allow yourself to fantasise. When you're looking at the Natural Cycles app on your phone the red no-sex fertile days take on a whole new significance. What the hell it would feel like if they were green-for-go instead of red-for-stop? And before you know it, the want has become an ache that won't go away. It's a very alien feeling for someone like me, who lives in the moment and tries to be happy as I am. Apart from those years as a teenager in love with Ross, I never allow myself to want what I can't have.

To put it in context, when Ross and I slept together the Natural Cycles app hadn't even been invented. When I lost Ross's baby all that time ago I felt bereft, but I made myself deal with it by filling the awful gaping hole with other things. I was sad for not having *that* baby, but I didn't immediately want to replace it with another. And it's taken until now, when I've met Millie, to fully come to terms with what I actually don't have. Back then I lost something that weighed ounces, but the last few weeks here the loss is suddenly huger. Somehow, the moment I met Millie the loss that's been dormant for so long did twelve years of growing all at once, and became person-sized. And from wanting to keep that secret tightly inside me all this time, suddenly I find it's fighting to come out.

I knot my cardigan taut around my waist and pull in a breath. 'I was like you, Sophie; I was pregnant when I was at uni. But I lost the baby at eighteen weeks, so instead of becoming a mum I went back to being just me again.'

Sophie's arms come around me. 'Sweetheart, I'm so sorry, we had no idea.' She's patting my back in the same way as she pats Maisie's, and it's strangely comforting.

My mouth is filling with sour saliva as Diesel's head arrives on my lap. 'Millie's around the same age mine would have been now. In spite of our huge family, I only ever told a couple of housemates about this.' I read the question in Plum's eyes. 'And the dad too, but he was away in the States.' I give a sniff. 'Meeting Millie and her being so amazing have made me realise what I lost. Everything I haven't had.'

Sophie's gently pushing my hair off my face. 'One day you'll have another, and that will be your rainbow baby. And I promise, they'll be just as strong and wonderful as Millie, but in their own, very special way.'

I'm wiping away a tear when Plum's voice cuts in. 'Maisie, put the yogurt down, there's a good girl.'

A second later there's a splat, and Sophie lets out a cry. 'Bullseye! That's all down my back.' She pulls a face and gently lets me go. 'Don't let Maisie put you off, she's our messiest yet, they aren't all this bad.'

Plum's already dipping into Sophie's changing bag. 'Clean T, Sophie Potato?' She's laughing as she scoops Petit Filou off Sophie's back with a serviette. 'When we were kids the only food Soph here liked was Smash.'

Sophie grins at me as she strips off her powder-blue top. 'I've made up for it since, Egg and Cressy, I can eat cake for England now.' A second later the dirty top's in a nappy sack and she's into her next one. 'This is my third today!'

Which reminds me to look at my phone. 'Anyone like any cake-to-take? We should get going.'

Sophie picks up another square of sponge. 'Thanks, Maisie and I have to run too, we're off to toddler trampolining then nursery.'

I can see Plum looking longingly at the three pieces left in the box. 'I take it you can handle these? We're baking

Roger's shortbread this afternoon. I need to leave room for that.'

Plum gives me a thumbs-up. 'And we'll see you later for another meringue night?' She brings out her phone. 'You've had lots more views since we've been talking. And all the comments now are saying the same – you need to get your revenge on Ross!'

And we're all straight on to the next activity, but somehow things have changed. It's not so much that I told my secret. It's more that I've found people who care about me enough for me to share it with them.

As Diesel and I head off across the deck I turn to the little group silhouetted against the sky. 'Thanks for being there for me, guys, it means a lot.'

They wave back at me as they call out, 'Any time, Cressy Cupcake.'

And it's wonderful to know they really do mean that. There's one more thought. 'And it's okay to tell Nell, and Clemmie too when she's home.' Now Charlie's happy again, there's no reason to keep him in the dark about something that happened so long ago.

And as Diesel and I make our way back down the hill to the harbour, I'm sadder because of everything I'm realising. But I'm also lighter, because it feels as if I'm colouring in a part of the past. Hiding my loss, closing it down, might have saved me from pain at the time, but as the years have gone by it has also made it feel as if it never happened. By sharing my secret now I'm finally allowing it to become real again. By acknowledging what I've lived, I'm affirming the person I am. And that has to be good. For me at least.

25

As the weeks here go by they seem to get busier and
more varied, and this one is no exception. After Plum
shouted about our plans for a village recipe book from the
rooftops the recipes flooded in. Judging from the piles
mounting up on the kitchen dresser, the book will be fat, not
slender. I'm spending every spare minute pushing on with
my own speculative book, and Clemmie, Charlie and Ross
are all chipping in to choose the bakes that make the final
cut on that one.

Sophie loses no time either. Her 'Be Whole and Happy at
Siren House' is taking place in two weekends' time and
now includes an appearance from Diesel and a session on
the benefits of dog ownership. Then she adds a tag line that
says 'featuring Cressy Cupcake', slaps the word 'exclusive'

At the meringue evening at Oyster Point
Stiff competition
Saturday evening

237

in very large letters across the advert, and triples the price we'd talked about. But she must know her market, because before you can say 'gravy bones' thirty places are snapped up. Gravy bones? They're the most recent doggy treats Ross has brought home, and Diesel's latest addiction.

As for me being an attraction, so many people have seen me baking now, I'm anything *but* special. After Tuesday's meringue night, we did a cupcake evening for twenty on Thursday, and pulled in a cheesecake demonstration for Sophie's sister-in-law and her besties on Friday afternoon. And now for our Saturday night special we're out at a converted boat builder's shed at Oyster Point belonging to Nell's friend Caroline.

We're back to meringues again, there are sixteen people watching, Millie's in charge of filming, and just to give her something to follow up on last weekend's super-popular YouTube clip, I may have a little surprise up the sleeve of my red spotty mini-dress. I catch her eye across the kitchen island as I do up my apron, and she sends me a little wave from the whitewashed pillar she's leaning against.

Sometimes when the internet followers are involved enough to shout for something really loudly it's only fair to deliver it, but if they're urging me to get my own back on Ross it has to be spontaneous rather than staged. But I will admit I tiptoed into his room earlier and brought along one of his clean T-shirts – just in case.

As the audience take their seats around the kitchen the routine is comfortingly familiar. Razorlite are singing 'I Can't Stop This Feeling I've Got' in the background, Nell's topping up the glasses, Plum's delivering mini meringues to everyone, and I'm tapping the toe of my pink Converse on the spotty plastic tablecloth under my feet – another precaution just in case I get my chance to take my revenge on Ross.

I clear my throat and smile around at the faces. 'Lovely to see you all here in Caroline's stunning kitchen. I'm Cressy Cupcake, sharing the baking love, and I'm about to fill you up with more meringues and cream than you'll ever have eaten in your lives.' As everyone claps I do a flourish with my hand. 'And this is my lovely assistant and right-hand man, Ross.'

Obviously I'm being ironic in every sense. And don't ask me how he came to get in on the introductions. I mean, not *that* long ago he wasn't even on the team. And it's not as if Sophie, Nell or Plum get their own shout-outs. I can only think it's because whenever we're starting he stands so close to wherever I am it would feel rude not to include him. Plus, he invariably makes himself indispensable within the first three seconds, so it saves making a big thing about who he is then.

And that's the other surprise about Ross, the-current-St-Aidan-version. Whenever he popped up in my head over the years, there was always a huge 'not there when I needed him' caption slapped across him that pretty much obliterated the rest. Which is why it's particularly funny to find him so ever-present now, to the point that I'm practically falling over him.

His voice is low. 'Those are your third-best Converse, what happened to your second-best ones?'

Damn. Only Ross would have been sharp enough to

spot I've downgraded my shoes in case of spillage, so I hiss in his ear. 'Last-minute accident with the bun mix.' I think I got away with that. Then I pick up my first egg from the tray and wave it in the air. 'Tradition is, I always crack the first egg on Ross's head so he remembers who's boss in the kitchen.'

'What?'

I watch Ross's eyes go wide and let out a laugh. 'Got you there, Cakeface.' Then I take in the delighted grins of anticipation around the kitchen. 'Only joking. For meringues we only need the white of the egg, so first I'll show you how to separate the yolks from the whites.'

I whizz on with the now familiar routine. The more of this performing I do, the more I get a feel for the audiences, and I can instinctively tell that this one is relaxed and up for fun. And when Nell and I privately ran the question of mess past Caroline earlier she assured us her polished concrete floor is indestructible. An opportunity like this may never come up again, so I need to screw up my courage and go for it.

I'm carrying on my chat. 'So I'm whisking the egg whites for approximately ten minutes or until the mixture is stiff enough to stay in the bowl when it's tipped upside down.' If I'm going to call a halt to the whisking while the mixture is still slippery I need to stop now so I flick the mixer off, and smile at the audience. 'As some of you may know, Ross accidentally tipped runny egg on my head last weekend when he picked up the wrong bowl.'

There are ripples of laughter around the table, and I pause while people get their phones out and show the ones who haven't already seen. At one time this would have thrown me off my stride but I'm much more used to making the most of these moments now. When I think back to how much it took for me to go out there in front of a handful of people to mix icing sugar with water that first time at Kittiwake Court, it's as if I'm a completely different person now. And it's not just that I care less about how impeccable my hair is; somehow I've found an ease and a confidence I've never had before. What's more, I love the banter and the to-ing and fro-ing; where the unpredictability and the unknown used to be terrifying, now it's exciting. And the thrill at the end of a successful night gives me the kind of rush I'm going to miss when I don't get it any more.

I tilt the mixer beaters to free the bowl, then pick it up and turn to Ross. 'Are you up for me to do the stiffness test over your head this time?'

He rolls his eyes, playing to the crowd. 'I'm living dangerously here, but as you're about to see, this moment is truly gravity-defying.'

Someone at the front calls out. 'Watch out, mate, it could be payback time!'

And seeing as they've guessed what I'm up to, I'm onto plan B – abandon mission. 'In which case, maybe I'll beat it a couple of minutes longer, just to make sure.'

Ross laughs and whips the bowl out of my hands. 'Leave this to me, I've got this.'

I let out a shot of protest. 'No, Ross, really, wait…' I've totally lost my nerve on this, but and before I can stop him he whooshes the bowl straight up in the air and over his head.

This time the egg white is almost solid but as the whole mass slides slowly out of the bowl to land on his hair and drop onto his shoulders he lets out a cry. 'Jeez, Bertie! What the hell happened to zero gravity?'

'It wasn't ready, Ross, *you weren't meant to grab it!*'

It wasn't premeditated but the women in the room are whooping with delight anyway. 'Nice one, Cressy!'

I grab a tea towel and push it towards Ross, then pull out his clean T-shirt with a flourish. 'Lucky I brought you a change of clothes. You'd better take a clean apron too.'

There's a lesson to be learned here; if you're going to tip egg white over yourself, runny egg needs much more clearing up. Where last weekend it took me the best part of an hour to sort myself out, a couple of swipes of the towel and Ross is already clean enough to be pulling off his shirt.

I turn to the audience. 'Anyone *not* wanting a view of one of the best six-packs in St Aidan, look away now.' Then, just to make sure this is the end of it, I turn to Ross. 'We're one-all now. How about we call a truce so we don't waste any more eggs?'

He's facing me, flexing disgustingly tanned shoulder muscles. 'Okay, no more egg throwing.' As his lips twist into a grin there's a glint in his eye. 'In future we'll go head to head with buns on strings – starting tonight!'

It's the last thing I'd be up for in an ideal world, especially face to face over the same bun, which is the rule Nell's singles club play by, but I'm not going to back down now. 'If the man wants cupcake wars he can have them – *if he's brave enough!*' I pause to let the reaction ripple around the island unit, then I take a breath and reboot. 'If we're going to make it home before dawn I need to get whisking!'

And this time I definitely won't be letting any out-of-control kitchen volunteer throw my mixture where he shouldn't.

26

The beachside Mamma Mia! singalong night
Meatballs, music and misunderstandings
Saturday, a week later

'We've got so many punters hitting the Greek brandy and lining up the ouzo shots, I reckon the second half singing will be even better than the first.'

This is Nell, a week later, chortling to Plum and me as we stand behind a trestle table on the beach below the swinging lights at the end of the Surf Shack deck where the large screen has been erected for tonight's event. True to St Aidan's principle of 'Why wait until tomorrow when today will do?', the *Mamma Mia!* evening is happening as we speak. Earlier we were dishing out moussaka and Mythos beer, and now we've moved onto the desserts. As I hand out baklava and spiced walnut cake, honeyed Greek donuts and rice pudding dusted with cinnamon, my mouth is watering.

Plum pops a mini filo pastry into her mouth. 'We'll still be singing louder than any of them.'

Nell laughs. 'Who'd have thought a fancy-dress themed singalong would fill the beach?'

It's true, this whole area is heaving. There are groups sitting on rugs on the sand in the centre in front of the screen, while others have set up their deck chairs around the side, and more still are standing in clusters beyond them. Wherever I look it's like being transported back to a Greek summer, circa 2008.

Plum's rolled up the legs of her navy dungarees, unhooked a strap and added a floaty white muslin blouse, Nell and George are in shorts and almost-matching cheese-cloth shirts, Nate's gone all Piers Brosnan in chinos and a striped open-neck shirt, and I'm wafting around in a voile dress with ruffles in unexpected places that I grabbed from the Cats' Protection 'everything for a pound' basket. The only downside to my outfit is the thigh-high slits in the skirt I only noticed when a freak gust of wind blew the wrong way off the sea earlier and showed everyone my pants. But as we're all female behind the table I got compliments about the pretty lilac colour rather than the over-exposure.

As Sophie comes over she's wafting too, in a dark turquoise dress she whipped from Nate's mum's cruise-wear wardrobe. She scans the crowd then turns to me. 'Where's Ross got to?'

I wrinkle my nose. 'Still not back from the emergency he rushed off to.' Elise called for his help again, but our musical clashes might be more to blame than her. 'I don't think Abba's his thing. When I was playing my warm-up mix, he wasn't really embracing the heart-pumping joy of the songs.' Me knowing *every* word to *every* song by Abba and Blondie goes all the way back to my mum playing her pop nostalgia playlist non-stop when we were kids. It can be too much.

Sophie shoots me a sideways glance. 'You and Ross are practically joined at the hip these days.'

I'm aiming to laugh this off. '*Not* when I'm belting out "Waterloo" at the top of my voice.' I'd never admit that I keep scanning the crowd for him this evening or that it feels a bit flat without him.

Nell gets her phone out. 'I can't stop watching the clips of you two battling it out over cupcakes-on-strings, they're hilarious.'

Plum hitches up her dungarees. 'People are going crazy for them. Have you seen how many views they've had?' She gives me a nudge with her elbow. 'You always look *so* determined to beat him.'

She's right about both things. I mean, a lot of the singles club people who go head-to-head over the buns end up in a full-frontal snog, and there was no way I was going there. In any case, growing up with five older siblings I learned how to fight my corner.

The first night I decided the only way to cope with being literally face to face to Ross with only a bun case between us was to take control, and I ended up ramming the cake and the icing all over his cheek with the side of my head. And after that it's somehow felt as if I've finally had the chance to channel my anger for the way he let me down. Which is why there has been so much icing crushed against various parts of his head and shoulders, and quite probably why there have been so many views too. We've just uploaded 'Cressy and Ross's Battle of the Buns Clip 5', and I'm proud to say, I've squished buns on him in all of them.

I laugh. 'I just call him Icing-head.' The only downside is that after my onslaught he's often ended up so sticky he needs a shower at the end of the night, and I can hardly make him go to the surgery so late. So I have to be extra careful not to collide with the guy in a towel in the hallway.

In fact all the clips I've put up are attracting attention of the right kind. There's a hysterical one with Walter telling everyone about cows giving birth while I make flapjacks in the background. People seem to love the ones of me looking for eggs up at Walter's place, and feeding time for the calves. I've even dared to put a couple up on the blog.

Sophie turns to Nell. 'The grand total for Kittiwake will be mounting up if we're getting this much support for all the events.'

I smile at her. 'Are you all set for next weekend?'

As she pushes back a strand of blonde hair her face lights up. 'The chromic yoga person put her back out, but we've got someone from the holistic exercise centre instead.' She drops her voice. 'It's quite a coup, their waiting lists stretch across the bay.'

Plum nudges me again. 'Watch out, it looks like they're settling down for the second half of the film. What's your favourite song from this part?'

I let out a groan. 'That's like asking Sophie which of her children she likes best.'

Sophie's handing bottles up out of the ice bucket. 'Beers

all round? My treat! Anyone need their wraps from under the table while I'm down here?'

As I sip my bitter and pull my cardigan round me I'm looking out at the wind ruffling the sea, the white horses streaking the surface as the sun slides down towards the horizon. As the first bars ring out across the sand, Diesel's nose is on my leg, and if I'm looking up and down the beach it's definitely *not* to see if there's a familiar figure making his way along the shoreline. For the next hour I don't give another thought to where Ross has got to because I'm singing my heart out, only pausing when customers come for second helpings of puddings.

In fact he's so far from my thoughts that as the light fades and the final credits roll and the whole crowd is swaying as one, arms in the air, to 'Thank You for the Music', when there's a tap on my shoulder, I jump back and bang into him.

'Hey, Bertie, how's it going?'

I suspect he's timed this perfectly. I unhook my hair from his polo shirt button then shuffle to a safer distance. 'The film's just finishing, but I could watch it all over again!' I hug my cardigan to me. 'How was your call-out?'

He pulls a face. 'It was a horse with colic, and unfortunately she died.'

My heart sinks for his crap evening. 'I'm sorry. Would a beer make it better?'

He sighs. 'Thanks, but I've had more than enough already. We called in The Yellow Canary for a debrief. Elise still thinks it's her fault if she loses a patient.'

I push out of my mind how young and beautiful she is.

And vulnerable too. That's a dynamite combination, according to the pangs in my chest. What's more, if he's been drinking on an empty stomach he may be totally rat-arsed. 'How long were you in the pub?'

'Long enough to make the world feel a better place.'

I'm not sure if what I'm looking at is a shrug or a drunken wobble. 'Don't worry, it's the after party next, you can dance yourself sober.'

'An on-the-beach Abba disco?' The line between his eyebrows deepens. 'It's been a long day, and I've got an early start tomorrow. I'd best head back.' Which seems slightly perverse when he's only just arrived, but it's his loss.

Nell frowns. 'You should go too, Cress, make sure he's okay. Top him up with iced buns.'

'Me?' As I take in her frantic throat-cutting gestures behind him I'm thinking of the night I hit the fizz and he caught me staggering along the landing and tried to save me. 'There are a lot of stairs to climb if you've been firing down beers.'

He gives a grimace. 'Nothing so lightweight, we were lining up shots.'

I blink to hide that my eyes just popped open. Not that I'm thinking of the worst-case scenario, but pissed people fall off balconies all the time and Charlie would never forgive me if I let that happen to Ross. Worse still, I know I used to groan at them, but the world would be a very sad place without Ross's dog jokes. 'I'll walk you home.' As I leap into action I'm not thinking of Elise any more, I'm concentrating on the best way to soak up the alcohol. 'How about some honey baklava? Or a cheese and filo turnover for the road?'

'It's fifty yards, Bertie, not fifty miles.' As Ross loops his thumbs into his pockets it reminds me – even if it's almost dark, I really need to keep my eyes at chest level. Or somewhere else entirely.

We say our goodbyes and we're making our way across the sand when Sophie calls after us. 'Tuck him up safely, I need him in tip-top shape for next weekend. My Happy Day wouldn't be the same without him.'

And for the first time in ten years I'd have to agree with her on that.

27

On the way home after the Mamma Mia! night
Mugs and heart-to-hearts
Very late Saturday

As we walk along the dune path towards the harbour Diesel trots ahead, cocking his leg on every reed clump, and Ross falls into step a yard to my right, but he's making no effort to be sociable. As for stumbling on the stairs, he takes them two at a time, and even beats Diesel to the top. But as he lets us in and still doesn't say anything it finally hits me – he probably hates that I'm here when he'd rather be alone.

As he throws the French doors open and clicks on a table lamp to illuminate the dusk I clear my throat. 'I'm sorry...'

He flops down on the pink velvet sofa. 'What's that?'

I take a deep breath. 'Sorry for implying you needed looking after. And for forcing myself onto you when I'm the last person you want to be around.'

The lines on his forehead deepen. 'Why would you think that?'

I might as well get to the bottom of this. 'You haven't said a word the whole way home.'

'Really?' He shakes his head as if it's news to him, then he blows out his cheeks. 'Truly, it's not about you, Bertie. But thanks for your concern.'

I slap my hand onto my forehead and regroup. 'There I go again, being self-centred. I always imagine being a vet is wall-to-wall cute puppies and forget about the ones that don't make it.'

He's stretching out his fingers, rubbing his palm on his knee. 'You can't win them all. Sometimes things go unbelievably well and you feel like a god, and then you lose an animal for no apparent reason, and crash back to reality again.'

I remember one of our family holidays in France, camping on a farm where a carthorse had died. There was something hugely poignant about the leaden lump of a body at the side of the lane under a tarpaulin. For the time it was there us kids rushed to get past it as fast as we could.

I'm thinking about the trauma Ross has been through this evening, and all that time we were whooping it up watching *Mamma Mia!* 'If a horse dies it's so much more significant than a hamster; it leaves a much bigger space in the world where it should be running free.'

As he looks at me his eyes are dark with pain. 'It's more than just the horse, Berts. Day to day, at the surgery, I can fool myself. But when I'm out in the field like we were tonight, that's when it *really* hits home – I'm a million miles from better.'

I'm kicking myself for reading the situation so wrongly. 'Maybe nights like this are part of you adjusting?'

As he swallows he looks so bereft my heart is breaking for him. I've got this urgent human need to throw my arms around him but it's the last thing I can allow myself to do. I fold my hands really tightly into my armpits but a second later, with no apparent input from me, I'm perching next to him on the sofa's edge.

When he looks up again he's close enough for me to see the individual stubble hairs on his chin. The lines at the corners of his eyes. 'I've got more tests the week after next. I'll know better after those.'

There's a small patch of fuchsia-pink velvet between his leg and mine. I tug the purple ruffles of my dress to cover my thigh, and as I put my hand down in the gap he's so near we're breathing the same air.

I also know I care about him on a whole different level from the way I've felt before. I'd do anything to make him feel less crap. 'You know we're all here for you if we can help in any way.' Here's me, with one all-encompassing wave of my arm, offering him the help of people he's known all his life. And then there's a more immediate suggestion. 'If you need a quick chocolate fix, I could make you a microwave mug cake?'

He cocks his head towards me. 'Which is…?'

'Steaming cocoa sponge in two minutes flat, topped off with a scoop of vanilla ice cream?'

There's a pause, then his face relaxes. 'You always know how to cheer me up.'

I need to put this in context. 'It's not a long-term answer, but it might give you a lift for the next ten minutes.'

He gives a grunt. 'It still deserves a high five.'

He turns and as he raises his hand mine rises too. Then, as my palm meets his, our fingers align and touch. I ignore the tingles zipping up and down my arm and for a few moments our hands hang in the air as if they're welded together. As they finally pull apart I gently grasp his wrist. Pull it until I'm cradling his hand across my leg. Tracing my fingers over the knotted scars on the folds of his fingers, willing them to heal again so hard my chest aches.

We stay like that, our eyes locked on the lights across the bay, snatches of Abba songs floating along the beach on the breeze. And as the seconds slide into minutes I shift my gaze to the hollows of his cheeks. The corner of his mouth. Imagine rubbing my hand across his jaw, the pricks of the stubble on my palm. How his face would turn, how my stomach would dissolve as his lips brushed my wrist. How it would only take one movement for me to slide, twist and be astride him, and everything would be hidden under the gauzy purple ruffles.

I pull myself up sharply. Me thinking of jumping him when he's hit the shots is well out of line. And that's before we get to the bit about him being the last person in the world I'd ever do that with. *Or is he the only person in the world I'd ever feel comfortable doing that to?* Either way, it's not healthy.

I allow myself one moment more to touch him, but his

low voice is penetrating the shadows. 'Maybe you could come with me – to the appointment.'

I gulp back my surprise. 'Of course.'

'It's a week on Tuesday.' This is so unexpected it has to be the alcohol talking. Which is fine. By morning it will be forgotten.

But it's broken the spell and pushed me into action. 'If you've got an early start, I need to make that cake.'

He stirs beside me. 'Really? Great. Fine. That sounds perfect. Exactly what the vet ordered.'

I'm already over by the kitchen door. 'You stay there, I'll call you when it's ready.'

It's an order not a suggestion and it must have worked, because Diesel's the only one who moves, and he settles in his usual place on the threshold between the rooms. I throw the dry ingredients into a mug, whisk in an egg, pop it in the microwave, and skid back into the living room.

'You'll hear the ping, it'll be ready one minute fifty-nine seconds from now. There's soft scoop vanilla in the freezer. Enjoy!' As I turn for the hall I don't know about Ross and his drinking, but whatever has sent my head to the places it just went, I'm better off well out of the way.

28

Diesel follows me to the bedroom, then I close the door softly but firmly and pull on pyjama shorts and a T-shirt. I push Pancake over so I can sit cross-legged by the pillows to let Ross get clear of the bathroom. And while I wait I'm tussling in my head. I don't mind that I care so much about Ross, even though it's a shock to find it cuts me so deeply to see him suffer. But I'm cross with myself for feeling attraction when he's proved himself unsuitable. For not getting that outrageous sizzle under control. For having those fantasies. But worst of all, for remembering how much I'd like a child of my own at the very same time he's rampaging around in my head.

I hear Ross's footsteps on the landing. The thundering crash of the toilet flushing. The click of his bedroom door.

Then I pull on my headphones for a quick blast of 'Mamma Mia! Here We Go Again' to give him time to settle down. But even after silently lip-syncing the words, I'm still left with a strange sense of not being satisfied and an emptiness in the pit of my stomach that won't go away.

I give Pancake's head a tickle, and tiptoe across to the bedroom door. 'Stay there, Diesel, I'm off to find cake.'

A large calorie intake should solve the problem. Except as I slip out into the landing shadows I crash head on into a naked chest.

'Shit, Bertie, I thought you'd gone to bed.'

I take a breath and a step backwards.' I decided I have space for a mug cake after all. What are *you* doing?' Surely he can't be washing up at this time?

He holds up his mug. 'Getting more ice cream. Do you know how delicious this is?' His frown turns to an expectant query. 'There's loads of it too, you're welcome to come and share it with me?'

'Thanks, but maybe not.' In that tiny room. Him in his jeans and no top. My eyes automatically follow the trace of hairs on his stomach all the way past his belt buckle and down to the bulge in his jeans.

It's almost dark, but that thing has happened where our eyes have locked on the same place in the same instant. In a bigger space strangers could get away with it. But crushed as close as we are and knowing each other as well as we do, it's impossible to ignore.

I smile. 'Nice Levi's.'

He rolls his eyes. 'The physical thing – it's still there, isn't it?'

I feel my jaw drop open. '*You* feel it *too*?' And damn that I gave myself away there when I should have kept my mouth shut.

He shrugs. 'Too many flashes of thigh, I guess.' And obviously the alcohol has robbed him of his inhibitions here *and* taken the lock off his tongue.

At least one of us still has their reality goggles firmly in place. 'As you say, it's pure *physical* attraction. We both know that means nothing by itself.'

His laugh is ironic. 'Very true, Bertie. There's a lot more to life than having the hots for someone. Even if it's blistering.'

What I said about the lost inhibitions, times ten. I flatten myself against the wall so he can pass. 'You'd better go before your ice cream melts.'

As he walks towards his bedroom his eyes are locked on my face. 'Thanks for helping tonight, Bertie. You take my mind off the bad stuff in a way no one else can.'

'You're welcome – any time.' I feel compelled to reassure him. 'It will all work out, you know. If all else fails you can come back to London with me and do stand-up comedy.' That was not at all how the reassurance was meant to come out, so all I can do now is make the whole thing sound jokey. 'Or The Hungry Shark are looking for a warm-up man for their karaoke evenings. You could do worse.'

He gives a low grunt. 'I'll definitely keep an open mind.'

This really is my last hurrah here. 'Good night then, and brace yourself for a stonking hangover in the morning.'

One eyebrow goes up in query. 'Why would *I* have a

headache? The shots were for Elise, *I* was on Pepsi Max all night.'

There are times when *What the actual eff?* doesn't come close. All I can do is close the bedroom door, dive under the duvet and pull a pillow over my head.

29

Sophie's 'Be Whole and Happy' Day
Pets at home and true confessions
Sunday, a week later

The *Mamma Mia!* evening turned out to be mega. Not only did it bring in the cash, but a whole week later people are still humming the tunes around the village. Luckily Ross carried on as if our late-night conversations never happened. For me, with three iced-donut evenings, finishing the village recipe book layouts for Sophie's team, and pushing on with my own book, life has passed in a blur. As Ross hasn't mentioned his appointment again, I completely respect that he's thought better of it.

And now we're on to the Siren House day, and Sophie – bless her heart – allocated Millie and Ross to help with my 'Ice Yourself Happy' sessions this morning, which were followed by an alfresco lunch of healthy salads followed by blow-out puddings. There's a real mix of women here, and the house is perfect for making guests feel treated in the best way.

Now I've publicly faced most kitchen disasters known to woman and come out the other side, my nerves have gone too. What matters today is that people have a good time, so my focus has been on them; if they go away more confident in what they can do, that's a win. And every single time that happens, the rush is so good it makes me want to do it again and again. As each session comes to a successful end, Sophie's smile is getting wider and wider.

With my work over for the day I'm on to supporting Diesel in his starring role at Ross's afternoon pet talks.

Plum arrives at my elbow as Diesel and I wait for our group to assemble on the lawn. 'You're looking fab now you've taken your pinny off. Is that a new dress?'

I haven't been treating myself. 'One of my old sponsors sent it by accident.'

Plum laughs. 'Or they've noticed your new clips and like what they see?'

'Me with icing up my nose?' It definitely can't be that.

'You never know.' She nods at the holistic personal training session already underway on the other side of the garden. 'Whatever's going on over there looks heavy-duty.'

It's Sophie's *pièce de resistance*. 'Sorrel and Saffron, the instructors, are rocking their orange lycra, and I'm guessing the guests are happy to sweat for a taster *that* exclusive. So many balls too!'

Plum shrugs. 'It's meant to give results *without* effort. That's why it's popular.'

She moves back to the cluster of easels on the patio and I

look down at Diesel, yawning as he leans against my leg. When we asked George to take him out and exhaust him beyond disasters, we didn't think as far as him being too tired to interact with the guests. We may both have relaxed too soon because I've just slightly embarrassed myself inside. When Ross asked me about pet sitting, I started talking about dog walks and ended up over-sharing how much they've toned my bum and how happy they make me.

My butt actually matters to me much less than it used to. And my state of contentment snuck up on me too. When my career plan failed so spectacularly I felt as if I was left with nothing. But for the first time I've had the space to fit things in that made me feel happy. My feeling of wellbeing might have happened by accident – but now it's here I don't want to let it go.

Our group is wandering out onto the grass now. We're going to watch a little Cavachon called Cora show off some agility, and then Diesel will take centre stage for a stroll along the beach.

As we sidle in next to Nell I can't help smiling. 'Look at Cora zipping off, she's really showing the contrast between giant dogs and pocket-size ones.'

When Nell claps her hands at Cora and Millie holds a hoop for her to jump through, I can't help noticing that the women wobbling on top of giant exercise balls are looking enviously in our direction.

Millie calls out: 'Come on, Cora! Big jump for a biscuit.'

As Cora speeds past so fast her little furry legs are a blur,

I'm patting us all on the back, because of how well it's all going.

Nell scoops Cora up into her arms. 'Okay, we're moving onto Cora's newest skill next – running through a tunnel! We've practised this earlier. Millie's going at the far end to call her through.'

Millie's kneeling at one end of the long blue nylon tube that's stretched out on the lawn, and Nell drops Cora onto the ground at the other. As Millie calls her name, Cora shoots into the tunnel.

We're clustered in a crowd, holding our breath as we wait for Cora to come into view at Millie's end. But as an orange ball of fluff shoots out past Millie's head instead of Cora, Millie gives a cry. 'Marmalade! You aren't meant to hide there!'

Ross laughs. 'So like a cat to steal a dog's thunder.'

As Diesel gives my leg an unexpected bump and almost pushes me into Ross, I'm hoping Ross hasn't noticed. Then Cora flies out of the tunnel, tracking Marmalade like a guided missile, and Diesel makes a sudden lunge to follow both of them. I tighten my grip on his lead, but he's gone.

Marmalade bolts towards the cover of the exercise class and Cora follows and shoots between the balls in the centre. Then as Diesel bounds over and tries to follow, the first guest tips sideways and slides off their ball, then it's like a domino effect. There's a series of shrieks, and a flurry of arms and legs. As I race across to help, I'm jumping over falling bodies and dodging bouncing balls. I make a dash to catch hold of Diesel, but as my hands close on his collar someone's legs tangle with mine. My feet stop dead, but the rest of me carries on and the grass is rushing towards me. There's a horrible jolt as I hit the floor, but at least I've still got hold of Diesel. As I roll over and stare up at the sky, I can see the bright purple balls rolling down the gentle sloping lawn towards the garden end, and disappearing, one by one, over the cliff edge. And then a shape appears against the blue, and Ross is smiling down at me.

'Don't worry, Bertie, I've got this.' He takes Diesel first, then his other hand comes down to catch mine. A moment later he sweeps me to my feet so fast I lurch forward and bump against his chest. I'm staring up into his face, and as our eyes lock, the world beyond slides out of focus. I have no idea how long we stand there for, but I'm filled with an overwhelming feeling that he's going to kiss me.

And then I come to my senses. Shake my head, force myself to blink. As I look beyond his arm the mayhem stretching across Sophie's garden yanks me back to reality and I let out a moan. It's hard to know where to begin with the apologies. Cora might have made one guest wobble; Diesel careering through was what totalled the area.

I step towards the guests, who are brushing themselves down. 'I'm so sorry for ruining your class. I'm the one in charge of Diesel, this is all down to me!' As I see Sophie hurrying over, my voice rises to a wail. 'And I'm *so* sorry for ruining your day, Sophie!' If I'm mortified on behalf of the other people, what I've done to Sophie's showpiece is off the scale.

Sophie clamps her mouth to my ear and hisses, 'That wasn't a work-out, it was a bloody boot camp. It's a miracle you ended it before anyone expired.'

The teaching assistant from Rose Hill pats my arm. 'Truly, Diesel coming along when he did saved our bacon.'

Her friend groans. 'If the dog group are going for a walk, *please, please, please* can we join you instead.'

I call across to Sorrel and Saffron. 'We're about to head to the beach, we could all go and round up your balls?'

Ross strides off across the lawn. 'What are we waiting for? Throwing sticks for the dogs is great for your biceps.'

Plum's looking at me sideways. 'I saw you two just before. Do you and Ross have history? *Were you and Ross an item?'*

Sophie's staring from Plum to me and back again, her eyes like gimlets. 'The thing we talked about, it wasn't—'

'Now's *really not* the time, Soph,' Nell interrupts. As she turns to me she's shaking her head.

Plum sighs. 'Nell's right, let's revisit this later.'

Sophie turns to them. 'You'd better hurry! Let everyone know there's a change of itinerary – we're going to the beach.'

A second later Plum and Nell are heading off across the grass, and I'm left looking at Sophie. Her pale-blue, perfectly outlined eyes are holding my gaze. 'No need to say another word, Cressy. But I'm *totally* in awe of what a professional you are, keeping that to yourself and not breaking. In the same flat too.'

As I smile at her my insides are relaxing, and for the first time ever, I'm understanding why girls hang out in gangs. There's the sharing that really can make your burdens feel lifted. And having each other's backs makes you feel so much stronger together than apart. 'For the record, me and

—' I pause and fill the gap with a little cough, '—we don't need your help. All the glue in the world wouldn't force us together.'

She gives a laugh. 'I'm not sure you're right about that, Bertie-bus. Let's wait and see.'

30

Sophie's 'Be Whole and Happy' Day
On the way out
Sunday

It's been a day of surprises. I came here this morning expecting to show people how to pipe buttercream flowers on cupcakes, but Siren House and Sophie have worked their magic for everyone. By the time Millie and I have handed out the goodie bags, and Sophie, Nell and Plum are waving people off from the front door, I'm floating on my own cloud too. As I head to the kitchen to pick up the last of my bags I'm even gushing to Ross.

'If Sophie ever decides to do this seriously, I'll be first in the queue to apply for a job.'

Ross frowns. 'I thought you loved London.'

'I do.' I can't deny that he's right. 'But we all need our dreams.'

Standing in Sophie's hallway, in a shaft of sunlight, I

can't actually remember ever spending a day in London with so many real, genuine, proper friends. And sooner than I know, it'll just be me and my phone again.

But I'm thinking of the positive things. 'Someone I used to work with rents a fabulous place she always promised to pass on to me. She emailed yesterday to say the flat's mine if I want it.'

There's a cry from Millie who's still standing by the hall table. 'But you can't go, Cressy, you belong here.'

I take a breath and try to explain. 'The spec-bake book is almost done and Charlie and Clemmie will be back soon. My holiday really is over.' I try not to notice how crestfallen Millie looks. 'I'll still be here for the launch of *A Slice of St Aidan* though.'

Ross gives a sigh. 'You're going to miss talking to Walter's calves and hens.'

I let out a cry. 'You've *heard me*?' Let me die now. 'I know I hated it at first, but since I started walking Diesel up there…'

As I tail off, Ross cuts in. 'Don't tell me you're enjoying it?'

I laugh. 'I was actually going to say, I hate it less.' Mornings without all those calves treading on my toes will definitely be sadder.

Ross is blinking. 'You are okay for Tuesday next week?'

My eyes snap open. 'O-of course. Don't forget to let me know a time.' I warned Jen there was an outside chance we might bake on Wednesday instead, so I'll confirm that. I'm trying to cover up that I hadn't actually thought it was going to happen. 'And Thursday afternoon I'm icing cakes at a baby sprinkle, which is a baby shower, only more low-key.'

He gives me a flash of a smile. 'I'll give you a hand as a swap for Tuesday.'

My stomach drops like a stone. 'Really, you don't have to.'

But he's shaking his head. 'Already decided. And we'll need to leave around two on Tuesday.'

'Great.' Truly it isn't. But I avoid the worst trap ever and don't say, *That's a date.* 'I'll get that in my diary.'

He's frowning. 'You have an *actual diary*, Egbert? How come *I've* never seen it?'

And luckily for me, before I have a chance to push him out of the house, across the garden and into the sea, everyone comes back in from outside, and Nate appears from the kitchen carrying a bottle of champers.

31

Ross's hospital appointment
Fashion tips and smart publications
Tuesday

'S o am I allowed to ask how you got on?'

Me coming with Ross all the way to the hospital in Truro without him giving me a full job description was the kind of mistake it was hard to put right once I'd agreed to it. Ross clearly didn't want me to go into the consultant's office, because he asked Diesel along too and it's too hot to leave him in the car. And then Ross suggesting I check through the proofs of the village cookery book while I waited confirmed that.

So while Ross disappears into the building, Diesel and I find a piece of grass next to the car park. As we sit in the flickering shade of a group of silver birch trees, I marvel at how fast Sophie's team have turned the document I sent her into finished page layouts. Ross has offered to give them a final proofread after me and then they'll be off to the printers.

Ross is spot on with his estimate of fifty minutes, so we're back in the car and on the return leg, speeding towards St Aidan inside the hour. But he's not exactly rushing to tell me how it went.

He taps his fingers on the steering wheel and glances at my knee. 'Is that another new dress?'

On balance, I'd rather talk about his tests, but he's right all the same. 'It's one more accidental freebie. I've emailed to tell them they've got the wrong person, so it should be the last.'

'And how is the book layout looking?' He's got his avoidance tactics off to a fine art here.

'They've done a great job. Still the same fab design we were talking about on the way here.' I'm sure he didn't only bring Diesel and me so we could enjoy the scenery and discuss my wardrobe. At the same time, if the news had been good he'd have shared it by now. So I try another way. 'How about an ice-cream stop?'

'I could work with that.' He turns to the back seat. 'And I'm sure Diesel could too. Do you want an ocean view or a picturesque village?'

I have to be honest. 'Ice cream always tastes better when you're looking out to sea.' And the distraction of watching the waves roll in to the shore *and* eating ice cream might be the dream combination we need. 'There's usually an ice-cream van in the car park where the road joins the coast. Let's try that.'

Twenty minutes later, the three of us are sitting shoulder

to shoulder on the grass at Oyster Point, looking out at the sun glinting off the deep blue water, and listening to the sound of the waves crashing onto the rock piles that push out into the sea.

Halfway down his raspberry ripple and dark chocolate ninety-nine Ross stops and sighs. 'It's ironic. When I went to the States all those years ago it was to make myself good enough for your family.'

That's not only a random choice of topic, it's also a strange observation considering how I remember things. 'But you were already brilliant. Apart from the size, our family was very ordinary.'

He's staring hard at his Flake. 'Ordinary my butt! Before uni I'd never been abroad. I can't actually ever remember going on holiday. You had a huge house in the home counties and the lifestyle to match.'

I'm squinting into the sun, and saying it like it was. 'We lived in a semi, and went to France in a tent!' Our house was small for the neighbourhood, and six kids made it feel smaller still. As for going abroad, camping was all we could afford; we stayed on the basic sites and took our own cornflakes.

He sighs. 'I was desperate to prove myself to you all, and excelling academically was the only hope of that I had.'

It's funny how he read us so wrongly. 'Our family don't judge people. We adored you as you were, because you cared and made us laugh.' I hesitate over the adoration, but talking on behalf of all of us makes it okay. 'I think you did it more for yourself than for us.'

He's got his elbows resting on his knees, cornet in one

hand, but in between sliding spoonfuls from the meaty sundae tub onto Diesel's tongue he's opening and closing the fingers of his other hand, flexing them. 'Whoever it was for, it was wasted effort, given where I am now… That's where the irony comes in.'

I'm making a wild guess. 'Do I take it the results weren't the best today?' From what I gathered, he was having wires stuck on him so they could measure the electrical impulses passing through his arms and hands, and so tell how well the nerves in his slashed fingers were mending.

He blows out a low whistle. 'Our ability to heal is remarkable, I see that every day with the animals I treat, but it doesn't always work out. More fool me for daring to hope.'

I blow out a breath myself to help with the shock. 'You're not even the *teensiest bit* better?'

He pulls a face. 'The lack of improvement was spectacular. Holding an ice-cream cone is pretty much the most advanced movement I can achieve.' He turns to me. 'Don't say it! *I know* I should be grateful I can still eat my raspberry ripple. That's why I brought you; I knew you'd make me focus on everything I can do, not what I can't.'

'It still sucks though.' At least I know why I'm here now, although he seems to be saying my lines, and me his. As for how he's going to readjust to being a much less spectacularly able human being than he was, my heart goes out to him. I know it's fatal to touch him, but I can't not. The most I dare to risk is to reach my hand out across his back and squeeze his shoulder. 'It may feel like your world is ending now, but it will be okay. You've got this, Ross, you'll find a way through.'

He gives a sniff. 'It's actually not the first time my life has come crashing down due to an error that was entirely my own.' The gaze he turns on me is so intense, I have to swallow hard before I can carry on.

'You're pushing forty. Messing up more than once goes with the territory.' It's my job to lighten this. Except, the night we argued, Ross said that what happened with us had shaped everything he'd done since.

It was actually days before I screwed up my courage to ring him to break the news about the pregnancy, but I could tell in the first breath how it was going to go.

... It's your final year, Cress ... and I'm on the other side of the world...

As if I didn't already know both those things. And after that we were on such different pages; him acting like it was an international catastrophe simply didn't relate to the tiny baby growing inside me. It was a small person I was already in love with, not a diplomatic incident that needed managing. And then he delivered one last spectacular boot in my guts for his parting shot, and I knew I was on my own. But by the next day, I also knew that if I wanted to follow my own path, I was going to have to dodge his calls, in case he tried to change my mind.

Even though he's already upset, I have to clear this up. 'You're talking about the mistake you made with me, aren't you – having a holiday fling with someone totally wrong.' The one that taught him to avoid casual sex with women who put wrecking balls through his life because they took their pills late…

His brows furrow. 'Hang on. There was nothing casual about it—'

My mouth's gone dry. 'There wasn't?'

'Not on my side. If I had my time over, I'd do it again in a heartbeat. Except this time I'd look after you better.'

All the air has gone out of my chest, and my body is limp. 'So when you couldn't bear to be around me here, it wasn't because you despised me for making a mess of your life?'

'I'd never have thought that.' His chest rises and falls as he takes another long breath. 'I've always blamed myself. Seeing you brought back the guilt and made it raw again.' He pulls down the corners of his mouth. 'Then, little by little, as I saw how together you are and what a success you make of everything you do, it became easier for me. I realised anyone as strong as you has no place in their life for someone who fails them. I'm truly sorry, Bertie. I couldn't apologise at first, I couldn't even bring myself to mention it, because I hated myself so much for everything I got wrong. But now I know who you are again, I can. I hope one day you'll come to understand.'

I'm opening and closing my mouth, trying to take it in; I think he may just have said he's sorry. And while it's great to know he doesn't regret what we had, it's going to take a while for my brain to readjust. I fully appreciate how he's been running to the ends of St Aidan to help me these last couple of months, and the effort he's put in, but it's still going to take time for me to erase the 'bastard' sign that's been slapped across the top of his head whenever he's popped up in my mind for the last twelve years … and replace it with one that says 'may deserve to be forgiven'.

He's staring down at his clenched hand. 'And here's the ultimate irony – there I was all those years ago trying to make myself better, and now I've got nothing to offer at all.'

My heart is aching for Ross and his situation. But I'm way out of my depth helping with his level of despair after the results he's had today. 'You can't deal with this on your own.' Bottling this up could be catastrophic for his mental health. 'We'll ask the mermaids, they'll know someone good for you to talk to.'

Ross gives me a sideways stare. 'That's strange advice coming from you. When we mentioned your pregnancy before, you said you preferred to deal with it by yourself.'

I can't deny he's right. 'At the time I had no one around that I felt comfortable to share that with. But I have now. So I'm not a hypocrite.'

His eyes flash open. 'You have?'

I smile as I think of it. 'For the first time ever I've had the support of a group of close friends. Meeting Millie brought a lot of things up for me; Sophie, Plum and Nell have been very helpful talking that through.'

He's trying to play this down, but he can't hide his incredulity. 'So *they know?*'

I nod. 'They do. And sharing did help. I feel much lighter and happier for it, which is why I'd recommend it.'

'For eff's sake.'

It was a mutter, but I'm straight back at him. 'For eff's sake what?'

He's shaking his head. 'It doesn't matter. Now's not the time. Just all of it. You haven't even talked to me about it.'

He's the last person in the world I'd ever have opened up to. 'I'm sure we'll talk if the time is right.' I just can't imagine it ever will be. I stare at the remains of my ice cream, then at the love in Diesel's eyes as he looks at it. 'Are you sure Diesel can't have this?'

Ross rolls his eyes. 'Not unless you want him up all night with an upset tummy.' He pushes the last of his own cone into his mouth. 'I could always help you out if you really don't want it?'

I hand my cone to Ross and give Diesel's hairy head a pat. 'Sorry, mate, that's the price you pay for hanging out with a vet.'

And five minutes later we're back in the car, racing back along the coast road towards St Aidan. I sneak a sideways look at the shadows on Ross's cheekbones and I can't help wondering – where the hell are we going to go from here?

It's not as if we have any time. It's two weeks to the book launch, Clemmie and Charlie should be back soon after, and that's me pretty much done. I'll be saying my goodbyes to St Aidan and everyone here. I just can't express how much that's twisting my guts every time I remember it.

32

The baby sprinkle at Tide's Reach
Men behaving badly
Thursday

'There have been lots of arrivals – I can see loads of kids and a few babies – but I haven't heard any men yet?'

We're at the baby sprinkle, in yet another of St Aidan's fabulous quirky cottages, and Ross is peering round the edge of the kitchen door, trying to get a better view of the guests in the living room.

This one's called Tide's Reach. It's got a glorious wood herringbone floor, and so many tall palms in the room we're in, it feels more like a hothouse than a kitchen. In fact, we've been to so many lovely places in the last few weeks, I'm tempted to write posts about country interiors as well as baking and Walter's farmyard. Obviously, as there's already a two-year-old living here, it's a bit like a toyshop too, but most of the kiddie stuff is in the dedicated party play area next door, which is filling up with small children as the guests arrive. And as it's only been mums arriving so far, there's no wonder Ross is feeling a bit left out.

His mouth was disarmingly close to my ear as he whispered to me. I don't know why I'm so jumpy about it. I was much closer yesterday evening as I was forcing icing into his stubble when we did our twenty-third buns-on-strings challenge. But that's different somehow. The clips are so well-watched our customers all shout for the event now; it's so expected it's simply become part of the job. It's also a matter of pride that he's never beaten me yet.

As for today, I did warn him. 'You knew it was a girlie do, but you still insisted on coming.'

His voice rises in protest. 'What the hell happened to St Aidan's obsession with equal opps?'

I wrinkle my nose. 'Hen parties, childbirth and men's five-a-side football are exempt.' I'm making it up but it sounds good to me. 'Just put on a pink stripy pinny, don't say anything and they'll be having too much fun to notice you.'

Nell's come along with the team today, and Sophie is here too, but as a guest with Maisie, so she's only meant to help out if we're stuck. Having said that, she's busy setting up my icing table next door while Maisie plays and I make buttercream.

We've been trying to fit in as many fundraiser evenings as we can while I'm still here, and we've done so many lately it's a miracle they've always come through with the helping-out. There's still lots of people wanting to see the donut making, and there's huge demand for brownie and blondie nights. And with my own self-imposed book deadline coming up I've finally finished all the test bakes and I'm adding the final touches to the chapter introductions. But I've still had to find time to squeeze in extra baking, because with the bake boxes it's the old saying: make it while you can. I know I'm sharing any profits with the Kittiwake Court fund, but it's good to get a bit ahead myself so I've got some leeway when I get back to London. I'd always assumed I'd pick up where I left off when it was time to go back, but unless things look up pretty fast on my blog traffic I'll have to find a new way of bringing in the cash all over again.

Ross grins. 'It's fine, I'm used to being surrounded by women at the surgery. I'll stick to my grey pinstripe pinny.'

I laugh. 'Or you could lose your T-shirt, add a bow tie and rock the topless waiter vibe?'

His voice rises. 'This isn't *The Full Monty*, Bertie, *there are children here!*'

As I go back to spooning the last of the buttercream into piping bags I can't help smiling at how real his horror is. 'They're toddlers and babies, they'd react more if you turned up in a lion suit than a diamanté thong.' As I shake my head to get rid of that image I'm also wondering why he's so clueless. 'How much experience do you have with kids?'

He pulls a face. 'Plenty with goats. Human ones, not so much. My sister hasn't got any, and most of my friends are late taking the plunge.'

'Remarkable.' With so many of my own sisters' tinies

around, it's easy to forget there are people like Ross who don't have contact with under-fives. 'Judging by the screams from next door, this afternoon should put that right for you.'

His eyebrows close together as he goes serious again. 'What's going on exactly? I only caught the bit about bathing the baby.'

'How about you forget all about baths, and we'll go from there.' I take a deep breath, and hope he can keep up. 'Amelia is the one with the baby bump and the two-year-old who's emptying the crisp bowls out onto the tribal rugs.' I check that his eyes are still bright to be sure he's keeping up. 'Amelia is having a party where friends "shower" her with gifts for the baby she's expecting next month, but because it's her second she needs less stuff, so it's called a sprinkle.'

'Right.'

I must have lost him with the last sentence. Due to his mystified expression I may need to expand here. 'So guests buy her little things like baby socks rather than big ones like Bugaboo pushchairs.'

His frown has deepened. 'So remind me where the water comes in?'

If I was doubtful about bringing Ross in case it was awkward between us, I needn't have been. He's so tied up with the mechanics, it's totally removed the focus from us on a more personal level.

I grin. 'No water involved at all, but there *is* a complication. People who want to know the sex of their baby usually find out around twenty weeks, and then they have a gender reveal party, with a big announcement and a special, colour-coded cake, prepared secretly in advance.'

'This is *so* involved!'

From the way he's shaking his head in total disbelief I take it he's with me this far. 'But Amelia only found out the sex of her baby by accident at her thirty-six-week scan last week, so for a bit of fun, she's going to let people guess the sex today at her sprinkle party.' I take a breath. 'And that's where I come in. First I'm doing flower piping for the party entertainment. And after that each person is going to ice their own cupcake in whichever colour they think is right for Amelia's baby.'

Sophie comes in on the tail-end of the conversation. 'So, pink for a girl, blue for a boy. Surely you know about *that,* Ross?' She eases Maisie off her hip and pushes her towards him. 'Do me a favour and hang onto this one for me for a second until I finish next door – she's doing her best one-woman-demolition-team impersonation out there. If she gets her hands on the icing bags it'll be all over.'

Ross's eyes go huge as Sophie turns to leave, and as he freezes I jump forward and catch Maisie sliding downwards somewhere around his knee level. 'Hey, what's the matter? She's not going to burn you!'

He sniffs. 'All the same, I'll leave the kiddie stuff to you experts. I'm strictly here for clear-up duties. There must be some tidying I can do?'

'You're too efficient for your own good. Right now, we're all washed up.'

Nell's smiling as she comes through waving another empty bottle. 'Don't think you're hiding in the kitchen *all* afternoon, Ross. Amelia's adamant, helpers are invited to join in the party too.'

Ross blinks and looks doubtful. 'Are you sure? I haven't brought any tiny socks.'

Nell shakes her head. 'Amelia won't mind, and at least you'll know for next time.'

I take it from his rabbit-caught-in-the headlight look that he won't be queuing for that, and spin Maisie round so she's propped on my thigh facing him and take a deep breath. 'Okay, Ross, there's nothing to be frightened of. Imagine Maisie is a puppy. Or a cat.' I remember him the night Pancake was ill, how capable his hands were, even though they're broken. How his grasp was firm, yet at the same time so very tender. Maisie's many kilos heavier, but he'll get the idea. 'Just cradle her bum in your elbow and wrap your other arm around her. Forget she's a scary human, and just hold on tight.' I'm slowly transferring Maisie's body across the gap and onto his forearm, and Maisie, sensing what's needed, is being like an uncharacter-istically angelic version of herself. 'There you go, you've got all her weight now. It's not so bad, is it?'

Ross swallows hard and pushes away a bit of prawn cracker that's fallen out of Maisie's hair and stuck in the stubble on his chin. 'If you say so.'

And then Maisie, as if sensing she's safe at last, turns and grabs a handful of his curls. Then as she wriggles side-ways Ross finally reacts and tightens his hold to the kind he uses on escaping sheep. 'Not so fast, you little worm. If you pull my hair I may have to turn you upside-down.' He turns to me. 'Will that be okay?'

I nod. 'So long as you're ready for squeals.'

Maisie lets out a shriek, and a moment later Ross has spun her over. 'There you go. It's not so funny down there, is it?'

Except to judge by Maisie's giggles, it's hilarious. After a few minutes of whirling her around upside-down while she lets out peals of laughter, Ross tips her upright again and Maisie grabs his nose. 'M-my daddy crawls on the floor and lets me ride on his back.'

Ross gives me a pleading stare. 'Jeepers, tell me she's joking?'

I'm biting back my smile. 'I don't think she is.'

Maisie nods her head. 'Like a h-horsey.'

I can't help teasing. 'If everyone has a turn, it's *really* fun.'

Ross groans. 'For eff's sake, Bertie, don't encourage her. She's already scalped me – I can't cope with more of them.'

Maisie whoops. 'Me first! Me first!'

Nell's laughing. 'There you go, Ross, looks like you've got a job for the afternoon. That'll be a job for life, once word gets around the Mums and Bumps group.'

I laugh. 'What are you waiting for? If you hurry you'll fit in three rounds of the living room before I'm ready to start.'

Ross rolls his eyes. 'You'll wish you hadn't done this when you're stuck with the washing up later.'

But Maisie's back on the floor now, tugging at his wrist with one hand, hammering his thigh with her other. 'C'mon, Boss, my little pony, my little pony!'

To be fair to Ross, for someone shuffling their way round a very smart living room on his hands and knees while the rest of the adults are all on the very comfy sofas knocking back fizz and chomping on canapés, he doesn't look *that* unhappy about it. In fact he is smiling quite a lot.

By the time my demonstration is done and everyone has iced their own cupcake, and we've all shouted hurrah at the news that Amelia's baby is a boy, and clapped furiously when we heard he's going to be called Maverick Jonson Jonas Johns, Ross is flat out on the floor, with small children perched right across his chest and legs.

As Nell goes past she stops and stares down at the pile. 'For someone who doesn't play with kids much, you're remarkably popular.'

I have to add my bit. 'He's so compliant too.' I stop to laugh. 'You don't have to agree to everything. It is okay to say "no" to them, Ross.'

He lets out a snort. 'You could have told me that earlier.'

Sophie gets up from where she's perching on a stylish Ercol chair. 'Okay, kids, how about we pack away some toys now, and move on to ice cream.'

Ross lets out a long moan. 'Please, I'm up for many things, but if it's a choice between being covered in Mr Whippy or helping clear the plates—' he gives me a look, '—I'm going to say "no" to the ice cream.'

I hold out my hand to him. 'Come on, up you get. I promise you safe passage to the dishwasher.' Somehow I resist the urge to both hang onto his hand and give his bum a smack as he passes me.

Then just before we make it into the kitchen he turns to look at Sophie from the doorway. 'You may think I'd have been too much of a tidier to hack this, Soph. But if things had turned out differently for Cressy and me, I swear, I'd have sucked it up.'

It takes a moment for it to sink in, what he's referring to, but when it does I round on him. *'What the hell are you talking about, Ross?'* In front of a whole room of people.

His thoughtful expression disintegrates. 'You said you'd shared with them? About the—'

I'm hissing at him to shut him up. 'I shared the bits about *me*, I never confirmed the part about *you*.'

His reply is low enough for only me to hear. 'Oh frigg. I've stuffed this up big-time, haven't I?'

I'm growling back through gritted teeth. 'That's the kind of question that doesn't need an answer.'

Sophie's got her smoothing-over voice on. 'After three months with you two, we'd all pretty much guessed the rest for ourselves.' She turns to the other women in the room, who are all sitting, eyes wide. 'Cressy and Ross had a bit of a thing back in the day, that's all.'

Nell rolls her eyes at me, then turns to everyone else. 'Which reminds me, ladies, we can't have a girlie party without teenage reminiscences! So, holiday romances – tell us your best and worst ones. I'll kick off with when I lost my heart to the guy in charge of the hog roast at the Young Farmers' camping weekend.'

And I have to hand it to Nell. That's totally taken the heat off us. As for Ross, I'll deal with him later.

So to make sure we don't have to spend too long in the kitchen together, I push all my icing stuff into a plastic box to wash up at home later, and then get called over by Nell to talk to another mum with a very small baby bump about fitting in a gender reveal after her scan next week, and someone else who wants a donut evening for her husband's birthday.

By the time I've made a few journeys to the car and I'm about to do a last sweep of the ground floor, Amelia has the children out on the decking finishing their cones. I'm just about to see if we're ready to leave when Nell steps into my path.

'Just rounding up Ross.'

Nell's eyebrows shoot up. 'Sophie's borrowed him for a moment.'

'What?'

Sophie comes up behind me. 'I was holding Amber's baby, Arran, while she nipped to the loo. But cuddles with such a tiny one were making me broody, so for everyone's sake I passed him on.'

Seeing Ross prone on the herringbone parquet with ten toddlers crawling over him, I was laughing along with the best of them. When he almost spilled our secret to the whole world, I was blazing. But stumbling across Ross leaning back in an Ercol chair, a tiny baby propped on his chest, perfectly still as he stares at the downy head, it feels like a size ten landed in my guts.

Nell's hand lands on my arm. 'Are you okay?'

I wince and clutch my stomach. 'Buttercream overload. It'll soon pass.'

She pulls me into a squeeze. 'Afternoons like this are hard for people like us.' She doesn't need to say more. We both know she's talking about the babies we love so much but haven't yet managed to have for ourselves. 'Don't worry, our turn will come.'

I slide my arm behind hers and hug her back. 'It will. It really will.' And for Nell, I really hope it does, because she gives so much to everyone else, she truly deserves some happiness for herself and George. For me, there's a lot less hope. I had my chance, and it didn't work out. I simply can't imagine any scenario now where I'm likely to get another opportunity.

And then there's a stampede of toddlers coming across the floor, and Amelia smiling in front of them.

'Don't forget, there are balloons for everyone before you go. And special *It's a Boy* biscuit favours made by Poppy from the wedding shop.'

I put my mouth to Nell's ear. 'I promise I'll make you Jammie Dodger blondies for *your* baby shower.' Then I remember Nell's special favourite. '*And* extra-sticky triple-chocolate brownies.'

Then someone pushes a balloon string into my hand, and next thing Maisie is bashing Ross over the head with hers. It's only as I swoop in to help Ross, who's holding out Arran, who's hollering like a baby who's been woken by a bash with a helium balloon, that I remember. By the time Nell might be eight months pregnant, I could have been back in London for almost a year.

And however close and cared for and wrapped up I feel today, I'm damned sure by the time that happens everyone will be on to the next thing. And Cressy Cupcake and her fabulous blondies will be a fading memory, like marks in the sand washed away by the tide.

33

At Clemmie's flat after the baby sprinkle
Hot air and cold turkeys
Thursday

'Bertie, you're here!'

Considering the teensy size of the flat, Ross doesn't need to sound *this* surprised to find me. The noise of me splashing at the sink should have been the major give-away I'd be in the kitchen.

'I was looking for you.'

I think I got that too, so I run the tap to give the piping bag in my hand yet another scrub.

'I wanted to say sorry for dropping you in it earlier at the sprinkle. I just wasn't thinking.'

That's an understated way to talk about broadcasting my most private secret to the entire village. He might as well have got a megaphone and shouted it across the harbour. *When Cressy got knocked up, Ross was the dad.* There should be enough fire inside me to rage about it for months. But right now I don't have the strength for that.

'It's over. Let's move on.'

The lines between his eyebrows fade as he relaxes. 'What shall I do with these?'

The two *It's a Boy* balloons in his hand are bouncing around the ceiling as they catch in the breeze from the open window. He's as qualified as me to make a decision on where to put them next.

I shrug. 'Hang them on your bed. Anything really, so long as you don't let them free outside.' I let out a sigh. 'Loose plastic helium balloons aren't exactly environmentally friendly.'

Ross's forehead furrows into a frown again. 'Something as precious as a baby, you'd think people would make choices that were kinder to the planet.' His frown deepens. 'We wouldn't have had these, would we?'

My mouth is full of saliva, and however much I swallow, it keeps coming back. 'No. We wouldn't.'

It's pretty much the first thing we've agreed on for twelve years. I sniff, rub my face with my upper arm, but when I lean back over the sink another drip off my nose lands in the water.

Ross's voice rises. 'Bertie, you're crying.'

'Am I?'

'Me and my big mouth. It's not even as if I can take it back.'

I don't know why I'm crying. All I know is the tears began running down my face as soon as I got to the sink, and now I've started I can't stop.

I sniff and rub my nose again. 'It's not your fault.' I gulp and try to explain. 'Seeing you sitting with the baby before, it brought back how much I wanted ours.'

His head tilts, and as he stares at me his Adam's apple rises and falls. 'So you didn't mind? You weren't devastated to be pregnant?'

I shake my head. 'Why would you think that?'

He pulls up his shoulders. 'The night we talked about it here you called it a mistake.'

'The only mistake was me thinking you'd step up. The rest was the opposite.' I stare out of the window by the sink, watch the white lines of sea foam moving towards the shore as I remember. 'I might have been pushing too much onto one tiny child, but all I could think was how wonderful a new baby would be after everything the family had been through with Charlie losing Faye. I know it wasn't planned, but when it happened it wasn't a problem; it felt like a gift.'

'Oh, Bertie.'

As I look along the kitchen Diesel's face is poking around the door frame, his brown eyes anxious, and Ross is moving a bright blue chair and a pile of boxes out of the way, and coming towards me.

I'm biting my lip, holding my tummy, and as I remember, the images flashing through my head are so sharp it might have happened yesterday. Those frozen January mornings, my stomach empty and aching from the retching. Walking the two miles to uni and back because I didn't dare to get on a bus. My pockets full of ginger nuts, bottles of ginger ale swilling around my bag to fight the nausea. Strangers staring at me by the basins in the ladies' loos when I'd been pushing my head under the cold tap to bring myself round. No one at uni really noticed; everyone just assumed I was partying so hard I had an endless hangover. And there I was, not minding any of it, because the reason was the baby. And she was already so much mine.

'It was the strangest feeling; for a nanosecond when I saw the lines on the pregnancy test my stomach left my body. Then in the space where my stomach had been there was just a whole rush of joy. Even that very first day I was ready to go to the end of the earth for her if she'd asked me to.'

As I stare out to watch the lines of breakers again, Ross slides in behind me, his hands light on my shoulders. And I've never really talked to anyone about this before, but now I am it's like a bottle being uncorked.

'We were only together for four and a half months, but she was *so* precious.' He turns me away from the sink, and as I twist to face him I let my head drop forwards until my forehead rests on his T-shirt. 'It sounds like nothing when you say it out loud, but those eighteen weeks were like a lifetime. We were in it together, she was already my friend. Then they mentioned there might be problems and I was desperate. When the doctor told me I was losing her, it felt like my heart had been ripped out of my chest. And then the contractions ramped up and I wanted to die too.'

'Oh, Bertie.' As Ross's arms close around me, his jaw is pushing against my temple. 'And by the time I walked into the hospital it was all over?'

I nod, because I can't quite bring myself to talk about that part yet. 'I hadn't even been home to tell the family. But it was such a good thing I hadn't, because it would only have upset them all over again.'

Ross lets out a long breath. 'That's you all over, Bertie, always thinking of other people. You shouldn't have had to go through this on your own, I should have made sure of that.' As his arms close tighter I glance up and see his cheeks are glistening. 'And you say it was a girl?'

'I knew all along she was.' I bury my fingers in the muscles under the soft folds of his shirt. 'I loved her so much.'

'I know you did.' His whisper is so low it's hardly there, but it penetrates right to the centre of my body. 'I loved her too.'

'Really?'

'Of course. I didn't know her, but she was a part of you. I hated that I'd made things so hard for you, but that didn't stop me caring. Or hurting.'

His chest is heaving against mine, and as we cling together shuddering, both of us crying for what we both lost, I'm wrapped in his warmth. Breathing his scent in and out, my cheek crushed against his chest as his T-shirt soaks up my tears, it's nothing to do with animal attraction anymore; it's just about solid human comfort. Someone being there for me now, even though they weren't before.

After a very long time our sobs subside and when it finally feels like I've no more tears left to cry I give a huge sniff. He reaches out and passes me a tissue from the box on the shelf and blows his nose too. It's hard to know how long we've been standing there, but the tide has come a long way up the beach. And somehow I feel different. There's a calmness I've never had before. A sense of things that were wrong now being right.

I pat my hand against his back. 'Thanks for lending me your shoulder.' Not that I'm going to go on about it, but it's brought a closure we haven't had before. 'We needed this.'

Ross sighs. 'We've both cried alone, but crying together is so much more healing, somehow. And talking helps too.'

It's twelve years too late, but it's still worth saying. 'I'm sorry I pushed you away that day at the hospital.' I pull in a breath to explain, but his finger lands on my lips.

'Don't. It's too late for recriminations. She'd have been very much loved by both of us, that's enough for me. We can both move forward knowing that.'

I unleash my grip on his ribs, and blow my nose. His arms are still around me and as he reaches across and pushes my hair out of my eyes I catch sight of his watch. 'Haven't you got surgery at six? And I've left a wet patch on your chest.'

His eyebrows lift, and he lets out a low curse as he takes in the time. 'Patients know, emergencies take priority over routine appointments.'

I smile at how his professional head is never far away, but all the same it's cool to think he'd put this first. 'I appreciate the chat, but you're good to go now.'

He's staring down at me, searching my face. 'Only if you're sure? If I'm going to make tonight's brownie evening for eight, I will need to get a move on.'

He's not the only one being sensible; I've got my practical head on too. 'Diesel and I will cadge a lift up to

Walter's with you to do the animals, then I'll walk him back along the beach, and get up to Honeycombe Cottage.'

'Good plan. I'll change at the surgery when I've done, and meet you there.' He takes a breath. 'Don't worry about the tears, I'll change my shirt.'

Then Ross takes one step back and as his arms leave my side the warmth and comfort drop away, and we're back to where we were earlier. It's like the time at the meringue evening. Everything is the same, but so much has changed. I can't begin to think about the enormity of it now.

For starters it's enough to remember – I may be prepped and ready to go for this evening's gig, but we're running almost an hour late. I need to get my ass into gear.

34

A blondie evening at Kittiwake Court
Winding down and winding up
Friday

'What happened to the cake-on-string clip of you and Ross from Honeycombe Cottage? It isn't up online yet!'

We're coming to the end of a really busy evening at Kittiwake Court. Millie and her friend Luce are spearing strings through the iced buns, and I'm hanging them from a tube suspended above my head. And I know the answer to her question is going to disappoint her.

'I'm afraid Ross had to rush off to help Elise with a golden doodle that needed a caesarean that night. Everyone else did the buns, but we didn't.' After the emotions of the baby sprinkle I was feeling like a wrung-out dishcloth, so it was a relief when Ross took the call and headed off. Even if it did mean a few more journeys up the stairs on my own,

I'd hate to have lost a buns-on-strings battle this close to leaving.

'Damn.' Millie looks so like Sophie when things don't go her way. 'We're getting so many views for them, it's a shame to miss out.'

I know I should be teaching her there's more to life than getting views, but I'm hoping I can make up for it. 'I thought it would be fun to film the residents here doing the buns-on-strings challenge tonight. They've all been on the clips we've put up for Walter, so our online followers already know them.'

Millie puts down her bun and flings her arms around me. 'That's a brilliant idea, they'll go down a storm!' To be fair, everything with Walter in gets lots of love. He delivers a wonderful combination of bluntness and honesty, and when you add in his farmyard references and the double dose of Cornish accent, he's bound to be a winner.

It's only what Millie deserves too, because lately she's proving herself to be a social media whizz. Not only has she been filming a lot of the various events and making clips that are hugely popular; she and her friends have also started a blog of their own. She's so good at editing now, she's uploading clips to my channel without my help.

If there's an end-of-term feeling to tonight's event, that's because there really won't be time for too many more. So when Jen suggested putting on a mega friends and family Blondie Special here, we all agreed; it will be a great way to bring in the cash and involve the residents too. And then we'll build up to a final hurrah for the St Aidan recipe book launch in two weeks' time.

Earlier today I made blondies in every variety known to baking bloggers. The Kittiwake residents have front-row seats in the Sea View Lounge and behind them there's pretty much all of St Aidan and most of Cornwall too. I've cooked up white chocolate blondies and Bakewell tart ones while they watched, and in between we've had tasting sessions. And now we're coming to the end of a raffle so large we may still be here at midnight.

So while Sophie and Jen take charge of drawing the numbers, and George and Nate and Ross go round the room delivering the prizes, we're putting the final touches to the hanging buns game so a few brave volunteers can round the evening off with a bit of fun.

A shout goes up from Walter, who's just won a spa day for two at the Harbourside Hotel, and under cover of the cheers Nell sidles up to me, talking out of the side of her mouth. 'Heard anything back from your agent yet?'

That's the other big thing about today that everyone's aware of, because the moment one person in St Aidan knows, everyone else does too. At nine o'clock this morning, after working late into the night checking the manuscripts of my own speculative baking book, I decided it was time to press send and waved goodbye to three months' work. So *Cressida Cupcake's Best Bakes Ever* are now on Martha's laptop, waiting for her to see if they're anything like good enough to take further. She replied straightaway to say they'd arrived, but I've no idea how long it's going to take for her to get back to me again. At best I'm expecting her to ask for a shedload of changes, at worst they may be no good at all, so there's a lot riding on this.

I grin at Nell. 'Ask me again in a month and I might have news.' I wave at Walter. 'Well done, Walter! Which lucky person is getting to go to your spa day with you?'

Jen turns and gives me a wink. 'He's going to be even more popular with the ladies now he's won that!' Then she holds up the next prize and shows it to the room. 'And now for the final four tickets, we have a car washing set, a Cressy Cupcake apron, a dozen freshly laid eggs, and then a meal for two at The Yellow Canary.'

Sophie's taking the bucket of tickets around the room so the winners can pick out the next ticket. As she moves towards Walter she turns to me. 'Have a look on your phone, you never know what might have landed from Martha.'

I hold up my icing-covered hands. 'Sorry, I'm way too sticky. My phone's in my apron if anyone wants to check for me.'

A nanosecond later Nell dips into my pocket. 'My hands are clean, let me look.' She's frowning at the screen, then she gives me a nudge. 'Hey, you do Natural Cycles too!'

She just announced my fertility app to the whole room, but so what? I'm well past being embarrassed. 'Along with most of the rest of the female population of the UK under fifty-five.'

What are the chances? Ross choosing this exact moment to walk right past me on his way to pick up the car shampoo and buffing cloths. 'Natural *what*?'

I roll my eyes, because I no longer give any shits. 'It's an app that tells you the days when you're fertile and when you're not.' I let that sink in for a moment.

Nell chips in, helpfully. 'Like a traffic-light system for nooky.'

Millie smiles sweetly. 'Good that wasn't around twelve years ago, or I would *definitely not* be here, and you'd have to find someone else to do the filming.'

Ross closes his eyes and bangs his fist on his skull. 'Jeez, sorry. I assumed it was to do with push-bikes, not contraception.' He's shaking his head. 'I don't know why I'm surprised. We vets have had tools to track animals' reproductive cycles for years.'

Nell looks at Ross. 'It's not only for stopping babies. Some people use it to help make them too.' She turns back to me. 'What's your book woman called again?'

I open my mouth to answer, but Ross gets in first. 'If you mean her agent, that's Martha.'

Nell's eyes pop open. 'Martha *Channing*? You're in luck!' She turns to the room. 'Fabulous news, Cressy's got an email from her agent, and the subject line says *A delicious delivery!*'

Sophie shouts from by the windows. 'We've all been holding our breath about this the whole day. Don't stop there, read it out!'

As Nell raises a querying eyebrow at me I nod. Not long ago I'd have been mortified for people to know my private business, but St Aidan's different because everyone is so invested. Going back to where no one gives a damn what their neighbours do because no one cares is not only going to be hard. It's going to be really dull too. I try not to think of how it's going to be when it's just me in my flat, with three real friends scattered across a city of nine million people.

Nell clears her throat and as everyone stops talking she begins. 'It says: *Well done, Cressida Cupcake, you've hit the icing jackpot with this! I'm sending your manuscript out to our original publisher, will be back in touch as soon as I have news, have a fabulous weekend, Martha xx.*'

As the room erupts into cheers I'm flapping my hands in front of my face, trying to take it in. 'So she thinks it's okay?'

Ross reaches over and squeezes my shoulder. 'Better than that, Bertie, I'd say you've nailed it.'

'Oh my, it never occurred to me she'd like it.'

Ross gives a cough. 'You had a very dedicated taster. It could be down to that?' He gives me a nudge in the ribs with his elbow. 'We all know the real secret – you're super talented, you worked your ass off and you're the best baking blogger there is. Enjoy your moment of glory.'

I grin up at him, wondering when he got so on top of this too. 'Thank you, I will.' After how far down I was when I arrived, even something as small as my agent liking what I sent is both unexpected and major. One thing's for sure; I'll never take anything like this for granted again.

Sophie claps her hands. 'If everyone's ready, we're going to round off the evening with a game.' An excited murmur runs round the room from the people who know what's coming. 'The plastic's on the floor, the buns are dangling and ready, and as Ross and Cressy are already hugging let's ask them to show you all how to play. The aim is to eat as much of the cupcake as you can, no hands allowed.'

'But we go last...' I open my mouth to protest but the words are drowned by more cheers. As Ross steers me over to the strings he murmurs in my ear, 'Maybe don't beat me up too much tonight, we don't want to upset the residents.'

I grit my teeth, and start to summon up my usual venom. As we move into our places facing each other I can see Millie standing on a chair by the wall, her phone poised to film. 'You're running scared, Ross?' Like I'd fall into that trap.

Nell grasps the cupcake, then she lets it go and steps back, and there's a collective gasp as everyone in the audience takes a breath.

Then Joanie calls out, 'Come on, Cressy!'

In front of me the brightly coloured sprinkles are spinning to a blur, the barely-set white icing is shining. And when I look up into Ross's eyes, instead of being all dark and flinty, they're soft and kind and friendly, with crinkles at the edges and brimming with... Who knows what the hell they're brimming with, but the fire is gone. For one time only I can't find it in me to ram my jaw against the cupcake and grind the sponge into his stubble. For a few seconds I'm so surprised, all I can do is open and close my mouth.

He's still standing back, dodging from side to side as he usually does, waiting for me to make my move. So I do a fake step to the left, then I open my mouth really, really, *really* wide – like wide enough to engulf the whole cake in one gulp – and move straight forward. A second later my nose nudges the paper case, but instead of my teeth closing on the cupcake, and the icing melting onto my tongue, the bun lurches and flies over my shoulder.

Ross lets out a low laugh. 'Bad luck, Egbert. Ready to try again?'

I'd be lying if I said I was ready for anything. Ross's cheekbone zoning in on my eye takes me completely by surprise. It's only a nanosecond, but I lose my concentration. Next thing I know, the cupcake is flying past my other ear. But that's nothing. So much worse is Ross's mouth, hot and soft and disgustingly delicious, landing on mine. If this is his diversionary tactic, it's low. But if I truly snog his socks off, I'll be able to hit the cake once it's over.

'You're well below the belt here, Bradbury.' I'm mumbling my protest against his lips, praying to any passing mermaid g-mothers not to let my knees collapse completely. From the shock. From the seismic electric pulses zinging through my body. From the immediate need to open up and completely engulf him.

He just laughs more, and mumbles back, 'Round twenty-five. It's payback time, enjoy the ride.'

At some point I must close my eyes, because the shouts of the crowd zone out and are replaced by some kind of symphony in my head that goes with the rainbow bursts and stars on the inside of my eyelids, and for who knows how long all I'm getting is a velvety taste of raspberry and almond. At least I'm still playing by the rules: my hands are still sticking out behind me, my neck is craned backwards, my face tilting upwards. It's one of those times when the world feels like it's stopped spinning, and I never want it to start again, because I want this moment to last for ever.

And then the crowd noise gets louder, we're slowly easing apart. And suddenly it's over, I'm gasping for breath, and pushing my hand over my mouth.

And Ross's breath is hot in my ear. 'Bakewell tart blondie. It might be my new favourite flavour.' Then he pushes the cupcake into his mouth with his hand and turns to the crowd. 'I'll let Cressy have that round.'

I take a step back, fall over a chair, and Nell moves in to steady me as she shouts to the audience. 'A win for Cressy there, everyone. She might not have got the cupcake, but the rest should have made up for it.'

Sophie's clapping again. 'So who's up next? It doesn't have to be couples, you can go for the buns on your own.'

Walter's already on his feet. 'Me and Joanie! If she wins she's coming to the spa day.'

And this is the beauty of St Aidan – they've already moved on. And with any luck what just happened with Ross and me won't have any significance in anyone's head. Especially not mine. As soon my heart slows down I'll be completely back to business as usual.

I can't help noticing. 'Hey, Walter, you've taken your cap off!'

He gives a gruff grunt. 'That icing looks a lot stickier than cow muck, I don't want it spoiling my Duke's tweed.'

Jen winks at me. 'There's no arguing with that, Walter.'

And someone has turned on Blondie's greatest hits in the background, and as Walter and Joanie move into position, and Millie waggles her phone at me, Debbie Harry is singing 'Heart of Glass'.

35

Down by the harbour
Another close call
Thursday

'When I go back to London I'll miss the sound of the breakers. And Crusty Cobs' croissants, obviously.' As Diesel and I amble across the harbour, me saying the things out loud is easier than bottling them up and being sad. 'I'll miss Pancake doing puddings with her paws on my pillow at four in the morning. The light glinting off the water like diamonds when the sun shines. How a black sky can turn the sea to slate in a moment. The way the wind whips the shingle off the beach and flings it against the windows on the wildest days.'

As a damp wet nose pushes into my coat pocket, searching out a last gravy bone biscuit, I come to a halt with my list, because I can't quite put into words the ache I get in my chest when I think of saying goodbye to Diesel. As for the joy of waking up every morning and *not* hearing Ross singing along to Radiohead on his beat box as he washes his cocoa mug from the night before and burns his breakfast toast – that's something else I haven't quantified yet either.

For months I've been desperate to put counties between me and Ross and his quirky habits and achingly beautiful thighs. But now that's in my sights, I catch myself humming tunes from his favourite *OK Computer* album as I wander around the flat or count the sheep up at Walter's. And when I find I'm word-perfect on entire verses, it throws me right off my stride. So, for now I'm putting my feelings about Ross on the too complicated pile.

It's Tuesday morning and Diesel and I are on our way back from our farm duties and beach walk. In fact there's a lot going on as I move into the last couple of weeks of my stay here. Obviously, the biggest thing of all is that any day now *should* be when Clemmie and Charlie find out if their second round of IVF has been successful.

Since Charlie rang us that awful night to say the first round hadn't worked they've given me endless input for my book, but they've never mentioned any more details of the treatment. But counting on from the night Charlie rang with the bad news, I know that this should be the make-or-break week, and I'm holding my breath, willing things to be okay for them. Needless to say I haven't taken my eyes off my message icon, but so far there's been no word other than our regular pet catch-ups.

I look down at Diesel, who's walking beautifully to heel on a slack lead. 'And you're so much better behaved than you were when I first arr—'

Famous last words. Before I can finish my sentence there's a tug on my arm, and next thing I'm being dragged past the cars to the front of George's office, where Sophie is just emerging, putting on her sunnies and buttoning her coat against the breeze.

She staggers back as Diesel's weight hits her. 'Hey, you don't *have* to put a paw on *both* my shoulders.' She gives me a wink. 'We could do with you to bring Millie back down to earth – her feet haven't touched the ground since she put up those latest clips over the weekend. I hope she didn't over-step with what she uploaded?'

'Seeing the number of people who are watching them, I'd say, go for it.' She ran them all past me first before she put them up, and the ones she took of the Kittiwake residents chasing buns are fabulous. 'Millie's too sensible to let the success go to her head. And I'm delighted to have the traffic.'

'They're all pretty popular, but there is one in particular that's streets ahead of the others...' Sophie's giving me a super-searching look through her Ray-Bans.

'Anything with Walter in, the views are exponential.' Then I have to admit, 'I'm feeling pretty proud of the blondie posts I put up too. I don't know if it's a knock-on effect from the film clips, but they had almost as much response as my posts before I went on TV.'

Sophie's eyes open wide. 'So you've done it! You've actually rebuilt your following again?'

I can't hold back my smile. 'I may be reaching different people now, but the numbers are good and the comments are more supportive than ever they used to be.' It's actually been a bit like an avalanche – what began as a trickle built up speed and this weekend the numbers came in a huge rush.

Sophie sweeps me into a hug. 'It's fabulous you've waved goodbye to the haters.'

I nod. 'They've gone, but I'll never forget the lesson they taught me.' I'm more grounded and less impressionable now, and I truly appreciate that on the internet you're only ever as successful as your last posting.

Last Friday's blondie event was the milestone that marked my posts taking off. But there are a few minutes of that evening in particular that have been playing on repeat in my brain ever since. No prizes for guessing which bit that is. And there are three questions I keep asking myself:

Why the hell did the buns-on-strings battle go so wrong when we'd done it so many times before? When my mouth did accidentally end up on Ross's, why did I stay there so long? And why the hell can't I stop thinking about it?

For the record, I'm thinking of it as a clash of mouths. Even in the darkest part of the night when I relive it, I refuse to call it a kiss.

And the other annoying thing – my heart keeps racing so fast, it's making me feel sick. Realistically, I admit there's an underlying problem; I do find Ross physically attractive to the point of finding it hard to keep my hands off him. I always have. But it's nothing new, I've coped with that for three months, and resisted. I'm hardly going to succumb to rampant animal desire this close to the end.

And just because he let me slobber all over his second-best T-shirt when I was a bit teary after the baby sprinkle, there's still a lot outstanding that I haven't got past yet. Sure, now we've shared a flat for two months it's easier to be around him. But if we've gone all these weeks and still haven't found any proper resolution, I seriously doubt it's going to happen before I leave.

I'm blinking up at Sophie, trying to drive the taste of Ross's mouth right out of my mind, as my phone rings.

I roll my eyes as I look at my screen. 'It's the people who keep sending me free clothes when they shouldn't.'

Sophie stares at the band of skirt fabric sticking below the beaten-up waxed jacket I've borrowed from Ross to do the animals. 'They're lovely. Is that one you're wearing now?'

It's a tribute to how versatile they are. On Friday the red flowery one got so many compliments at Kittiwake Court, and today the calves were equally impressed by the blue one with yellow pineapples. 'They're so easy to wear and wash, I barely take them off. This won't take long to sort out.' I press accept on the FaceTime call. 'Hi, how can I help?'

'I'm Catey, Maudie Maudie's new marketing assistant. We're following up on the dresses?' It's only as she smiles out at me from the screen, her eyebrows and lips as perfect as her sleek blonde bob, that I remember the state I'm in.

If only she'd called earlier, before I'd opened the packs and worn the dresses to destruction. I'm slightly bluffing here. 'I completely understand there's been an error, would you like me to send the clothes back?' If I drop them by Iron Maidens, the cleaners, and pay enough, I'm sure they'll make them look like new again.

Catey's voice rises in surprise. 'Why ever would we want you to do that? We're excited that you're enjoying them.'

'Excuse me?' I can't quite believe what I'm hearing.

Her smile widens. 'We quite understand that you wanted to dip out of view for a while, but now you've bounced back into the public eye we're more than happy to pick up where we left off.'

She can't possibly mean that. 'Have you seen how I look?' The hair escaping from the scarf I tied into a bow has been whipped to a mass of beachy waves by the wind.

Her eyebrows arch. 'Your new Cornish style is great for our customer base. Relaxed seaside vibe and sand-blasted hair are a perfect fit.'

I think she might mean salt-sprayed, but whatever. It's their choice.

Not that she's being pushy, but it feels like she's trying to close a deal here. 'Tag us in your posts. I assume your bank details are the same? If you're happy to start again, we'll get our new collection over to you asap.'

My mouth's hanging open in shock, but it's such a bad look, I snap it shut and say, 'Fab.'

Her face creases into a smile. 'We particularly like the spotty gumboots and the animals.'

I give Sophie a nudge because she's listening in, and they are *her* wellies.

Catey's still going. 'The dress you were wearing in the kissing clip that's gone mad has sold out already.'

That's so much good news. 'The red one with daisies is so pretty. Lucky I was in shot cheering Walter on.' If anyone was going to go viral, it was always going to be him.

Catey's querying. 'I had the name of the guy on the tip of my tongue. I didn't think it was Walter.'

I can definitely put her right on that. 'There's only one ninety-odd-year-old stand-out star from Friday night.'

Catey's frowning. 'The guy I mean was a hottie.' As her smile comes back it's wider. 'But you probably know that anyway.'

Walter's going to be stoked when I tell him about this. 'Walter definitely looks great for his age.'

She gives me a bemused look, then firms up again. 'Anyway, whatever… We're getting more made up of that style, so tell your followers to order away!'

I know from the past they like to know what's coming up. 'We're launching a community recipe book here soon, if there's anything you'd like to showcase for that.'

Her eyes light up. 'That sounds great, I'll get straight onto it.'

And then she's gone, and I'm left staring at Sophie and an empty screen. 'I can't believe that just happened.'

Sophie suddenly looks serious. 'It's down to sheer hard work, Cressy. Don't question it, just enjoy.'

I'm not boasting, but I know Sophie will enjoy the news. 'I've had other approaches too. There's a national holiday-let company wanting to talk, and my original make-up sponsors got back in touch too.' Not that it's a problem but I'm only using a fraction of the amounts I used to. No doubt that'll change again when I'm back in London where everyone's standards are more exacting.

Sophie's eyes are shining. 'That's so exciting! It's all coming back together. This time round might be bigger than ever.'

'Wooohooo! And it's all thanks to you mermaids and the lovely people of St Aidan.' I should be thrilled, so I don't know why my whoop feels so hollow. I truly don't want to sound as if I'm ungrateful, because I'm not. But when something's blown up in my face so spectacularly once, it feels odd to be putting my trust in it again. This time I need to be more careful, I mustn't put all my eggs in one basket.

Thinking of hens reminds me. 'I can't wait to see Walter this afternoon, and tell him Catey called him hot.'

Sophie frowns. 'You don't think Catey may have got her wires crossed with that?' She lifts up her Ray-Bans. 'Or the wrong end of the stick?'

Sticks and wires and eggs in baskets. 'I know exactly the clip she's talking about.' It's especially cute. 'I'm cheering on Joanie, and Walter swoops in and gives her a peck on the cheek.' There's nothing quite like oldie romance to make the views rocket.

'I thought she meant another one entirely, but if you're sure, it doesn't matter.' Sophie drops her sunnies again. 'I'd better get back to the office.'

'And we're off to Kittiwake Court later to make New York cookies.'

Sophie nods. 'I'll see you up there then.' As she takes in my bemused blinking she starts to laugh. 'Nell told Plum and me, so we're coming along to lend a hand too. You surely didn't think we'd miss a cookie afternoon?' As she rushes off to her shiny SUV she points upwards. 'Don't forget to bring your umbrella, there's rain on the way later.'

Looking at the cornflower sky above us, I seriously doubt it. As for what Sophie's talking about with the clips, I can only think that, with four kids, a multinational company and all the fundraising events, she's got so much on, she can't be right all the time.

36

Up at Walter's after the New York cookie afternoon
This way to the beach
Thursday

'Hey, Diesel, Sophie was wrong about us needing an umbrella.'

It's later on Thursday, and Diesel and I are striding out across Walter's meadow in the early evening sun, our legs dusted yellow with buttercup pollen. Nell dropped us off at the farm after Kittiwake, and I've done most of the regular jobs for today. But as I've eaten my body weight in sticky cookies this afternoon I'm walking them off by going to the far field to top up the sheep water. We've turned for home, and we're still a couple of fields away from the yard when I spot a figure by the next fence waving.

It takes approximately half a second to take in the beaten-up denim jacket slung over his shoulders. As soon as he's in earshot I call, 'Ross, what happened to evening surgery?' As a smile spreads across his face I can't help thinking how much more relaxed he looks than he was when I first arrived.

He opens the gate for us as we get near. 'The first appointment isn't for an hour, and there's something I want to run past you.'

As my heart skips a beat I trip over a tuft of grass and end up crashing into the fence. 'That sounds exciting.'

He runs his fingers through his hair. 'But there's something else I want to say first, because it feels like time's running out for us.' He's staring at me intently. 'I don't want to dwell on what can't be changed, but you gave me your insight last week, so I want to return the favour.'

My tummy has dropped so far, I grab the fence rail. 'Right.' I can't see it will alter anything, but it's only fair. He's wrong-footed me though; I was primed and ready earlier, but now I've let my guard down because I've given up expecting it. 'Fine, fire away. I'm listening.'

He turns to lean beside me on the fence and his Adam's apple bobs as he swallows. 'I'm not here to make excuses. I know how badly I handled things. But this is my one chance to let you know how it was for me.' He stops and pulls in a breath. 'The day you rang with the news you were pregnant, I felt so responsible. So guilty. But it was the same day the faculty asked me to extend my stay from one year to two, so I was already really torn and confused.'

'Confused about what?'

'I hadn't expected to miss you so much. I was weighing the upside of making myself good enough to deserve you, against the desperation of being so far away from you for so long.'

'And then I dropped a baby into the mix…'

He nods. 'The moment you told me, I was already going through a million options in my head.'

'And that's when you said you couldn't make any promises.' My mouth is dry, but I can't keep the recrimination out of my voice. That moment, the devastation of hearing that he wasn't going to be there for me, is still etched so sharply in my mind, it could have been yesterday. The hurt is still so raw. I've carried it with me for twelve years. It's strange to think how clearly that single second changed the course of my thinking, and shaped my entire future.

Ross blows out his cheeks. 'It wasn't until afterwards that I realised how wrong I'd been to say that. What I meant was that I didn't want to give you false hope until I knew what was possible. I thought saying, "Leave it with me, and I'll try my best to work this out" would be enough. All I wanted was enough time to do the very best by you.'

He steps back and kicks the ground. 'With my warped masculine pride, I totally missed what you were going through. You weren't answering my calls, but I carried on blindly, trying to sort out the details on my side. And the irony is that when I arrived to see you the day you were in hospital, it had taken for ever, but I'd finally got all my ducks in a row.' He's staring out towards where the one tiny patch of sea visible in the distance meets the sky. 'There was a media masters scheme out there, they'd agreed to give you preferential treatment down the line if you'd wanted to join it. But I'd actually arranged to come back here for a couple of years at least. What took me so long was that I had to wait for the faculty committee to agree to the deferment before I came back here for good. As soon as I had that, I took the next plane I could.'

My chest feels as if it's collapsing. 'So you weren't only here on a visit?'

It's as if the sun is echoing my despair, as the clouds close over it, and the grass in front of us goes dull.

He shakes his head. 'It was a one-way ticket, I came back to make it right, to be with you if you wanted me, but I was too late.' His voice is low now. 'I could understand that you didn't want to see me that day, so I hung around, I kept trying. When I finally understood that you wanted nothing more to do with me, because I wasn't there in the right way when you actually needed me, there was really nothing to stick around for. They let me go back to the States again. I'm sorry I got it so wrong.'

So he was there for me all along, but I just didn't know it. 'It's so tragic it's almost funny.'

He sighs again. 'As a hopeless guy I was working towards the nine-month due date. I had no idea those early weeks would be so rough or so lonely for you.'

'Oh frig. I'm sorry.' There's nothing more I can say. I cut him off because I thought I was on my own. My heart is bleeding for him for the lengths he went to, all for nothing, and for me, because I had no idea. 'We both got this so wrong.'

He raises his eyebrows. 'You went on to achieve everything you deserved. That's all that really matters.'

I'm trying to let my brain take it in. I'm not looking at the biggest wimper-outer in the world. It's just that somehow he didn't say the right words at the right time. And in my turn, I failed to understand him.

'Thank you for explaining.'

There's a buzz in my pocket, and as I pull out my phone I mouth, 'It's my agent' at Ross as I accept the call.

He gives a grimace. 'What was I saying about achievements? You're the only person I know with one of those.'

'Martha!' My stomach's plummeting for a second time. A call from her this soon can only mean one thing – they don't want the book.

She's sounds irate. 'At last, Cressy, I've been trying to get you all afternoon.'

'Sorry, the network's patchy here.' If I tell her I've had my phone switched off she might explode.

'The news is so much better than last time we talked – the publishers love the book you've sent so much that they're offering you a new contract for two books, and this time they won't be backing out. Are you up for that?'

My mouth's dropped open, I'm nodding furiously, but nothing's coming out.

Ross chips in. 'She says, yes, Martha! Yes, please!'

I'm biting my lip, and suddenly it's like a dam of emotion has burst, and there are tears streaming down my cheeks. 'But why?'

She snaps straight back. 'Because you've written an amazing recipe book, Cressy.' She pauses for a second. 'You do know you've gone viral?'

I gulp back a sob, and scrape the water away from under my eyelashes. 'With Walter and the buns on strings?'

'No, nothing to do with Walter, this is you pashing the face off that gorgeous man you usually plaster in icing.'

'For frig sake!' I let out a groan. 'Surely not?'

'It got you noticed, that's what matters. An advance *this* size on the back of *one* kiss – don't knock it!' She doesn't pause for breath. 'Congratulations, the contract is digital, I'll send it over now for you to look over. Sign right away and we'll get them tied in.'

And then she's gone as fast as she appeared.

Ross stares at me. 'That's another good thing about this location, it's got signal.' He hands me a hanky. 'I couldn't help overhearing. Well done for that, great to see you back at the top again.'

There's one very urgent question I have to ask. 'Did you know about the clip?' I had no idea that *particular* one had been uploaded. There's another point too. 'Whatever she says, it wasn't a kiss. You were there, you can back me up on that, can't you?'

As I scrub his hanky under my eyes and sniff away my tears, his lips part as he takes a breath to reply. Then, as I see his expression falter and he hesitates, there's a long, low rumble in the distance. 'What was that?'

He glances up at the sky. 'That was another thing I came to tell you. There are storms on the way.'

'But the sun was out a minute ago.'

He shrugs and gives a nod towards the coast. 'The Cornish weather is renowned for being mercurial. It's black over Oyster Point – the storm's coming from there.'

As I follow his gaze towards the darkness in that direction and pull my cardi around me against a sudden gust, I can see he's right. The rain is already blowing towards us in squalls over the fields, and we hear its rattle on the ground before it hits us. Then a huge drop of water splashes a dark stain down the front of my dress, then another lands on my cheek.

Ross has already pulled Diesel and me through into the next field and slams the gate behind us. The clouds above us are smoky purple, the daylight darkens and, as a thunderclap crashes over our heads, Diesel lets out a yelp. Ross yells over the sudden rush of air that's flattening the grass. 'Run for the yard! We'll shelter in the barn.'

And the next moment the water is falling from the sky in bucketloads and we're all running as fast as we can across the fields towards the farm buildings.

37

In the hay barn at Walter's farm
Damp but not quite finished
Thursday

I t's true we can't change what's done, but as we reach the last gate and race across the cobbles with the rain pelting down on us so hard my skin is stinging, between my gasps for breath and pushing the water out of my eyes so I can see, I'm puzzling. As I follow Ross across the yard and clutch at the stitch in my side from running so far so fast, there's still an unease about why I read him so badly all those years ago.

He grabs my arm, and pulls me through the curtain of water falling off the roof and into the shelter of an open-sided shed piled with bales. The rain is ringing on the metal high above our heads, the water is sluicing down the sides where the gutters are overflowing, my hair is hanging in rats' tails, my soaking dress is sticking to my body, but I'm laughing with relief that we've made it to the shelter. I breathe in the sweetness of the newly mown hay I'm leaning against, though it's pricking my back through my dress.

I blink at Ross through sodden eyelashes, take in that he's approximately a millimetre away, and a seismic shudder passes through my body. 'I couldn't be any wetter if I'd been dipped in the sea.'

He shakes his head, then shrugs off his jacket. 'Here, it's wet, but it's better than nothing. Put it around you, you're freezing.' He slides it over my shoulders and around my back, then, as another clap of thunder echoes off the stone wall opposite, he drags on the jacket lapels and pulls me in against the hard planes of his body. 'These summer storms are fierce, but they don't usually last too long.'

And then the answer to my puzzling rushes into my head like an express train. 'I've remembered the thing you said that really let me know how you felt; it was *What a disaster!*' And we went downhill from there. But at least that explains to me why I reacted as I did.

His hair is falling in long strands across his forehead. 'What's that?'

My breath is still juddering, but at least the burn in my throat is fading now I'm getting my breath back. 'When I rang to tell you about the baby, that's how I knew you were appalled. How much you hated the idea. And I had to block your calls in case you tried to make me change my mind.'

He lets out a moan. 'The disaster wasn't the baby, Bertie. The disaster was that I'd let it happen at all. That I was responsible for demolishing your last year at uni, and probably your future too. That I cared for you *so* much, but had been *so* careless.' He pushes back my hair, and when I look up, his eyelashes are clumped too. 'I only began to think about the baby as a living, breathing reality when I arrived to see you at the hospital. But I always, always wanted her.'

My sigh is heartfelt and I swallow back a mouthful of tears. 'And by that time we'd already lost her.'

The hollows in his cheeks are dark as he stares down, and his voice is heavy with regret. 'You know, I didn't ever get to see you when you were pregnant. I never even put my hand on your tummy.'

I could weep for both of us for the hurt we've caused each other. And I have so much catching up to do. Knowing what I do now means I need to reassess my fear of putting my trust in someone. Because however it felt back then, he wasn't running out on me. He came all the way through for me, but it was just too late.

I let out another sigh, because I want to explain. 'All my life-decisions since then have been based on only relying on myself so I wouldn't be let down again. It's made for such a lonely journey. And you hadn't failed me at all.'

His face is resting against my temple. Then he pulls back, tilts my chin upwards and looks down at me. 'At least you know the truth now. I was there for you then, and that will never change; I'll always be here for you.'

As he rubs his thumb across my jaw, my heart is beating so hard it's practically jumping out of my chest. There's a gaping need in the pit of my stomach as I crush my hips against his groin. That's raw desire. I swallow hard and bite my lip, aching to bury myself in him, to taste the sweet, dark velvety heat of his mouth again.

I feel his chest expand against me as he drags in a breath. 'So what are you thinking, Bertie?'

I'm thinking that if he's going to kiss me I won't mind at all because I'm finally ready. More than ready. And even further in the back of my mind there's also the green-for-go on my Natural Cycles app this morning. How if he'd like to sit on a hay bale and lie back, I'd be fine to take it from there. Ease him out of his jeans, button by button. Then quietly pull up my dress and kneel across him. That I don't know about him, but I'm so fit to burst that I'd probably last all of two seconds…

I push that as far out of my mind as I can and clear my throat and try to say it like it is. 'I've got a week left in St Aidan; that feels scarily like *déjà vu*. But it's exciting to have cleared so much baggage out of the way.' I send it back to him. 'How about you?' I'm close enough to see his individual eyelashes in the half-light, and I hold my breath as I wait for his answer. There were so many barriers between us, but we finally heaved the last one aside. All I can I hope is that he feels the same.

He's looking into my eyes. 'I agree about the baggage. But I'm thinking, with your advance and your sponsors you're back to where you were.' He gives a grimace. 'I also know, once you and your bicycle app are back in London, you won't have time to give any of us in St Aidan a second thought.'

I take a moment to steady my breathing. So that's his way of, very politely, saying he's not interested. I mean, I always knew what we had was coming more from my side than his. Our accident happened because of something I'd pushed him into. He didn't regret it, but obviously he wouldn't be going there again. I'd be crazy to think anything else. Which is great for me, because knowing that for sure might make me feel as empty as if my insides had left the building. But at least it puts the brakes on my heart rate.

I'm frowning at him. 'You'll still be here, then?'

His eyes open wide, then he blinks. 'It's all a bit up in the air for me.'

It comes out in a rush before I engage my brain. 'You wouldn't like to come – to London?'

He pulls a face. 'The last thing I want to do is hold you back. So we both know that's a no.' He screws up his face, then his voice lightens. 'So how does it work then – this famous app of yours?'

There's nothing like a change of subject to clear the air. But then maybe he's only making conversation until the rain stops. We can hardly stand here in silence. 'Okay, so I tell the app lots of vital details like my temperature and my period days, and in return it tells me if it's a green day or a red day.'

He nods. 'So green means safe?'

He's got me there. 'It used to. But then I changed it around, so now it means those are my fertile days.'

'Jeez, Bertie! What the hell?' His voice is so full of horror he might have read my mind just before, but he can't have.

Ten more days – maybe less – then I'll never see him again. It's amazing how liberating that thought is when it comes to frankness and spilling secrets. 'I'm sure I'll change it back again soon. It's just being around so many kids in St Aidan has really made me want a family of my own.'

He practically chokes. 'Cripes! I don't know if I'll ever have kids.'

It's great that we covered this. The extremity of his reaction is making the fact he just closed me down feel like a lucky break. 'Really? Why ever not? Don't tell me – your taste in music is too bad to pass it on?'

'Of all people, I'd think it would be obvious to you.' He gives an eye roll. 'I screwed it up so badly with you, what if it happened again? *What if I failed the kids in the same way?* No, children are definitely off the table, I could never trust myself to get it right.'

There are images flashing through my brain. I'm thinking of toddlers, six-year-olds, ten-year-olds, teenagers. All miniature versions of Ross, all as adorable and irresistible as he is. I raise my palm, rest it against his face. 'One day you might want to rethink that. Forget the past – what about all the donut evenings you've come to, all the boxes of kitchen equipment you've hauled up and down the stairs at Seaspray Cottage, all the times you rush off to the rescue with animal emergencies? You really are the most reliable guy I've ever met. For the man you are now, I honestly can't think of anyone who would make a better dad.' He's just been super clear about where we stand, so he knows I'm talking generically here and definitely not for myself.

In fact now it comes to it, the thought of him having a baby with someone other than me is pretty crippling. But at least I won't be around to see that.

He leans his face into my hand. 'Stop, before the compliments go to my head! Thanks for the reassurance, but it's still not on my to-do list for any time soon.'

Another thought powers into my head, and as steel fingers close around my stomach and make me feel sick, I'm kicking myself for not realising sooner. 'It's Elise, isn't it? You two are more than just work colleagues, aren't you? You're an item!'

His face folds in disbelief, then it relaxes into a laugh. 'Hardly! Elise has a lovely girlfriend who lives in Rose Hill. You've been here three months, how have you missed that?'

If I wasn't so frozen, I'd be bright red with mortification for everything I've given away with that comment. As it is, my blood vessels are too cold for my cheeks to be anything other than ghost-coloured. As for the whoosh of relief that's flooding through me, I'm not going to own up even to myself how big that is. It doesn't matter anyway. But it'll easier for me when I'm sitting in my nice, new-to-me studio flat if I don't have to think of him with his arms entwined around an actual specific person.

I cough away my embarrassment and take back my hand. 'Anyway, did you say earlier you had something to run past me?'

His eyebrows rise, then his eyes cloud again. 'I may have done, but we've probably moved on from that now.' He brightens up. 'You know those ideas, they seem brilliant when you have them, then you think again and realise they're total crap. It was one of those.'

That's the end of *that* conversation then, but I can't bear the thought of silence. 'If you want to do a Rolling Stones singalong until the rain stops, I know all the words to "Gimme Shelter". Or "The Man Who Sold the World".'

He sniffs. 'The David Bowie version, or the Kurt Cobain one?'

Seeing how well he knows my teenage self, I'm surprised he has to ask. 'Kurt Cobain, obviously.'

He just stares down at me. 'How about Dolly Parton's "I Will Always Love You"?'

Oh frig. I'm word-perfect, and he knows too. How the hell can I tell him that's the one song I couldn't manage now? I'm digging deep, summoning up my excuses, when there's a distant thumping that gets louder, and then the notes of a car engine coming along the lane.

Just to be sure no one arriving gets the wrong impression, I take a jump and land a clear three feet away from Ross. Then I send him my best 'Hi, I'm Cressida Cupcake' beam. 'Expecting visitors?'

He looks at his watch and his face slides into a smile. 'Any time around now Jen should be dropping by with Walter and Joanie on the way back from Walter's hospital appointment. That was the other thing I came to tell you about.'

I'm imagining how this would have played out if my fantasy had gone to plan, and at this moment I'd been straddling Ross halfway up the hay stack.

Which only goes to prove, you should be careful what you wish for, though at the same time it reassures me that I probably do have a secret fairy godmother after all. And more than that, however crap I feel right now, I know she must be really looking out for me.

38

At Walter's farm
Great expectations and long goodbyes
Thursday

'What's happened to you two? You look like you've been dipped in the duck pond!'

Walter appears round the corner of the house first, bobbing up and down as he walks with a stick in each hand, then Jen and Joanie come into view a few moments later, Joanie in her smart flowery going-out dress, and Jen in jeans, Doc Martens sandals and a fluorescent pink and green tie-dye T-shirt.

Ross is right about the changeable weather. Not only has the rain stopped, but the sun is breaking through the clouds and making steam rise from the stone flags in front of the farmhouse.

Walter's peering past us to the hay barn. 'How did the

contractors get on? They charge me an arm and a leg, and they never stack the bales as tight as I tell them.'

Ross looks over his shoulder at the barn we've just left. 'They've done a great job, the hay smells wonderful.'

Jen laughs. 'I should hope so, seeing as they're family.' She turns to me. 'Nell's dad's brother and his son did the first hay cut for Walter. He just won't let any of us forget how much it's cost him.'

Walter gives Ross a wink and grins at me. 'If you've had a roll in it, no one's going to mind.'

I pull a damp hay strand out of my hair. Sometimes the best way of closing something down is to tell the whole truth, then people assume you have to be joking. 'No such luck. I asked but Ross wasn't up for it.'

Joanie shakes her head at me. 'Take no notice, my beauty, Walter's only being cheeky because he's pleased with himself.'

That sounds like an invitation to ask the question I'd have hesitated over otherwise, knowing how ill he was when I first arrived. 'So did it go well this afternoon?'

Jen and Walter are beaming, and Joanie replies. 'The consultant was very pleased. He called our Walter a walking miracle!'

Walter butts in. 'When he saw me in spring, he thought I was a goner.'

Joanie pats his arm. 'All Jen's good food and making you take your tablets at the right time, she's properly brought you back from the dead.'

Jen is quietly proud as she smiles at Joanie. 'I suspect the love of a lounge full of good women also helped with that.'

Walter chuckles. 'I reckon the manure I put in my boots helped too.'

Joanie laughs at Walter. 'All that grumbling you've done – Kittiwake Court hasn't done so badly for you.'

Walter lets out a grunt of indignation. 'Grumbling? When have I ever grumbled?'

Ross turns to them. 'We'd maybe best not get into that. There's more good news too. Cressy just heard, she's landed a book contract.'

As they all turn to look at me, I'm suddenly shy. 'I'm very pleased, but honestly, it's nothing compared to yours.'

Ross shakes his head at me. 'That's why I had to tell them, I knew you'd underplay it.' He laughs but he isn't smiling. 'We're having so many deliveries from her sponsors, we're running out of space at the flat. That's what it's like living with a celebrity.'

Joanie reaches over and gives my arm a squeeze. 'Well done for that, Cressy. I hope you're going to treat yourself, my love!'

The sudden idea of buying myself some pretty lingerie is completely ridiculous, given the flat-out knock-back I just had ten minutes ago, so I push the thought of balcony bras and matching knickers out of my head and think of something more grounded. 'The fish, chips and fizz are on me tonight!'

Ross winks at Joanie. 'Not forgetting, the ketchup has to be Heinz.'

Walter waves his stick at the farmhouse and turns to Ross. 'Are you two still up for a look around inside the house before you head off to celebrate, lad?'

Jen looks at her watch. 'Walter had me breaking the speed limits so we'd get here in time to catch you.'

I'm trying to hide my surprise, because I'd rather they didn't know I had no idea this was coming. I can't say how much I'd love to know what's inside those honey-coloured stone walls, to look out of those small-paned sash windows, instead of only seeing as far in as the tattered net curtains as I pass.

It's only as I'm standing here now by the front door, with its paint that's so old and faded you can't tell what colour it was meant to be, looking across to the quaint old caravans where I collect the eggs up by the orchard, thinking how sweet they'd be to stay in, that I ask myself: am I really ready to go back to London? Or would I rather hide away here, and let my holiday go on for the rest of the summer? Carry on feeding the calves. Maybe help Clemmie when she comes back and starts up her proper Little Cornish Kitchen again.

Ross glances at my soaking dress clinging to my legs. 'All things considered, we're probably best to leave it for a time when we're drier.'

If I needed confirmation that I accidentally got in the way here, that is it. And that's another thing I'd need to consider. If Ross is staying here, how hard would it be for me to be here too? It's not even as if we'd be hanging out together. And I know that I hated being round him at the start. But somehow I've come to enjoy being around him. And being here, but not seeing him, would actually be excruciating. Which confirms my idea of living in a caravan for the summer as the total non-starter it is.

I see their three faces fall in disappointment at Ross's rebuff, but I'm sensing he isn't about to change his mind, so I hand him the out he needs. 'Truly, I wouldn't feel comfortable making puddles on your carpets.'

There's definitely a tension, and Joanie's trying to ease it by joking. 'You have carpets, Walter? All these years you told us you had straw on your floor!'

Jen gives Ross a hard stare. 'You'll never know if you don't go in. Now's your chance. Surely you don't want to miss it?'

I'm not sure what they'd arranged or how exactly it's gone wrong, but I'm going to tell the truth again, and bring the awkwardness to an end. 'I'm actually really cold. I'm so pleased your appointment went so well, Walter, but I'd best head home for a shower now.'

Ross is straight in there. 'My car's here. If we leave straightaway I've got time to run you back down to town before surgery.' He drops his arm around Walter's shoulder. 'I'll get back to you about the other. We can do it together tomorrow or Saturday.'

'Whatever suits you, lad.' He leans against the wall, and pushes back his cap. 'Today I've been given a gift I didn't think I had. Believe me, when time's running out, it makes a chap like me think very hard. That's why I'd hate to see you throw away an opportunity.'

Joanie and Jen nodding like they understand makes me wish I did too.

Walter clears his throat. 'So all I'll say to you, son is – YOYO!' He turns to the women. 'That's right, isn't it?'

Jen smiles. 'I think what you mean is YOLO, Walter – you only live once.'

'Aye, that's the one.' Walter shuffles his weight from one foot to the other. 'And if times are tough for you, Ross, all the more reason to have someone beside you to help you through. Take it from me: life is precious, don't waste a second.'

I'm swallowing back a lump in my throat, hearing Walter being so profound.

Ross's expression is grave. 'I'll certainly bear that in mind Walter.'

Joanie's words come out in a rush. 'Take it *to heart*, Ross, that's a better place to put it.'

Walter nods. 'Joanie's right. She always is. She keeps me on the right track. That's what we men need sometimes – a woman to sort us out.'

Ross says, 'I remember you quoting Beyoncé at me not long ago. Something tells me you're the one who should be putting rings on things, not me!' He winks at Joanie. 'Just saying.'

There's an extra twinkle in Joanie's eye as she smiles at me. 'We single ladies in St Aidan can look out for ourselves, thanks all the same, Ross.'

Ross's eyes open in surprise, then he grins at her. 'I'm pleased to hear it. In that case, unless you're planning to go down on one knee right now, Joanie, we'd better get a move on.'

Joanie tuts at Walter as we turn to leave. 'And I thought you were bad.'

It's only as we get to Ross's car I realise that in the

excitement there's something else I've missed too. I pull open the back door to let Diesel jump in and look at Ross across the roof. 'The care at Kittiwake Court that has made all the difference for Walter. We *have* to get that money together, we *have* to save it so he can carry on living there.'

Ross pulls a face. 'Even with grants, there's still a long way to go. And time's running out on that too.'

I'm gritting my teeth. 'One last big push, then.'

I don't know how I'm going to do it, but I *have* to make this happen.

And that's the last thing we say all the way back to the harbour.

39

On the deck at Plum's gallery
Popping corks and cutting to the chase
Friday

'Crusty Cobs' strawberry tarts really are heaven in a box.'

This is Plum talking, a shower of pastry crumbs falling from her lips as she speaks.

And as I bite into the last of my own and the smooth vanilla custard merges with the fruit chunks on my tongue I have to agree. 'As we're celebrating me signing my cookery book contract I *should* have baked them myself.' But this is one of those times when instant gratification trumps an hour or two in the kitchen. I grin at them across the table made from hewn oak sleepers, and glimpse the shimmering turquoise of the sea far below us. 'We did chill our own champagne.'

It's actually Friday afternoon before we get to celebrate.

Somehow the slap-up fish and chip supper I'd promised Ross yesterday got swept aside due to a springer spaniel that got hit by a car. And as the girls were all enjoying a rare night in, I was happy to submerge myself in a hot, deep bath and leave the cork-popping until today. It might not have been a bad thing. From the heavy silence in the car on the way home from Walter's, it wouldn't exactly have been a lively evening with Ross. I'm not quite sure what went wrong up at Walter's. One minute we were chatting openly and easily, then everything seized up, and Ross withdrew.

Left to me, I wouldn't have made a big thing about the contract. When I had the offer first time round I didn't do much more than ring Mum and Charlie. But as Plum needs to be at the gallery, it's actually lovely to sit quietly in the sunshine on the deck perched way above the harbour, and have a catch-up with just the four of us.

Plum opens another bakery box and hands us all second helpings. 'We never even started to explore tarts with your evenings, Cress.'

Nell's giving me a hard stare over the rim of her flute. 'Your Little Cornish Kitchen On Tour has the legs to run and run. You do know that, don't you, Cress?'

Plum agrees. 'What we're trying to say is, there's everything you need here for the basis of a whole new career. If you wanted one, that is.'

Sophie's topping up everyone's glasses with fizz as we settle in for a second round. 'What you're all forgetting is, we're here celebrating that Cressy has not only reinstated her old career, she's done more. Her celebrity status is there for the taking – if she wants to choose it.' She stops to squeeze me into a hug. 'All we ask is, if you do decide you have to leave, please don't forget about us. You have to come back at Christmas. And in summer. And every weekend in between.'

My leaving date isn't actually fixed yet, but it's a lot more certain than anyone's making it sound. We all know Clemmie and Charlie are due home this week or next, and whatever the outcome, they'll need space. So I'm planning to head off very soon after they get here.

Plum's leaning forwards, and drops her voice. 'And what about Ross? I haven't seen you for a proper debrief since the baby sprinkle, but the others said he'd let slip that you two were properly involved all those years ago.'

Sophie says it how it is. 'We all know he was *the one*. But has he said any more?'

This is where we were sitting the first day I talked to them about any of this. It feels so long ago now, and I feel so different about everything now too. And he announced it to the entire party, so I'm not breaking any confidences. 'He was the dad. It happened over a short Christmas holiday in St Aidan. It was a fling for both of us – he went off abroad afterwards and it really felt at the time that he didn't want anything to do with the pregnancy. But we've managed to sort a few things out now.'

Nell's looking at me. 'Ross is so quick to jump in and help people, it's hard to think he wouldn't step up – but the best of guys struggle with an unexpected baby. Some even struggle with planned ones.'

I pull in a breath. 'It's completely tragic in some ways. He actually had everything finalised to leave the States and come home. He just didn't ever manage to tell me until yesterday.'

Sophie gasps. 'Wow, that's so, so sad. At least you know now.'

I look around at their concerned expressions. 'Understanding what happened has resolved a lot for me. It's shown me that I can put my trust in people after all.'

Nell smiles. 'That has to be a good thing going forward.'

I nod at her. 'When I bumped into Ross that first afternoon, I couldn't have imagined how my time in St Aidan was going to turn things around. But it feels like the path ahead has been cleared. And I've learned so much along the way.'

Nell laughs. 'We've learned from you too. Cupcakes here will never be the same again.'

There's another change that can't pass without mentioning it either. 'When I came I was determined to only rely on myself. But St Aidan's taught me you can achieve so much more if you work together, and that friendship is one of the most important things in life.'

Sophie nods. 'St Aidan certainly proves what a force for good a community can be.' Her foot catches a carrier that's next to my chair and her eyebrows rise. 'Hey, a fuchsia-pink bag from Sheer Surf!'

Plum winks. 'They use that colour carrier exclusively for their lingerie sales.'

They've got me here. 'And there I was, thinking I was buying my new knickers and bra under the radar.'

Nell snorts. 'Secret shopping in St Aidan is *not* a thing!'

Sophie gives me a nudge. 'Can we have a peep?'

I'm making my excuses as I open the bag, because it's nothing exotic. I just left home a little early, and called in at the girlie surf place by the harbour on the off-chance. 'Just a navy bra, and matching Brazilians, with a teal-coloured flower or two and some satin ribbon.'

Nell lets out a hoot. 'Good call on the panty line. I can't do thongs either, they get right up my crack.'

Sophie sighs. 'Pretty. And very you.'

As Plum nods her approval her eyes are bright with interest. 'So are you buying with anyone *particular* in mind?'

I wondered that too at first, then, as I was at the till, I worked it out. 'It's actually for me – as a promise to myself I won't give up on my love life.'

Sophie frowns. 'But what about Ross? You two look so good together, you seem to get each other.'

I try to keep the disappointment out of my voice. 'I think he signed off. A long time ago.'

Nell's smile fades. 'George mentioned a high-flying job in the Midlands. Has he shared that with you?'

'Not yet.' I shake my head and try to ignore the wave of panic that idea causes me.

Plum leans across the table again, her voice urgent. 'If there's any chance at all you have feelings for Ross, you need to give it a go while you're both still here.'

I screw up my face. 'I'd hate to throw myself at him.'

Nell shrugs. 'Sometimes that's the only way. It took years for me and George to get together. I wish now we'd both been less resistant.'

Plum lets out a low laugh. 'He didn't look reluctant on the clip.'

I round on her. 'You saw it too!'

Plum grins. 'Along with a million other people.'

I'm still pushing this. 'Who put that up?'

She laughs. 'I'm not sure, but there was no holding back on Ross's side. It would make Top Ten Snogs on YouTube.'

I have to hold firm on this. 'It wasn't a kiss.'

Nell just looks at me sideways. 'No, you were both just having your cake and eating it.'

Plum's voice rises to a shout. 'Of course it was a kiss!'

Sophie's sounding thoughtful. 'If you don't try, you'll never know. If he does say no, all that's hurt is your pride.'

Plum's right in my face. 'Mermaid's honour. Promise us you won't leave before you've tried to jump him. Bewitch him with your magic lingerie.'

There's only one answer they're going to accept here, so I relent. 'Okay. I'll try.'

Sophie grins. 'That's all we want to hear.'

While we're all here, I have to let them know how much times like this have meant to me. 'The best part of being in St Aidan has been finding you three. I've never been part of a friendship group before, so I never really knew what I was missing. But you've all been here for me, you've all helped me, you've all had my back. You've taught me how much better life is when you have people around you to share things with. And that has been the biggest gift of my stay.'

Plum grasps my hand and as Sophie's pulling me into a hug I'm swallowing back my tears. And as Nell comes round the table and joins in, so does Diesel, who puts his nose in my ear. 'Sorry, Diesel, obviously you've been awesome too.'

'You really are a mermaid now.' That was Sophie, patting my back.

Plum's joining in. 'Not just an honorary one. You've been here for all of us, but just look what you've done for St Aidan and Kittiwake Court too. You're a fully-fledged, nuts-and-bolts, real-life one, who skipped the first thirty-five years and dolphin-flipped onto the team.'

Sophie raises her glass and holds it up to the sky. 'How about we drink to us – to best friends, and to mermaids in particular.'

Nell joins in. 'Not forgetting Clemmie.'

Sophie gives a cough. 'To best mermaid friends, both here and far away.'

And we all raise our glasses in the air, then gulp down our champers.

Nell's shaking her head. 'If someone had told me four months ago I'd be best friends with Cressida Cupcake, I would not have believed them.'

I have to fess up. 'The new-look Cressy isn't quite the same as she used to be.'

Nell laughs. 'But you're *our* Cressy now, with all the benefits of a St Aidan makeover. Very few people who come here go away the same.'

And I don't actually mind that at all.

Now Sophie's started organising us, there's no stopping her. She's pointing her finger at me. 'Thinking about Cressy Cupcake, for the book launch next week – if you can drop by Plum's and sign as many copies as you can before Saturday, next to your foreword, that would be great.'

Plum's taken a notebook out of her dungaree pocket and

she's jotting things down. 'I'll let you know when the books are here. And you are okay if I get you a mermaid's tail made up for the after-party?'

I know I'm a fully-fledged member of the mermaids' club now, but on balance, I'm probably okay without. 'It'd be a shame to go to all that trouble.' I can tell by their faces I need to be more insistent. 'So much work for one outing seems a waste.' I have to find something to put smiles back on their downcast faces. 'But don't worry, I'll make you all proud. I'll throw myself at Ross so hard the man won't know what's hit him.'

And their shouts of 'Go for it, Cressy!' are so loud, people probably heard them all the way around St Aidan Bay.

40

At Clemmie's flat
Optimism and indigestion
A week later, Thursday

When I came back to Seaspray Cottage last Friday after our little party on Plum's deck I was buoyed up and fully determined to keep my promise to the girls.

I tore up to the flat and into my new underwear, ripped open my latest package from Maudie Maudie and chose a dress made of a few teensy scraps of navy chiffon. In fairness it was probably more suited to a fairy than to a fully grown person like me. But, what the hell, it seemed to cling in the right places so I pulled it on anyway. Five minutes after landing I was curled up with Diesel on our favourite pink sofa, sucking in my stomach so far even I could tell my boobs looked astonishing. Then I waited.

My first strategy was to pop up on my five-inch velvet stilettos – so lucky I packed them! – as Ross walked in.

Before he got his breath back from the climb I'd already have jumped him.

When he still hadn't turned up quarter of an hour later I started breathing again and decided I'd get him to share the box of bite-sized brownies and bottle of fizz I'd brought with me and take it from there.

By the time I'd come to the end of the brownies *and* the bottle I was lying with my legs hanging over the sofa end thinking I'd wing it. Five episodes of *Outlander* later I called off the mission for the day, due to the non-arrival of the target.

And this has pretty much been how it's gone all week. Six *entire* days later, I haven't had one opportunity. Not one! He has definitely been back to the flat, because I've seen crumples on the duvet where he's been sitting on his bed. He's just never been here at the same time as me. Isn't it always the way?

When it came to the meringue evening last Saturday, Plum coming in his place at the last minute felt like one of those unavoidable things. It was quiet without him, but it was only the once. By the time he'd sent replacements for the brownie and blondie evenings and the donut one too, no one said, but it was starting to feel like this was the new normal.

No one had made any firm commitments, least of all Ross, so I know I was wrong to have built up my expectations. But somehow the picture of my last week in my head had me laughing and joking, with Ross realising I was too hilarious to live without. Instead, with every no-show from Ross the mood got gloomier. Our final evening last night we all made the effort, but it still petered out. Talk about ending in an anticlimax!

So much for my bigger ambitions with Ross. As the week went by, and his silence grew metaphorically louder, I'd just have liked to see him to find out why he was upset, and if there was any way I could help.

He wasn't even around when Charlie messaged to say he and Clemmie will be travelling back next weekend, times to be confirmed when flights are finalised.

As the week went on, even Diesel's high spirits waned. With Diesel, quiet is always relative; he still tried to steal my muffin off my plate while I was staring out into the distance across the bay at breakfast this morning.

I know when Ross was first moving in, I was dreading the sound of his key in the door. But being here now, knowing I'm *not* going to hear him breezing in saying, *Bertie, there you are!* is actually making me physically ache for him to come home. I know it's wet and weedy, and that's not who I am at all. But there's just this gaping hole at the pit of my stomach, a hollowness that makes me feel like crying and throwing up both at the same time. I'm the first to admit, it's taken me by surprise. I'm just so used to thinking of him as annoying yet super sexy, I had no idea I'd miss him so much when he wasn't here. Without him everything just feels so dull and dead and faded.

Last Friday I was riding a wave, and primed for him to walk through the door. A week on, my expectation of seeing him has dwindled hour by hour, and I'm totally deflated. It's starting to feel completely possible that the time will come for me to leave without our paths ever coinciding.

And I can't quite cope with the constrictions of panic that thought sends through my chest.

And the undies are tossed on the chair by my bed like a mocking reminder of how wrong I got this.

But as the days have passed, it's become clear; Ross's absence isn't an accident, it's a deliberate choice. There's no mistake, he *is* avoiding me. And as that realisation has gradually sunk in, my once fluttering heart has slowly turned to stone.

My whole life since uni I've been so self-reliant. Letting a man determine how I feel isn't like me at all. Similarly, there's little point second-guessing the reason. All I know is the change seems to go back to the day of the storm up at Walter's; he must be so adamant he doesn't want to take things further, he's going to enormous lengths not to be anywhere near me. Playing for time, until I disappear out of his orbit for ever.

This evening, it's almost a week after we drank fizz at Plum's, and I'm expecting to spend the evening dashing up and down the stairs as people call to collect a stack of bake boxes. There's so little going on at home now, but I refuse to wallow, so I've started on try-outs for my next book. That's another thing about Ross being around less; there's a whole lot more baking left over than there would have been otherwise.

I've taken the cookie theme further, and as everyone knows we're doing a last big effort for the Kittiwake funds, so there are cookie bags too, and the regulars will be dropping by to pick those up.

As I come back up after quite a chat with the third doorstep customer of the evening I find Diesel slinking out from the kitchen, so I give him a gentle reminder he's not supposed to be in there. 'Hey, boy, I hope you haven't been helping your-self?' When I go in to check there's a tea towel on the floor by the sink, and a cooling tray, so I pick them up. 'I don't know where you found these, but thanks for not wolfing the cookies.'

He gives me a wounded look and flops down on the rug by the sofa. Every time I make a trip downstairs after that I shut the kitchen door, just to be sure. But Diesel doesn't move again. When Clemmie and Charlie do their video call just before eleven, he's so fast asleep he barely lifts his head and we all laugh at how loudly he's snoring. I go through to the bedroom to show them Pancake, who manages to open one eye when I tickle her behind her ear, and then they sign off.

Before I go back through again I glance down at the chair by the bed just to remind myself I bought the bra and pants for me, not anyone else, and to promise myself I will wear them for the book launch on Saturday. Then as I pick up the bra I see the knickers have gone.

Damn. There's only one knicker-stealer in this flat, so I raise my voice so he hears me. 'Diesel, carrying socks in your mouth is cute, running off with my new briefs isn't funny.'

I do a sweep of the hall and the bathroom to see where he's dropped them, and when they aren't there I get on my hands and knees and scour every last corner of the kitchen. I do the same in the living room, and I'm coming round the corner from the back of the sofa when Diesel lets out a long groan that makes my blood run cold.

'Diesel, get up now!'

He lifts his head, then drops it and grunts again.

I scramble to my feet and rush through to the kitchen and come back with a handful of gravy bones. 'Come on, up you get, I've got biscuits!'

A whiff from fifty yards is usually enough for him to pelt along the beach at a hundred miles an hour. But he doesn't even stir, and even when I put a biscuit under his nose, he just turns his muzzle away.

I close down the screams in my head and try to stay calm. 'Okay, Cress, your pants are nowhere to be found in the flat, Diesel's flat out and moaning, what's the *logical* conclusion?' One thing's for sure, Clemmie didn't cover this in her manual of instructions.

I'm breaking out in a sweat as I perch on the sofa arm and pull out my phone. I open Google and type 'dog eating panties'. There's are loads of opinions, all coming to similar conclusions:

Dogs that ingest underwear are at risk of blockage of their digestive tract or intestines.

The groan I let out as I read that is louder than Diesel's. I skim further down the page.

If in doubt, call your veterinarian.

Wouldn't it just say that? But I can't afford to put my

personal preferences in front of Diesel's health and wellbeing. He's not as young as he was and gastric blockages aren't great at any age. My chest constricts as I follow that thought. *What if he dies?*

I mustn't get ahead of myself. All I have to do is ring Ross. As I press call, and wait for a connection, I'm staring out of the French windows into the darkness, counting the string of lights around the bay, praying that he answers. I get to three when I hear his voice.

'Cressy?'

I'm so relieved, the words come tumbling out. 'It's Diesel, he's eaten my lacy Brazilian knickers…'

There's a beat of silence. 'Since when have you had lacy knickers? I thought you wore…' He stops and coughs. 'Sorry, remind me, what size are Brazilians?'

I'm shaking my head that I'm having to explain. 'They're bigger than a thong, but smaller than granny pants, cut back on the bum so you don't get a VPL.'

I hear him sigh. 'How long ago did it happen and how does Diesel seem in himself?'

Saying it out loud I'm cringing with guilt. 'A couple of hours ago maybe, but I only realised now.' As I look down at poor Diesel, I'm swallowing back a sob. 'He's groaning and he won't get up.' Then another awful thought hits me like a juggernaut. 'I can't get him downstairs.'

There's a second of hesitation, then he says the words I realise I've been longing to hear. 'I'll come straight over.'

'Thank you.' Then a different wave of guilt sweeps over me for forcing him to do what he isn't comfortable with. 'I'm sorry, truly, I didn't mean this to happen.'

His voice is quiet. 'I know you better than to think that, Cressy. Keep him quiet, and don't worry. I'll bring the portable scanning machine, and we'll see what's going on.'

And it's a measure of how grave the situation is that Ross didn't mention baked goods once.

41

At Clemmie's flat
Lost causes and helicopter rescue
Thursday

'There isn't any obvious obstruction I can see at the moment.'

Ross is kneeling on the rug at Diesel's side where he's been for the last half-hour, and he wipes off his scanning pad and puts it next to the portable screen he set up on the coffee table. 'I'll stay here and keep an eye on him and we'll see how he is in the morning.'

I'm crouching next to Ross, stroking Diesel's flank with one palm, still holding the dustpan I've been using to brush up the wisps of grey fluff Ross clipped off Diesel's tummy earlier. 'Are you okay with that?'

Ross's mouth tightens. 'I wasn't ever going to get much sleep. There's more I haven't told you yet; they phoned from Kittiwake just after you called, to say Walter isn't well.

All I know so far is he had some kind of funny turn, and they've taken him to A&E.'

'Oh no.' Hearing that makes my stomach spasm all over again. 'Should you be with him?'

The shadows on Ross's cheeks darken as his jaw clenches. 'Jen's there, and Joanie too. They promised to ring as soon as they know more.' A gust from the open French windows lifts the hair from the dustpan. 'All we can do now is wait and hope for the best for both patients.'

I can't bear to say the words out loud. But Walter's come so far, it would be tragic for him to be snatched away now when he's found another chance at happiness. As I'm willing him with all my strength to be okay, I feel guilty for finding the space to think how much more like home the flat feels with Ross on the rug, tidying the kit back into the holdall he brought with him. At least the stethoscope around his neck is there to remind me this is a duty call and not one he'd have made of his own free will. When two such precious characters are suddenly in danger, it's hard to imagine the trivial worries that were filling my head a couple of hours ago.

Ross slides his bag in beside the chair and the bookcase and sinks onto the sofa. 'Is that another new dress?'

If he's resorting to small talk to pass the time, I may as well join in. 'Maudie Maudie have gone mad this last week. It's their new collection.' I pull a face. 'You know me, I have to test-drive them before I wear them out in public.' The print of this one is lovely. As I remember how much it reminds me of the buttercups and dandelions up in Walter's meadow, I'm swallowing hard. The wrap-over top will definitely need a pin or I'll be showing my boobs every time I bend over.

Ross blinks. 'I like the front.' He thinks for a few seconds. 'And Maudie Maudie sent the Brazilians too?'

If only they had, it would be less of my fault. As it is, I'm kicking myself for ever buying them; if I hadn't been so self-absorbed, Diesel would still be running round the flat. As it sinks in that he might have to be operated on, and as an older dog his heart might stop under the anaesthetic, I have to come clean.

'I actually bought them myself.' I'm imagining Diesel stretched out at the surgery, tubes in his mouth, Ross and Elise in their scrubs leaning over him, and I know I won't feel right until Ross knows the whole damn thing. 'I had this crazy idea to wear them for a surprise seduction.'

His eyes cloud with horror. 'Who *the hell* were you going to seduce?'

I'm blinking at him. 'You, of course. Who else would it be?'

He leans back against his cushions. 'Okay. That's not so bad then.'

'I know it's the last thing you'd want, but I didn't want to go back to London without trying. I needed to know for sure the answer was no – then I could get on with the rest of my life.'

He's shaking his head. 'Your usual pants would have done the job fine.'

'Excuse me? How do you know what pants I wear?'

He looks up at the ceiling. 'Bertie, I've lived with you for two months, I have eyes. There was that dress you wore for the *Mamma Mia!* evening. And Diesel has also turned up in my room quite a few times with them in his mouth. And dropped them around the flat.'

'Right.' I'm a lot less calm than I sound.

'Obviously I put them straight in the laundry basket.' He leans towards me. 'Hey, it's fine, there's no need to cry…'

I choke back a sob, and wipe my eyes on my sleeve. 'But Diesel could die, all because I couldn't accept you didn't want to be with me.'

Ross lets out a long sigh. 'I don't know where you got that idea from.'

My eyes flash open. 'Ross, you haven't been near the place all week! Why else would you be avoiding the flat like it's a plague village?'

His Adam's apple bobs as he swallows. 'It's a lot more complicated than that, Bertie. I was working on something good enough to offer you, but then all your sponsors came flooding back, and when your publishers came through too, I simply couldn't compete.'

'So that's why you stayed away?'

He nods. 'I care about you too much to ask you to settle for less than you deserve.' He takes a breath. 'But I'm pleased you told me you were thinking about taking a last chance while you could, because these last few days on my own I've done a lot of thinking too. And with Walter suddenly in hospital, it's reminded me again, I shouldn't put off telling you…

'A few weeks ago the worst thing I could imagine was not being able to do my job properly because of my hands. But then you arrived, and my whole world brightened. And now when I think of those problems with my hands, they're nothing.' His eyes are shining with tears. 'The worst thing I can think of now is a future without you in it. I thought I was going to be able to tough it out, but I can't. I messed things up between us before because I didn't say enough, so I'm going to put myself out there now. For the first time in my life I'm going to be really selfish, but I'm going to have to ask you to accept less than perfect. Because the only thing that really matters to me is that we can be together.'

'Oh my.' As I sink down onto the end of the sofa, I can hardly believe this is happening.

His eyes are dark with anguish. 'I've always been so hung up on getting everything mapped out. When I went to the States my career plan was all in place, I'd been crafting it for ever, and then we spent that time together here over Christmas and after that all that mattered was that I'd fallen in love with you. I was trying to see a way forward that would work for us both and then you told me about the baby and the world turned upside down. It all went so wrong that time around, I can't bear to lose you all over again.'

I'm two feet away from him, breathing in his scent, taking it all in. 'You were in love with me *then*?'

He gives a grimace. 'I've always been in love with you, Cressy. That's why I've always been so obsessed with making myself better. I hadn't meant to make a move until years later, but when we kissed on that holiday suddenly my love wasn't one-sided any more. As it became real it exploded into something bigger than I'd ever imagined possible; it was all I could think about. We both know everything came crashing down for us so soon afterwards. But since then I've never, ever stopped thinking about you or loving you.'

Maybe this explains my obsession with him too. 'I think I've been the same; even as a teenager, I lived for your visits. I've loved you so long and so hard – apart from when I hated you, obviously. But even then there was a part of me that still couldn't bear to let go.'

He pulls me round to face him. 'I've been tossing some ideas around – so *just assuming* you might want to be with me, how would you feel about staying in St Aidan?'

For me he couldn't have said anything better. 'I have such good friends here. For the first time ever in my life, I love the version of Cressy I am when I'm here.' I've been thinking about it a lot the last few days. 'I love my blog, but until I was here I didn't know how much I enjoy being face to face with real people. I thought I was happy before, but the happy I've found here is on a different level.' Then my heart sinks. 'But haven't you had a fabulous job offer some-where else?'

His eyes narrow. 'Heading up a team developing joint supplements is a prestige position for someone, but I think we can both do better than that.' He grasps my hand. 'Remember at Sophie's wellbeing day, how you said it was your dream to run residential courses?'

'I do.' I'm nodding furiously because that would be a dream come true, but I can't imagine where he's going with this.

He takes a big breath. 'How would you feel about you and me taking over Walter's place and doing that there?'

'What?' My jaw drops so far, it's practically on my chest.

'It's a big project, but he's very keen we should do it.'

I let out a moan. 'Poor Walter. I hate to think of him in hospital, struggling again…'

Ross's chest heaves against mine. 'He's found so much to live for, I can't believe he'll give up the fight now.'

I have to agree he has a point. 'He's got a whole new sparkle in his eyes.'

Ross nods. 'It helped when he felt we'd be there to carry on the farm for him. There's not just the house and outbuildings, we'd be allowed to build cabins up where the caravans are. We could do baking and animal care courses, and that would link well with the surgery too.'

'So that's what we were supposed to be looking round when Martha rang about my contract?'

Ross nods. 'I'm sorry I lost my nerve that day. I promise it won't happen again.'

My smile feels like it's wider than St Aidan Bay. 'That would be amazing. There's so much interest in country crafts now.' But stuff the country crafts, what I really care about is being with Ross. I swing across the sofa, and put a leg either side of his thighs and bury my mouth in his. Then his arms close around my back, his fingers are raking through my hair, and this time around the sweetness has nothing to do with cupcakes or blondies, the warm velvety taste of his mouth is all him.

It's a long time before we come up for air. And as we do he's pulling his hand out from under one of Clemmie's velvet cushions. 'Don't get your hopes up, but I may just have found something important.'

As he holds his finger in the air a flash of turquoise satin makes me gasp. 'You found my knickers?'

Ross's laugh is low. 'Not for the first time. That's Diesel's second favourite hiding place. If I hadn't been so distracted by the thought of seeing you I'd have looked there straightaway.'

'Hang on!' I know this is a vet I'm talking to, but there's something he's overlooking. 'So what's wrong with Diesel?'

Ross gives a low whistle. 'I came in earlier and made an extra-large cake. It was supposed to be a *please be with me and love me forever* cake, I was planning to give it to you tomorrow along with my speech. I left it on a cooling tray on the dresser, with an *I heart St Aidan* tea towel over it so you wouldn't notice.'

It's the tea towel that rings a bell. 'I found a cooling tray and a towel on the floor earlier, but there was no sign of cake.'

Ross lets out a moan. 'There were twelve eggs in that mix.'

'Twelve? But that's huge!'

There are creases in Ross's cheeks as he smiles. 'It was a massive thing I was asking you. Anything smaller wouldn't have cut it.'

I nod down at Diesel. 'I think that explains why someone is groaning in their sleep.' I look down at Ross. 'I hope there weren't any avocados in there, or chocolate? Or chives or macadamia nuts?'

Ross shakes his head. 'It was lemon drizzle that hadn't been drizzled on.' Then his gaze hardens. 'Where *did* that poster go?'

I know if we're going to be together we should be telling the truth all the time, but I'll start after this. 'I was going to put it on the door but it was too big, so it's still folded up on the table.'

He blows out his cheeks. 'In an effort to always be honest, I may have dropped that round mostly to make sure you had my phone number.'

I laugh. 'If you were hoping I'd ring you and invite you round for hot sex, it worked in the end.'

As he smiles the crinkles at the corners of his eyes actually make my heart squish. 'Twelve weeks wasn't too long to wait.'

Talking about being truthful, I've another question to ask. 'You remember the clip of us *not* kissing that went viral? I still don't know who uploaded that.'

This time his laugh is so low, I feel the vibrations in my tummy. 'I'm afraid that was me.'

I'm already thinking of what I'll be doing to punish him later. 'Stealing Millie's film, that's disgraceful!'

He coughs. 'It wasn't actually Millie's. It was from my phone, held that evening by Nell. I always used to get someone to film our battles, because I knew one day I'd get to win, and I knew you wouldn't upload it.'

'So you planned all along to snog my face off?'

He laughs. 'I thought you said it *wasn't* a kiss, Bertie?'

My eyes widen as I follow it through. 'So my book contract is all down to you?'

He's shaking his head. 'Oh no, the credit for that is all yours, I just put up the hashtags. I knew it would go wild because of all the ones before it.'

I have to hand it to him. 'In that case, thank you for your good judgement.'

He gives a cough. 'I do have an idea for a follow-up…'

'Come on then. If you see potential you have to tell me.'

His grin is sheepish. 'How about we do a little Mr and Mrs happy-ever-after post featuring the St Aidan recipe book?'

I roll my eyes. 'Are you going all Beyoncé on me?' Not that I'd be complaining if he were, but it's best to be clear.

He laughs. 'I mean Mr and Mrs in the loosest sense. If it's okay with you, I'll leave my big proposal for a day when Diesel *hasn't* eaten the cake.' He's already got his phone in his hand. 'You have copies of the book here, let's do a shout-out and tell the world we're an item before you change your mind.'

'What, now?'

He gives a slow smile. 'What I'd really like is to take you to bed right away and stay there for a week, but…'

I'm hesitating too, resting my forehead on his. 'Neither of us will be able to settle until we have news of Walter.'

He's pulling me in towards him. 'So how about we do our piece to camera, then we'll wake Diesel and see if we can get him down to the garden. And we'll take it from there.'

There's a lot to be said for decisive action. Fifteen minutes later our brief but very cute selfie clip goes live, so 3 a.m. today will go down in history as the time Ross and I officially came out to the world as a couple. And ten minutes and quite a few kisses after that, as we make it down into the garden and out onto the beach, Ross's phone pings with a text that lets us know that Walter is okay, and staying in overnight for observation, but due to come home in the morning. The moon is playing hide and seek between the clouds, sending splashes of light quivering across the water. As I walk with my shoulder against Ross's chest, with the strong grasp of his arm around me, we fall into step and follow Diesel down to where the wavy lines of foam are running up the beach.

Ross stops, stoops for another soft and very delicious kiss, then pulls me into a hug. 'There you go, I told you Walter wouldn't let us down.'

I push back my hair as the wind catches it. 'I don't know about his heart rate being raised, he certainly raised ours.'

Ross turns to look at Diesel, whose head is up sniffing the air. 'One patient on the mend. All we need now is for Diesel to pass a motion, and the world will be right again.' He laughs. 'That's one of the hazards of falling in love with a vet – if we're not covered in poop we're probably thinking about it.'

I smile up at him. 'I just hope you can cope with loving a baker – you realise you can never say "no" to tasting the cakes?'

'As if that would ever happen!' He's grinning down at me, and then his smile fades and he pulls me into a sudden squeeze. 'We've got our second chance here, Bertie. I never dared to hope we would.'

And suddenly as we stand there, our bodies fused together in the warmth of the night air, I know. 'We would have been all right, wouldn't we? If we'd had our baby, I mean.'

Ross looks down at me and nods slowly. 'I think we would.'

It's silly. It doesn't relate to anything that's actually real. But somehow it's a comfort to have that confirmed. To agree on it as the people we are now. On behalf of the people we used to be. It's a strange realisation to get to, when I've spent so many years thinking the opposite. But after two and a half months of being with Ross every day, he might not have been there the actual second I needed him, but I know now he would have come through for us all. And with his massive heart, we'd have become that same team we are now.

He's looking down at me. 'We can always try again. So long as you don't mind that none of those three-year-olds got my jokes.'

I laugh. 'You'll have plenty of time to polish your comedy. In the meantime, Diesel is just coming through for us. Which means once we've picked up we can go home and work on the rest.'

And as we walk back towards Seaspray Cottage there are salty tears rolling quietly down my cheeks. I'm the happiest woman in St Aidan, because I'm with the man I've loved since the start of time, and I know now there's no one in the whole world who is a better man for me.

42

The book launch at Kittiwake Court
Silver fish and new hair
Saturday

Let's face it – any book launch in St Aidan is always going to be well supported. When it's for a book so many people have their recipes in... By two o'clock on Saturday afternoon Kittiwake Court is bursting, and residents, staff and visitors are all bursting too, with excitement.

Ross and I are a full three minutes late arriving, which is unusual as Ross is famous for turning up everywhere at least half an hour ahead of schedule. Obviously, with the local grapevine being as healthy as it is, everyone knows we're together. But as it's our first outing in public as a couple, we're both feeling a little bit shy as we skirt the crowds going round to the doors on the beach side. As we head for the entrance next to Jen's office Ross drops his arm from my shoulders, grasps my hand tightly and grins at me. 'Now you're mine I don't want to let go of you for a second.'

I grin back at him and drop a kiss on his cheek. 'I love where you're coming from there, Bradbury, but spot the deliberate mistake. We've come in without any of the unicorn cupcakes I've made, so one of us needs to go back to the car and get them.'

He curses under his breath then he grins at me again. 'Mind-blowing sex is known to cause memory lapses, so that explains that one.' He hands Diesel's lead to me and puts in the code to reopen the door. 'You go on in, I'll be back in with the booty.'

Now Ross has somewhere better to be – ahem, in bed with me – he's calling in all the favours he's due up at the surgery. So this morning we raced out early to take Diesel along the beach, and then headed home with a big bag of warm croissants for a very lazy breakfast in bed. Talk about last-minute baking; I literally stuck in my last unicorn horn in the buttercream swirl and we ran out of the door to head over here now.

You have to hand it to the people of St Aidan, they certainly know how to party. As I walk into the Sea View Lounge it's fuller than I've ever seen it, and people are fanning right across the terrace and onto the lawns beyond. Sophie has had everyone baking, Millie has brought Luce and her friends from school to circulate with trays and hand it out, and Jen and the staff are all wearing fabulous new aprons with baking-themed prints, kindly made up and donated by Helen from the fabric shop. Sophie's Nate has Maisie perched on his shoulders and Marcus and Tilly at his side, and the drinks are disappearing from the bar table as fast as George and Nell are popping corks and filling the flutes. And obviously, as promised, Sophie, Millie, Nell and Plum are all in their spangly fishtail skirts, with starfish in their hair, and glitter on their eyelids.

Joanie, Walter, Pam and the gang are thankfully dressed as smart versions of themselves, and are sitting in a cluster of easy chairs behind Jen, who is rocking her newly-dyed reverse-ombré hair-do. It only takes a couple of claps of her hands for the roar of chatter to subside around the room. As she welcomes everyone, Ross is tiptoeing in behind her, giving me a thumbs-up. Then before I know it, she's handing over to me.

As I take my place at the front, I twitch the cornflower-blue version of the dandelion and buttercup dress to make sure I'm not exposing too much boob, but there's no time to be nervous.

I take a breath and go. 'Hi, I'm Cressy Cupcake and I did the foreword to the book that's been written by *all of you!*' As I look sideways, Kathleen and Madge catch my eye, and their smiles are so proud, I have to stop to swallow, and purse my lips to bite back a sudden rush of emotion before I start again. 'The book grew out of the lovely chats we had when I came here to bake with everyone a few months ago. We all had our favourite recipes, and it felt like a wonderful thing to do to collect a lifetime's worth of tried and tested baking secrets in one place so other people could enjoy them too.'

I pause for the murmur of agreement to die down, then I hold my copy in the air. Everyone's familiar with the sugar-dusted-butterfly-cake cover now, as Sophie has made sure every shop in the village has a poster in their window, and has hung blown-up versions around the walls here, but holding the book in my hand now is very special.

'With bakes as startling as mucky golf balls, and as tantalising as ginger cloudburst cake, let's celebrate putting St Aidan on the map one delicious recipe at a time. So please give *A Slice of St Aidan* a wonderful launch! And now Joanie and Walter are going to cut the ceremonial ribbon.'

Two nurses help Joanie and Walter forward and Jen hands them a giant pair of Helen's fabric scissors. As they slice through the silver satin ribbon draped between two chairs, Walter lets out a whoop. 'There, it's out in the world! Now you all put your hands in your pockets, and buy as many copies as you can.'

Then Nell and Plum squeeze between a side table stacked high with piles of books, and before they've had time to open up their cashboxes the queue to buy already stretches out across the terrace.

Millie comes by with a tray of millionaire's shortbread, and as I bite into a slice Sophie and Nate arrive too.

As Sophie turns to me her voice is urgent. 'Have you seen where the book sales have gone this morning?'

I shake my head and swallow a mouthful of caramel. 'I was pretty busy with the cupcakes.' Obviously I've had my mind on sex, not sales figures, but I can think of better places to discuss my decade-long dry spell's sudden end. I force myself to concentrate. 'Since Maudie Maudie put our Mr and Mrs clip with the recipe book on their Insta feed, their followers have gone bananas.' I can't take the credit. 'That clip was all Ross's idea, and the rest was one of those perfect storms that just happens sometimes. Maudie Maudie texted to say they'd already had thousands of pounds' worth of orders for dresses.'

Sophie nods. 'The book sales are phenomenal too. You've done so well for us all with this.'

I have to tell her. 'Ross was the one who uploaded the other clip that went viral too, that's what started it all off to begin with.'

Sophie punches the air. 'I knew there was something odd about that, I tried to tell you but you wouldn't have it!'

I give a grimace. 'Good thing I didn't know or I might have tried to make Ross take it down.'

I feel a warmth behind my back, and Ross slides in next to me. 'Talking about me again? I hope it's good.' He's looking even more pleased with himself than he was when we arrived, holding a rainbow cupcake up for me to look at, and he isn't waiting for a reply to his previous question. 'So what do you think of this?'

'I'm thinking it's a unicorn cake…'

He rolls his eyes in frustration. 'What I mean is, they'd be perfect for our baby party if we were having boy and girl twins. Or for the sprinkle, when the time comes, that is.'

I can't help shaking my head. 'You're getting way ahead

of yourself, but yes, I like your thinking. So yay! Let's go with those! Just eat that one quick before Diesel gets in first.'

This is how unbelievable the change is. Two days ago I was coming to terms with being alone for ever. Now I'm with the guy I love, and we just settled on cakes for our baby shower. But it sounds more spur of the moment and flippant than it is; we have known each other for eighteen years and more. I truly do feel I know what I'm getting with Ross, and I couldn't be more thrilled.

Sophie lets out a squeak and pulls us into a hug. 'How sweet are you two?' She looks over her shoulder at Nate. 'Do you remember when we were like this?'

Nate grins at Ross. 'Enjoy it while it lasts. After child number four you're definitely outnumbered.'

We all laugh, and beyond them, I hear Plum let out a whoop. Then Nell's voice saying, 'Well, I never.'

Then Diesel lets out a bark and starts running on the spot. As his lead tugs through my fingers I hear a familiar voice resonating.

I let out a gasp, because I can't quite believe what I'm hearing, and as I turn to follow Diesel I lock eyes with Ross. 'That sounds like Charlie!'

Ross's relaxed smile shows no surprise at all. 'So it does!'

How Diesel forces his way right across the room is a sign of his dedication, but people step back, and somehow he passes. He reaches his target, and the only casualties are a couple of empty wine flutes, upturned on a tray he dislodges on his way.

As I follow him through I catch sight of Clemmie's

auburn curls, half-caught up in a bun on top of her head. And as Diesel's paws land on Charlie's shoulders Charlie flings his arms around Diesel's grey hairy neck. It's quite a while before Diesel's doggy leaps subside. He's covered them both in huge sloppy licks, but neither of them mind.

As Diesel flops over onto his back and puts his legs in the air Millie's at my side, whispering in my ear. 'Clemmie's wearing her favourite orange dress with the white stars on. I think that's a good sign.'

As Charlie stands up I stare into both their faces searching for a clue, but I can't bring myself to say the words. And then their faces relax into smiles, and without even asking I know it's all right. The tears are rolling down my cheeks as I fling myself at Charlie.

'It's okay – it is okay, isn't it?'

Then I step back and look at them again, and Charlie nods. 'It's very, very early days. But for now it's all good.'

I pull Clemmie into a tiny, gentle air kiss, because that's all I dare do. 'Well done. I'm so happy for you.'

Then I rush back and hurl myself at Ross, and sob into his chest, because suddenly all the aching and hoping and willing I've done for Clemmie and Charlie is over. And when I eventually pull away he hands me a bundle of serviettes and waits until my nose is wiped and my face is dry again. Then I stare at him, and say, 'Did you know about this?'

Ross's smile says he's guilty as charged. 'They wanted to surprise you.'

I sniff and rub my nose again. 'For one time only, I'll let you off. The surprise was lovely.'

Clemmie's next to me, her hand on my arm. 'We hear you've got together too? How great is that?'

I shake my head at Ross. 'Who said men didn't talk?'

Then Charlie is rubbing his hands, saying, 'Hey, where's the end of the queue? We need to buy some books before they all go.'

Sophie's hissing at me behind her hand. 'The printers are delivering more tomorrow, we're going to need them!'

Plum's sitting back in her chair, visible again now the book piles have gone. 'Okay, Cressy, Maudie Maudie have had their money's worth of exposure now, it's time for you to change to match the rest of us.'

'It is?' My mouth is open.

There's a victorious note in Plum's voice. 'I *knew* it would be worth making you a tail. Just think of the wear you're going to get out of this now you and Ross are going to be here full-time.'

It's obvious the green and turquoise flowers on my dress aren't cutting it as much as I thought they were.

Millie's tugging my arm. 'It's in Jen's office. Come on, Luce and I will help you into it.'

I send a final pleading look to my new helper and protector, but he shrugs. 'This is mermaid business, I'm not sure a vet should intervene.'

I hiss in his ear as I pass, 'I'll deal with you later.'

He just laughs. 'That's exactly what I was hoping.'

I have to be honest, I'm playing for time here. If I do this really slowly, most people will have gone home anyway. So when Millie wants to fluff up my hair and put electric blue and pink spray in and plait shells and ribbons through it, I let her. She gives me one of Sophie's over-sized watery blue T-shirts, which fits me like a glove, and when they take at least twenty minutes gluing sequins to my eyelids, I'm happy to comply. Then I stand up while they spend another quarter of an hour wrapping me up in sacking and gauze, which is the nearest I've been yet to being trussed in a fishing net. And then they step back and nod.

I stare down at myself. 'So what's the verdict?'

Millie's grinning. 'You look awesome.'

I have to be honest. 'I had no idea it took so long to become a mermaid. Maybe that's why we see so few around.' If we're making time comparisons, it's more like I used to be when I was getting ready when I was in London, which feels really strange somehow.

Millie nods. 'So what are we waiting for? Let's go and show you off.'

My ankles are fully tied together. 'You're expecting me to walk?'

Millie lets out a peal of laughter. 'Shuffle for now, you'll soon get the hang of it.'

Which is why I swear it takes another twenty minutes for us to get along Ocean Boulevard and back to the lounge. As a measure of how long we've been away, by the time we get there, there's only staff, residents and mermaid families left. And Charlie and Clemmie too.

As I inch into the lounge there's a cheer. And everyone claps me until I make it to a very nice chaise longue they've saved specially so I can lie with my tail horizontal, then Ross perches next to me, his hip next to mine.

Nell clears her throat as I finally ease into place. 'We all wanted to say a private and special thank you for everything you've done to help everyone at Kittiwake.'

Jen takes over. 'Without your ideas and evenings, and the recipe book, we'd only have a fraction of the funds we've got now. We've still got a little way to go to reach our target, but I'm told that book sales will be ongoing, so thank you, from the bottom of all our hearts.'

Sophie's giving me a hard stare. 'We could have a best-seller on our hands here! It's all down to you!'

I'm looking round at all the lovely residents, thinking how they've encouraged me, how they were the ones who first edged me out of my comfort zone, how their enthusiasm showed me what was possible. Without them I'd never have taken the leaps I have.

I swallow hard. 'I'm actually the one who has to thank you. When I arrived I felt like a pretender, but with your help I've learned to perform in front of people. And that has made me feel real and genuine. After all the experience I've gained in St Aidan, I wouldn't be stuffing up on *Internet Special Bake Off*. But with what I know now, I wouldn't actually be going on it either. I'm too busy living a much better life.'

Joanie's dabbing her eye. 'We're all very proud of you, Cressy, we always were. And now you've got to learn to be a farmer's wife.'

Ross gives a strangled choke. 'Hang on, it might be me learning to be a farmer's husband, more like.'

Walter gives a cough and taps his stick on the floor. 'That's another thing I meant to tell you. *This* farmer's going to have a new wife too!'

I'm thrilled, but surprised. 'Really? That's wonderful. But when did this happen?'

Walter slaps his thigh. 'You're not the only fast workers round here, you know!' His eyes are twinkling, then he stops teasing and carries on. 'I asked her in the car on the way back from hospital the other morning.'

Joanie looks shamefaced. 'That sly fox, I'd been so worried, I said yes straightaway.'

I beam at them both. 'There's nothing wrong with quick decisions, so long as you know your own mind.'

Walter grins. 'That's what I like about you, Cressy, you've got your head screwed on. I reckon you'd be the right person to grow watercress down in the brook. It would go nicely with your hens.'

I laugh with recognition. 'Egg and Cressy? That's what I used to be called at home as a child.'

Sophie's eyes are shining, and she nudges Clemmie beside her. 'We mermaids all have our childhood names. Clemmie Orange, then there's Nelly Melon, Sophie Potato and Victoria Plum. And now we have an Egg and Cressy too.'

I look down at the sequinned tourniquet around my ankles. 'Before I take on the challenges of being a farmer, I reckon I need to master walking in my mermaid tail.'

Millie sashays over to me, her scales glinting in the sunlight. 'If you step over here, I'll give you a few tips.'

And as I let go of Ross's hand and falteringly lurch after her, I look back at him over my shoulder. As our eyes meet I know he's the only person in the world I'd want to make a family with, and I feel so lucky that the time is finally right for us to be together. It's also a wonderful feeling to be surrounded by our St Aidan family too, because I know they're the ones who've helped me make a life I can be proud of, and brought me more happiness than I could ever have wished for.

PS

I f anyone had told me four months ago that I'd only ever go back to London for a weekend, I wouldn't have believed them. But here I am, like Charlie before me, a brand-new fully fledged resident of St Aidan, looking forward to starting my apprenticeship as a Cornish person. It helps that I have Ross to keep me right. And Walter, Joanie and all my friends at Kittiwake Court, not to mention my wonderful mermaid friends.

And like the waves that rush up and down the beach along the bay, nothing in St Aidan stays still for long…

Walter and Joanie lose no time. Six weeks after the book launch they say 'I do' in a tiny ceremony at the local church, and celebrate in style with a singalong *Sound of Music* evening back at Kittiwake Court.

There's more good news from there too. Even with phenomenal sales on the cookbook, and a mud run that broke local records, we were still struggling to make the target for the renovations. But it wasn't the end of the line.

So Walter is adding a chunk from the sale of his farmhouse to the fund, because, as he rightly points out, if it wasn't for Kittiwake Court he wouldn't be here at all, and he definitely wouldn't be a happily married man for a second time around. And Charlie is chipping in to make up the rest, because that's just the kind of loaded he is.

As for Ross and me, Clemmie and Charlie insist that we should stay on in Clemmie's flat at least until we sort out the basic work on the farmhouse. Clemmie has been feeling as rough as you do when you're newly pregnant, but she and Charlie are sipping ginger tea together, and taking Diesel out for lots of fresh air and blowy walks. And truly, they haven't stopped smiling. There's a long way to go, but somehow we know in our hearts that this time they're going to get there.

The garden at Seaspray Cottage is filled with curly green metal chairs and tables again, I've been helping Clemmie out with her summer events, and carrying on with my own tour of St Aidan's homes in the name of The Little Cornish Kitchen. For breaking news of caramel evenings, watch this space. And anyone with recipes for the next St Aidan village cookbook, drop them in the Deck Gallery, or Kittiwake Court.

Thanks to Ross cutting his ties with Scotland and the fact, as he insists, that he's barely been out in twelve years, he, George and Charlie have had their heads together. Between them they've come up with a scheme for Ross to buy the farmhouse and farm buildings from Walter along with the orchard and nearby fields, and to rent the rest of the land we need. So our rare breeds country living centre with log cabins, glamping, shepherd's huts and vintage caravans is on course to emerge very soon.

And when Ross comes up to London with me to pick up my stuff, we do all the things that tourist couples do. We go to the zoo – so he can show off his awesome animal knowledge – and lie in the sun in Regent's Park with our meal-deal picnic, take selfies by the Thames with the London Eye in the background, and have double-decker burgers and chips with Heinz ketchup at the Hard Rock Café so he can sigh over famous guitars.

We also spend a lot of time in bed, because we seem to have so much time to make up for in that department. Then just to show our minds aren't completely one-track, we call in to a rare breeds farm on the way back through Devon. And it's all lovely, but I have to admit, when I'm back in the far field counting sheep next day, it feels a lot like coming home.

Then on a sunny day in late September, Ross and I borrow Diesel and walk into the wind, along the beach and out to Oyster Point. And we clamber out to where the ocean is swirling, now and then colliding with the rocks, and take the bunch of mauve daisies and cornflowers we've picked from Walter's orchard. Then one by one we toss the flower sprigs into the sea, and think about our little one.

The only marker we have of her now is the day she should have been born. But remembering her together, our hands tightly clasped, watching as the petals bob on the swell and sweep out towards the horizon before they disappear completely, makes the moment all the more precious. And afterwards, as we eat ice cream, sitting shoulder to shoulder on the same grassy bank in the car park where we sat on our way back from the hospital appointment in Truro, we can already feel the history we're making here. Then, hand in hand, with the wind buffeting our backs and Diesel lolloping in the surf, we get blown all the way back to St Aidan again.

And then one day a few weeks later, with the hoods of our waxed jackets clamped around our heads against the rain, we call by George's office to pick up a large bunch of keys – and Snowdrop Farm is officially ours. It's one of those unbelievable pieces of luck that isn't really about luck at all; it's more about Walter knowing we'll love and care for the place with as much heart as he has for the last seventy-five years, and being certain he can trust us to look after it in the way he wants. No pressure there then; but Ross reckons we've got this, and it's just as much my dream as his now. I only love him all the more for having it in the first place.

As we run through the horizontal rain around the front of the house, the leaves blowing from the pear tree in the garden are gathering in the gaps where the cobbles are missing. Then as we get to the faded front door, the sun breaks through the slate-black sky, and as we shake the rain off our faces and put the giant key in the lock, the meadows light up.

Ross pulls me inside his jacket, and into a rain-soaked kiss. 'A rainbow arching right across High Hopes Hill. I hope you appreciate how long it took me to organise that.' His laugh vibrates through my chest. 'I'm truly sorry it's taken so long for us to get here, Bertie – but are you ready for the next bit?'

I can't actually reply straightaway because he sweeps me into a kiss, then as he picks me up and shoulders the door open, I'm shouting, 'Yes, Cakeface! Yes, yes, yes, I am!'

Then we switch on the light and walk into the large whitewashed kitchen, and it's wonderful to know we're going to spend the rest of our lives here – together.

CRESSY'S RECIPES

In case this book has made your mouth water, here are a few of Cressy's recipes to try for yourself at home.

Cressy's Chocolate Mug Cake

Cressy makes a two-minute mug cake in the microwave to cheer Ross up. If you love chocolate it really is a high-speed answer to instant happiness. It's also a great way to enjoy chocolate cake if you'd like one piece rather than a whole cake.

Bear in mind that everyone's microwaves are slightly different, so the perfect cooking time for yours may be slightly shorter or longer. And like Cressy, you'll need to make sure you use a mug that's microwave-safe, and large enough that it doesn't overflow when the cake rises.

Serves one.

4 level tablespoons self-raising flour
4 level tablespoons caster sugar
2 level tablespoons cocoa powder
1 medium egg
3 tablespoons sunflower oil
3 tablespoons milk
A few drops vanilla essence
For extra luxury add 2 tablespoons of chocolate chips

Find the largest mug you have.
Put in the flour, sugar and cocoa and mix them together.
Add the egg and mix in as much as you can.
Add the milk, oil and vanilla essence and stir until smooth.
Add the chocolate chips if using.
Centre your mug in the microwave and cook on high for one and a half to two minutes.

Delicious eaten hot or warm, straight from the mug. Cressy likes to eat hers with vanilla ice cream.

Cressy's Chocolate Brownies with Walnuts

Of all Cressy's many brownie recipes, this is one of her favourites. She makes it in a tin that's 13 inches by 8 inches and 2 and a half inches deep. Some days she lines the tin with parchment, but if she's in a hurry she wings it and cooks without. Again, temperatures of different ovens may vary, and you may want to vary the cooking time to get a stickier brownie too. Remember the brownies will carry on cooking as they cool.

    375g butter, at room temperature
    375g dark chocolate if you're feeling posh (cocoa is
    fine if you don't have that)
    6 large eggs
    1 tablespoon vanilla extract
    500g caster sugar
    225g plain flour
    1 teaspoon salt
    300g walnuts, chopped

Preheat the oven to 180°C/160°C fan/gas mark 4.
Grease the tin or line with parchment.
Melt the chocolate and butter together in a heavy
based saucepan and put aside to cool.
In a bowl, beat the eggs with the sugar and add the
vanilla essence.
Sieve the flour into another bowl and mix in the salt.
When the chocolate mixture is cool, beat in the eggs
and sugar.
Stir in the flour and beat until the mixture is smooth,
then stir in the nuts.
Transfer to the baking tin and bake for about 25 mins.
Check often at the end to make sure not to cook it for
too long.
When it's ready the top will have a paler brown
crust, but the inside will still be dark and sticky.
Leave to cool and then slice into pieces.

Cressy's Custard Cream Blondies

There are as many variations of blondie as there are brownies, but custard cream blondies are one of Cressy's faves. Some fancy bakeries have a custard cream biscuit topping every slice of blondie, but Cressy suggests putting all the custard creams into the mixture. That way it's easier to cut the finished result into smaller snack-size pieces.

175g butter
200g muscovado sugar
125g golden caster sugar
4 tablespoon custard powder
2 eggs
2 teaspoon vanilla extract
250g self-raising flour
A pinch of salt
15 custard creams
150g white chocolate

Preheat the oven to 180°C/160°C Fan/gas mark 4.
Put the butter, sugar, and custard powder into a
heavy based saucepan, and stir gently over a low
heat until all the sugar has dissolved.
Leave to cool for ten minutes.
Break in the eggs and stir, one at a time.
Then stir in the vanilla, flour and a pinch of salt.
Crumble the custard creams into pieces, cut the
white chocolate into chunks, and stir these into the
mixture.

Put the mixture into a greased or lined baking tray, and bake for 30 minutes.

Once it's out of the oven let it cool in the tray. Then put the tray in the fridge to chill, before cutting into snack sized pieces.

Cressy's Bakewell Tart Blondies

Another of Cressy's favourite blondies, these are my personal faves because I love the jam. Yum yum.

250g butter
125g soft brown sugar
125g white granulated sugar
3 eggs (medium)
100g ground almonds
225g self raising flour
200g white chocolate, in chunks or chips (optional, but extra delish)
250g raspberry jam
50g flaked almonds

Preheat the oven to 180°C/160°C fan/gas mark 4.
Grease an 8 inch by 13 inch baking tin or line with parchment.
Put the butter and sugars into a heavy based saucepan, and stir gently over a low heat until all the sugar has dissolved.
Leave to cool for ten minutes.
Add the eggs one by one and stir.

Add the flour and ground almonds and beat for a short time until thick and sticky.

Add the white chocolate chunks or chips, and fold through the mixture if using.

Pour the mixture into the baking tin and spread out evenly. Dollop the jam in lumps across the surface, and gently swirl this through the mixture.

Sprinkle almond flakes evenly over the top, then bake in the oven for thirty minutes, until the surface begins to wave.

Once it's out of the oven let it cool in the tray. Then put the tray in the fridge to chill, before cutting into snack sized pieces.

Then enjoy.

Love, Jane xx

AUTHOR'S NOTE

To my readers…

Thank you for choosing this book. I may write the words, but it's the hearts and imaginations of readers that bring the stories to life.

St Aidan is a fictitious place, but I feel as if I live there, and some readers feel the same. If you've enjoyed your time in St Aidan, you may like to visit again.

All my St Aidan stories are standalone reads. The books run chronologically, some characters appear in several books, but not everyone is in every story. For anyone who'd rather avoid accidental spoilers, this is the order they were written in:

The Little Wedding Shop by the Sea
Christmas at the Little Wedding Shop
Summer at the Little Wedding Shop
Christmas Promises at the Little Wedding Shop
The Little Cornish Kitchen

A Cornish Cottage by the Sea (aka *Edie Browne's Cottage by the Sea*)
A Cosy Christmas in Cornwall
Love at the Little Wedding Shop by the Sea
Welcome to the Little Cornish Kitchen

Happy reading and lots of love, Jane xx

ACKNOWLEDGMENTS

First, thank you to my wonderful readers. These books are all for you, I'm so grateful to you for enjoying them. I love hearing from you and I can't wait until we're properly back out in the world so I can have the opportunity to meet up with you again.

A book is so much more than just the words, and lots of people helped to make this one. Back in 2012 Charlotte Ledger pulled my first manuscript out of her e-submissions pile, and signed me to HarperCollins' brand new digital fiction line. It's been an amazing personal journey for me since then, from the slush pile to over half a million book sales worldwide. And wonderful Charlotte has been there all the way, with her amazing warmth, friendship and professional brilliance, making all of that happen. There are no thank you's big enough, or enough words to describe my love and admiration for you, Charlotte.

Huge thanks and love too for Amanda Preston, my agent. I couldn't do this without you. Whatever I need, you are there with it, I love how much fun we have alongside the serious stuff. And I'm so proud you got Bailey.

Thanks to Kimberley Young and the team at One More Chapter and HarperCollins, for wonderful covers, production, promotion and support. To my lovely friend Emily Yolland and the fab foreign rights team, not forgetting the team at HarperCollins Germany who work their own magic with my books over there. And a special thank you to my editor Emily Ruston; you helped so much when I was setting up this story. I love that you've got a fab new job, but that doesn't make me miss you any less.

To my writing friends, especially Zara Stoneley and Debbie Johnson, who keep me sane on a daily basis. To my wonderful Facebook friends who constantly support me, especially Wendy McClaren in Australia. To the fabulous book bloggers who spread the word, especially Rachel Gilbey who delivers the most amazing Blog Tours.

Jess Cushway began lockdown as someone who made great brownies and ended it with a fully fledged baking business. Congratulations on creating Cushway Cakes, Jess, and thanks for all the baking inspiration and advice you've given me along the way. I loved how you and Cressy both independently came upon with the bake box idea at the same time. And your blondies are truly sensational!

And last of all, huge hugs to my family, for cheering me on all the way. And big love to my own hero Phil … thank you for never letting me give up.

ONE MORE CHAPTER

One More Chapter is an
award-winning global
division of HarperCollins.

Sign up to our newsletter to get our
latest eBook deals and stay up to date
with our weekly Book Club!
<u>Subscribe here.</u>

Meet the team at
<u>www.onemorechapter.com</u>

Follow us!
 <u>@OneMoreChapter_</u>
 <u>@OneMoreChapter</u>
 <u>@onemorechapterhc</u>

Do you write unputdownable fiction?
We love to hear from new voices.
Find out how to submit your novel at
<u>www.onemorechapter.com/submissions</u>